I0760957

STRENGTHENED BY LOVE AND FIRE

STRENGTHENED BY LOVE AND FIRE

THE HOUSE OF WARD BOOK THREE

A.R. ABBOTT

Published by Lost Warren Books LLC

Paperback ISBN: 976-1-967520-10-7

Hardcover ISBN: 978-1-967520-12-1

ALSO BY A.R. ABBOTT

Founded on Blood and Magic: The House of Ward Book One

Bonded by Friendship and Fate: The House of Ward Book Two

For my sister—my ride or die, my partner in crime, and the keeper of our shared history. Your faith in me carries me further than you know.

1

LUCIA

Normal felt strange after so much change. It was good to be back at work, even if the location was different. The new shop still smelled like fresh paint and sawdust, a reminder that Sara didn't need us hovering anymore. My sister and I had stepped back, letting her build her own place, her own life. It was the right thing to do—at least, that's what I kept telling myself. I sighed when I thought about how that had gone initially, but now it was time to pitch in and lend a hand.

"Aunt Lucia, you okay?" Sara asked from the other side of the counter, where she was working on a new herb display.

"Just fine, I don't know why you would think anything was wrong," I said.

Sara just raised an eyebrow and went back to arranging bundles of rosemary.

I bent my head back over the supply catalog I was flipping through. Sara was a good girl—no, woman—I reminded myself. She had changed since she lived with us, but overall, it was for the better. Even I could admit that much. Her mother and I might not have been initially thrilled that she'd decided to move in with a bunch of vampires or that she'd had a bonded shifter as a boyfriend, but we saw how happy she was, and in the end, we loved her and wanted her to be happy. And her fiancé and roommates were actually quite nice.

"Okay, I think I'm finished here," Sara said, walking over.

I glanced up into her smiling face. The smile could only mean one thing. "I assume you're off to spend time with your man?"

She pursed her lips. "No, I was going to invite you to dinner."

"Not tonight. I'm afraid I already have plans," I said, setting the catalog aside.

"Are you sure? Mom's coming, and Bruce and Silas are cooking. We're having roast beef." She smiled and tilted her head.

She knew how much I liked it when the boys cooked together. Individually, they were both good cooks; together, they were phenomenal.

"I wish I could," I said honestly. "But I have been invited to attend the Elders' meeting tonight."

Sara's eyes widened at the pronouncement. She understood how rare it was to be invited to a meeting and the possible importance of my invitation. "Do you think they intend to make you an Elder?" she asked in a hushed tone, as if trying not to let the Fates hear.

"I have no idea," I said. "I guess I'll find out at the meeting. I wouldn't be surprised, however; I am the oldest in our family, and our mother was an Elder before she passed." It didn't always mean that a family member would be invited into the exclusive group of decision-makers for our kind. There were limited spots; not all families could be represented, but ours was an old, proud line, and I had a hunch.

"Well, I'll be thinking about you and sending you good vibes," Sara said.

"Vibes," I scoffed. "I'm not sure what kind of witchcraft you're practicing, my dear, but *vibes* don't play into it."

"It's just a saying, Auntie," Sara said. "I can burn an offering, too, if you need me to."

"I'm sure that's not necessary, but thank you," I said. "Tell your mother I'll be home late, would you?"

"You didn't tell her about the meeting? I'm surprised."

"I was only invited this morning, by phone, after I arrived here at the shop. While you were still asleep, I might add."

"I told you, we don't officially open until after lunch these days, no matter what time you arrive," Sara said, resting her hands on her hips. "We keep near vampire hours these days, so that we can spend time with all the roommates."

I sniffed. "I see. Well, I certainly don't keep vampire hours. And since I can see Kate anytime I want now, I don't see a reason to. Still, I do like that little one, E. She's got a rather peculiar name, though."

Sara had the nerve to smirk at me. "Uh-huh. I know you like the rest of them, too. You were awfully chatty with Felix at dinner last week."

"Well, he is a very intelligent young man, and interesting to talk to."

"That young man is over two thousand years old, Auntie. Of course, he's interesting. He's lived a lot of life," she said.

"If they *are* alive," I said in a low voice.

"Fine, I'll see you tomorrow, I expect," Sara said. "Not too bright and not too early, though."

"I'll be here when I get here," I said. "Unless you plan to take my keys away."

Sara huffed out a laugh. "I don't want to get my fingers burned off," she said. "Lock up when you go?"

"Of course, what do you take me for?" I asked.

"Love you, Auntie," Sara said as she opened the door to the passage that led to the main house.

"Love you too," I called after her. She really was a good girl.

I tidied away the items I'd been working on and moved around the shop, turning off the lights and shutting down the computer in the back. I tried to work efficiently, avoiding haste in my tasks. There was plenty of time before the meeting, I told myself. I didn't want to arrive early and seem overeager or presumptuous. I would arrive exactly at the scheduled time, not a minute earlier or later.

My stomach fluttered when I thought about what would happen tonight. Although I'd told Sara that I wasn't sure, I had a pretty good idea about the purpose of the meeting. I was close with one of the Elders, a witch named Ruth. She was several years older than I, but we met for tea now and then, and she told me last fall that I was being considered. I'd been waiting for the invitation ever since.

I smoothed my damp hands over my linen trousers and looked around the shop. It still had all the beautiful antique furniture we had always used to display our goods, but the building itself was larger and more open. It was built in the style of the main house, with a mix of unfinished logs and whitewashed walls. Heavy beams hung overhead, and the lighting was just right to make the place glow in the afternoon without being so bright as to harm the products. It was beautiful. My parents would have loved the improvements.

I thought of my mother, a proud woman and fire-wielder like myself. She had been an Elder for over thirty years by the time she died. I like to think she would have been proud of me for following in her footsteps and representing our family, as well as the rest of the witch community, as an Elder like her. I swallowed the lump in my throat and straightened my shoulders.

I grabbed my bag and coat and headed to the front door of the shop. The bell rang as I stepped out into the cold, damp night. The air was chilly but dry. Although we lived in Western Washington, a place known for its rainfall and gray overcast days, our valley was usually sunny and relatively dry. It was nice to live in an area with Water and Air Witches, who also enjoyed the sunshine. Any two of them, together, could affect the weather in the valley with little effort. The same way that an Air and Energy Witch could ward a building when working in tandem. It was yet another reason witches tended to live in groups. We were stronger when we worked together.

After locking the door behind me, I headed to my car. The new shop and Sara's house were on the opposite side of the river from the main town where Sybil and I lived, as well as where the meeting would be. The house was built as a skier's lodge by a couple from the city. They weren't witches, and no one in town would sell them property for their business venture. Ultimately, they bought a piece of land just outside the town but still in the same valley. The drive back to town was short, but I took my time.

I steered my car over the narrow bridge, glad that it was a two-lane road across the river. Some of the crossings up and down the valley were smaller suspension bridges with only enough room for one car to drive along the wooden tracks. Crossing one of those was always unsettling, no matter how many times I'd been safely across.

I pulled onto the main street of our small town. It was only a quarter mile long, but it held most of the businesses along with the only official government building. It was a gas station, a food market, a diner, and sometimes a post office all in one, but we just called it the General Store. It was also across the street from my destination, and the lights from the gas station lit up the front of the building I was heading toward. Several cars were already parked out front. I was right on time.

The building itself didn't look like much. Like nearly every other building on the street, it was made of wood and stone, giving it a rugged, mountain-like appearance. It looked right at home here among its peers and the scattered pines. The two-story structure was built specifically for small gatherings and meetings among the community's Elders. It was the place where the valley's governing actually happened.

I parked my car just as another pulled in beside me. I got out and recognized Ruth's red Toyota. I waved as she shut her door and looked in my direction. She started to raise her hand in response, but once she met my gaze, the smile on her face faded, and she lowered her hand. I smiled tightly and nodded at the older woman, her grey hair neatly bound in a halo of braids. I understood the importance of propriety better than most. It wouldn't look good for her to appear friendly with a prospective Elder. She would have to vote on my approval, after all.

I paused and gave her a head start, so it wouldn't look like we were entering together. When I stepped inside, I was alone. A low rumble of voices told me that those who were already here were in the main room. I dropped my jacket and bag in the cloakroom next to the front door and took a deep, calming breath before joining the others.

The main room was laid out with a long table along the far end, facing the front of the building. A large assembly of chairs was arranged before the table, filling the rest of the large room, and was used for community-wide meetings. The seven Elders all sat behind the table waiting; the chairs were empty. I was the only non-Elder in attendance, further confirming that this meeting was for me and me alone.

I walked forward on legs that felt wobbly beneath me. This was it. This was the moment I'd dreamed of for the past two decades of my life. I was finally achieving what I had sacrificed so much for. The thought of those sacrifices brought a lump to my throat, but I swallowed it down and continued to the front of the room to stand before those who waited for me. After this night, I would be one of them. I would be a community Elder, the most revered of our kind, trusted to make decisions for the good of the community as a whole.

There was a single chair pulled forward in front of the others, and I stood in front of it facing the Elders.

"Lucia Heartwood, thank you for answering our summons. Please be seated," said Theo, the older man at the center of the table.

I bowed my head and sat as instructed. Glancing down the table in either direction, I was met with stony faces. Everyone was the picture of professionalism and composure. I, too, kept the smile off my face and sat waiting patiently, hands folded in my lap.

"We are happy you have come voluntarily," Theo said. "We have always admired your dedication to our community, and you have always, in the past, conducted yourself properly."

Voluntarily? Why would you have to drag anyone before the Elders for a nomination, I wondered. A feeling of dread gathered in my stomach.

Something was wrong.

"We trust you to be honest with us," said Diane, the ghostly-looking, stooped woman beside Theo. She gazed at me with milky blue eyes that, despite their years, bore into me with an intensity.

"Of course," I whispered. My mouth had gone suddenly dry. I cleared my throat. "Of course," I said firmly.

"Good," Theo said. "We have asked you to this hearing to answer some questions about the recent introduction of vampires into the valley."

"The... the vampires?" I asked. "You mean Kate? Uh, Katherine Ward and her housemates?"

Theo lowered his brows and took a deep breath. "Yes, we understand that the vampire known as Kate was offered temporary sanctuary in our valley some months ago and has yet to leave."

"Worse," said Ruth from farther down the table. "She has enthralled a witch, your niece, who lives with her and the one from their Council."

"Enthralled? What do you mean?" I asked, trying to control my rising anger. The idea that the vampires were somehow controlling Sara, and the fact that it was Ruth of all people who was making the accusation, was just too much. "Sara and Kate have been friends since they were young. I've met and spent time with all four vampires living at the house, and they don't control anyone."

"Four?" Diane said, her eyes wide. "That is news. I know I would remember approving the addition of four vampires to our valley. We did not. They are all here without our permission and will have to leave immediately, taking with them any humans or witches they have under their control. We will not have blood magic in the valley."

"Now, wait a minute—," I began, but was cut off by yet another Elder.

"Everyone knows that vampires are killers. They are probably feeding on humans up and down the river. Soon we will be blamed for allowing them to hunt nearby," said one Elder from a neighboring community.

"Hunting?" I said. "That's ridiculous. Their meals are served from plastic bags. If you would just—," but I was cut off again.

"How do we know that this woman herself isn't enthralled to the blood drinkers?" Ruth spat.

I stared at her with wide eyes. How could she make such an accusation? Not only was I outraged, but I felt betrayed. I opened my mouth to argue, but Theo stopped me.

"This has clearly gotten out of hand," Theo said before I could object to Ruth's lunacy. "I think we've heard enough for now." He looked up and down the table at the stony faces and sighed. Turning back to me, he said, "Lucia, please leave us so that we may discuss what is to be done about this problem privately."

"*Problem?*" I mouthed. I couldn't believe what I was hearing. How could they believe that I would allow anyone to control Sara or me, or practice dark magic? This was ridiculous. "Please, I think you may have misunderstood—," I began before it was Theo's turn to cut me off.

"Thank you, Lucia. You are dismissed," he said in a tone that left no room for discussion.

Dismissed? My blood heated, and my hands grew warm with the urge to pull on my gift, but I couldn't let it show. I wanted to yell, to shout that they had it all wrong, but I found myself rising to my feet and walking back out the way I'd come.

I paused on the sidewalk, composing myself to go back inside. *I would not be dismissed that easily. Why had I walked out? How had I let them treat me that way?* But I knew. I'd held the Elders on a high pedestal my whole life, and being brushed aside in that way was a shock. I was in shock, I thought. There was no use in going back now. I would only make things worse. The heat drained away, and my whole body felt numb as I walked back to my car.

My mind cleared as I climbed behind the wheel. This was not how I had pictured the evening going. The Elders clearly weren't going to accept me as one of their own. Worse, it seemed the House was no longer welcome in the valley.

What would this mean? Where would they go?

And, would Sara go with them when they left?

2

KATE

My latest engraving was taking shape nicely. It was a small piece, a ring. I stuck with my usual motif of leaves and flowers, although the canvas I worked on left little room for embellishment. At least, the design was recognizable. But it wasn't the design that mattered. As I engraved the small surface of the gold ring, I poured determination and strength of will into the object itself. I wasn't exactly sure how I achieved this, but it worked. After creating several similarly imbued objects, mostly jewelry, I'd developed a sense for when it was taking hold and when I needed to focus more intently to get the job done. The witches called them Relics, and as far as we knew, I was making the first new ones in centuries.

I leaned back and rested my fingertips on the locket I wore against my chest. The love and gratitude I'd infused the locket with swelled inside me, bringing a smile to my lips. I hoped that whoever bought this little ring would find as much comfort in it as I found in my locket. And, I hoped it would fetch a nice price at auction too.

I'd only auctioned one piece so far. It was a pocket watch filled with calm and serenity, something I figured anyone would want. Sara had found the perfect auction house, and it sold for nearly thirty million dollars. Even after the auction house took its cut—thirty-five percent—, we ended up with plenty of money, more than I ever imagined earning. After a few splurges, like buying a new car for myself, we still had plenty left, but I was learning that it took a lot of money to run a House, even a small one like ours. I'd never considered the taxes we owed to the vampire Council—over fifty percent of our take—along with regular expenses like bills, insurance, mortgage, Bruce's salary, and the hefty cost of blood for three vampires—Bruce covered Felix's needs. I also wanted to boost our funds to upgrade the house so we could accommodate more people—humans, vampires, or witches if needed.

Being a leader, especially of a group of supernaturals, was not something I ever imagined for myself. I had no idea how much satisfaction I would gain from helping people like Bruce, our human housemate. Spending the money to provide a place for those who needed it felt like the right thing to do. Vampires, especially, were at the mercy of their sires and the Council. A vampire in a dispute with either had nowhere to seek sanctuary. Sara and her family kindly took me in when I was in trouble and had nowhere else to turn. I wanted to do the same for others. And I was starting with E.

E worked for the Council until she was mistreated while trying to help Bruce. She had lived at the Council's house, and when she chose not to return to her job, she lost both her home and her livelihood. She was staying with us until she figured out what she wanted to do. She was my test case. I just wished I could feel more generous toward her than I did.

It wasn't that there was anything wrong with E. She was great. You couldn't help but be captivated by the small vampire with the easy smile and the bubbly attitude. Everyone loved her. And that was the problem.

She was a long-time friend and former housemate of Marcus. The two were close. Very close. Like sleeping in his room each day and walking around the house in his old t-shirts, close. I should have been happy for them. I should have been supportive of my friends, but I was struggling for some reason.

Marcus and I were friends, nothing more. But there was something about seeing the two of them together, knowing they were sharing a bed just across the hall. It irritated me. The mere thought made my pulse quicken and my fangs descend, as if I were ready for a confrontation. Which was stupid; E wasn't my rival, she was my guest. And even if Marcus were single, it was impossible for me to be with a vampire. My past experiences had proven that point.

The sound of the door at the bottom of the basement steps opening and closing interrupted my thoughts, reminding me that the vampires in question were now awake and heading upstairs. I sighed and pushed away from the table where I was working. I knew I should go upstairs, too. There was a House dinner that evening. At least once a week, Bruce and Silas would cook up something special for those who ate, and we would all gather around the table. It had quickly become a tradition I loved. I took a deep breath and straightened my shoulders. It was time to be the leader, to act like I knew what I was doing, to be in charge.

I smiled to myself as I climbed the stairs to the main floor. It was ridiculous that I was any kind of leader at all, let alone the leader of this particular group of people. I was by far the youngest and least experienced among them. Well, okay, Sara and I were the same age, but she had her act together long before I did, and I relied on her like an older sister most of the time. I shook my head and thought about my good luck. Sure, I'd been murdered by a crazy vampire and turned against my will, I'd lost my job, my family, and my home, but I'd found a new life and family I was growing to love very much. I gripped my locket again and headed for the dining room, where the sounds of playful banter could be heard over the clatter of dishes and glassware.

The savory aroma of roast beef, garlic mashed potatoes, green beans, and fresh bread filled the air as I approached the dining table. I wish I could say it smelled enticing, but it didn't. Sure, it smelled good, but not like food anymore.

Sybil, Sara's mother, was already seated, along with Marcus and E. Sara was delivering food from the kitchen, and Felix was pacing, a book open in his hands, head bent over the pages.

"Good evening, Sybil," I said as I came up behind her.

"Hello, Katie," Sybil replied, turning to give me a warm smile. I squeezed her shoulder and leaned in to give her a peck on the cheek, inhaling her scent—a mix of herbs, oranges, and fresh green growth. She was a Garden Witch, also known as a Green Witch, and was like a second mother to me, especially now that my mother thought I was dead.

Straightening up, I paused briefly and glanced at Felix. At first, I assumed he was poring over one of his old journals. He'd found a possible answer to my strange differences by combing through them. He was convinced that I was part fae. I was eager to see if he would make any more discoveries that could point us toward finding who the fae were and where they'd gone. The only fae anyone had heard of were stories and legends. But, like my memories of my father, which were gone completely, Felix was convinced that the fae had left and taken most traces of themselves along with them.

The blond proto-viking's lips twitched as he tilted the cover of the book he was reading to give me a peek, but it wasn't a journal he had in his hands. It was, of course, the next romance in the series I was currently reading, about a demon hunter and her vampire lover. I rolled my eyes and then deliberately ignored him, not willing to give him the satisfaction of an outburst he was clearly fishing for.

As I turned toward my assigned chair, Sara gave me a wink and a sly grin. I should have known. "Did you tell him what I was reading?" I demanded. All the romance novels I'd been reading lately came from Sara's very large collection, and I depended on her recommendations, which were excellent—unlike her discretion, apparently.

"I wasn't aware that it was a secret," she said matter-of-factly as she set the dish of beans down and turned back toward the kitchen.

I snorted, then remembered myself, realizing I was supposed to be the hostess that evening and that we had guests. I nodded politely to Marcus and E, who smiled back at me. Marcus was dressed in civilian clothes—jeans and a grey T-shirt, the same color as his eyes. Seeing him out of uniform seemed odd, even though he hadn't been acting as an enforcer for the Council for a while. He still had his close-cropped military haircut, though, and I suspected that was how he'd worn his hair when he was changed. Our hair never grew past the length it was when we were turned. E had a short blond bob, wore an adorable red blouse with tiny black hearts—at least she wasn't in Marcus's clothes—and looked like she was trying not to laugh. I couldn't blame her. We were not your average vampire House.

"Sorry," I said and took my seat. It took me a while to get used to sitting at the head of the long dining table, but it felt like my spot now, and I settled into my chair and picked up my napkin. The place settings for vampires were fairly simple: a black placemat, a black napkin, and a wine glass. The rest of the table was beautifully set with modern dishware, a decorative centerpiece, and candles. It looked right out of a home decor magazine. The entire house did, ever since Bruce moved in and made it his personal project to overhaul the place. He'd fallen into the roles of manager, chef, and advisor—all things he excelled at.

As I straightened the napkin in my lap, Sara returned with another dish, followed by her fiancé, Silas, and Bruce. Bruce placed a steaming stainless steel carafe next to my placemat and one next to E's. Marcus received the third from Silas, and everyone was seated. We passed around the food to those who ate and poured ourselves a glass of our preferred beverage. It was O-negative for me.

Felix had tucked his book away and taken his seat next to Bruce, draping an arm around the back of the man's chair and running his fingertips across Bruce's back. Bruce was not one for overt public displays of affection, but he smiled at Felix and placed a hand on his knee. And despite the fact that he was a vampire, there was no wine glass for Felix. Although it was awkward to see him sitting at an empty placemat, I was grateful that he didn't eat at the table. The only blood he consumed these days came from Bruce, and was a thoroughly private afair.

I cleared my throat. "I wanted to offer a toast," I said, holding up my glass. "To family, near, far, and gathered around this table. Thank you all for being part of my life and each other's."

"To family," everyone said in unison, and sipped from their glasses. All but Felix, who nodded cheerfully as everyone took a drink.

"And to Bruce and Silas for the wonderful meal," Sara added, raising her glass toward Bruce and gifting Silas with a radiant smile.

Everyone echoed their agreement, and I studied my best friend sitting beside her mate. Not long after the two had made their relationship official, Silas admitted he'd bonded with Sara—something that was permanent and beyond his control. Luckily, my witchy friend had been in love with the massive, yellow-eyed wolf shifter for quite some time. The two of them had gone from dating to mated and engaged in a matter of days, but it had come as no surprise to the rest of us. Sara set her glass down and glanced back at Silas. The way the two of them looked at each other made my heart ache, both from joy and want.

I took another sip from my glass, more to distract myself than because of hunger. But I couldn't help it when my gaze drifted to Marcus and E sitting side by side. Even though the two had been sharing a bed for weeks, I didn't see much romance between them. At least, that's what I told myself. I had resources at my disposal that others at the table didn't, and it would be easy for me to peek at their emotions, but I really tried not to.

I'd become so skilled at shutting out my housemate's feelings that I had initially missed the connection between Bruce and Felix altogether. My eyes drifted from Marcus and E over to Felix and Bruce. Felix was gazing at Bruce with the sweetest expression on his face. Now, looking at the two of them, it was laughable that I hadn't realized what they felt for each other.

At that moment, Marcus said something that made E laugh, and she placed a hand on his shoulder. My muscles tightened, and I clenched my jaw, looking away, trying not to show my reaction. *My reaction.* It was then, with my eyes averted, that the reality hit me.

I was jealous.

Not jealous of any relationship. Not jealous of love—it was all around me. No. I was jealous of E, because somewhere along the line, I'd developed feelings for Marcus.

I swallowed hard before taking a sip of blood, trying to calm myself. I turned my attention to Sybil, grasping for a distraction. Sybil was seated to my left, the only other single person at the table. She was taking small, neat bites of roast beef as she listened to the conversations around her. I wondered, not for the first time, if she still missed Sara's father. It wasn't something we'd talked about much. He had died of cancer before I met Sara, and Sybil had never remarried or dated, as far as I knew.

"How's the food?" I asked, getting her attention.

She dabbed at her mouth with a napkin. "It's wonderful. Those boys really know how to cook," she said, then paused to look at me. "Do you miss it?"

"Yeah, sometimes," I admitted. "I miss the ritual of it, and the variety. What I eat now is satisfying, but it's not the same." This was good. The conversation was what I needed. I took a deep breath and let it out, feeling much better.

She nodded. "I can imagine. I'm glad you all join us for meals, though. It's nice to all gather together." She smiled at me, wrinkling the soft skin around her deep brown eyes, and I felt a lump in my throat that had nothing to do with Marcus and everything to do with the woman sitting beside me.

So much had changed in the past six months. It hadn't been that long ago that I'd snuck downstairs in the Heartwood family home to eat privately, not wanting to upset Sybil and her sister, Lucia. And now they both sat happily around our table at least once a week, not bothered by the glasses of warm blood or the display of fangs. One thing that hadn't changed was the love the women showed me, and I was grateful for it every day.

Reaching out, I squeezed her arm and smiled, but stopped when I heard a car pull into our drive. I glanced up, and Marcus, E, and Felix were all staring toward the front of the house. They'd heard it too.

"I'll go see who's at the door," Bruce said, pushing his chair back.

"No, you sit and enjoy the meal," I said, getting to my feet. Bruce frowned at me, but I waved him off. “Please, let me.” He nodded, and I headed for the front door.

Crossing the living room, I went to the foyer and looked outside. I was surprised to see Lucia’s car pulling up out front. She was supposed to have a meeting that evening, and from what Sara had said, it was an important one.

“Did you come to celebrate?” I asked as she climbed out of the driver’s seat and shut the door. When she turned to face me, however, my joy for her vanished. Her face looked more stern than usual, which was saying something.

“I’m afraid I’ve come with some bad news,” she said, her tone strained. This was about more than her pride, more than her not being appointed as an Elder; she was nervous. In a moment of weakness, I dropped my internal wall and let her emotions reach me on the porch where I stood. I hadn’t known much to bother Lucia. All in all, she was a fairly stoic person, so the dread and uncertainty coming off her was enough to make me gasp.

We were in trouble.

3

MARCUS

The table stayed quiet as Lucia recounted what happened at the meeting of the Elders. She twisted an embroidered napkin in her hands, but her voice remained steady, and her tone was resigned. E reached over and took my hand. She didn't like confrontation, and the tension rising in the room at Lucia's words made her nervous.

I glanced at Kate, but she was completely focused on Lucia. Lately, I'd noticed the way Kate looked at E and me when she thought I wasn't paying attention. I'd gotten the impression that my relationship with E was a problem for Kate. I knew Kate liked E. She'd said so, and she'd never been anything but kind to her, but something felt off. I valued my friendship with Kate, but I couldn't deny that E was an important part of my life. She'd been an important part of my life for decades. It would complicate things greatly if the two didn't get along. I would have to talk to Kate soon, I thought, but as Lucia's story unfolded, it seemed we had more urgent matters to handle.

"It was unexpected," Lucia said when she finished telling us how she was dismissed by the Elders and decided to return to the House to share the news. "I'm sorry, and we will, of course, help in any way with the move." She leaned back in her chair and placed the napkin back on the table.

"I'm sorry," Sara said, staring at her aunt. "And just who do you expect is moving?"

"Well, it seemed fairly obvious that the Elders are going to vote to expel the House. I can't imagine it going any other way, not with the attitudes in that room." Lucia sniffed and crossed her arms. "I'm sorry, but the House will have to relocate. The vampires, at least," she said softly as if it would hide her desire that Sara remain behind.

"The House isn't going anywhere," Sara said. She glanced at Kate. "Are we?"

Kate shook her head. "I don't want to move. And I have no plans to leave this house. If the witches think they can vote us out of our home, they are mistaken."

"They pushed the last owners of this property out," Lucia continued. "If they want you gone, they can make life here very unpleasant. Besides, they are your Elders too, Sara. You'll have no choice."

"The hell I won't," Sara replied. "This is our property. We own it, and our business is located here. I'm not going to let their bigotry force us out of the valley." She glanced back at Kate.

Kate sat up in her chair and gazed around the table. "I agree with Sara, but this isn't a dictatorship, and I would like to know how the rest of you feel. Bruce?" she asked, turning first to the tattooed human on her right.

"I like this place. I've put a lot of work into it, and I've got plans. I say we stay," Bruce said.

Felix spoke up next. The ancient vampire glanced at Bruce and then back at Kate before cracking a smile. "I agree with our House leader," he said. "We stay."

Silas sat next to Felix, and all eyes turned to him. "I'm not an official member of your House, but I go where my mate is. If she's staying, then I'm staying."

Everyone knew what Sara thought. Across from her sat Lucia, who had also made her feelings known. The next person around the table was E. She shrugged, "I don't think I get a vote," she said in a small voice.

"I'd still like to know how you feel," Kate replied, and I was grateful she thought to include E. It was a nice gesture.

"Oh, well, then I say you stay. This house is so pretty. It would be a shame to have to leave it," E said, quickly glancing at me to go next and take the focus away from her.

"I'm assuming there is no law that can force the House to relocate, no matter how the Elders vote," I said, glancing first at Sybil and then at Lucia. Both witches shook their heads. "So it would only be a matter of their preference for who gets to reside in the valley? We are technically outside of the town's boundaries, am I correct?"

"You are," Sybil confirmed.

"I see. Then they have no right to make us go, and I would leave the decision to our leader, but I would like to remain. We've had enough upheaval, and I don't like the idea of running away." I looked at Kate, and she smiled.

She took a deep breath and glanced around the table. "We aren't moving. It's final. The witches can try, but we won't be bullied," Kate said. "I'll stand up for our home and everyone in it, vampire, human, shifter, and witch. We all have a right to be here."

Lucia sighed, and her sister, Sybil, patted her on the arm. "It will be okay, the Elders can be made to understand. I'm sure we can work it out, somehow," Sybil said. "Besides, we don't know how they'll vote. They could still vote to let them stay."

"They don't get to *let* us do anything," Sara said to her mother, her tone softening. "They don't have any say over what this House does or doesn't do."

"But we could at least try to reach out and smooth things over. They are our neighbors and our community. Plus, as you pointed out, Sara, our business is here. It could risk our livelihood to go against the Elders. We need to tread lightly," Sybil said.

Sara lowered her brows. "Fine, but they don't get to decide if we stay or go."

No one seemed to have anything further to add, and dinner came to an end. We all helped clear the table, and the older witches excused themselves and headed home, while the rest of us stayed downstairs in the living room. There was a strange energy in the House, and none of us was eager to leave the group.

Sara and Silas took their usual spot on the loveseat, while Bruce and Felix claimed one end of the large leather sofa facing the massive riverstone fireplace. I took one of the side-by-side chairs across from the loveseat, and E the other, curling her legs under her, making her look even smaller than she was. Kate was the last to join us and sat at the other end of the sofa, near the chair where I was sitting.

We all quietly stared at the fire, crackling merrily in the hearth, until Felix spoke up. "So what did the witches do last time to make the humans leave this place? It would be good to know."

All eyes drifted to Sara. She snorted. "Plenty. They threw everything at them that a witch could without giving themselves away. Rain, wind, lightning, and overflowing streams. They even made it seem as though the place was haunted."

"How did they pull that off?" Bruce asked.

"Earth Witches can move all kinds of solid matter, not just earth. They had a rotation of Earth Witches who would hide nearby, move objects around, and open and close doors at random," Sara said. "It seriously freaked the humans out."

"I can't see how any of that would scare us off," Kate said. "We know they're witches, and short of burning the place down, I don't think they could get us out of here."

Her words hung heavy in the room. Fire, while one of the rarer gifts, was a talent several of the witches in the valley possessed, not only Lucia.

"Do you think they would go that far?" I asked Sara.

She sat contemplating before she answered. "I don't think so. The witches in the valley hold life sacred. I don't think they would put lives in danger to drive us away. Or at least I hope they wouldn't."

"Are we in danger?" E asked, shifting in the chair beside me. I glanced at her, but it was Kate who answered.

"No. I won't let anything happen to you," she said, her tone gentle and reassuring. "You're safe here."

E nodded and gave a small smile, but didn't look entirely convinced.

"I think we may be getting ahead of ourselves here," Felix said, noticing E's distress. "We've heard nothing directly from the Elders, and it's quite possible that Lucia misunderstood the situation. I say we don't worry until we have to. The house is warded, and we are a fairly capable group."

"Yes, we are," Kate said, placing a hand on her locket.

"Well, I hate to break up the party, but I have to get to Seattle tonight to meet with the new Council," Felix said, standing and offering a hand to Bruce.

"Are you going too?" Kate asked Bruce.

"No, but I'll see him off, and then I have a list of things to do tonight. Let me know if you need me, though. I'll be around," Bruce said, following Felix out of the room.

I wasn't surprised when Sara and Silas, who'd been gazing at each other in the way newly mated couples often do, excused themselves next. They each had some mumbled excuse about chores and work tasks, but they left together, and their footsteps echoed on the main stairs and down the hall to their room. I didn't blame them; in fact, I envied their love and the connection they shared.

I glanced over at E. She was watching me with a sad smile on her lips. "I think I'm going to go down and take a bath," she said. "You don't need the bathroom for a bit, do you, Marcus?"

I shook my head. "No. Take your time. I'll be up here with Kate," I said.

She rose to her feet with the fluidity of a ballet dancer, unfolding with a precision and grace that made me smile. She waved at Kate and then kissed me on the cheek before heading downstairs. I watched her leave the room when Kate got my attention.

"You don't have to stay up here just to keep me company," Kate said. "If you want to go with E..."

"Oh, no. I want to give her her privacy. And I've got nowhere to go and nowhere to be these days," I replied.

Kate cocked her head as she regarded me. "Do you miss it? Your job as an enforcer?"

"Yes. I miss it very much," I said. "Don't get me wrong; I didn't agree with all the Council did, or every law I was asked to enforce, but I miss it."

"You had a purpose," Kate said quietly, and I nodded.

"I did." I smiled at an early memory her words sparked. "You know, my very first job was also in law enforcement?"

"When you were a human?"

"Yes. I was a police officer before the war, for almost five years."

"The war? I assume we aren't talking about any war I lived through."

"World War Two," I said, watching her eyebrows rise and wondering why I'd mentioned the war. I usually avoided the subject.

"Of course," she said with a smirk. "I think several of my great-grandfathers fought in that one."

"I'm sure they did," I said. "A lot of us did, and a lot of us didn't come home after." Memories I hadn't examined in a long time sprang to mind. A small two-bedroom cottage with yellow curtains in the window and a red rosebush out front. My throat grew tight, and I tried to banish the image and the thoughts swimming in my head.

Kate grew quiet then, watching me. I wondered if she could feel what I was feeling, if she sensed emotions I'd accidentally summoned by bringing up the war. I cleared my throat. "Sorry, I didn't mean to get so dark," I said. "What I was trying to say is I've always been drawn to the same type of work, trying to make the world safer and better for the people I protect. I can't picture myself doing anything else."

"You could go back," Kate said. "Felix said that you've got a job if you want it."

I thought about what she said. Felix had made me the offer soon after I'd walked away, after the Council had been exposed for ignoring their own laws and manipulating the system for the benefit of the few. It had been a wake-up call. I'd been looking the other way for decades, telling myself that I was making a difference and preventing bigger tragedies than the ones I saw unfolding. But I knew who I worked for. I knew how they behaved behind closed doors and how little regard they had for both human and vampire life. I'd been wearing blinders for far too long.

"I believe that Felix is a good person and has good intentions—probably always has—," I said. "But I need time. Maybe when there's been some real change in our culture, I can feel comfortable about going back."

Kate nodded. "You don't have to explain to me. I understand better than most," she said.

"I don't want you to think that I'm miserable," I said, smiling. "I'm not. I'm glad to be here, and I'm thankful for you giving E a place to stay. She's having a harder time than I am. At least I'm still in my home with my people."

Kate's smile fell, and she gazed down at her hands folded in her lap. "I'm happy to be able to help her," she said, glancing up at me. "I want to help more people, vampires, shifters, whoever. It seems there's a need."

"There is," I replied, hoping this was a good time to bring up Kate's feelings about E. "Kate, I know you want to help E, but if you don't feel comfortable having her here for some reason—," I started to say, but Kate cut me off.

"No. I like her. She's kind and friendly, and gets along with everyone in the House. Hell, even Lucia likes her, and that's saying a lot," Kate said. "It's not her. I promise. And, I'm happy for you two. I really am."

Us two? I thought, understanding finally clicking into place. "Kate, do you think that E and I are together? Like a couple?" I asked.

She stiffened and sat upright. "Well, it's none of my business. I just assumed because you're sleeping together, but honestly, I have no idea how most vampire relationships work. I mean, I don't care if it is just sex. Like I said, it's none of my business."

I waited for her to finish. I could have stopped her and put her out of her misery sooner, but seeing her so flustered was more than a little endearing. "Kate," I finally said. "We aren't a couple. And, we aren't sleeping together."

Kate's forehead creased in confusion. "But you are, I mean, she's sleeping in your bed..."

"Yes, she's sleeping in my bed during the day. She has nowhere else to sleep. But I sleep on the floor, and we are not having sex."

Kate glanced down at her hands again, but this time there was a smile on her lips, and I didn't have to read emotions to know that my admission pleased her. My chest constricted, and my fangs tingled at the thought. I'd been drawn to Kate from the moment I'd met her in a club on James's arm. She had a curiosity and straightforward way about her that intrigued me. She was unusual for a vampire. I hadn't learned how unusual she was until later, when she'd been covered in her own blood after a brutal attack by her sire. She was different. A half-human, half-fae, turned vampire. She was irresistible, and not just to me, but to all vampires who scented her blood.

Despite her smile, I knew Kate was reluctant to allow herself to get too close to any vampire, even a friend. In the first months I'd lived with her, she used her abilities to push back against me, to turn me off her scent. She'd been afraid of what living in the same house would push me to do. It had worked. But when I found out, I'd put an end to it. I didn't want her manipulating the way I felt, and she'd stopped.

That had been the beginning of a slowly building attraction to her. I was convinced it was about more than just her blood. Yes, every time I was around her, I found myself wanting her. I wanted to be near her, to hold her, to brush my lips against her soft neck. But I felt the same when we were apart. I was falling for her. I nearly said so in that moment, but I stopped myself.

"Are you okay?" Kate asked, shifting on the sofa. "Do you need something? Some blood, perhaps?"

I smiled and shook my head. "No," I said. "I'm fine. It's just been a lot to take in tonight." I gazed into her worried brown eyes. "Don't worry about me," I said. "You have enough on your plate. I can take care of myself, I promise."

She nodded and smiled. "What a relief," she said, mimicking wiping her brow. "Now all I have to worry about is a town full of angry witches, a homeless vampire, and being the maid of honor at the wedding between my witchy best friend and a shifter; two cultures I know nothing about."

"Sounds like a Tuesday around here," I said, and got to my feet. "I'm not running away, but I hear Bruce in the kitchen, and I thought I'd go offer to help with the dishes. Care to join?"

She screwed up her face, wrinkling her nose. "Ugh, I think this is one of those times I'm going to play the leader card and say no," she said, and gave me a wink.

"Say no more," I replied, and reached out, placing a hand on her shoulder to give her a squeeze. Before I could withdraw my hand, however, she covered it with hers, resting it there and trapping me in place.

I sighed, suppressing my desire and forcing myself to relax. I knew that with direct touch, she could feel my emotions clearly, and I didn't want to upset her. She'd been pursued by an obsessed vampire once and attacked by another. I didn't want her to worry that I was becoming a problem, someone she would have to protect herself against once more.

Then she lifted her hand, and I was free.

As I left the room, guilt replaced desire. *If she knew how I felt, would she still want me here?* If I confessed, would she allow me to be as close as we were, I wondered. I was afraid it would ruin the friendship we already had, and I didn't want to risk it. She'd been through a trauma, and I didn't want to retraumatize her.

I would not become a James to her.

4

SARA

The sun was high, shining through the thin curtains of the bedroom and filling it with a bright glow. Silas was asleep. My head rested against his chest, and his breath came deep and steady. Every morning, when I woke, I still couldn't believe he was here, that he was real. No matter how many times he touched me and I touched him, it was a revelation.

I should have stayed quiet and let him rest, but I couldn't help it. I raised my hand and traced a finger across his opposite shoulder, over the rounded muscle of his chest, letting my hand rest against the tanned skin of his flat stomach.

"Mmmm," he mumbled, and took a deep breath. He brought his hand up and covered mine, grasped it, and pulled my fingers to his mouth, kissing them. He inhaled again, opening my hand and placing a kiss in the center of my palm.

"Good morning," I said, wrapping a leg over his and burrowing closer, then pushing myself up to reach his neck. He tilted his head, and I nipped at the scar where his neck met his shoulder—the spot I'd bitten, marking him as mine, my mate. It wasn't something witches did, or that I'd ever imagined doing before I met this powerful shifter. But seeing that mark on him and knowing I bore his mark on my neck was thrilling.

He moaned as my lips sealed over the scar, and I bit down gently. He inhaled sharply, and before I knew what was happening, I was on my back with Silas above me, looking down with hooded yellow eyes. "Good morning," he said, nudging my legs apart with a knee as he settled between my thighs. "Did you want my attention?"

"Yes," I said, biting my lower lip. He leaned down and kissed me. His kiss was soft and slow, but I didn't want soft and slow. I'd lain beside him for over half an hour, fantasizing about this moment. I was ready. I raised my hips and pressed myself against the hard length of him.

"Gods, woman," he breathed. He moved back slightly and, in a well-practiced move, seated himself deep within me.

I sighed and pulled him closer, enjoying the sensation of being stretched, filled. The rocking of our bodies and the growing pleasure were, at the same time, familiar and a wonder each time we reached for each other. Always more than I could have imagined and never enough.

I wrapped my legs around him, gasping as the intensity increased. I dug my fingers into his arms. Mindful of my gift, I channeled my energy deeper into my body and away from my hands. I'd shocked my mate so many times during sex, I wasn't sure he even felt it anymore, but I really tried not to.

As the pressure continued to build, I gently pushed against his chest with my hand. Sensing my cue, he leaned back, sliding a hand between us to touch me. It was exactly what I needed, and he muffled my cry with a kiss as waves of pleasure overtook me, flowing through my body and threatening to erupt from my fingertips in arcs of electricity. I loosened my grip on Silas just in time, clenching my fists as blue light engulfed my hands and then sputtered out. Exhausted, I lay gasping while he thrust harder, growling deep in his throat, and following me over the edge. He stilled, letting his head drop to the pillow beside mine.

I turned my face toward him. He lay with his wavy dark hair

partially covering his closed eyes and a smile on his full lips. "Hey, I didn't electrocute you that time," I said.

His smile grew wider, but his eyes remained shut. "No, you didn't," he said. "But, I don't mind so much when you do." He paused and flicked a golden eye open. "If you ever want me to finish early, feel free to give me a jolt," he said with humor in his voice.

"Seriously?" I asked and let out a small chuckle. "Is that what you like? When I torture you?"

"And when you laugh like that while I'm still inside of you," he said, leaning forward to kiss my mouth as I laughed at his comment. "Yup, just like that," he said against my lips.

"We could try it again," I said. "I could shock you if you want me to..."

He groaned. "No... we should probably get up." He sighed and rolled to the side, but left his hand resting on my stomach, not moving to get out of bed.

"We could pretend we're sick and stay in bed all day," I suggested.

"There is no way the vampires in the house aren't aware of what we've been doing up here, not with their hearing. They would certainly call us out if we tried to claim we were too sick to get out of bed."

"You're probably right," I said. "Besides, I'm sure there will be things to do and fires to put out, especially after last night."

His hand on my belly tensed. "It's going to be okay, though, right? You don't think they could actually make you leave?"

"I don't think so. I'm more worried about my family's relationship with the town. The witches here are our community, and they take their cues from the Elders. If they're against us, it could get uncomfortable. Already, I've noticed some tension. There are fewer and fewer customers in the shop these days, and I've seen the way people look at me and watch me when I'm in town. They've all heard about the vampires living here, and they all know I'm engaged to a shifter."

"Does it bother you?" he asked. His tone was curious and kind.

"A bit," I admitted. "I haven't always lived here, but these are my people. No one likes to be an outsider. Especially now that we're planning our wedding, I want to feel like my community supports me. I don't want anything ruining our happiness."

"Do you regret it?"

"Regret what? Asking Kate to live here or letting the House use this place as our home?"

"No," he said tentatively. He circled his fingertips over the skin of my stomach as if distracting himself. "The part about being engaged to a shifter."

"Not for one minute," I said without hesitation. "I'd move from town to town my whole life just to spend it with you."

"Well, let's hope it doesn't come to that," he said, stilling his hand. "But I'm glad to hear you say it. And I meant what I said last night. Where you go, I go."

"I don't plan on going anywhere," I said. "This is my home, our home." We were both quiet for a moment, then I asked, "Do *you* regret it? Bonding me instead of a shifter? That whatever children we have someday will be half witch?"

He spread his tan fingers across my dark skin, extending from nearly one hipbone to the other. "Not for one minute," he echoed. "I am honored to be yours. I have no regrets. And our children will be perfect because they will be ours: yours and mine. I don't care if they aren't shifters or witches. Hell, they could be puppies and I wouldn't care," he said.

I wanted to laugh, but I had to ask. "They couldn't really be puppies, though, right?"

He chuckled. "No. We don't shift until sometime around puberty. Whatever children I give you will be human. Or at least look human," he said. "As for what abilities they will have or won't have, I've no idea. I've never known a witch-shifter couple."

"Me neither," I said. "But we won't have to worry about that for a while yet. I may be ready to walk down the aisle, but I'm not so sure about being a mom just yet."

"There's no rush," he said. "Keep drinking your morning tea, and we can just keep practicing for now." He leaned closer, brushing the curls away from my face to get at my ear, nipping as his hand wandered south of my belly.

I put my hand over his, stopping its descent. "If we start again, we won't get out of this bed until after noon," I said.

"Is that a problem?" he asked, his lips against the shell of my ear.

It was very tempting to say no, but I did have things I needed to do. "Ugh, yes. Beth is coming in early today. I'm supposed to be there when she arrives." We didn't open until three in the afternoon for the few customers we had in person, but today we had a ton of online orders to fill, and I needed to be there to help.

"Okay, but can we promise to pick up here later?" he asked, moving his fingers enticingly.

"Oh yes," I replied, already regretting putting on the brakes.

He kissed my cheek and then climbed out of bed. "Do you mind if I jump in the shower first? I promise to be quick," he said.

I stared at him, standing there in the soft light, taking in every muscle on his perfect naked body. He was beautiful, he was mine, and he clearly still wanted me.

"Sara?" Silas tried again.

"Um, I'm sorry. What were you saying?"

"My eyes are up here," he joked, noticing my wandering gaze.

"On second thought, I'll join you," I said and hopped out of bed after him.

It was just before noon when I finally arrived at the shop. Despite the long shower, I still had time to grab a quick lunch on my way past the kitchen. Beth showed up shortly after, Arrow, her German Shepherd, in tow.

I loved it when she brought her dog. Arrow was the best-behaved dog I'd ever met. She was a trained search-and-rescue dog specializing in HRD (Human Remains Detection). Arrow was the one who had led Beth to discover my unusual housemates before the rest of the community caught on. Arrow had smelled Kate's breakfast and headed straight for the kitchen, following her training. She'd been so proud, and Beth had taken the news about the existence of vampires well. As it turned out, Beth was somewhat of a vampire fanatic and thrilled to learn that not only were they real, but several lived next door to her workplace. As the human daughter of a woman who married into our community, Beth hadn't known about vampires or shifters before coming to the valley.

It was about an hour after we'd started in on filling orders that I finally got up the courage to ask Beth the question that had been on my mind. "So, have you heard anything from your stepdad about what's been going on with the Elders?"

Beth stopped mid-packing and gazed up at me, her blue eyes wide. "The Elders? No. Why? What's been going on?"

I filled her in on what my Aunt had said when she'd come back from the meeting. Beth nodded, looking troubled. "I knew there were some in town that had a problem with the vampires, but I didn't know it had gone that far," she said.

"What are people saying? If you don't mind me asking?"

"No. It's fine. They speak openly in public, so it's not as if they expect their opinions to be kept private. I've heard some people say that blood magic doesn't belong in a valley of Nature Witches. That blood magic is forbidden, and that the vampires are undead and therefore… Unholy, I think is how they put it." She winced. "I'm sorry. I know it isn't true, and my stepdad isn't saying those things. Not every witch in the valley is against the House, I promise."

"Don't worry about it," I said. "The ones who are talking that way obviously don't know Kate and Marcus, haven't talked with Felix, and have clearly never been around E." I knew I was trying to reassure both Beth and myself. I suspected people were saying things along those lines, but it was still upsetting to hear it was true.

"Clearly," Beth said with a grin. "But, I'll keep an ear out and let you know if I hear anything more sinister. Okay?"

"Thank you," I said. "And, I hope it doesn't lead to people treating you badly in town."

"Ehh, I'm a human, so I've already got one strike against me.

What's one more? Plus, I don't need the approval of anyone who would hate Kate, Marcus, Felix, or E, just because they're vampires. Who wants to be friends with those people?"

She gave me a wink and a smile to show she was unbothered, but I was sorry to hear that she wasn't treated like the rest of the community. It must have been hard to live here without being a witch. Sometimes I forgot that the vampires and Silas weren't the only outsiders in the valley.

That gave me a thought."Hey, would your mom and stepdad accept an invitation to dinner sometime, do you think? And you too, of course," I said. "Once a week, the boys cook up something special, and we'd love to have them over sometime."

"That would be really cool," Beth said. "I'll ask them, but I'm almost positive they'll say yes."

"Great. Let me know, and we can plan an evening."

It was a start, I thought. It might be a small step, but at least it was a step in the right direction. I knew we couldn't host dinners for the entire valley, but it was a place to begin. Both to show the witches that not all vampires were violent killers, and to demonstrate to the vampires that not all witches were bigoted vampire-haters.

I just hoped Beth's parents wouldn't be put off by a little blood and fangs with their roast beef.

5

KATE

"So you invited them to dinner?" I asked my best friend, as we sat in the overstuffed, dusty pink chairs I'd come to think of as ours. They were positioned in the library corner of the great room, and we were surrounded by the colorful spines of Sara's many romance novels.

She shrugged. "It seemed like a good idea. The witches of this community need to get to know you and the others if we are going to find harmony here, and I thought this would be the easiest place to start."

I nodded. "Okay, I see your point. Beth is great and gets along well with everyone. It will be nice to finally meet her mom and stepdad,"

Sara offered a satisfied smile. I appreciated her effort to make things work. I knew she had more at stake than I did. It was her community, after all, and I wanted to do my part to help smooth things over if I could. She was right; Beth's parents were a good place to start.

"Hey, is Silas around today?" I asked. "I've got a project for him and Bruce."

"He's working on the other side of the Pass on a renovation with his brothers. He should be back for dinner, though. What's up?"

"We need a vampire guest room. Specifically for E," I said, not able to keep the smile off my face.

"Oh, did they break up?" she whispered, leaning toward me.

"You don't have to whisper. They're still asleep," I said, and I proceeded to tell her what I'd learned the night before.

She gave me a hopeful smile. "You like him," Sara said.

It wasn't a question. She'd seen me around him from the very beginning. She also knew the reasons why it wouldn't work. "It doesn't matter how I feel," I replied. "I've known, since Alexander and James, that I can't be with a vampire. It can't work, not with the way vampires seem to react to my blood. I'm hoping something in Felix's journals will tell us more about why that is. But for now, I don't see it happening."

Sara tilted her head. "You could at least give it a shot. I mean, he wouldn't have to bite you."

I winced. "If we were together... yeah, he would." I licked my lips, and when Sara continued to stare blankly at me, I went on. "It's a vampire thing. Not quite like the shifter marking but..." I sighed. "We bite. I don't think either of us would be able to control it."

"And you know this because?" Sara asked. She knew I'd never slept with a vampire. She knew I hadn't slept with anyone since I was turned.

I looked away, but it was a mistake. Everywhere I looked, my eyes met with shelf after shelf of romance novels. Sara followed my gaze, and her mouth dropped open. "You mean, when you... Umm... When you're alone, and you... You bite?" she asked, sounding confused. "But you're by yourself." I nodded. "You bite yourself?" she asked in disbelief.

If I could have blushed, my cheeks would have been bright red. I covered my face with my hands, mortified. I don't know why, but it was an embarrassing admission.

"Hmm, okay. It's okay. At least you heal fast," she said. "But doesn't it hurt?"

"Ugh, God. Can we stop talking about this, please?" I begged, looking up at the ceiling.

"Yeah. Yeah. No problem. So, another room for vampires," she said. "I'm sure Silas would be happy to help, but you can talk to him tonight."

"Thank you. I'll do that," I said, feeling some of the mortification drain away. "I'll offer her my room for now, and I can take one of the two guest rooms upstairs, since I can handle the light. But I like having my permanent room downstairs near my studio. Plus, I don't think I could sleep on the same floor as all the happy couples. Not with my hearing," I smirked.

"You say that, but we both know it's just because you're jealous," she said. "We seriously have to find you a man. Maybe a human?"

"Nope. Not going there," I said. "I'd probably kill the poor guy."

She nodded thoughtfully. "Well, that would be a problem." She raised her eyebrows. "But not the first body we've buried on the property."

"Okay, I'm out of here," I said, getting to my feet.

"Sorry," Sara said with a laugh. "I didn't mean to drive you away."

"You didn't," I said. "I'm going to go find Bruce and tell him about my idea." I moved toward the foyer just as rain started to fall outside, heavy rain. "Oh, hey. It's raining," I said over my shoulder to Sara.

"That's strange," she said. "It's only five o'clock."

"What does the time have to do with anything?" I asked.

"Haven't you noticed that it never rains during the day here in the valley? Didn't you ever think that was strange for this part of the country?"

"Up until a month ago, I was asleep all day, believing that I would burn to a crisp if I stepped foot outside my room before sunset, remember?" I said.

"Oh yeah," she said and grinned at me. "Sometimes I forget you're only recently a *daywalker*."

Now that she mentioned it, though, it was strange. I'd lived in Washington my whole life and was very familiar with how cloudy and wet it typically was. But she was right; over the past month, I had never seen it rain during the day here. "Are you telling me that the witches only allow it to rain at night?" I asked.

"Of course," she said. "The plants still need water."

"No. I mean, they keep it from raining all day?"

"Yes. It takes two witches at a time, but from what I understand, it's fairly simple," she said with a shrug. "But the rain doesn't usually start until after ten or so. I don't know what they're up to today."

"Hmm. Well, I think it's kinda nice," I said, peering out the window next to the front door. The rain was pelting the steps and driveway. It was the heaviest I'd seen in quite a while, but it felt cozy being inside with the hard rain falling all around.

I turned to the sound of a door opening and closing upstairs, followed a moment later by Bruce's footsteps on the front stairs. I watched him as he came down. He was wearing his usual jeans and black button-down shirt with the sleeves rolled to the elbow, showcasing his muscled, tattooed forearms, and open at the neck, revealing that the ink flowed all the way up to his hairline.

"Crazy weather we're having," he said by way of greeting. "I haven't seen it rain this hard in years."

"We were just talking about it," Sara said, coming to join us in the foyer. "Some witch must have forgotten it was their afternoon to work the weather."

"You don't think it could be raining just here, do you? Over the house?" I asked.

"No. All weather is local, but not that local. I don't know any pair of witches who could be that precise. If it's raining here, it's raining all throughout this part of the valley, at least over the closest town," Sara said.

That came as a relief. I seriously hoped this wasn't the witches messing with us. But if it was, at least they were getting wet too. Besides, I liked the rain.

"How's our roof?" I asked Bruce. As our House manager, he was well acquainted with every part of the property.

"Ship shape," he said. "Silas went over it just after Sara purchased the place. He says we won't need a new one for a few years yet."

"Good," I replied. "Because I have another project for the two of you." I outlined the problem: there were too many vampires and not enough light-proof bedrooms. He listened, nodding and staring off in the way he did when I knew he was working through a problem. I had no doubt that with him and Silas working on it, we would have a solution in no time. "Oh, and Sara's invited Beth's parents to dinner," I said.

He raised a black eyebrow. "Oh, that's a great idea," he said. "Do we know when? I'm sure I could pull something together as soon as tomorrow evening."

I gave him a fangy grin. "I have no doubt," I said. "Sara?" I glanced at my best friend, who had her phone out and was focused on the screen.

"Texting now," she said. "And... Tomorrow evening is good."

I turned back to Bruce. "Perfect. Beth, her human mother, and her witch stepfather. Let's make sure to include Lucia and Sybil. We could use a redo after last night's family dinner."

"On it," Bruce replied.

"And, Sara," I said, getting her attention. "Have your mom and aunt arrive ahead of time so they can get all the griping about the Elders out of the way before the others arrive. I want to try to keep the conversation light."

"I think that's a good idea. I'll give my mom a heads-up, and she can help handle Aunt Lucia. She's been doing it her whole life after all," Sara said, giving me a wink. She glanced back at her phone and wandered into the living room, leaving Bruce and me in the foyer.

I watched her walk away and then flicked my gaze back to Bruce. He was standing with his head cocked to the side, watching me. "What?" I asked.

"It looks good on you," he said, the corner of his mouth curving up in a rare smile.

I looked down at my outfit. It was my usual oversized cream knit sweater and jeans. "What does?" I asked.

"Leadership," he replied.

I let out a sigh. "Don't go telling Felix, he'll just tell me how proud he is and make a fuss," I said.

Bruce shrugged. "He's been awake for hours, just waiting in our room so he doesn't get a sunburn. I'm sure he's heard everything we've said."

Oh great, I thought. I knew he was going to give me a hard time later. I should have realized from the start that he was much older than the rest of us, just by how supportive and calm he was all the time. Felix was the ultimate father figure in many ways, and a total child in others.

"Okay," I said. "I'll deal with him when he comes down. For now, let me know if you need any help getting things ready for tomorrow."

Bruce paused for a moment before replying. "I've been wanting to hire some additional staff, if you don't mind, of course. I've already contracted with a landscaping company, but I'd like to bring on some help for inside the house. It's a pretty big place, and it's getting bigger. It would be nice to have a housekeeper and maybe someone to help with serving when we have guests."

"You're in charge of the house. If you need more help, by all means, hire staff. We've got plenty in the bank, and I trust you and Felix can work out the legal details and hire good people," I said.

"Would you like to vet them before we sign any contracts?" he asked.

I thought it over. "Sure. It could be a good idea. I could give you an idea of how the person was feeling, in case that was helpful. But, like I said, I trust you." I squeezed his bicep and gave him a smile before he headed off toward the kitchen, presumably to get dinner ready.

Listening to the rain on the roof and all around me, there was only one thing I wanted to do with the rest of my evening. I wandered back into the library and considered my options. Felix still had the next book in my demon-hunter series, and I would rather have died than ask him for it. I ran my gaze over the shelves of candy-colored spines. There was so much to choose from. In the end, I picked the first in a series of cat-shifter books and sneaked back downstairs for some private reading before supper.

6

LUCIA

We walked up the front steps of what I thought of as The House. All the other homes in the valley had names similar to ours: The Heartwood Family Home. There was Thornbrush Manor, Kindlewood Home, and Stormwind House. I supposed this place would eventually have a proper name once the House was forced to move out, and it was a regular witch home, I thought. It was a shame. I knew the vampires were trying their best, and overall, this lot was a good group. I loved Kate, of course, and the rest weren't so bad.

"We were just here two nights ago," I said to Sybil as I climbed the last few steps. "Why the rush to entertain?"

Sybil glanced my way and gave me a smile. "Stop complaining. I know you don't mind. You love it when someone else cooks."

"It's not that. It's just, I'm not sure having community members over for dinner is such a good idea. The differences between... our kinds will only be highlighted. I don't like it," I said.

Sybil snorted as she reached for the door. "I'm sure Beth's parents are nice people. I don't think we have anything to worry about." She paused before opening the door and gave me a hard look. "Promise me you will be on your best behavior?"

"Me?" I said. "It's not me that's started tongues wagging all over town. It's not me who's broken tradition by living with vampires, or her shifter boyfriend... Before they're even married," I added under my breath.

"You're not helping," Sybil said, sounding irritated, before turning and going inside, leaving me on the porch.

Why she was upset with *me* was beyond my understanding. The only reason I agreed to come was that I didn't want the evening to turn into a complete disaster. It wasn't like, by inviting random witches over, the House was going to influence the Elders. We still hadn't learned how the meeting had ended, and Sybil thought that was a good sign, but I wasn't convinced. I knew it was just a matter of time. I heaved a sigh and followed after Sybil.

Bruce was waiting in the foyer and greeted me as I entered. "May I take your coat, Ms. Heartwood?" he offered. He was such a gentleman, a human, and sleeping with a vampire of all things, but a true gentleman.

"Thank you, Bruce," I said, handing it over. "Whatever you've got cooking smells good. I hope it's enough to distract from the fact that half the table won't be eating."

He nodded. "Thank you. We'll be having a fresh green salad, followed by lamb with mint sauce, roasted potatoes and carrots, and chocolate mousse for dessert. Would you like a cocktail or a glass of wine while you wait? I chilled the white you like."

"Yes, that would be nice. Thank you," I said and went to join the others in the living room. Before I'd made it two steps, Felix approached with my wine. "Were you listening in, young man?" I asked the tall vampire with long, messy hair. He was a lawyer, and supposedly older than dirt, but he still looked like a kid to me.

"Lucia darling, the very sound of your voice makes my ears prick up. I can't help but hang on your every word. Besides, it brings me pleasure to serve you," he said cockily as he handed me my glass.

"You're far too cheeky. You know that, right?" I said.

"Oh, I am entirely aware. May I escort you in?" he asked, offering me his elbow.

I sighed but took his arm. He was trying. We walked slowly past the library—if you could call it that. It was full of nothing but smut, I'd checked. It was completely inappropriate to display such books. What one read—or listened to—was personal. "When do the special guests arrive?" I asked, trying to distract myself. I hadn't seen any strange cars in the driveway, and I assumed we were early.

"In thirty minutes or so," Felix confirmed. "Do you know Louis and Maureen?"

I sniffed. "I've known Louis for years. I haven't had the opportunity to meet Maureen yet," I said. "She's human, you know?"

"Yes, I've been told," he said.

"Do you anticipate that being an issue?" I asked.

"I will restrain myself. I assure you," he said with a wink. While he *had* bitten and bedded the only other human in the house, I was sure that, after all his time on Earth, he was well in control of himself.

"Not you," I said dismissively. I tilted my head and dropped my voice. "But the others?"

"Don't worry," he said, patting my hand with his cold, smooth one as we joined the group.

As we entered the main living room, Felix let me go and went to help Bruce. Everyone was there: Sara, Silas, Bruce, who was handing out drinks, and the four vampires. Sara was talking with her mother, Sybil, and Silas was beside her as usual. The vampires were spread throughout the room, and I moved toward E, who sat alone on the sofa.

I took a seat beside the small blonde vampire and sipped from my glass. The wine was excellent. "How are you this evening, dear?" I asked.

She beamed at me with her usual cheerfulness, but I could tell her heart wasn't really in it. "Good, thank you," she said, her expression stiff.

"Okay, let's cut to it," I said. "What's the matter?"

E blanched and looked at me with wide eyes. "Oh, no. Nothing's the matter. Really, I'm fine—"

"Save it," I said, cutting her off. "Tell me what happened." The thought that anyone had been rude to E or upset her in any way made my blood heat.

She sighed and offered a sad smile that was more convincing than her first. "Nothing happened," she said. "It's just, I've been feeling a bit lost lately. I miss my job and my friends. I miss my old room and the city." She shrugged. "I guess I'm just feeling sorry for myself."

I nodded. "I understand," I said. "It can be lonely out here. What are your plans? For the future, I mean."

She shook her head. "That's the problem. I have no plans since I quit my job and moved out of the Council house. I thought this would feel like a vacation, a chance to rest for a while, but I just feel like I'm in limbo."

I patted her on the knee. "Give it some time. Who knows, you may find yourself back in the city before long," I said, taking another sip.

She seemed to consider. "Maybe you're right," she said.

"Don't worry, dear. I'm sure you'll figure yourself out," I said just as Marcus and Kate came over to join us.

"I think our guests are arriving," Kate said. "Bruce has gone to get the door. I'm feeling nervous." She smoothed her hands down her fitted black trousers, which she wore paired with a simple red blouse and black heels; she looked quite nice. Her long, dark hair was loose in waves down her back, and her pale complexion glowed slightly, indicating she had been out in the sunlight earlier. It was just good to see her out of her sweater and jeans for once. She looked like a real grown-up. Not that she would actually grow up, I thought.

It was a shame. I was glad she wasn't dead, of course, but I deeply regretted what had happened to her. She would never know what it was to age, to watch your body change, to carry a child. I banished that thought and refocused on what she was saying.

"I'm sure it goes without saying, but let's try to avoid the subject of the Elders and their issues with the House tonight. I want to keep the conversation light, if possible. Tonight should be about getting to know Beth's parents and them getting to know us," she said.

I couldn't help but feel the statement was directed at me, and when she looked my way for confirmation, I shrugged. "Why would I bring it up?" I asked. "I want to keep this conflict as quiet as possible." That was true. I hoped everything would be settled quickly and to the Elders' satisfaction. Maintaining harmony in our community was important. You couldn't have so many magical individuals in one place without harmony and strong leadership, and that was the job of the Elders. People respected their decisions and followed their guidance. It was the way it had always been, and it had kept peace in the valley for as long as anyone could remember.

Kate nodded and smiled at me, showing the tips of her canine teeth before turning away to greet her guests. Seeing her fangs was a reminder of how much had changed, not just for Kate but for our family and the valley itself. It wasn't me the Elders were concerned about. The House would learn that you couldn't go against the Elders' wishes and tradition. Eventually, the House would have to relocate. It would be sad to have them farther away, but we would visit. This would all be over soon, and things would go back to normal, I reassured myself. And, most importantly, our family would regain the community's respect.

But that was a discussion for later. I wouldn't want to involve Louis and his wife in House business or Elder politics. We just needed to get through the night without incident. We didn't need to give the witches of the valley any more ammo against the vampires or our family.

Louis looked just as I remembered: tall and slim, with sandy brown hair streaked with grey and a grey beard, cropped close to his chin. His wife, Maureen, looked a lot like Beth. She was of average height, probably in her fifties, with long blonde hair and blue eyes. She had the toned body of an athlete, and Beth told me that she and Louis met while windsurfing in Oregon.

Introductions were made, and Kate led everyone back to the living room. We arranged ourselves on the various sofas and chairs to chat while Bruce and Silas put the finishing touches on dinner.

Conversation was, indeed, light. Louis recounted how he and Maureen met, and Beth sat quietly with the rest of us, listening with a warm smile. Maureen spoke of their trips back to the Gorge in

Oregon. She and Louis drove a camper van from spot to spot to find the best surfing during the season, only returning to Washington when the weather got too bad to surf. The travel sounded nice, but I couldn't fathom sleeping in a van at my age.

Twenty minutes later, Bruce came in to announce that dinner was ready. We all proceeded to the dining table, which had been set with extra touches for the evening and had been expanded to accommodate all twelve of us. All the place settings matched for once, and there were several low arrangements of fresh flowers at either end of the long table, as well as lit candles. We took our seats, and the boys brought out the food. It looked and smelled amazing. I suspected it would be awkward, with only two-thirds of us eating, but at least there wouldn't be pitchers of blood on the table. Or so I thought.

After setting the last dish down, Bruce and Silas went back to the kitchen, came out carrying the familiar stainless steel carafes, and started depositing them beside the vampires. I grabbed Sybil's arm. "What are they thinking?" I hissed.

Sybil snapped her head in my direction. "What is the matter with you?" she asked.

I let out a breath. "With me—" I began, but was interrupted by Kate.

"Lucia, is there a problem?" she asked pleasantly.

"No," I said, but I could hear the strain in my voice. I took another breath. "I just assumed, given the company tonight, that you all would have eaten ahead of time." As I looked around the table, I saw Marcus tip his pitcher into a wine glass, filling it halfway with the thick red liquid. Why couldn't they see how inappropriate it was to drink blood in front of a witch and a human who weren't family or House members? I was sure that Louis and Maureen were not only offended but disgusted by what was happening. I glanced back at Kate.

"This is our home, and my House," she said. "We eat together, like always. I'm not going to hide what I eat, nor would I ask the others to do so. I'm sure that when they accepted the invitation, Louis and Maureen understood that we were vampires."

It was then that Louis spoke up. "Really, we have no problem with it. I assure you," he said.

Kate inclined her head and then poured herself a glass as well. I was mortified, not for having spoken up, but for the spectacle that was unfolding. It never crossed my mind that they would drink openly in front of strangers. It had taken Kate a long time to drink in front of Sybil and me, after all.

I filled my plate when the food came around and tried not to imagine the thoughts going through the minds of our guests, or the stories they would tell the next day in town, about watching the vampires consume human blood while everyone else ate. The food was delicious, however, and the meal, along with the pleasant chatter, somewhat mollified me. We just needed to get through the meal without any more embarrassment.

I turned my head when Maureen addressed Felix, curious to see what topic of conversation they would strike up. For all his flirtations, Felix was a very interesting individual. "I see you're not drinking this evening. I hope having us here isn't making you uncomfortable," Maureen said as if it were possible to make Felix uncomfortable.

He smiled broadly at her comment. "Not at all. I am quite comfortable," he replied. "I thought about inviting Bruce to sit on my lap so I could have a bite, but I thought that might be too much for our first meal together, and Bruce is a tad shy." He flicked his gaze in my direction and gave me a wink.

I nearly dropped my fork, but Maureen burst out laughing. "It's probably good. I'm afraid that might have made me blush," she said.

"That might be worth it. What do you say, Bruce?" Felix said, turning to the man.

Thankfully, Bruce raised an eyebrow and shook his head. "You'll go hungry if you keep it up," he said.

"I'm afraid he has the last word," Felix said with mock sorrow.

Maureen might have enjoyed the joke, but I did not. If the idea was to invite two members of the community over to show them how normal the vampires could be, they were doing a poor job of it. I couldn't imagine a worse impression to make.

Louis must have felt things had gone far enough because he took advantage of the pause in conversation to change the subject. "So, Sara and Silas," he said, turning to the couple. "Do you two have a date set for the wedding yet? Beth has mentioned it could be as soon as this summer."

Sara nodded. "Yes, actually. We decided to have it under the Strawberry Moon," she said.

"But that's a full nine days before the solstice," I said. "Are you planning on having two ceremonies?"

Sara's features hardened. "No, Auntie. We are having one ceremony, and it will take place on the evening of the full moon, not the Solstice. It's a shifter tradition to celebrate important events on the full moon. We wanted to honor that, and have the event after sunset so all our friends could be included."

"That sounds lovely," Maureen said. "Will it be local or on the other side of the Pass?"

"It will be here on the property," Sara said to Maureen. It could have been my imagination, but it seemed like Sara was avoiding looking toward my end of the table.

I glanced at Sybil, wondering if she knew about these plans and was keeping them to herself, as Sara had. She was definitely avoiding my gaze. "Did you know about this?" I asked quietly.

Sybil turned her head and nodded. "Yes. She told me yesterday, and I support her choice."

"Of course you do," I murmured. "It's not you who wants to lead this community someday. What do you care if the next generation flaunts our traditions?"

"Lucia, please," Sybil whispered. "Drop it."

I clenched my teeth, making my jaw ache. Why had I even come? It was a mistake to attend this dinner. Yes, Sara was my niece, and I loved her, but I didn't want to be associated with all this, not in front of a member of our community.

"Would someone please pass the potatoes?" Maureen said from across the table.

I exhaled sharply and reached for the platter of potatoes in front of me. But as I pushed the dish toward Maureen, it bumped into the carafe in front of Marcus, knocking it over toward her. Time seemed to slow, but try as I might, I couldn't reach the pitcher in time. I watched, horrified, as it spilled onto its side, the mouth of the pitcher aimed directly at Maureen, drenching her in a liter of human blood.

7

MARCUS

My head was turned away from Lucia when I heard the sound of porcelain hitting metal. I thought little of it at first, but the gasp that followed drew my attention. If I had glanced over a split second earlier, I could have stopped what happened next. Sadly, I didn't. By the time I realized what was going on, a wave of blood was already splashing toward Maureen, and there was nothing I or anyone else could do about it.

The table sat frozen for a heartbeat, everyone staring at the human woman, blood soaking through her shirt, pooling in her lap, and splattered across her face. She blinked, her expression one of shock, red droplets clinging to her lashes and running down her cheek.

And then all hell broke loose.

Before the others could move, the vampires launched into motion. I pushed back from the table, standing up and searching for a way to help as the others rushed over. Beth screamed, calling out to her mother, and Louis tried to get to his feet but was blocked by Felix. Sara and Silas sat as if stunned, watching what would happen next, while Sybil yelled Kate's name, trying to get her attention. Lucia gripped her sister's arm, her mouth open, but no sound came out. It was pure chaos, with Maureen at the center of it all, covered in blood and surrounded by vampires.

I paused, realizing what this must look like to Louis and Maureen. As the thought crossed my mind, Kate's voice rose above the others. "Everyone, just stop," she bellowed. The dining room fell silent. "I think we have too many helpers. Everyone, take a step back."

As we did, Maureen let out a shuddering breath, and Louis fell back into his chair, his face damp with sweat.

"Okay, let's move slowly and get this cleaned up," Kate said, and although her voice was strong and commanding, I could hear the slight lisping caused by her elongated fangs. "E, would you please take Maureen down to my bedroom—your room—and help her get washed up and changed? There should be something of mine that will fit her in the closet."

E nodded, moving to Maureen's side and holding out a hand, a small, closed-lipped smile on her face. She was a good choice to help the woman. Maureen took E's hand, and the rest of us stepped back farther to give them space.

"E, please bring me her clothing when you return," Bruce said. "I'm somewhat of an expert on removing bloodstains." He also offered a reassuring smile to Maureen, and she smiled back through her mask of gore.

"I suppose you would have to be around here," she said and chuckled.

The tension in the room eased with the sound, and we all took a collective breath. As E led Maureen from the dining room, I looked at Lucia. Her mouth was closed, but her expression looked haunted. I imagined the only way this could have gone worse in her eyes was if we had all actually attacked poor Maureen, and Louis had run from the house to tell the whole town.

"I am so sorry, Louis," Kate said. "I'm sure this has been upsetting—."

Louis held up a hand. "No, please don't apologize. Accidents happen; it was just a surprise, is all."

"Why doesn't everyone go to the living room while I get this cleaned up?" Bruce suggested. "I'll serve dessert there after Maureen and E return."

It was a good suggestion. Moving away from the blood-soaked table was the right decision. Felix stayed behind to help Bruce, and the rest of us headed back to the living room while they worked. Kate was the last to leave the dining room, and I waited as she talked softly with Bruce.

"How are you doing?" I asked in a low voice when she was finished. "You feeling as strong as you look?"

She snorted. "I wish. That could have gone better, but at least no one got hurt." She moved her tongue around in her mouth.

"Did you get enough to eat?" I asked. "I can bring you something or make excuses while you go feed."

She shook her head. "No, I suspect it was a combination of the spilled blood and the scent of fear in the air," she said. "I'm fine. I just can't always control my body's reactions."

"Understandable, but please let me know if you need help. You're not doing this alone," I said, squeezing her arm as we joined the others. The group was milling about, and I suspected everyone was feeling a bit unsettled. I saw Lucia deep in conversation with her sister, edging toward the foyer and escape. She shook her head, her face staring stone-cold and resigned, but Sybil wasn't giving up. I turned away, giving them privacy.

Louis was the first to take a seat on the large riverstone hearth in front of the fireplace. The night was cool, but not cold, and no fire was burning. Beth sat down beside him, and they talked quietly. It wasn't long before Maureen and E returned. Maureen was thankfully free of blood, wearing fresh trousers and a blouse. Her hair was damp, but she had a smile and looked relaxed. She gratefully took a glass of wine from Felix, who had also joined us, and she sat between her husband and daughter.

I hadn't realized we were waiting for her to come back before we could all finally settle down. But as soon as she sat, the rest of us found seats and quieted. I was happy to see that Lucia stayed with us, sitting close to her sister, although her expression hadn't softened. The silence stretched until Louis spoke.

"That was a lot of excitement. Is dinner usually that eventful around here?" he asked, with humor in his voice.

Kate smiled but shook her head. "No. We like to put on a show for special guests," she teased, but then her tone grew serious. "I'm sorry we scared you both. We react quickly and move fast, but I promise, no one here would have harmed you in any way."

Maureen nodded. "I was scared at first, but it became clear that you all were just trying to help. I think it'll just take me some time to get used to being around vampires."

She was very gracious about the whole thing. I wondered if most humans or witches would have handled it as well. But she had married a witch, so she had to be pretty open-minded.

Lucia huffed out a sigh. "I should be the one apologizing," she said. "It was my carelessness that caused this mess. I hope it doesn't reflect badly on the House."

"Don't worry," Louis said. "Beth told us about the Elders. We aren't here to judge any of you," Louis turned to address Kate. "I just want you all to know that not every witch in the valley feels the same way the Elders do."

Kate nodded. "Thank you, that means a lot. I understand that what we're doing here is new," she said. "I know that not everyone is comfortable with having us here or the fact that there are witches, humans, vampires, and shifters under one roof. It's not traditional, as some have pointed out, but it works for us, and I see no reason why we should have to keep apart."

"I couldn't agree more," Louis replied. He reached over and took his wife's hand, squeezing it. "I feel we are stronger together, with those we love most."

"Well put," Sara said. "I only wish everyone else shared your view. It would make life a lot easier." She glanced at Silas sitting beside her, and the corner of his mouth turned up.

The discussion was interrupted by Bruce, who brought the

dessert, followed by another round of drinks. The conversation turned to less heavy topics, and when the mousse was gone and the wine glasses were empty, the guests rose to leave.

I was surprised when Maureen stepped forward and pulled Kate into a tight hug. "Thank you for having us over. This is the first invitation we've gotten since I arrived here in the valley." She stepped back. "And thank you for accepting my daughter. I know she loves working next door and being included here in your home." She smiled. "Oh, and I'll get your clothes back to you tomorrow," Maureen said as they made their way to the foyer.

"No rush," Kate replied as they reached the door. "I can send your things back with Beth once Bruce has worked his magic. And thank you for being so understanding and accepting of us."

I hung back with E as the goodbyes were said and more hugs were exchanged, and noticed that Lucia and Sybil also took the opportunity to leave. I sincerely hoped Lucia would forgive herself for the accident and the rest of us for being what we were. She was a tough one. You didn't have to be an empath to see that she was struggling, trying to walk a fine line between her community's traditions and the people she clearly loved.

Once again, we found ourselves back in the living room, gathering to debrief. We all gravitated to our usual spots, and Bruce had been kind enough to serve glasses of fresh blood to Kate, E, and me. I was grateful. None of us had fed enough before dinner was interrupted. I sipped from my glass and stared across the large coffee table to Sara, who was leaning back against Silas and shaking her head. "I don't know if that went well, or very badly," she said.

Felix laughed. "Either way, it was entertaining. I'm glad Maureen was such a good sport," he said. "I just can't believe it was Lucia who made a scene."

Sara huffed out a laugh of her own. "Yeah, if it was going to be any one of us, I'm glad it was her. She needs to lighten up."

"That's not her way," E said from the chair beside me. She looked thoughtful but not amused. "I know she's been hard on you and the

House, with everything going on with the Elders, but I think she's doing her best. She's going to have to come at this from her own angle."

The room grew silent after her remark. It wasn't often that E shared her opinion on anything, especially about someone. It made me realize that the two of them had become friends over the past month, and I was glad to see it.

"I think overall, it turned out well," Kate said. She was curled up at the end of the leather sofa, her legs tucked under her, her head tilted to the side. "I think, even with the mishap, it showed them who we are, and I like who we are."

"Me too," Sara said. "So, what's next?"

Kate blinked at her best friend. "What do you mean?"

"If this was the test run, what's next?" Sara replied.

I cleared my throat. "I think we need to get Kate out into the community," I said. "Provide an opportunity for more people to meet her, maybe during the day?"

"It's not a bad idea," Felix said. "It might make them see you as less of a threat if you are out in the daytime."

"Typically, when a woman in our community is getting married, she has a gathering, like a wedding shower," Sara said. "I hadn't thought about having one, with everything going on, and our marriage being... unique, but it could be good. And, I kinda want one." She looked at Kate, her eyebrows raised, looking for confirmation.

Kate let out a breath. "Yeah, I think I could do that," she said. "As long as you're willing to coach me through it."

"Of course," Sara agreed. "I'll talk to my mom and aunt, and we'll plan something. Maybe it will help repair things with Lucia a bit to plan for a traditional bride's gathering." The thought seemed to please Sara, and I suspected some of the traditions meant more to her than she was willing to admit.

I finished my glass, and Bruce rose to take it from me. "I can get it," I said. "You've put a lot of work into this evening. You and Felix relax, I can handle the clean-up."

"Thanks," Bruce said, settling back down on the sofa. "I appreciate it."

I got to my feet and started gathering glasses. When I reached Kate, she stood up and offered to help me in the kitchen. I followed her, holding bloody wine glasses in each hand. "I wanted to thank you," I said when we entered the large industrial kitchen situated between the dining room and the foyer.

"Thank me for what?" Kate asked me over her shoulder.

"For giving E your room, so she has somewhere lightproof to sleep until she gets one of her own. It was a kind gesture, and I do appreciate sleeping in my bed again," I said.

She grinned at me. "I'm sure. But it's no problem. I should have asked when she moved in. I just assumed..." She sighed. "Anyway. She's welcome to it, and I'm glad you're sleeping more comfortably."

Scanning the kitchen, there was very little for Kate and me to do. Bruce was apparently one of those clean-as-you-go types. We washed the glasses, stored some of the leftover food, and wiped everything down. We were about to head back to the living room when Felix poked his head around the corner. "Kate, I wanted to tell you I finished that book," he said with a grin. "The next in the Demon Hunter series. I left it on your bed in the guest room."

"Okay, thanks," she said, sounding bemused.

He disappeared only to reappear a second later. "Oh, and I wanted to warn you," he said. "This one gets really spicy. Try not to chew an arm off, okay?" With that, he ducked back around the corner and was gone.

I glanced at Kate, who was staring after Felix in shock. "Would you prefer that I forget he said that and pretend that conversation never happened?" I asked.

She nodded silently, pressing her lips into a thin line before walking out of the kitchen, leaving me alone. I watched her walk away and fought the urge to laugh at her obvious embarrassment. I tried not to think about what Felix must have overheard that prompted the remark. I tried *very* hard not to think about it, but most of the evening, it was all I could think about. I was twice as grateful to

Kate for deciding to give E her room that night. Later, lying in my bed and trying—and failing—to stop thinking about Kate, I found myself with my fangs buried in my own arm.

8

KATE

The book Felix left in my room was only making me feel worse. Sighing, I let it fall onto my chest as I stared at the ceiling. It had been several nights since the incident in the kitchen, and I'd been avoiding Marcus. I couldn't believe Felix said what he did right in front of him. If Felix had been listening, he also would have known I had feelings for the former enforcer, but maybe that was the point. Felix had always been the one to push me out of my comfort zone, usually for my own good, but not this time. There was nothing to gain from trying to push me toward Marcus or anyone else at that point.

I had to accept that I might spend my existence alone, relying on romance novels for escape, without the companionship I deeply longed for. I didn't think I could handle being with a human; I wasn't experienced enough as a vampire to trust myself with one. And vampires seemed out of the question. That left witches and shifters? Neither of those options appealed to my senses. I rolled over in the guest bed I'd been sleeping in, and my current novel fell closed, losing my place. The truth was, I didn't want anyone but Marcus.

I didn't know exactly when it started, but somewhere between helping me recover from James's betrayal and supporting me as the leader of this new House, I developed feelings for the grey-eyed vampire. He was incredibly handsome, with an amazing body and a beautiful smile, and he smelled so damn good. He was confident and strong, and being around him made me feel steady and capable. But I worried those feelings might be unearned. Sometimes I felt I was stealing the best parts of him for myself when we touched, but the truth was, he made me a better vampire, a better person, and when I needed strength, I reached for him.

It was almost easier when I thought that E was a barrier to any romantic relationship between Marcus and me. It was more comfortable to believe he was out of my reach because he was with someone else. After I found out they weren't together, I was forced to admit it was me. I was the problem. I was the one blocking myself from pursuing something more. My blood was a drug, and I was a thief, unable to tell my emotions apart from his.

At that moment, I heard my housemates' voices downstairs. Everyone was awake and going about their routines, chatting happily. I buried my face in the pillow, pressing it over my ears. I wanted to block out the world. I wanted silence and peace. I wanted to escape my own self-pity. I wanted to be held. I didn't want to be alone anymore.

A knock at the door startled me, and I sat up. "Yes?" I called out.

"It's Sara. You coming down?" she asked softly from the other side of the door.

I pushed off the bed and went to the door, cracking it open.

"Oh, honey. You've been crying," she said, her brown eyes full of concern. "What's the matter?"

Crying? I wiped my face with the back of my hand, and sure enough, there was a streak of bloody tears. I shook my head. "I'm okay, just... a bit sad, I guess."

"You want to talk about it?" she asked. "I'm here, if you need me."

"Thanks. I know you are, but I'll be alright."

"Ok, well, why don't you wash your face and come downstairs if you want some company. Okay? I'll be in the shop."

I nodded and smiled. "I will," I said and closed the door again.

Twenty minutes later, I finally felt ready and headed downstairs. I had washed my face, brushed my hair, and tried to look as presentable as I could. Just before leaving my room, I saw my locket on the dresser and put it back on. It helped, and I didn't want my sour mood to affect the others in the house. It was important for me to get my emotions under control as much as my appearance.

Feeling steadier, I went down to the kitchen, where I found Bruce and Felix. I hesitated a beat when I saw the blond vampire, remembering the last encounter we'd had in this kitchen. His expression was soft, however, not playful, and his eyes showed his age. "Kate," he said. "I've been meaning to talk to you in private, to apologize."

"Would you like me to leave?" Bruce asked his lover.

"No. Please stay, I've embarrassed myself in front of you plenty," Felix said with a smile. "As long as Kate doesn't mind."

"I don't mind," I said. "And an apology isn't necessary. I know you were just teasing."

He shook his head. "It is necessary. Very little in this house is private, simply because of what we are. I knew that teasing you about that particular subject in front of Marcus would embarrass you." At the mention of Marcus's name, my head whipped around, listening. "He's not in the house. He can't hear us just now," Felix continued. "I take it too far sometimes, and I'm sorry, Kate."

"Thank you for that. I appreciate it," I said. "I can usually handle a joke, but it's been... harder lately." Felix nodded.

Bruce put down the knife he was using and looked at me. "Do you like him? Is that what's causing you distress? I can imagine it would be a tough situation, considering you are the leader of our House and have half-fae blood. If I'm correct, and you do like him, I think you should talk to Marcus about how you're feeling. I think you might find he's struggling too."

I blinked at Bruce. "Marcus is struggling? I highly doubt that. I'm keeping my guard up, it's true. But every time he's patted me on the arm or squeezed my hand, there's been no hint of attraction or frustration. He's solid as a rock. But even if he were interested, there's the little difficulty of my blood. It's just too dangerous for both of us."

"I think you're wrong," Bruce replied. "It might be uncomfortable, but I doubt it would actually be dangerous. You've got pretty good defenses if he did lose control. But as you said, he's a rock. Plus, there are ways around biting each other when you're... together."

I stared at Bruce, but he didn't say anything more; he just stood there, his cheeks flushing. I turned to Felix. "You're going to have to spell it out for me," I admitted. "I have no idea what he's talking about."

Felix grinned, and his playful, teasing side was back. "What he means, darling, is that if I bit him every time we had sex, he'd probably be dead. I often bite myself instead, when the urge arises. It's not impossible to keep your fangs to yourself in the heat of passion; it just takes some forethought and a bit of control."

"Ahh, I see." I looked back at Bruce, who had gone back to prepping dinner. He was red from his chin to his hairline, and he wouldn't meet my eye.

"But..." I turned back to Felix and lowered my voice. "Don't you wish you could? Are you satisfied with having to hold back?"

Felix held my gaze, and his eyes sharpened. "It would be nice not to have to worry," he admitted. "But, I'll take what I can get... for now. Speaking of which," Felix said more loudly. "I believe Bruce wanted to talk with you this evening as well."

"Bruce wanted to talk to me about sex?" I choked out.

"Gods no," Felix said. "More about developments in his and my relationship."

I raised my eyebrows. "Are you two getting married?" I asked, feeling happiness bubble up at the thought of another wedding.

Felix cut a glance at Bruce and chuckled. "Not exactly. I'll let him explain. But it would require your approval as leader of our House," he said, and gave me a wink before leaving the kitchen.

Bruce heaved a sigh and set his knife back down, wiping his hands on a towel. "Kate, can I heat a glass of O-negative for you to sip on while we talk?" he asked.

My stomach clenched at the mention of food. "Yes, please. That would be great." I sat down at the small kitchen table and watched him move around the room with efficiency and precision. Before long, he had a warm glass in front of me and was sitting across the table.

"I wanted to talk to you about the housekeeper I plan to bring on. I've contacted someone I used to work with at the Tap House. She's professional, hard-working, and reliable. I explained the position, and she agreed to drive up for an interview," he said. "I told her I would ask if the job would include housing. It's something you and I haven't discussed yet, and I didn't want to make the offer without approval."

"Yeah. I have no problem with it. It would make sense for the new staff member to live here if they weren't a witch, that is. I imagine it could be challenging to find housing nearby due to the current situation between us and the community," I said. "Did you consider advertising within the community to see if a witch wanted the position?"

He hesitated. "I did. There were no applicants. I was forced to look farther away, and I figured it would be safest to seek someone already familiar with vampires."

I nodded. That made sense. "But what does this have to do with your relationship with Felix?" I asked.

He licked his lips. "Well, I thought it was best to train someone we could rely on to run the house during the day, in case I'm no longer available during daylight hours."

"Are you thinking of only working the nights so that you and Felix can have more time together? Why would that require my approval? You can work whenever you want."

He shook his head, the corners of his mouth lifting. "No. I'm thinking of becoming a vampire."

"Oh," I said. I don't know why it surprised me, but it did. Bruce had said he wasn't looking to be turned when he agreed to come work for us and join the House. I guess I never thought he might change his mind. But I understood. I smiled at him. "I assume it was Felix who changed your mind," I said.

He nodded. "Yes. He's very convincing. I want more time with him."

I reached over, holding my hand above Bruce's, waiting. He nodded, turning his hand over, and I placed my palm in his. The flood of his emotions was like a cool wave on a hot day. He was happy, excited, and completely at peace. I shivered with happiness and grinned from ear to ear. "I'm so happy for you," I said. "If you need my approval, you have it." But then I had a thought. "I hope you don't need me to do it, though, as your leader, I mean. Marcus said it will be years before I'm able. I don't want you to have to wait."

"Don't worry," Bruce soothed and squeezed my hand. "With your permission, Felix will do it."

"Oh, good. Yes, that seems like a better choice. I'm sure he's done it many times. He'll know exactly what to do," I said in relief.

"Actually, it will be the first time for him," Bruce said, and I could feel through our clasped hands that the thought pleased him very much.

"Even better," I said. The thought that this would be a first for both of them was somehow sweet. It made my eyes prick with tears, and I felt the need to change the subject. I cleared my throat. "Let me know when the interview is. I'd be happy to meet..."

"Chelsea," Bruce said.

"Right. Chelsea. I'd love to meet her. I'm sure she'll be great." I squeezed Bruce's hand one more time and then let go. "And when does Felix plan to turn you?" I asked.

Bruce straightened up and considered. "It will probably be some time yet. I want to get someone in place here first, and then there are a few things I'd like to do beforehand."

"Like what?" I asked. I hadn't been given a choice when I was turned. I often wondered what it would have been like if I had been allowed to plan it out.

"I want to enjoy a few more sunrises, eat a few more special meals, and maybe get a few more tattoos," he said. "It will likely happen after Sara and Silas's wedding, though. I don't want anything to disrupt their ceremony. I'm going to be busy until then."

"Great. And take some time off after. You're familiar with our world, but actually becoming a vampire might take some getting used to."

"We'll see," he said, getting up from the table and returning to his meal prep.

"By the way, where is Marcus?" I asked.

Bruce glanced up from his work. "Oh," he said pleasantly. "He went to visit his wife."

9

SARA

The lone customer was making her third circle around the store, picking up and setting down items at random. It was nice to have someone in the shop for a change. It had been two weeks since anyone had darkened our doorway. I had a feeling, though, that this witch in particular was curious about the local herb shop run by a witch engaged to a shifter and connected to a house full of vampires, and wasn't there to do any shopping.

The middle-aged woman kept glancing around as if expecting a vampire or wolf to jump out at any moment. She would be sorely disappointed if she actually encountered one. None of my roommates were particularly prone to theatrics in front of customers, and the most exciting thing they were likely to do was help shelve inventory or ask to borrow a book.

I was about to ask for the second time if I could help the witch find anything when the door to the house burst open, and Kate rushed in vampire-fast, causing the candle on the counter to flicker and sending a pile of papers flying. She came to a stop right in front of me, seemingly unaware that I had a customer. "Sara!" she exclaimed. "Did you know that Marcus was married?"

"Um, yeah. I did," I replied, then raised my eyebrows and tilted my head toward the witch who was staring open-mouthed at the two of us.

"Oh, crap. Sorry," Kate said, wincing. "I didn't realize there was anyone here." She turned to the witch, who had managed to close her mouth but still stared in awe. "Sorry, ma'am. I didn't mean to interrupt." The woman nodded but didn't look away. Kate turned back to me. "I'll be in your office. Come talk to me when you're free?" Her expression was both apologetic and anxious.

I nodded. "Of course. I'll be right there," I said with a tight smile.

It was another ten minutes before the grey-haired witch left. She didn't buy anything and kept glancing at the office door. Finally, she must have grown bored and decided she'd had her only glimpse of a vampire for the evening. I locked the door after she left and put up the closed sign. I was reasonably sure we wouldn't get any more customers that night, but I wanted to ensure we weren't disturbed.

As soon as the door was shut, Kate appeared behind the counter. "So you knew?" she asked. "And still encouraged me to give it a shot with him?"

"Whoa, hold on," I said. "I only found out he was married tonight, just before he left. He asked Bruce where he could pick up some flowers on his way to visit. But I don't see why it's a big deal."

"Not a big deal?" Kate said, placing her hands on her hips. "He has a wife, and he never thought to mention it, or that she lives within driving distance."

I couldn't keep the smile off my face. She was obviously into Marcus, or she wouldn't be this pissed, but I had to put her out of her misery. "Kate, she doesn't *live* anywhere. She's dead, Sweetie. She's been dead for ten years. He said he was going to visit his late wife's grave. And when I said I was sorry for his loss, he told me she'd died ten years ago. That's all I know."

Kate's face softened, and her expression grew concerned. "I asked Bruce where Marcus went, and he told me he went to visit his wife... I just assumed. Oh."

"You didn't think to ask Bruce to clarify?" I asked.

"No. I was so shocked. I just fled the kitchen and came to find you," she said. "How come he never told me?"

"I don't know, you'll have to ask him," I replied. "It didn't seem like a secret, but it was the first I'd heard about it. Maybe he's just a private person?"

"Yeah, I guess I never thought to ask either. He's always just been Marcus. I never considered what his life was like before he moved here," she said, her brows drawing together. She leaned forward, resting her hands on the counter and dropping her head. "I feel like a terrible friend."

"You reacted like a jealous girlfriend," I said with a smirk.

She jerked her head up. "I...," she began, but paused. She took a deep breath. "I like him, Sara. I really like him."

"I know, Sweetie," I replied, reaching over to place a hand on hers. "You're going to have to work it out. And the first step is talking to Marcus."

"Bruce said the same thing," she said.

"Bruce is very smart. You should listen to him," I said with a wink.

She straightened up and smiled. "Yeah. He is pretty smart. I can't promise I'll spill my guts, but I will talk to Marcus. There is clearly a lot we need to talk about."

"Great. Now that we have that figured out, what are you going to do until he gets back?" I asked.

"I don't have anything planned. Do you need any help around here?" Kate offered. "I notice you're alone."

"Yeah, Beth is training Arrow this evening, Mom is away at a Green Witch's retreat, Aunt Lucia is planning my Bride's Gathering, and Silas is with his family for dinner tonight."

"You didn't want to go?" she asked.

"No. I wanted to go, but someone had to open the shop, and I have to finish addressing the wedding invitations."

"I could help," she said. "Vampires write almost as fast as we run." She quirked a smile. "Sorry if I scared away your customer, by the way."

"Oh no. You didn't scare her away. You probably made her

whole week," I said. "The only witches we get in here these days are those coming to gawk at me or trying to catch sight of the local vampires."

"Is it hurting your business?" she asked, looking genuinely worried.

"No. Not at all. The money we make from in-person sales is almost zero. The only reason we have a physical location at this point is to provide locals with a place to buy supplies. It would upset business greatly if we had to relocate, but only for logistical reasons. Given our current traffic, I'm not sure why we're open to the public at all," I said. "I should just turn this place into a warehouse for our online orders."

"It would be a shame," she said. "This place is beautiful. I love being here. It feels so cozy and rustic, with all the old furniture and herbs hanging everywhere. I love it."

"Thank you. I hope people keep coming by to enjoy it," I said. "Want to work in here, or spread things out on the dining table?"

Kate grimaced. "The dining room still has bad vibes," she said. "It's going to take at least one uneventful dinner there before I can get over the last one we had."

I laughed. "Are you squeamish about the blood?"

"Well, no. But seeing a human, covered in blood and reeking of fear, was... challenging. I didn't like how it made me feel."

"And how was that?" I asked, already knowing the answer.

"Like a vampire, I guess." She shrugged and smiled, showing her fangs.

"I have news for you, hon," I said, smiling back. "At least you didn't eat Beth's mom. That would have been bad form, for sure."

She rolled her eyes at me. "It wasn't that bad. I was in control, just... interested."

"Hmm. Have you given any more thought to having more traditional vampire meals?" I asked.

Kate swallowed, and I watched the tips of her fangs slide out from under her upper lip. "I try not to," she said with a slight accent.

I pressed my lips together, trying hard not to smile. "Yeah, I see that," I said. "I'm sure Bruce could hook you up if you needed someone to sink your teeth into."

She shook her head. "Felix would rip my head off," she said.

"Not Bruce himself," I said. "But I'm sure he knows dozens of people who would be willing to feed you, if that's what you wanted."

She seemed to consider it. "How would you feel about that?"

"Me?" I asked. I paused to consider. "If you had asked me when you first came to stay with my family, I would have answered differently, but I have no problem with it now. I'm getting more comfortable around shifters, humans, vampires, and even half-fae vampires. I think I appreciate our differences more now than I used to. I might not want to watch, but I'm supportive."

"Thank you," she said, sounding more like herself. "Ok, where are these invitations? Let's get these things knocked out, and then go watch some sappy '90s movie."

"Sounds perfect," I said and went to get the large box of supplies.

It took us hardly any time to finish the rest of the invitations. Kate had the speed of a vampire, combined with the dexterity and control of an artist. She wrote so quickly I could barely keep up while she worked, and all I was doing was stuffing envelopes. Twenty minutes after we began, we packed everything up again to take to the post office the next day.

"I didn't know you still had family in the South," Kate said as we put everything away.

"Yeah, some distant relatives, mostly my mom's side. I'm inviting my dad's sisters too; they live in Virginia, and I haven't seen them since his funeral."

"How long has it been?" she asked. "Fourteen years?"

I nodded. "Almost fifteen. I was twelve at the time."

"And how long since you've seen your mom's family?

I had to think. We used to see each other at least once a year when I was young, but not so much in the past couple of decades. "I guess it would have been around the same time," I said with a shrug.

Kate grew quiet then, thoughtful. "I noticed you didn't invite my mom," she said. "And I totally understand why. But I can't help but think of her and how, if this had never happened to me, we would probably both be at your wedding."

I wished she were right. I would have loved to invite Melanie. But even if we could think of a way to prevent her from seeing Kate, it still wouldn't work. "Given everything that happened, we decided to keep it to just family and members of our communities," I said.

Kate smiled. "And housemates, I hope," she said.

"Of course," I said. "You're my maid of honor, and I consider you family. I wouldn't dream of getting married without you—or the rest of the gang. Most of the people attending will be my mom and my aunt's friends, as well as Silas's large family. I'm counting on you being there for support."

Just then, there was a flash of light followed by a clap of thunder.

"Is that normal for around here?" Kate asked.

"No. It's not," I mumbled. "And it's not natural either. I would have felt an electrical storm coming. This one came out of nowhere." Another bright flash lit up the windows in the front of the store, followed quickly by a loud boom.

Kate and I inched closer to the windows to look out. It had started raining again. As we moved toward the front door, a bolt of lightning streaked from the sky and hit on the other side of the road from the shop. It was a distance away, but the sound was deafening. I covered my ears with my hands and turned away instinctively. When the spots cleared from my vision, I looked at Kate. She was lying on the floor, hands pressed to her ears.

"Are you okay?" I asked, but my voice sounded strange in my ears.

She had her eyes squeezed shut but gradually opened them. "I think so. I'm pretty sure my ears were damaged, but they seem to be healing."

I nodded, feeling anger sparking inside. "They're doing this on purpose," I said.

"Witches?" she asked, getting to her feet.

"Yes, and there are only a few who can wield electricity like me, but with the power and skill to summon lightning." As I spoke, another bolt struck nearby. Not as close this time, but still loud enough to make us both wince.

"Can you do anything to stop it?" she asked.

I shook my head. "Not with my gift. I'm not strong enough yet, or practiced," I admitted.

"I could make them stop," Kate ground out. "If I could just get my hands on them."

"I understand the feeling," I said. "But I don't think we are in real danger. I suspect they're doing this to scare us."

"It's working," Kate said under her breath, as another peal of thunder rumbled through the air, shaking the shop's windows.

10

MARCUS

It had been a long time since I visited my wife's grave, but the ground around the headstone was clear, and the stone itself was free of dirt and leaves. The cemetery staff were meticulous, and I was glad her family had chosen this spot. I wasn't sure how often her children came to see her, if at all, and I felt guilty for being away for so long.

I tried to visit once a season to say hello and catch her up on everything that had happened. I'd been fairly consistent over the past decade, but I'd been away for too long this time. A lot had changed recently, and I had much to tell her.

I placed the flowers I'd brought against her headstone. They were a mix of blooms, mostly white and yellow, her favorite color. I stepped back and sat on the ground at the foot of where she rested. The night was dry, and the grass felt cool beneath me. I sat there for a while, gazing at her stone, unsure of where to start. Mary Elaine Thomas, it read. She'd been Mary Wallace when we met, and Mary Sullivan after she became my wife. I closed my eyes, remembering her that day. She'd been so beautiful and so young. We were both little more than babies when we agreed to be together until death.

And yet, here we both were, ten years after hers and more than eighty years after mine.

I blew out a breath and began. I told her about meeting Kate and James. I explained how I came to live with Kate and Sara, and how the House had expanded since then. I told her about the fight with the Council and Felix, the Relics Kate could create, and Kate's suspected fae heritage. My voice trailed off after that. It was several more minutes before I spoke again.

"Kate's different," I said. "Not just because of her blood, or who her father might have been. She's special to me." It felt good to say it out loud. "I have strong feelings for her, but it's complicated."

I took a breath of the cool evening air, tinged with the smell of freshly cut grass and newly turned earth. "I've felt this way before, though, with you. When I first saw you, I knew right away you would change my life... It was the same with her," I admitted. "It was exciting, but sad at the same time. She's not replacing you in my heart, but I think there might be room in there for her too."

I smiled at the thought of what Mary would say if she could actually see and hear me right now. She would tell me I was being a sentimental fool. She would say I should do the same thing I did when I first met her—buy her a bouquet of flowers, tell her she was beautiful, and say I'd love to take her out sometime. It worked nicely the first time around.

"I don't know," I sighed. "It's been a long time since I courted anyone. I don't know if I still know how. I'm not so sure she would welcome my feelings." The silence stretched out, and I knew I'd said all I came to say.

I stood and brushed off the loose grass that clung to my clothes. I knew in my heart that coming here was for me, not for Mary. I'd gone to war when she was twenty-three years old and never came home. To her, I was dead, and she'd moved on, as I hoped she would. She'd lived a full and beautiful life afterward. I knew because I'd watched it unfold. I stepped forward, pressed my fingers to my lips, and touched her stone. "Until next time," I said and turned to leave.

The cemetery was near Everett, roughly halfway between Seattle and the valley. The drive back was quick—too quick. Before I realized it, I was pulling into the driveway and parking beside Kate's new Toyota Camry. It made me smile. She'd earned millions from the auction of the pocket watch but insisted on buying one of the most affordable and reliable cars available because it was "a smarter choice." She still wasn't comfortable with money or with spending it, and that was okay. It took me decades to see money as a tool. I learned that most people tie their emotions to money; in Kate's case, it was apprehension and fear. But she was right, too; it was a smart choice.

The house was nearly empty for that time of night. I found Kate and Sara watching a movie in the living room, but I couldn't hear anyone else around. I decided to see if they minded company. I didn't feel like being alone at that moment.

"Hey," I said by way of greeting. "Titanic. Nice choice. Mind if I join?"

Sara paused the movie, and both women smiled up at me from the sofa. "Not at all," Sara said. "I was just going to get up, actually. You can have my spot."

"Oh, no. That's okay," I said. "I didn't mean to interrupt."

"You're not interrupting. I have... stuff to do," she said, glancing meaningfully at Kate as she dropped the throw blanket she'd been wrapped in back on the sofa. Sara gave Kate a quick kiss on the cheek and waved goodnight before disappearing upstairs. It made me suspicious that the two were up to something. I hoped they were. Kate had been rather down lately; she needed a bit of a distraction.

I took Sara's vacated seat, scooting a bit farther from Kate as I realized just how close the two had been sitting. "Where is everyone tonight?" I asked.

"Oh. Um, Silas is having dinner with his family, Bruce is grocery shopping, and E convinced Felix to go clothes hunting with her in Seattle."

I nodded. "It's strange to have it so quiet around here," I said.

Kate snorted. "You should have been here an hour ago. I don't think my hearing has fully recovered," she said, and then told me about the lightning and their suspicions that it was the witches trying to intimidate the House.

I didn't like the sound of that one bit. I hoped their show of force didn't escalate past intimidation. I didn't know what we would do if they started aiming directly for the house.

I glanced at Kate. She sat holding the remote, but didn't restart the movie. "Have you seen this one?" she asked.

"Titanic? Yeah, it's been years, though."

"Does it remind you of when you were young?" she asked with a slight smile.

"The Titanic sank five years before I was born, so not really." I looked at the frozen frame on the screen. It featured the main character and her mother, both dressed in 1912 attire, with multiple layers and large, fancy hats. "The styles had changed considerably by the time I started making permanent memories. But I do miss hats sometimes."

"Hats?"

"Yeah, everyone wore hats—especially men," I said. "I wouldn't have left the house without a good hat."

"When did people stop wearing them?" she asked.

"I don't know, the '50s, '60s? It's hard to say, but I miss it. Clothing was more formal when I was human. We had fewer clothes, but we dressed up more."

Kate nodded but then grew serious. She took a breath and licked her lips. "Bruce said you went to visit your wife tonight," she said.

I swallowed. "Yes. It had been a while. It was time."

"I didn't know you'd been married, or that she'd died," Kate said, her tone soft, careful. "I'm sorry."

"Thank you. And, I'm sorry I never mentioned it."

"How was she killed?" Kate asked.

"Killed? She wasn't killed," I said. "She just died."

Kate's brows fell, and she frowned. "She wasn't a vampire?"

I smiled and shook my head. "No, she was human. And she hadn't been my wife for over seventy years by the time she died."

"Oh," Kate said, surprise written all over her face.

I took a deep breath. "I kept track of her over the years, but to her, I was dead. I died during the war."

"You were changed while you were at war?" she asked. "While you were away?"

"Yeah," I said, shifting in my seat. "I didn't intentionally choose this life either. I didn't know what I was signing up for at the time, and I didn't meet my sire until years later."

"But how? I don't understand," she said.

"I was selected for a special mission. All I knew was they were going to perform a procedure that would make me stronger, faster, and heal better. I should have asked more questions," I said and smiled. "Agreeing to the procedure was one of the biggest mistakes of my life. And yet, I don't regret where I am now, or the fact that I have a long life ahead of me to look forward to. But when I woke up, when it was over, I realized I could never go home again."

"That's awful," Kate said. "I can't believe they would do that to you without telling you what you would become."

I looked at her and smiled. "It's not much different than what happened to you."

She huffed out a laugh. "Yeah, I guess you're right." She paused, her eyes taking on an edge as she looked at me and then asked, "Did you make them pay?"

"...Fuck yeah, I made them pay," I growled, shutting down the flood of memories that washed over me. Flashing lights, broken glass, and blood. So much blood. I shook my head to clear my thoughts. "But that was a long time ago," I said.

Kate looked at me and raised an eyebrow. "So you're like Captain America," she said.

I chuckled. "I was a soldier who got caught up in more than he bargained for. Something so dark and secret, not even the people in charge knew what was happening in that lab. It's hardly a superhero story."

"I'm not hearing you say you're not Captain America..." she teased.

"I'm not. I assure you."

"Maybe a more gothic, raven-haired version? Could you say that?"

I laughed. "No. I could not."

"Fine. But I can still think of you that way. You can't stop me," she said.

"Very well," I conceded. "But, seriously. I'm no superhero. I'm a vampire. I was made a killer, a being who lives off the blood of others. I wouldn't have chosen this for myself."

She grew quiet then, and I regretted crushing her mood, but I didn't want her to think that I considered myself noble or that my transformation was some patriotic sacrifice. It was a violation, just as hers had been.

"I guess that answers my next question," she said.

"Which is?"

"Why didn't you offer to turn your wife when you came back?" she said.

"I thought about it," I admitted. "I was a mess. I wanted to go home. I wanted to be with her, to let her know I wasn't gone. But by that time, I'd learned of the vampire laws, and I knew I'd endanger her if I let her know what I'd become. I couldn't do that."

"I'd like to say I understand," Kate said. "But I've never been married. I don't know what it would be like to love someone like that and have to make that choice. I don't know what I'd do."

I paused for a moment. I wasn't sure if Kate would understand or think my choice was inappropriate. Either way, it was the truth, and I wanted her to know. "I chose to stay close to my wife," I said. "I never let her see me, but I watched over her." I shrugged. "I just couldn't leave her. I'd promised to protect her, stay with her, until death, and she was still alive and all alone. Later, when she remarried, I kept a greater distance, but I checked in occasionally to ensure they were all okay. When she moved with her husband and children to Seattle, I followed. I got a job with the Council here to stay close to them."

"And all that time, you never went to her? You never talked to her?" Kate asked, her eyes full of concern.

I sighed. "Only at the very end," I said. "I went to her just before she died. By that time, she wasn't fully aware anymore, but she did recognize me." I smiled at the memory of her eyes lighting up when I appeared in her care room. "I wanted to hold her one more time." I swallowed, my throat feeling tight. "I've never told anyone that before," I said. I hadn't told anyone most of that story, actually. Very few people in my past knew about Mary or her family. It was safer that way. But things were different now. Kate and the rest of the House weren't like most vampires. I no longer felt like my past or what I said would be used against me, as I once did.

I flinched when Kate put her hand over mine. I was so lost in thought that I hadn't noticed her move. "Sorry," she said, starting to jerk her hand away, but I caught it and held on.

"No. It's okay if you want to know how I feel," I said, trying to shift my melancholic mood to something more steady, more calm.

"It's not like that," she said. "I was trying to offer comfort, I guess. I… I'm sorry." She shook her head.

"What?" I asked. "What's the matter?"

She tugged on her hand, and I let go. "I'm sorry you assumed that I was trying to sample your emotions. It's a bad habit I've gotten into. When I want comfort. And I'm sorry for it."

"You don't have to be sorry," I said, confused. "I want to help, if I can, when you need it."

"But that's just it," she said. "I shouldn't lean on you like that. It makes me a parasite."

I quirked the corner of my mouth up. "A vampire?" I teased, trying to lighten the mood.

"Ha," she said in a mocking tone, but she did smile. "Yes, a vampire sucking down your emotions instead of your blood. You should not be comfortable with that."

The thought of her sucking my blood made me uncomfortable in an entirely different way, and I fought to keep my fangs from sliding from my gums. Instead of letting my thoughts wander in that particular direction, I held out my hand. She looked at me, confused, but put her palm in mine. I let her see how I was really feeling, underneath what I tried so hard to project for her, underneath what most people saw on the surface, underneath what I'd gotten used to burying all those years.

Kate gasped. "Oh, Marcus. I..."

"I've only ever given you what I wanted you to have." I smiled. "You really do have your walls up, then?" I asked, trying to distract her a bit from the depth of the sorrow I felt after visiting my wife's grave.

She gave me a sad smile. "Yeah. It's second nature now," she said. "I thought it better to use touch here in the house. That way, you will all be aware that I'm doing it. It's too icky otherwise."

I nodded. "Thank you," I said, withdrawing my hand. "Does it bother you?" I asked.

"Does what bother me?" She tilted her head, looking at me.

"That I still love her, my wife, that it still makes me sad to think about her from time to time?"

"No. It doesn't bother me," she said. "I would hope that if someone loved me like that, they wouldn't stop just because I died."

It took me a moment to gather myself enough to respond. "Good. That's good," I said, my voice rough. "Because I don't think that will ever change. And, well... if I were ever with someone else, especially if they could sense my emotions, it would only work if they were okay with how I feel."

Kate just stared at me. She didn't respond, and I was afraid I'd made a terrible mistake. Staring down at my wife's grave, I'd made the choice to tell Kate how I felt. I knew it might ruin everything. I knew she might not respond well, but I thought she deserved to know that I was interested in more than just a friendship. What I really wanted to say was that I adored her, that I wanted to try again, to hold her and show her what it was like to be loved like that. I suspected she wasn't ready for that, however.

I waited, not breathing, while she processed what I'd implied. Then she slowly nodded her head. "I could see where that would be important," she said cautiously. "And, if I were to be with someone who had loved before and lost that love, I wouldn't resent him for that. Just so that you know."

I smiled, feeling bolder. "I like you, Kate, very much. And understand why that could be complicated, or make you uncomfortable, but I wanted you to know."

She nodded, looking uncertain. "I'm glad you told me," she said, her eyes flicking to mine. "I..." she swallowed, holding my gaze. Slowly, ever so slowly, she leaned forward until our mouths were no more than a few inches apart.

I dared to breathe in, savoring the scent of her so close. She closed her eyes, and I crossed the distance, pressing a soft kiss against her mouth. I felt a tremor go through her body, and she leaned into the kiss, tilting her head ever so slightly.

I raised a hand, cupping the back of her head as I pressed in closer, kissing her slowly, gently. I slid my hand down the side of her neck, and she froze. I pulled back, not too fast; I didn't want to alarm her further.

When I opened my lids, she was staring back at me, her eyes full of worry. "Listen. I need to...," she trailed off. "Umm." She glanced toward the front of the house, as if looking for an escape.

I'd pushed too far. I scooted back to give her space. "It's okay," I said and smiled at her. "It doesn't have to change things if you don't want it to." I held out my hand again, and she looked at it like it might bite her. Slowly, she reached forward and placed her hand in mine once more. Her body seemed to relax, and she nodded. I knew what she would feel. I was calm and in control. There were no hard feelings or resentment. I let some of my warmth for her peek through, but just a little.

"I'm going to need to think about this," she said, removing her hand from mine. "I'm not saying I don't want this, but I just... need to think." She raised her gaze to mine, and her eyes were troubled.

"There is no rush. I'm not going anywhere. And that's true no matter what you decide or how you feel. I'll be here as long as you want me to be. As long as you need me," I said.

11

LUCIA

When I was younger, I loved traveling. I would spend months planning my next trip. It all began with an idea, a dream, a desire to see something new. I wanted to meet new people. To disappear into an unfamiliar city and immerse myself in its sights, smells, and sounds. It was the best part of travel, and I never minded being a stranger in those new places.

Now I was a stranger in my own town. I was on the outside. I never thought I would find that feeling in the place I had lived my whole life. Instead of the excitement of adventure, however, it felt cold and lonely.

Things had been escalating. Ever since news about the vampires spread, I had been getting strange looks from familiar faces and mumbled greetings from close friends. I figured it took time for people to adjust to something new, and I assumed it would be the same here. I was wrong. It only got worse.

We still hadn't received official word from the Elders, but it was obvious what was coming. The House wasn't welcome in the valley, and the cold stares and whispers served as their message. I wished our family weren't so involved in all of it. I had no regrets about helping Kate, or Sara's ongoing friendship with the vampire, but it would have been easier if they had chosen a place farther outside town, or even in Seattle. Maybe I could persuade them to move to the city, I thought. I knew that would make E happy.

I sighed and glared at the woman behind the counter at the small grocery store. "Excuse me? Could I get some help, please?" I said, unable to hide the annoyance in my voice. I'd tried to ignore the rudeness over the past week, but it was becoming too much.

"Oh, Lucia. I didn't see you there," she said, her words dripping with condescension.

"Of course you didn't. You were too busy looking at your phone instead of doing your job," I replied.

The woman's fake smile disappeared, but the Light Witch still rang up my purchases, and I managed to leave the store without further issues. I may not have been an Elder myself, at least not yet, but I still deserved more respect from the witches in our town, especially from someone like this witch. She was at least a decade younger than me and had never organized any community events or volunteered for any committee. She rarely attended gatherings at all, for the Gods' sake.

I carried my bags half a block back to my car and loaded them into the trunk. The day was overcast and misty, and the gloomy weather was soaking into my skin and affecting my mood. Had I been in better spirits, I might have reacted differently when I spotted Ruth's red Toyota two cars down. But I was not in a positive frame of mind. Nor was I feeling particularly cheery when Ruth herself got out of the vehicle, locking eyes with me over the top of the other cars. Instead of waving at her, as I would have in the past, I simply stared.

Instead of nodding or attempting any type of politeness, Ruth had the nerve to shake her head and level her gaze at me, as if I were the one who had betrayed a friendship. As if I were the one who led the other to believe she was meant for something great, only to pull the rug out from under her and humiliate her in front of everyone. It was only her status as an Elder that stopped me from flipping her off or shouting some insult. My bridges were shaky, but I wasn't ready to set them on fire just yet.

A wave of heat spread over my skin, and I looked down to realize that my gift had other ideas. Flame had sprung up in each palm and quickly started to engulf my hands. Fortunately, I caught it in time to avoid singeing my favorite coat. I was also thankful that Ruth, who had turned and walked away in the opposite direction, didn't see. Losing control of your gift was almost as bad as fraternizing with vampires, almost. I took a deep breath, got into my car, and headed home.

My sister had returned from her trip the night before and was puttering around in her kitchen garden when I pulled in. I'd hardly made it to the side door when she called out. "How was it?" she asked.

I understood what she meant, and she wasn't asking if I had found what we needed for dinner. "It was fine," I replied. There was no need to go into how rude everyone had suddenly become. I saw no reason to explain the ongoing punishment from the community or the embarrassment I suffered due to what was happening a short distance down the highway. It was what it was, for now.

I was putting everything away in its place when Sybil came in to wash her hands. "It was really okay?" she asked.

"Like I said, it was fine," I replied.

"Hmm," she commented. "Because it's been rough for me. The past few times. Ever since... You know."

"Hmm," I responded.

"It would be understandable if it made you upset or caused you to worry. The way people have been acting, I mean," she went on.

I sighed, shutting the cabinet door, and began to fold my shopping bags back into neat little squares.

"I don't think it will go on forever," she said. "Eventually, they will come to know the members of the House, and all will be forgotten."

"Stop," I said, flinging down the bag I'd just folded. It landed with a soft thunk. I wished it had been heavier or made of a different material. "You've got to stop believing that this will all just go away. The community has made it clear: the vampires are not welcome. I wish it were different, I really do. But you and the House will soon have to face the facts. They will have to move. There's no other choice. The sooner Sara tells her housemates what has to be done, the better. In fact, we should get her over here and talk to her together, away from the others."

"We will do no such thing," Sybil said, placing her hands on her hips. "We made a promise that we would stop interfering in Sara's life. We would let her make her own decisions and live it the way she chooses. Even if that means living with vampires, marrying a shifter, or going against the Elders."

"You can't mean that," I said, my voice rising. What was she talking about? *Going against the Elders.* It was like turning your back on the community, exiling yourself.

"I do mean that," she replied, and for a Green Witch, there was a fair amount of fire in her eyes. "We will not put any more pressure on Sara than there already is."

"Well, you can do as you please," I said. "But I'll be speaking with her about this. She's ruining her standing in our community and damaging our reputations. It's not like I'm asking her to give up her friends or her membership in Kate's House. I'm just asking that they respect the wishes of the Elders and relocate for the good of everyone."

"No. You won't say anything," Sybil spat. "Maybe it's because Sara spent much of her life living under the same roof as you, but you need to remember, she is my daughter, not yours."

It was a low blow, and I thought I saw a flash of regret on her face, but it vanished in an instant, replaced by cold resolve. "Fine," I said as calmly as I could, despite the fire raging in my veins. "But then you can be the one to explain to her why only one person from the community RSVP'd that they planned to come to the Bride's Gathering. And that person was Maureen, a human. What good is it to have a witches' celebration with no witches in attendance?"

"We will be there," Sybil said. "Her family, who loves her, believes in her, and respects her choices."

I didn't respond. I stood there with my arms crossed, staring at my sister. She meant well. She really did, but she didn't understand the importance of community cohesion. She'd left at one point to raise her daughter in the world, only returning when Sara was nearly grown and the business needed her help. It wasn't her future she was putting in jeopardy. It wasn't her who wanted to lead this community one day. It wasn't Sybil who had given up so much to remain here, to be the witch everyone needed her to be.

Sybil didn't back down, but her eyes softened as she looked back at me. "You may have to make a choice someday soon," she said gently. "Your standing in the community and the respect of the Elders, or your family." She paused and looked down as if gathering her thoughts or courage. "I know you've made this choice before, and I'm not saying you chose incorrectly at the time, but I ask you—was it worth it? Will it be worth it this time if it means losing Sara? If it means standing with the Elders instead of with Kate, Marcus, Bruce, Felix, and E? Could you live with that?"

The heat in my body cooled as I listened to her speak. That was the question indeed. And she was right, I'd been fighting it, but I saw it now. It was coming. The only problem was, I wasn't sure how I would answer.

12

KATE

The rain had been falling steadily for days and nights. At first, it was only occasional downpours with intermittent lightning. Over the past week, it rained constantly with no breaks, but thankfully, there was no more lightning. I couldn't believe I'd liked it at first. The cozy feeling the rain once brought had been replaced with a sense of being trapped. And damp. Everything felt damp.

To make matters worse, I'd been kicked out of my studio by Bruce and Silas. They were having a construction meeting down there with one of Silas's brothers, Lucas. I was invited to the meeting, and could have stayed, but, honestly, I was sure that whatever they decided would be great, and the technical aspects were a bit boring.

When Beth learned that one of Silas's brothers would be making an appearance that evening, she found plenty of reasons to stay late after work. Sadly for Beth, Lucas was the older brother who was mated and had kids. She was still bugging Sara to introduce her to Silas's other older brother, Beau, who was thirty and still unmated. I was sure that when construction began down there, all the brothers would eventually show up. Whether they told Beth or not was up to them.

With art off the table for the evening, I went looking for company. I left my temporary room on the second floor and listened carefully. My stomach fluttered as I listened for sounds that would tell me who was up and about. There was really only one person I was listening for. It had been several days since our conversation in the living room —and our kiss—, but it was all I could think about.

I wanted to talk to Marcus again in private. I wanted to kiss him again, too, if I was being honest, but I hadn't worked up the courage yet. I wanted to tell him how I felt, but I was also terrified. It had been easier to want him when I thought there was no real possibility for us. After speaking with Felix and Bruce, discovering that he had feelings for me, and then the kiss... everything was becoming too real.

I touched my lips, remembering the feel of his mouth on mine. I felt a spark of hope, but at the same time, I was filled with dread at the thought of actually having him so close again. I thought of our kiss and imagined holding him, pulling him closer. I flinched as memories of Alexander at my throat flooded my mind, the savage way he'd bitten into me, how I'd feared for my very survival. I shivered, shaking off the memory.

Agitated, I jumped off the bed. I needed to move. I didn't hear anything, but I decided to head downstairs and look for myself.

The first person I found was Felix, his head bent over a book in the reading area. I'd thought he was going into the city again, but was pleased to see that I was wrong. He was sitting in Sara's chair, and I sped over and plopped down in mine. Felix's eyebrow twitched. "Hi," I said, settling myself into a comfy, curled-up position. "Did I surprise you?"

He didn't lift his head when he replied, "You clomped down the steps with all the grace of a three-legged goat." He smiled and lifted his gaze to mine. "But yes, I'm continually surprised by you."

"Good," I said. "I wouldn't want to be predictable. What are you reading? Something you stole from my TBR pile?"

He raised both blond eyebrows now. "No, actually. It's something from mine." He held up a leather-bound book with no markings on its worn cover. "It's one of my journals," he explained. "I've only gotten through a few hundred years. This one dates back to the nineteenth century. I thought I might start with some of the most recent and work my way back. Unfortunately, I don't have several of the more modern volumes on hand. They're stashed away in various places, but I'm having them all sent here."

"What have you found out?" I asked. He'd been looking for any mention of the fae. He firmly believed that my father, whoever he was, had to be at least part fae. The only problem was, no one remembered the fae, including Felix, who'd written about his encounters with the beings over the years. It seemed that if they were, in fact, real, they had the ability to affect memories.

He sighed and placed the book on his knee. "I found one mention of vampires and fae," he said. I leaned forward. This wasn't what I'd been waiting for, but he had my full attention. "I wrote about trying to curb what were called Hunting Parties."

"Hunting Parties?" I asked.

He nodded solemnly. "It's what it sounds like," he said. "Vampires who would band together and hunt... fae." He looked over at me, and when I didn't respond, he continued. "They were after a transfer of abilities. As we found out, with Alexander, drinking from a fae would temporarily transfer the fae's abilities to the vampire."

I looked down at my hands clasped in my lap. "We should have guessed," I said. "It makes sense. It's disgusting, but it makes sense. I suppose that's a fairly good reason to disappear."

"Indeed," Felix said. "I've found entries where I named individual fae that needed protection because their magic was particularly sought after. I've been keeping notes on these names. They were all associated with the type of magic you've displayed. None of them has appeared in the more recent entries, however."

"Do you think they were found? Killed?" I asked.

"Or maybe they found a way to protect themselves," Felix offered.

"Well, keep looking. If you don't mind," I said. "I would really like to know what happened. And I want to know if there is anything I can do about it."

"Do about it?" he asked, a look of confusion on his face. "Why would you want to do anything about it? Your gifts are extraordinary, Kate."

"Sure, they're great. However, it would be nice to be able to turn them off sometimes. You know, touch someone without feeling all their emotions. Or, I don't know, get into a relationship with a vampire that doesn't put my life at risk or drive him insane."

"Hmm, yes. I can see where that would be helpful," he said. He flicked his eyes toward the stairs to the lower level and then back again. "Any movement on the discussion we had the other night?"

I bit my lip and considered. "I don't know," I said. "I just can't see myself getting into a relationship with a vampire unless I had some sort of guarantee that it wouldn't turn into a fight for my life." That thought gave me an idea—something I might actually be able to do about the problem. I put it aside for the moment and refocused on Felix. "I'll work on it, but I'm also hoping that you find some answer in one of your journals. You had contact with the fae. Who knows? Maybe you dated one?" I teased.

"Ha! I wish," he said, shaking his head. "You'd think I would remember that?"

"You'd think I would remember my own father?" I replied.

He nodded, conceding the point. "I'll keep reading," he said. "I know we talked about going to your mother. Revealing yourself, what you suspect of your father. Maybe she would—"

"No," I said, interrupting him. "We could learn something; it's true. She might even know how to contact him, but it's not worth it." I took a deep breath, trying to organize my thoughts. "I want to learn more about the fae. I want to know what happened to them, why they disappeared from the world, and what it means for me. But I don't want to find my father," I said, searching for a way to explain the complex feelings that arose when I thought of my father. "He left and took my memories with him. I don't want either of them back. And most importantly, until you've overhauled the laws, or whatever it is you're doing with the Council, I don't want to put my mother in danger. I don't want her involved with all this."

Felix tilted his head. "It seems to me she is already involved in *all this*, as you put it. That is, if your father is what I think he is."

I shook my head. "Still not going there," I said. "I wanted to when I was first turned. I resented that the laws meant she couldn't know about me, that I couldn't have any contact without filing paperwork and agreeing to monitoring. But now, now that I've seen more, I'm grateful she's been kept away from our world. She may know about the fae, if she still has any memories of them, but that doesn't mean she knows about vampires, and I want to keep it that way if I can."

"Very well," he replied. "I'll let you know when I find more in my journals, and when the Council finally gets its act together enough to start doing some real work. I'd forgotten how long these things take, and just how stubborn we all are."

I smiled at his frustration. "Thank you, Felix. I appreciate all you're doing. I don't tell you enough."

"Don't mention it. It will only go to my head," he grinned. "Just don't hog all the best romantasy on the shelves, and that will be thanks enough."

I chuckled. "And here I thought you were just reading them to tease me," I said. "I'm starting to think you actually enjoy Sara's smutty book collection."

"Oh, I do," he said with a wink. "Just ask Bruce."

"I most certainly will not," I replied, getting to my feet. "I think the poor man would die from embarrassment before you got a chance to turn him."

Felix's head snapped up at my comment, and he watched me, probably looking for a reaction. I smiled at him. "I'm happy for you both. He's a good man… and you're not so bad yourself," I said.

"You really don't mind then? That I'm making another vampire?" he asked. "Given your history, I would understand if you were against the practice."

"I'm all for free will, and I can't imagine a better reason to become a vampire than wanting more time with someone you love," I replied. There was a question I wanted to ask, however, and it seemed like a good opportunity. "Bruce mentioned you've never made a vampire before. May I ask why?"

Felix nodded, looking thoughtful. "My own transformation was... traumatic. I didn't stay with those who'd made me for long, and after traveling and meeting more of our kind, I decided there were probably enough of us. It was quite some time before I met the other two of The Three, and we chose a different path. We thought that if vampires could live within a framework—a code of laws—it might protect not only ourselves but also the human populations we rely on. We worked for centuries to change our culture. It didn't always work. The laws aren't perfect, and the different Councils we established across the world have each handled things their own way." He shrugged. "That was my attempt to contribute to our society. I didn't want a family or to belong to a House until recently."

"Have you given up then?" I asked. "On trying to make it better? On being one of The Three?"

"No. Not at all. I just realized that the path is different from what I first thought. And it's not one I want to walk alone anymore."

"I'm glad to hear it," I said. "I plan to live for a long while. It would be nice if things got better. For everyone."

Felix dipped his head in agreement and refocused on his journal. I didn't want to stick around and distract him from his reading, so I decided to go in search of Sara. I knew she had to be close. Silas was home after all.

I found her in the shop surrounded by bridal magazines. "How goes the search for the perfect dress?" I asked. "Any closer to picking?"

She lifted her head and frowned. "No. It's hopeless. I love parts of several, but not everything about any one of them."

I nodded, pretending I understood what she was talking about. "Could you just buy several and have them pieced together or something?"

Her frown deepened. "No. I'm pretty sure that's not how it works."

"Well, you could always have one made, just the way you want," I suggested.

“That would cost a fortune, and I’m not sure we have the time. There are only three months until the wedding.”

“I’m sure you’ll find the right thing,” I said, leaning against the counter as she scooped up her magazines into a neat pile. “I do have some good news,” I said.

“Really? You ready to take a chance on dating again?” she whispered, her frown disappearing and a spark lighting in her eye.

I quirked my lips and pulled the ring I’d been working on out of my pocket and presented it to her.

“It’s sweet, but I’m already engaged,” she said sarcastically, fluttering her eyelashes for extra effect.

“Just take it,” I said, rolling my eyes.

“Oh, this one’s nice,” she said, slipping it onto her forefinger. “It’s beautiful too.”

“Determination and purpose. That’s what I meant to put in it anyway.”

“Nailed it. I feel like I could take on the world,” she said. She paused, tilting her head. “I suppose we can’t make sure someone with good intentions buys the thing.”

I winced. “I didn’t think about what might happen if someone with a dark purpose bought it.”

“It’s something to consider,” she said. “I suppose any feeling could be weaponized if you tried hard enough, but maybe for auction, we should stick to happiness, love, and contentment. That sort of thing.”

She took the ring off and handed it back. The boost of determination helped dispel my frustration, and I nodded in agreement. “I’ll fix it. It shouldn’t be too hard.”

As I slipped the ring back into my pocket, the door to the house opened, and Silas came into the shop, followed by Lucas and Bruce. “You guys done already?” I asked.

“For tonight,” Silas said, going to Sara and slipping his arms around his mate. I glanced at Lucas, who wore a smile as he watched his brother.

“We are going to need you out of your studio for a period of time during construction," Bruce said. "I'll set up a temporary space for you upstairs until then."

"How long do you think the project will take?" I asked.

Bruce turned to the two shifters. "It depends on the rain," Lucas said. "We need to bring in equipment, and there's an awful lot of mud back there."

"I thought you guys were just going to put up some walls in the existing storage space to make a new bedroom," I said.

Both the shifters looked back at Bruce. "There might have been some changes," he said. "Given that we expect some guests to stay with us for the wedding, I thought it might be best if we make a larger project out of it."

"Larger project?" I asked.

"We plan to add a sizable addition off the back," Silas said. "With your permission, of course." He wasn't talking to me, however.

He looked down at Sara, and I realized he was right. It was her house after all. "Oh, Sara. I'm sorry," I said. "I should have checked with you and not assumed."

She blew a breath out between her lips with a pffft sound. "This is *our* house. I might hold the deed, but I trust you all. Whatever the House needs," she said. "Plus, you're only increasing the property value."

"Great," I said, turning back to Bruce. "In that case, proceed."

He gave me a sharp nod. "If you'll excuse me? I have an architect to email and orders to place." With that, he retreated back to the house, leaving me with Sara and the shifters.

"Architect?" I mouthed. "How many overnight guests are we expecting for the wedding?" I asked. The wedding was going to be held on the property, but I hadn't really thought about where the out-of-towners would stay. There weren't a ton of hotels nearby, however, so it made sense that they would stay with us.

"I'm not really sure yet," Sara said. "I've received RSVPs from both my aunts in Virginia, who will be coming, but I still haven't heard from my family in Louisiana. Maybe another one or two?"

"I'm sure Bruce will work it all out," I said. "And he's bringing on help. We're meeting with someone next week for the housekeeper position."

"I'm glad he's going to have help. He deserves it," Sara said. "But, it's a little crazy to think of having a housekeeper, though."

"How is it different than having Bruce as your butler?" Lucas asked.

Both Sara and I burst out laughing. "I dare you to call him that," I teased. "Besides, he's not really our butler. He's our House manager. And he's... Bruce. He's one of us."

Lucas nodded, but I could tell he wasn't convinced. "Well, this has been fun, but I have to get back. Lara is home with the pups tonight, and I promised I'd be back before she fell asleep."

Silas walked him out to his truck to say goodbye, and Sara and I went back to the house. "How's it going with Silas's family?" I asked when the guys were out of earshot.

"Really great, actually," she said. "I know the witch community hasn't been super welcoming, but it's different over there. Bonded is bonded. I got a few shocked reactions when some of his extended family found out I was a witch, but they would never object to our union. It would mean condemning Silas to a life without his mate. They would never want that for him."

"That's refreshing," I said, waving to Felix on our way to the kitchen.

"Don't get me wrong," Sara said. "They would all have preferred I were a shifter. They just aren't going to make a fuss now that he's bonded."

"Well, it's still nice that they are accepting of you guys. Now we just have to get the witches on board," I said. "With all of us. Any progress on that front?"

"Have you seen the weather today?" she asked rhetorically, going to the fridge. She pointed to my shelf, and I nodded.

"At least they aren't trying to blow us up with lightning anymore," I said, catching the bag of O-neg she tossed me.

"For now," she mumbled, pulling out a glass bottle full of premade smoothie. She shook it as she closed the fridge.

"Maybe things will improve after your gathering," I suggested as I took a seat at the kitchen table with my snack. "It will be the first chance for most of your community to meet the House members after all. Maybe we'll charm them."

Sara came to join me, smoothie in hand. She sat, placing the bottle between us, but didn't open it. "There isn't going to be a Bride's Gathering," she said.

13

MARCUS

The four walls of my room were starting to close in around me. I'd spent more time than I cared to calculate shut behind my door the past week. Since my visit to the cemetery and my discussion with Kate, I'd decided to give her a bit of space. I didn't want her to feel I was obsessed or hounding her. But I also didn't want her to feel as if I was withdrawing and punishing her for pulling back. I just needed to act normally, I thought. And normally, I would seek her out. I made up my mind and went to see how she was doing.

I found her at the far end of the dining table. It looked like half her studio had been set up around her, and she was busy drawing, her head bowed over her work, her dark hair falling to hide most of her face. She was so absorbed in what she was doing that she didn't notice my presence. I stood and watched her. She was so beautiful. I loved the look of concentration on her face as she worked. Her dark brows were knitted together as she focused on the paper in front of her. It felt wrong to interrupt, but I couldn't look away.

"Kate," I said.

She lifted her head, eyes wide. "Oh, hi. I didn't hear you come in," she said, smiling broadly and setting her pencil aside.

"I know you're busy," I said. "I just wanted to check in, see how you're doing."

"I'm good," she said, attempting to get to her feet. "Actually, I wanted to talk to you. Just give me a minute to get out of this." She disentangled herself from the sketchbook on her lap, the artist's board she'd been working on in front of her, and the cart pushed close to her chair. I had to smile at how confined she'd been. Finally free, she pointed toward the living room, and I nodded.

"Shall we sit?" I asked when she just stood there looking at me.

"Oh, sure," she replied, taking a seat on the leather sofa.

I chose the closest chair, not wanting to crowd beside her.

She took a deep breath, and I waited. "So," she said. "I made you something."

"You did?"

"Yes," she said, digging an object out of her pocket. She pulled out something small and round.

She held it out, and I extended my hand. She dropped a coin into my palm. "Ah, you've been defacing money?" I said, letting the humor show through in my voice. "But honestly, it's beautiful."

"I asked Felix for something the right size and thickness," she said, shrugging. "I figured he probably had foreign coins that would work, and I'd been right. I'd ground down the surface of a British Pound coin—sorry Queen Elizabeth—and then engraved it with my own design."

I examined the side facing up. It was covered in small leaves and flowers, a common theme of hers. I flipped the coin over, and the other side had a rabbit encircled by a wreath of leaves. It really was beautifully done. "What does it do?" I asked, feeling a bit nervous, but hopeful at the same time.

"Well, I've been thinking about what you said, about how you feel about me," she said. She licked her lips, and I realized she was as nervous as I was. "I thought that if I could have some sort of insurance, it might be okay."

"Insurance?" I asked, not quite getting what she was saying. I indicated the coin. "What am I supposed to be feeling?"

She winced, as if telling me was going to upset me. "Resolution, determination, calm."

"I see," I said. "And this is supposed to...?" I needed her to say it—to name her fear—so we could address it directly.

"I thought, if we were going to be more than friends, like you suggested, it might come in handy. You know, help you not want to bite me," she said.

"Because you're afraid that if I bite you, I'll lose control and hurt you."

She nodded, still looking troubled. "Do you think you could be in a relationship, a romantic relationship, without biting the other person?"

It was a fair question. Biting was part of the deal when you were a vampire, and I had to admit, the idea of biting Kate was very alluring. However, I understood her fears and their source. "Yes, Kate. If that's the way you would want it, I would refrain from biting you. It's probably a good idea," I said. "You forget, I've smelled your blood before. I understand the risks."

"Because I like you, Marcus. I'm attracted to you," she said, stealing my breath. "And, it's been hard for me to be around you lately, knowing how you feel about me."

"Hard for you?" I asked.

She nodded, biting her lip. I thought I saw a sheen of pink across her eyes. "I'm afraid that your feelings for me are just about my blood. I'm afraid that the way I feel about you might be only because of the way you make me feel calm and strong when I touch you. I don't know what's true or not anymore, but I do want you."

I sat there, unable to respond right away. I'd thought about what might happen if she wanted me back. But in each scenario, it was all about me convincing her I could control my impulses and not go too far. I hadn't considered that she wouldn't believe that I was attracted to her for more than just her blood, or that she might doubt her feelings for me.

I thought for a moment and then called out, "E, could you come up here for a minute?"

"What are you doing?" Kate asked.

"Just give me a moment," I said. "I want to ask E something that may clear this up."

She sighed but waited.

E came into the room a moment later. Her steps were slow and hesitant. "Am I in trouble?" she asked, creeping closer.

"No. Not at all," I assured her. "I just have a question. Would you mind coming over here and sitting beside Kate on the sofa?"

E moved forward with more confidence. "Sure," she said cheerfully. "What is it?" she asked as she took her seat.

"Do you remember when you first met, Kate? The night at the club?" I asked.

E wrinkled her brow. "Of course, it wasn't that long ago. We shared a lovely dessert, as I remember," she said, smiling at Kate.

"Yes," I said. "And do you remember biting her?"

At my question, E blanched. "I... I did?" she asked. "I'm so sorry. I get a little bitey when I've been sipping from a drunk human."

"You did. And don't worry. I'm not upset or anything," Kate assured her.

"E," I said, refocusing her attention on me. "Some vampires seem to have a reaction to her blood. I was wondering if you have been craving her, or struggling in any way when you are in her presence."

"Oh," E said. "Not really. She smells really good. Like, really good. But I'm not having an issue with it. I know Kate doesn't feel that way about me, which is cool, so no. I wasn't planning on asking her out or anything."

"But you do feel an attraction?" Kate asked.

E looked at her, frowning. "Well, who wouldn't? You're gorgeous."

I glanced at Kate, my eyebrows raised.

Kate sighed. "E," she said. "Would you mind going back downstairs and pretending you can't hear everything we're saying up here?"

"I'll do you one better," E said, bouncing to her feet. "I'll put my headphones on and crank up something with a heavy beat."

"Thank you," I said as E left the room. When we heard the door to

E's room open and close, I continued. "E has actually bitten you and tasted your blood. She's not struggling. Alexander drank quarts, and he didn't attack you the next time he saw you," I said. "And James was just a creep."

She looked thoughtful, but didn't speak.

"I've smelled your blood, and while you do smell divine, it's not why I want to be with you. I feel the same way about you, whether I'm standing in front of you or a hundred miles away, no matter how long it's been since I was in your presence. I don't need this coin to be in control of myself, but if it makes you feel better, I will keep it with me. As for your feelings, I can't say. You'll have to work that out for yourself."

She seemed to consider that. "Okay," she said. "I... I think I'd like us to try."

I smiled and blew out a breath. "Can I hold you?" I asked. I didn't want to overwhelm her, but the urge to touch her was strong. I longed to hold her, to prove to her that it could be good between us. She nodded and scooted back on the sofa, giving me room to sit next to her.

As soon as I was seated, I wrapped my arms around her and pulled her close. As I did, her body shook against mine, and I realized she was crying. "Are you okay?" I asked, breathing into her hair.

"Yeah," she said, her voice thick with tears. "It feels really good to be held."

I pulled her even closer, inhaling her scent, and desire washed over me. I felt her stiffen in my arms, her breathing catching in her throat, and then all desire left me, all feeling left me. I was numb. "Kate," I said gently. "It's okay. Please let go. Let me feel this. I won't hurt you, I promise."

She let out a sob, and my emotions crashed back into me with a force that nearly knocked the air out of my lungs. I struggled not to react. I breathed in steadily as the wave of emotion ebbed and settled into a soft longing. Only then did I rub my face against her silky hair, inhaling her scent once again, letting it fill me up.

This time, she relaxed into my arms. Her breathing evened out, and I felt the shift. She was no longer afraid. She tilted her head, letting her hair fall back, and I brushed my lips over the shell of her ear. She turned her head toward me, not breaking contact, and captured my mouth with hers.

As much as I wanted this to go on—and I did—I gently pushed her back. "Hold on just a moment," I said, smiling at her worried expression. "I think it might be easier for you if we do this differently this time."

She nodded, her expression shifting to curiosity.

I kissed her hand as I pushed myself away, leaning back against the couch. I opened my arms, letting her come to me if she wanted. And she did. She didn't hesitate. She straddled my hips, placing both hands on my chest, and looked into my eyes. I'm not sure what she saw, but it must have given her confidence because she leaned in and kissed me again. There was no reservation in her kiss. She was fierce and hungry, and her desire fed my own.

As soon as her soft mouth met mine, I gasped, and she slid her tongue between my parted lips. My first impulse was to crush her against me, to deepen the kiss, to show her how much I wanted her, but I didn't. I held still. I opened for her, letting her explore, letting her slide her tongue against mine, taking what she wanted, what she could handle.

Our mouths pressed together, and I felt her fangs slide from her gums, growing long, and I knew she wanted me. The thought of her sinking her fangs into me, biting me, sent a thrill of pleasure down my spine. I wanted that. I wanted so much more, but for now I was content to have this—to have her in my arms.

She pulled back, breathless. "That was okay, right?" she asked, sounding uncertain.

I swallowed, my own fangs crowding my mouth. "It was more than alright," I said.

She looked shyly up from under her dark lashes. "Maybe a bit more?" she asked, her voice smooth and sure.

My hands rested lightly on her hips, but as the kiss went on, I dug my fingers in, holding tight, urging her closer, deeper. She rolled her hips against me, and I gasped again. I longed to feel the smoothness of her skin against mine, and slid a hand under the hem of her sweater.

I cupped the curve of her breast and ran my fingertips along the edge of her bra, gently pushing it aside. As we kissed, I brushed my thumb over her taut nipple, and she moaned into my open mouth. She whimpered as I increased the pressure, then pulled away slightly, throwing her head back.

I didn't even think about it; I leaned forward to kiss her smooth neck. The moment my lips touched her throat, she froze, and I knew I'd screwed up. I stopped what I was doing, pulling my mouth away and removing my hand. She pushed herself back on my legs, staring down at me with wide eyes. "I'm sorry," I said, but she shook her head, her dark hair waving around her shoulders.

"No, it was me," she said. "I… I can't help but think of…"

"It's okay," I said. "I understand. We can go slow. And I won't touch you anywhere that makes you uncomfortable."

She nodded but pushed herself off my lap. "I think I just need some time," she said, hugging her arms around herself. "I'm not saying I don't want to do this, I do. It's just going to take some getting used to."

I swallowed down my wanting; I understood. It was completely reasonable, and I could do whatever she needed to feel safe. "May I stand? Give you a hug?" I asked. "Nothing more."

She smiled and stepped back, giving me room to get to my feet. I approached her slowly and put my arms around her. She leaned into my embrace, placing her head on my shoulder. It felt good. I gave her a squeeze and kissed the top of her head. "It'll get better. You'll learn to trust that I'm not going to hurt you. Until then, I'm here." I kissed her silken hair again and stepped back.

There were tears again in her eyes. "Thank you," she said. "Could we sit for a while, maybe, and just talk?"

"Of course," I said, feeling relieved that I hadn't scared her away completely. We settled back on the sofa, Kate beside me, leaning against my shoulder. “I should have opted to get you flowers and ask you out properly,” I said, one arm around her.

She shook her head. “I think we’re past the dating stage,” she teased. “We’ve been living together for months.”

“I don’t think you ever get past the dating stage,” I replied. “At least not past the romance part.”

She tilted her head back to look at me. She was relaxed, with a smile on her full lips. “Maybe we can get all dressed up sometime. That sounds nice.” She gazed back at the cold fireplace, and we were both quiet for some time. “I want to do this again,” she said after a while. “I… I really like being with you, touching you, kissing you.”

I felt my body respond to her words. I wanted that, too. “Any time you want me,” I said in a husky voice. “I’m yours, Kate.”

She sighed and pressed closer into my shoulder. “Thank you,” she said softly.

I kissed the top of her head again and was content.

14

SARA

Kate's new car hugged the curves of the mountain road as we drove back from a quick shopping trip to the nearest larger town. We could get a lot within a few miles of the house, but there was still plenty we couldn't find, like good art supplies or the shampoo I liked. We had been going on more of these small excursions as the weeks went by. Since the weather turned dreary, we found ourselves in need of an escape. That afternoon, it gave Kate and me a place to talk without being overheard by every pair of ears in the house. I sometimes felt seriously left out of the gossip because of my witch hearing, which was no better than a human's. Even Bruce had sharper ears these days—not that I wanted to think about why.

"Sooo," I said, trying to drag more out of my best friend. "Are you and Marcus together or not?"

She blew out a breath and shrugged. "I don't know. He told me how he felt, and I admitted I liked him too. We kissed, and it was amazing, I mean, really, really good. And then I freaked out."

"You freaked out?" I asked. "What happened? Did he try to bite you? Or come all unhinged?"

"No," she said and then winced, absently touching her neck. "I just couldn't get the images of Alexander and James out of my head.

He kissed my neck, and it was just too much." She shook her head. "He says it's alright, and he understands, but I feel awful. What if I can't have a normal relationship? What if I never get over the fear?"

"Well, I hate to tell you this, but you're probably never going to have a normal relationship ever again, at least not the way you're thinking. You're a vampire now. And that will affect anyone you're with. Would it be easier with a shifter, a witch, a human? I don't know, Kate. You have to determine where your new boundaries are and find someone who can live within them. It sounds like Marcus is willing to try."

"Easy for you to say," she mumbled.

"Is it?" I shot back. "I'm not saying it's the same thing, but I'm over here dating outside of my own species. I'm marrying a man who has bonded with me for life. I'm sticking my neck out for my best friend and defending her and our House against my own people. I'm facing being shunned by my community. You don't think that scares me a bit?"

She glanced over at me, her eyes full of regret. "I'm sorry, Sara. You're right. I don't give you enough credit for all you've put on the line. I'm being selfish. I didn't mean to upset you."

I waved a hand. "Don't worry. I'm not really mad at you, I'm just frustrated with the situation we've all found ourselves in. And I am sympathetic to what's going on with you and Marcus. Don't forget, I was there when Alexander attacked you. I remember," I said softly. "I just think, if Marcus is someone you want, you should go for it. Don't let Alexander take this away from you, too."

Kate reached over and took my free hand, which was resting on my lap. "I love you, Sara."

I squeezed her hand and smiled.

As we drew closer to the house and the town just beyond, the weather deteriorated, and soon the wipers were going, and the road ahead was a haze of fog and rain. It was really getting old. I would have given a lot for just one day of clear blue sky and sunshine.

We parked next to the house, and both sprinted to the porch for cover, shaking off as much water as we could before going inside. I hated to create more work for Bruce if I didn't have to. As soon as we were inside, I recognized Silas's voice, and it didn't take supernatural hearing to tell that he was arguing with someone.

Kate and I rounded the corner into the dining room to find Bruce and Silas standing next to the table, bent over a large sheet of paper. "It's not that big a deal," Bruce was saying. "And it just makes sense. From a practical standpoint."

"No. We are not putting in a doggie door," Silas said, his tone low and firm, his arms crossed over his massive chest.

"It's more of a flap," Bruce argued.

I bit my lip to hold back a laugh and glanced at Kate, who looked to be struggling just as much as I was. "Everything okay in here, guys?" Kate asked, unable to hide the mirth in her voice.

Bruce straightened up and turned to face Kate. "We were just discussing my plans for the new locker room," he said. "I was explaining that with a sizable *flap*, the wolves could come in, shift, and then there will be showers and lockers for dressing. That way, when shifters are here to visit, like for the wedding, for instance, no one has to walk through the backyard naked."

"And I was telling Bruce that shifters have no problem with nudity and will not come and go like house pets," Silas said. His expression made it clear he would not be budging on this point.

"I think you're going to lose this one, Bruce," I said. "Especially considering who your contractor is."

Bruce sighed, turned back, and pointed to a spot on the plans in front of him. "Fine, but then we are planting privacy hedging around this entire area. We can create a sort of Shifter's Garden around the door with a path leading to the forest."

"That I can live with," Silas replied. Then he softened his voice to nearly a whisper. "A few bowls of water wouldn't hurt. The wolves do come back thirsty from a run."

I quickly covered my mouth with my hand, but a loud snort escaped through my nose. Silas gave me a dirty look, but then his lips curled into a smile.

"We'll leave you to it," Kate said, wrapping an arm around my shoulders and guiding me back the way we came. I waved and winked at my mate before disappearing around the corner.

Back in the foyer, Kate shook her head, a grin on her face. "Next, Bruce will be suggesting flea collars and chew toys, and we'll have wolves running around here in holiday sweaters," she said.

"We can still hear you," Bruce called out from two rooms away.

I smothered another laugh. "What are you doing for the rest of the afternoon?" I asked. "Feel like hanging out in the shop?"

"I would love to," she said. "But Bruce and I have House stuff to do today when he finishes with your fiancé. Is your mom or aunt going to be here this evening?"

I shook my head. "Nope. There's not much to do tonight, so it'll just be Beth and me. She's got some computer stuff to figure out, and I'm there for any customers or gawkers who happen to stop by."

"Sorry, I won't be there to put on a show," she teased, but then her brow flattened, and her eyes sharpened. "But if someone gets out of hand or you need something, just call out. I'll be there quickly."

The look in her eyes made my hair stand on end. Sometimes I forgot that she was a vampire, a lethal being who was quite capable of protecting what she felt was hers. I swallowed. "I don't think it will come to that, but thanks," I said, trying to lighten the mood.

She relaxed somewhat and nodded. "Okay, but I'll be around," she said, before giving me a quick hug and going up to her room.

Several hours later, I was in the shop with Beth. There was more work than I'd expected, but I was having a hard time summoning the will to do it. "How do you get anything done with a dog?" I asked from the shop floor. I'd started out petting Arrow, which turned into scritching, then a belly rub, and now I was just using her as a pillow while she lay on her side. She didn't seem to mind, and I was too cozy to get up. Her energy was as soothing as her short, soft fur.

Beth laughed through the open door of the office where she was working. "It's hard sometimes," she said. "You have to learn to be tough. Tell her to go lie down if you're busy."

"She *is* lying down," I protested. "It's not helping." Arrow's tail started to thump rhythmically on the floorboards. She knew we were talking about her.

"Are you snuggling her again?" Beth called out.

"Maybe," I said, burrowing into the warm fur behind me.

"You're spoiling her," Beth replied. "But, speaking of cuddling with canines, any word on when Silas's single brother might make an appearance?"

"Who? Elijah, the twenty-year-old?" I teased, fully aware that's not who she meant.

"Ugh, probably not," she said. "I was thinking of the one who's been out of high school for more than a couple of years. I may look young, but I'm pushing thirty, you know?"

"Hmm, we'll see. If it keeps raining like this, you might have to wait until the wedding, which will have to be a cramped affair in the living room," I said, my mood souring at the thought of the wedding. I was excited to marry Silas, but the actual event probably wouldn't match my expectations. "Although at this rate, it might just be our two families, the House, and you and your parents."

"I don't know, that could be kinda great," Beth said, appearing in the doorway and leaning against the frame. "You know, something small and intimate."

"Yeah, I know. It's just not how I pictured it," I said, reaching behind me to scratch Arrow's head. "I was never particularly invested in our community, not the way my aunt is, but now that this milestone is approaching, I want to be celebrated. I want the large wedding with my family, friends, and neighbors all there. I want it to stop raining so it can be outside, in the fresh air, under the moon, like the Goddess intended."

She smiled down at Arrow and me. "Whatever it ends up being, you'll be married to Silas and surrounded by those who love you."

I glanced up at her. "Thanks," I said. "That is really what matters most. We're already mated according to his family and his pack; the wedding is more a formality, a witchy ritual for me." I brought my fingers up and touched the scarred bite mark on my shoulder and smiled to myself. Even if we didn't end up with the wedding of my dreams, I still have everything I needed.

Just then, the headlights of a car shone through the shop window. Someone was here. It was time to act like a professional. I reluctantly got up and brushed off the dog hairs from my blouse. Beth called Arrow into the office and shut the door before joining me behind the counter. Most of the people who entered the shop didn't mind the dog, but there were always exceptions. I just hoped this wasn't another local witch come to size me up or check the place for vampires.

I was fussing with the back of my hair, trying to fluff out the flattened curls, when the bell over the door chimed and a figure in a dark raincoat entered the shop. She stomped her booted feet and drew her hood back, shaking the water off her shoulders. When she turned to face us, I froze. This was no local witch. This wasn't anyone I'd ever laid eyes on before. And yet...

She was tall, maybe five feet eight or nine inches, and probably in her early twenties. She had black, curly hair, cut close to her scalp, and skin that was just a shade darker than mine. She was dressed all in black, from her raincoat to her vintage combat boots. But none of that was what caught my attention. She also happened to look exactly like my Aunt Lucia, except for the eyes. This woman's eyes were a light, whiskey-brown, where my aunt's were dark pools of umber.

"Hi," she said as she approached the counter.

Beth leaned closer, until she was right beside my ear, and whispered, "Are you seeing what I'm seeing?"

I nodded, not taking my eyes off the stranger. "Hello," I managed, watching her as she walked closer. Even her gait was the same as my aunt's.

"I'm looking for Sara Heartwood," she said in a firm but friendly tone.

"I'm her... I am she... That's me," I stammered. I folded my arms and then uncrossed them, fidgeting. *Who the hell was this?*

The girl stopped, raising both eyebrows. "Okay, great," she said, digging in her pocket. She pulled out an envelope I recognized immediately as one of the wedding invitations I'd sent out. "This arrived addressed to a friend of mine, and I came hoping you could help me."

I glanced at the envelope as she held it up. It was one of the ones I'd sent out to my mom's relatives in Louisiana. "Umm, sure," I said. "What is it that you need?"

"I was hoping you could help me find my mother," she said, and sniffed in a way I recognized all too well.

15

KATE

I'd asked all the questions I could think of. But since Bruce ran the house, I wasn't sure what I needed to know when interviewing a housekeeper. Luckily, Bruce seemed to have it all under control. Chelsea had been sitting at our kitchen table for nearly an hour, patiently answering everything asked to the satisfaction of Bruce. I kept the barrier in my mind—the one that blocked out others' emotions—lowered so I could sense the woman and Bruce's reactions at the same time. As far as I could tell, it was going well.

"And, what makes you want to leave your current place of employment?" Bruce asked, glancing down at his notes.

"Well," Chelsea said. "I've been thinking about it for a while. It's not that I'm unhappy there, quite the opposite, but I'm not sure I want to work nights forever, and the work takes a physical toll. When you called and mentioned there was an opening here, I thought it might be a good opportunity for a change." She tucked a stray auburn curl behind her ear and looked at me. "I was told the position wouldn't involve serving anyone's blood needs. Is that correct?"

I swallowed at the mention of fresh blood. "Yes," I said. "We primarily eat bagged." Chelsea nodded, looking relieved. Bruce told me that humans who worked for the various Houses were typically used at the complete discretion of the House members, with no say of their own.

"However," Bruce said, clearing his throat. "We will soon have need of such services. Not from you, of course. But if you know anyone who might also be in need of a change, we could easily meet or exceed their current salary and benefits. This House is a human-forward working environment with flexible hours. The position would come with the standard contract for employment only, not transformation."

I looked at Bruce, and my mouth started to water. He saw me staring and shrugged. "Felix will need someone new to feed from eventually, and I thought it might be a service others in the house would want to take advantage of." I nodded but didn't reply.

"I'll ask around," Chelsea said. "Discreetly, of course." She smiled, dimpling her pretty, round face.

"Do you have any questions for us?" Bruce asked, placing his notes aside and resting his forearms on the table.

Before she could answer, we were interrupted by the clatter of nails on wood, as Arrow shot into the kitchen. I'd been so absorbed by the thought of feeding that I hadn't noticed her approach. She ran right past us, nose in the air. She rounded the island and came to a halt in front of the large industrial sink where I'd deposited a dirty tumbler just before the interview. She sat, tail wagging, and began to bark.

"Sorry," I said to Chelsea over the barking, just as Beth appeared to retrieve Arrow.

"Arrow, no. You are not working," Beth chastised as she quieted the dog. "You are turning this into a hobby. I'm not rewarding you with your favorite toy. I don't even have it with me. But you're a good girl. Come on." She patted her leg, calling the dog to her. "Sorry, everyone," Beth said as the two left the kitchen.

"Beautiful dog," Chelsea said, her brow creased. "Does she do that a lot? Bark at the sink?"

"Oh, no. Well, yes. She's trained to sniff out blood. She thinks she's working and takes her job seriously," I tried to explain.

The crease in Chelsea's brow deepened. "In case you lose a snack?" she asked.

I choked on a laugh, and Bruce shot me a look but was kind enough to take over. "No. She belongs to Beth, who works in the shop next door. The dog is trained to help in police investigations. It's a bit of an inconvenient coincidence that she ended up in a house with blood drinkers." Chelsea nodded but still looked confused. "I explained that this was a somewhat unusual House," Bruce said.

"Well, I've known you for a long time, Bruce. I trust that wherever you are happy, I'd be happy too. And it says a lot that you and your House were willing to stand up for Bruce against Margaux and Étienne," she said to me. "I don't know many vampires who would have done that. Or any, actually."

"We protect our own here," I said. "We're a family." I glanced at Bruce, and he gave me a rare smile.

Chelsea watched us with a smile on her face as well. "I can see that," she said. "Along with the impressive facts sheet that Bruce e-mailed me, that's all I need to know."

"Great," Bruce said. "I expect us to make our decision within the next week. Would you like a tour before you drive back?"

"That would be great," Chelsea said, rising along with Bruce and me. She shook my hand and followed Bruce out of the kitchen.

I waited a moment, then went to see what was happening in the living room. I'd kept half an ear on Beth and Arrow when they left the kitchen, and now I heard three voices and a dog panting in the living room. The voices were low, and aside from Beth and Sara, I had no idea who else was here.

I found the trio, along with the dog, in the reading area. Sara was sitting in her chair, facing me as I entered. Beth, with Arrow at her feet, was sitting beside the stranger on the small sofa with their backs to me. When Sara saw me, her eyes widened slightly, and she gave me a strange look. That was when I realized my walls were still down as I took in the emotions in the room. The stranger was calm but excited and full of curiosity. Beth was nervous and amused. Meanwhile, Sara was quietly freaking out.

Her emotions fluctuated rapidly between excitement, worry, astonishment, and alarm, making me feel like I might have a fit myself. I quickly reestablished my defenses and took a deep breath. Whoever the stranger was, it was personal to Sara, and she wasn't sure how to feel about it.

As I drew past the sofa, the stranger turned her head, and I came face to face with a younger version of Sara's Aunt Lucia. It was uncanny. Same cheekbones, mouth, nose, even the cock of her head. She even smelled the same. Only the eyes were different. "Hi," I said, looking from the woman to Sara and back again.

"This is Juno," Sara said, and I could hear the hysteria in her voice. "She is visiting from New Orleans. She's come in search of her mother..."

"Oh. Right," I said. "It's nice to meet you."

I held out a hand, and Juno shook it politely, but then her eyes brightened. "Vampire?" she asked, her tone friendly, not accusing, matching what I felt through the connection.

"Um, yeah," I replied. I glanced at Sara, but she just shrugged. "So, any luck locating your mother?" I asked, wondering just what this woman knew and how far the conversation had gotten. It was clear that Sara wasn't aware of Juno's existence until now.

"We were just asking Juno what she knew about her and what brought her here specifically," Sara replied.

"Yes, I was saying that I've always known I was adopted and that my birthmother lived somewhere in the Pacific Northwest, but it wasn't until I was twelve that I found out I was a witch," Juno said. She smiled warmly, and the expression looked alien. I wasn't sure I'd ever seen Lucia smile, especially not like that. "My mom, adoptive mom, has family connections with witches, so it wasn't as big a shock as it could have been, but that was when I realized my birth mother must have been a witch."

"But you don't know her name?" I asked.

"No. It wasn't until I saw that invitation on my friend's fridge—she's a witch too—that I started asking the right questions. I discovered that the witches in Washington mainly live in one area, and that our family connections reach this far north. I snagged the envelope the invitation came in and thought this might be a good place to start."

"Your friend is a Heartwood?" Sara asked.

"Yeah. She's the daughter of Jace and Ruby Heartwood, Kendra," Juno said.

"And your last name?" Sara asked.

"Everheart."

Sara nodded, as if she recognized the name. "How old are you, if I may ask?" she said.

"Oh, yeah. I'm twenty. My birthday was in January." Juno sniffed, crossing one long leg over the other. I shook my head at the familiar gesture.

I could see Sara counting backward, trying to figure out where she was at that time and whether Lucia had been around. Because if I had no doubt, then Sara wouldn't either. This girl had to be Lucia's daughter. "Well, I didn't live here at that time," Sara said carefully. "But my family has lived in this valley for generations.

"What's your gift?" Beth asked brightly. "My stepdad is a Water Witch."

"Fire," Juno said. She raised her hand, snapped her fingers, and flame sprang up from her fingertips.

Sara shot me another look, somewhere between pleading and shock. I could tell this was too much for my poor friend. It was time to get Juno out of the house so we could talk about this whole situation.

"Well, we would love to help," I said. "Where are you staying while you're here? We can make sure to let you know what we find."

"Oh, I hadn't thought that far ahead," Juno said. "Is there a decent hotel in town?"

"There is nothing in town," Beth said. "You'll have to drive back the way you came as far as the fairgrounds."

Juno frowned. "Oh, I didn't realize. In that case, it's getting late, and I should probably get going. It's already been a long day, and I don't want to fall asleep on the road," she smiled again and got to her feet.

We all stood, and I glanced at Sara, who was staring at Juno. The look on my best friend's face was conflicted, somewhere between worry and guilt. It wasn't a huge shock when she blurted out, "You could stay here."

Juno tilted her head, considering. *God, she looked like Lucia when she did that.* "If you don't mind, that would be great," she said. "It would make my search that much easier."

I swallowed a giggle that threatened to bubble up out of my throat. Her search couldn't get much easier, I thought.

Sara nodded. "Right. Well, if you want to get your things, I can show you to one of the guestrooms."

"I was just about to leave," Beth said. "Arrow and I can walk you out." Juno agreed, and Beth glanced over her shoulder at us as the two walked out. She mouthed, "*Call me*," before leaving through the front door with Juno.

As soon as the front door closed behind them, I turned to Sara. "Did you have any idea?" I whispered.

Sara shook her head, her eyes still wide in shock. "None. At. All," she said. "I've never heard one word of Lucia having a child. Do you think my mom knows?"

I shrugged. "Are you going to tell her?" I asked.

Sara grabbed my arm, sending waves of panic through me at the connection. "I have no idea. What do I do?" she asked.

I carefully unwrapped her fingers from my arm and patted her hand before stepping away. I didn't need her turmoil; I had plenty of my own. "I don't think it's your responsibility to do anything," I said. She furrowed her brow at me. "I mean, it's not you who's been keeping a secret. It's not you who gave up a child. Maybe you should call your mom and aunt and ask them?"

"You're right. Lucia should be the one dealing with this. Not me," Sara said. "Okay. Yeah. That way, she can decide if she wants to tell Juno or not. It's not up to me." She nodded, looking more confident.

A moment later, Juno came back into the house, carrying a small hard-sided suitcase and a backpack slung over one shoulder. Before I could go relieve her of her burden, Bruce and Chelsea appeared at the top of the staircase, looking down.

"Hello," Bruce said, descending the stairs. "Let me get that."

"Umm, Bruce, this is Juno. She's going to be staying with us," Sara said.

Bruce looked in our direction, raising one dark eyebrow. I shook my head. He refocused on Juno. "It's a pleasure," he said, taking her bags.

"Bruce is our House manager," I explained. "You guys can go up and find a room." I turned to Bruce. "Unless you're not done with your tour, Bruce."

"We were just finishing up," he said.

"I was on my way out," Chelsea said. "It was nice to meet you, Ms. Ward."

"Kate, please," I said, walking her to the door and saying goodbye.

Bruce took Juno's raincoat. "You can follow me or grab a bite to eat, and I can settle your stuff in the guest room," he said.

"Oh, I am hungry actually," she replied. "Would you mind?"

"That's my job," he said in a friendly tone, and turned to carry her baggage up the stairs, leaving the three of us alone in the foyer.

"So," I said, "let's get you a snack?"

Juno blinked at my question. "Food?" she clarified.

"Of course, food," I said. "Bruce cooks most nights around here. I'm told it's good, although I've never tried it."

"That would be great," she said.

I looked to Sara, but she still seemed at a loss for words. "Why don't we go to the kitchen?" I said.

She nodded in agreement, and it wasn't long before we had her seated at the kitchen table with a plate of cheese and fruit I found in the fridge and a sparkling water. I poured a tall glass of red wine for Sara, and she smiled gratefully as I set it in front of her.

I heard movement in the foyer and assumed it was Bruce returning until I heard the front door close sharply. "Where is everyone?" a voice called from the front of the house.

Sara froze, and I could practically smell the adrenaline dumping into her system. The wine glass in her hand began to shake as the voice called out again, closer this time.

"I have news. The Elders have finally decided," Lucia said as she appeared in the kitchen doorway. She spotted me first. "Oh, there you are." She crossed her arms, not yet seeing Sara or Juno sitting at the table. "You'll have no choice now," she said, sniffing. "They never change their minds on issues like this."

I held my breath and glanced at Juno. I couldn't help it. She sat up straight in her chair, her mouth slightly open. The look in her eyes was wonder, hope, and fear.

My eyes traveled back to Lucia, and I watched as her gaze slid sideways, taking in the other people in the room. Her expression froze on her face, and then she shook her head. "I'm sorry," she said, her voice breaking. "I... can't." She turned and walked out of the kitchen and out of the house, leaving us staring after her.

16

MARCUS

I looked over at E as she picked apart the paper coaster her drink arrived on. The bloody wine glass sat empty beside her as she peeled the layers of the coaster into thin rounds. She seemed deeply focused on her task, but I knew she was thinking about what I'd told her, and I was happy to wait while she processed.

After my interaction with Kate, the first person I wanted to discuss it with was E. It was also important that we had privacy, and I knew she was dying to get out of the house and escape the rain-soaked valley. A trip to Seattle for a few hours was exactly what we needed.

Finally, she took a deep breath and set her project aside. "I think Kate has legitimate reasons to be afraid," she said, glancing up to meet my eyes. Whatever she saw there made her sigh and offer a sad smile. "Would you agree that I know you better than anyone alive?" she asked softly.

I nodded. Not only was she my oldest friend, but she had been with me since shortly after my transformation and had seen how I struggled at the beginning. E was the only one I told about my wife before she died. I never had to watch myself around E. I never doubted her loyalty or love.

She reached over and placed her hand on mine. "I haven't seen you interested in anyone like this in years. Maybe ever," she said. "I know you wouldn't ever hurt her, but I think you might be pushing her too fast. She hasn't even been a vampire for a year. I know she seems a lot older than she is, but she's got very little experience to go on, and most of it's bad."

"You're right. Maybe it was too soon to tell her how I felt. To engage in... " I stared down at my drink.

She paused, then softened her tone. "Have you told her about Mary?" she asked.

I nodded. "I did. I told her about the war, too, and what happened to me. I didn't go into details, but she knows the basics and how I ended up here."

"Did you tell her about me? About our relationship?" E asked, a crease forming between her blonde brows.

"No," I admitted. "I thought, since you were staying with us, it would be better to leave that to you. It didn't seem like my place to tell her your story."

"It's okay," she said. "I don't think I would have minded. I know we've kept our connection quiet for safety reasons, but I don't believe Kate is like that. I don't think she would ever use it against us, play one of us off the other."

"I think you're right," I said.

"Would you mind the House knowing about us?" she asked.

I shook my head. "No, I don't think so," I said. "It just wasn't a choice I wanted to make for you. And it felt wrong to talk about it."

"Well, thank you," she said and then cocked her head at me. "I think the fact that you told Kate about Mary is telling."

"How so?"

"Have you ever told any of the women you've been with about her?" she asked.

I shook my head. "No. Never."

"Not even the humans you've slept with?"

"No. It wasn't something I wanted to share."

"Until now," she said. "Because Kate means more to you than those other women?"

"Yes, she does," I admitted. Over the years, I'd had a few lovers and more than a few one-night stands. I'd never considered telling them about my wife. I never wanted to share that part of myself with them. It was always about a physical connection, not an emotional one.

"Hmm, maybe I'm wrong," E said, getting my attention.

"How so?"

"Maybe you could both be good for each other. Healing."

"I don't need healing," I protested, but the look E shot me had me considering.

"Marcus," E said gently. "I've known you almost your whole life. And I've seen you hold yourself back from everyone, everyone but me. You've never told those closest to you about our relationship, about Mary, about your life before or after you were turned. I think there is a deeper reason for those things than you've led yourself to believe."

I started to protest, pointing out that many of those secrets we had kept together for safety, but she stopped me. "No. I know all the reasons already. And I agreed with them at the time," she said. "But you're safe now, we are safe now, and you're only now starting to open up because of Kate. I think that says a lot."

I thought about what she said. I saw the wisdom in it, but I'd never considered things from that point of view before. "So, what is your advice?" I asked.

"Don't give up, but go slow with Kate. And don't wait to start letting people in, either. I think it's time to bring down some of those carefully constructed defenses you've built," she said.

Her comment made me flinch. I forgot sometimes just how well she knew me and how well she read people. She wasn't wrong, but the idea of sharing more about myself with the world in general made me uneasy. I'd spent a lot of time protecting those in my life with my secrets.

E and I paid for our drinks and decided to head home. As I drove,

I reflected on how things at the house had changed since E's arrival. I hoped she would choose to stay, but I knew there wasn't much for her to do out there—for either of us to do out there. She'd been so happy when we moved to Seattle. I came out first and wrote to tell her all about it. It wasn't long before she joined me and built a life for herself here on the West Coast.

I glanced over at her in the passenger's seat. She was looking out the window at the city lights, a smile on her lips. "Do you think you'll stay and join Kate's House?" I asked.

She shook her head. "I still don't know. But if I don't, I promise I won't go far." She patted my shoulder and went back to quietly looking out the window.

Wherever she ended up, I was sure we would always stay in touch. It had been that way from the beginning, and I couldn't imagine living far apart.

When we returned to the house, a strange car was parked out front, and beside it was Lucia's Subaru. "Were we expecting guests tonight?" I asked.

"Not that I know of, but I'm happy to see Lucia is here," E said brightly. "I haven't seen her in days."

Before we'd gotten out of the car, the front door opened and Lucia shot out onto the porch. She walked down the front steps, her posture more rigid than usual, and I briefly wondered if she was fighting with Sara again. I shut my door as E climbed out, her attention on Lucia. E glanced back at me. "Something's wrong," she said, and started walking toward Lucia, who had made it to her car. "Lucia," E called out.

Lucia opened her car door, ignoring E, which was unusual. She might be occasionally rude to the rest of us, but no one, including Lucia, was rude to E.

E stopped walking and called out again. This time, Lucia did turn to look, her face a blank mask, devoid of any expression, yet tears streamed down her face. She blinked once and then climbed into her car, starting the engine.

I walked up next to E and put a hand on her shoulder. She

glanced up at me, worry written all over her face. "I wonder if something happened with the Elders?" she said.

"Whatever it is, it must be bad," I said, turning toward the house. "Let's go find out."

I led the way into the house, E right behind me. There was a murmur of voices coming from the kitchen, and I headed straight there. As soon as I stepped into the kitchen, I had to stop and do a double-take. I was sure I'd just seen Lucia drive off in her car, and yet here was a woman who looked like she could have been her twin—a much younger twin—and yet the similarities were remarkable, right down to the tear-covered cheeks.

I knew the exact moment that E caught sight of the stranger, because whereas I had frozen, she grabbed my arm and gasped. I glanced down at the vampire, who was clutching my arm like she was about to tip over. The look on her face could only be described as awe.

I looked back at the trio sitting around the kitchen table. Kate looked worried, Sara appeared to be in shock, and yet they both seemed to be doing better than the woman in black. She sniffed and lifted her chin to look at E and me. "Hello," I said. "I'm sorry, we're clearly interrupting." I turned to go, putting an arm around E, who was still staring at the stranger.

I half pushed, half dragged E back out through the hall and into the foyer. "Did you see her?" E whispered, "Or am I losing it?"

"No. I saw her," I said, just as footsteps sounded from the hall.

A moment later, Kate appeared. I steadied myself as she drew near. I felt my heart pick up from its imperceptible beat to a steady rhythm. I took a deep breath and watched her, the sway of her hips, the graceful movement of her hair, loose around her shoulders. My stomach dropped, and my fangs began to tingle.

"Hey, crazy, right?" she said as she reached where E and I waited. She came closer as if I was pulling her toward me with my desire. She stood beside me, slipping her hand into mine, and I felt the rightness of it. I wanted to pull her against me, feel more of her body, but now was not the time.

I cleared my throat, trying not to get sidetracked. "We just saw Lucia tear out of here and came to find out what happened. We thought it might have something to do with the Elders and their decision, but considering what we just walked in on, I'm guessing that woman had something to do with it."

Kate led us farther from the kitchen, toward the reading area. "Yeah, that's Juno. She came here searching for her birthmother and just found her," Kate said.

"Lucia has a daughter?" E whispered. "Did anyone else know?"

"No," Kate said. "It seems no one knew. At least neither Sara nor Juno, at any rate."

"And she just ran away?" E said, hugging her arms around herself.

"I think it was a shock. I'm hoping she'll come back, for Juno's sake if not her own," Kate said.

"Juno," E said, like she was testing out the name. "Is she okay? Is there anything we can do?" She glanced back toward the kitchen like she was ready to run back in and help in any way she could.

"She's pretty shaken. I don't think she imagined it going quite like that," Kate said with a wince. "Sara and I just met her, however, so I'm not sure how she'll take it. She seems nice. Sort of like Lucia, but she smiles." Kate cracked a smile of her own.

"That would be something to see," I said as Kate's head whipped toward the sound of someone on the stairs.

She patted her hand against my chest. "Hey, that will be Bruce. I'm going to head him off and fill him in. I don't want him to walk into the kitchen unprepared. He's already met Juno, but he wasn't there when Lucia showed up," she said, and went to stop Bruce.

I looked over at E. She was still staring toward the kitchen, her brows drawn together with worry. "I'm sure she'll be okay. Listen," I said, cocking my head to the side. It was easy to hear Sara and Juno talking quietly at this distance. They seemed to be getting along. "You can hear that everything is alright."

E nodded and turned her gaze on me. "Talk about a shock," she said, and I couldn't tell if she was talking about her own feelings or those of the Heartwood women.

I was about to suggest we go downstairs and give Sara and Juno some space when E and I both looked up as we heard the two leave the kitchen and head toward us. E grabbed my arm again as we waited, and I could feel the trembling of her muscles. This really had shaken her up, I thought. She was close to Lucia, and I could understand where something like this might affect her deeply, but I'd never seen her this way.

"Hey," Sara said as they came into view. "I wanted to introduce you."

"I'm sorry again about barging into the kitchen," I said. "We didn't mean to—"

Sara held up her hand. "No. It's fine. It's your kitchen too. Guys, this is Juno, my... cousin," she said and smiled up at the taller young woman.

Juno smiled back at Sara and then nodded at us. "It's nice to meet you," she said, and even her voice was like Lucia's.

E surprised me then by dropping my arm and stepping forward. "Hi, I'm E," she said, holding out her hand for Juno. "And this is Marcus, my little brother."

17

LUCIA

Driving was tough through all the rain. I could barely see the road in front of me. I kicked the wipers up higher, to no effect. Sighing, I reached up and wiped my face. That was better. Turning off the highway just a few miles ahead, I crossed the bridge and let my car find its way home. The route was automatic after driving the same road since the day I got my license.

Blinking, I caught sight of the house through the trees. The same house I'd spent almost every day in since moving here when I was a little girl—except when I took trips, of course, or during those six months I stayed with relatives in Louisiana. No. I had to stop that thought right there. I pulled into my parking spot and turned off the engine. It took me over five minutes to get out of the car. The messy emotions kept spilling out, unwanted and unasked for. I couldn't go into the house like that. I waited until I'd regained my composure and my face was free of tears.

Taking a deep breath, I bit the insides of my cheeks and went inside. I saw my sister sitting at the kitchen table and bit down harder, the pain helping to clear my head and keep the tears that pricked my eyes at bay. I couldn't get caught here in the kitchen. I wasn't in the mood for a chat. I needed to get to my room, where I could think without her asking what was wrong.

"Hey," my sister said, looking up from her phone. "I heard the news."

I froze in place and looked at her. Her features were calm, with no sign of pity, no outpouring of emotion I might have expected.

"You were right," she said. "I didn't think they would actually do it, but they did." Confusion must have shown on my face because she clarified, "The Elders," she said, tilting her head and looking at me. "I would have thought you'd be more upset."

I shrugged and hung up my bag, careful to hide the shaking of my hands.

"I just don't know what to do next," she said. "If there's anything to do at all. And I'm not sure ordering the House out of the valley will do any good. Sara and Kate seemed pretty determined to stay. And why shouldn't they? It's a free country, after all. The Elders don't have any legal right to make the House leave. I don't want this to turn into a fight, though." She heaved a sigh and waited for me to respond.

I cleared my throat and tried to focus on what she'd just said. "I'm sure the Elders have their reasons. We will have to wait and see how the House reacts."

"Do they know? Sara and Kate?" she asked. "Maybe we should go over and tell them directly. It would be better coming from us than one of the Elders."

I flinched. "I just stopped by. They know," I managed to say in a fairly steady voice.

"Oh. How did they take it?" Her features softened, and her look of concern was almost overwhelming. I knew it wasn't about me or how I was breaking inside, but it still took my breath away. I shook my head, unable to speak, and turned toward the kitchen staircase. "Lucia," my sister called after me. "What is it? What did they say?" Her voice trailed off as I reached my room and shut myself inside.

I leaned my back against the familiar wooden door. I took a deep breath and let out a muffled sob. *How could Juno be here? How was this possible?* I stumbled to my dresser and yanked open the bottom drawer. I pulled out a worn envelope and backed up until my legs hit the side of the bed, then eased down until I sat on the edge of the mattress.

I stared at the envelope through a haze of tears. Sniffling, I opened the flap and pulled out the stack of photographs. The top one was a Polaroid of a newborn baby with black, curly hair, wrapped in a white blanket edged in blue. It was taken at the hospital shortly after Juno was born. I recognized the background as the room where I delivered her.

The next few photos were on photo paper with "1-hour photo" stamped on the back, featuring the same baby at about three months old. As I flipped through the stack, the baby grew into a toddler and then a young girl. The photos started to skip more and more time, and the images became sharper while the paper changed to a popular home printing brand. The last photo was taken at Juno's high school graduation. She stood in a yellow cap and gown, a beautiful smile on her face—the same face I'd seen staring at me from Sara's kitchen table.

I had received the photos over the years from Juno's adoptive parents. I never asked for them, but kept them. They were the most valuable things I owned. If the house ever caught fire—not that I would let it get out of hand—, these would be the items I would take to safety. For the past twenty years, since the first and last time I held my daughter, the pictures were all that I had of her, my only contact, until she showed up at Sara's. My vision blurred again, and I clutched the stack of photos to my chest as the tears rolled down my face.

Part of me—a large part—wanted to get back in the car and drive to her as fast as I could. I wanted to explain. I wanted to tell her that I had always loved her and always wanted the best for her, but I couldn't. She probably hated me. She was probably relieved that I'd left and didn't have to face the awkward confrontation of demanding to know why I'd given her up. She didn't have to watch me fall apart while I tried to explain, trying to take away a hurt I know I'd caused.

My phone rang in the pocket of my linen trousers. I pulled it out and glanced at the screen. It was Sara. I clicked the button and turned it off, tossing it onto the bed beside me. I couldn't talk to anyone right now, especially not Sara. *What must she think of me?* How could she accept that I'd given up my family? Given up a daughter, knowing how her parents cherished her? I'd spent so much time with Sara; she was like my own. I could only imagine how she felt finding out about Juno and that I'd kept her a secret all these years.

My thoughts were interrupted by a soft knock on the door, just before Sybil cracked it open. "Hey, Luc," she said. "Sara just called." She eased into the room, as if I might explode. I didn't move. I didn't even look up. Maybe I was afraid I might explode too. The bed dipped when she sat down beside me, and then her arms were around me.

I turned into her embrace and wept. Truly wept. Here I was, a grown woman, being comforted by my little sister, and all I could do was sob into her shoulder as she gently stroked my back, rocking me slightly like I was a child. And I needed it. "Shh," my sister said. "It's all going to be okay."

Sybil and my parents knew about Juno. I came home pregnant after one of my solo trips, when Sara was about six years old. I hadn't known I was pregnant for a few months, but I suspected it. By the time I told them it was time for me to leave town if I wanted to hide the pregnancy.

They all said they would help if I decided to raise her. They had been so kind, but I wasn't ready to do that. I was unmarried, working full-time at the shop, and helping care for my aging parents. Sybil was married and lived several towns away, raising her own daughter. I couldn't ask everyone to change their lives because of me. Plus, I couldn't bear how the community would react to my pregnancy. I didn't want to be the talk of the valley. I didn't want to limit my chances or what I could achieve because of what I'd done. If the Elders seemed old-fashioned now, it was nothing compared to twenty years ago.

So I'd given up my baby. I'd left her with strangers who promised to love and take care of her. And I'd faced the reality of my life. I'd taken care of my parents until their deaths, and I'd kept the shop going afterward. But I'd never forgotten about my daughter. I'd never stopped wishing things could have been different.

After a few minutes, I pulled back. Still clutching the photos, I wiped at my face with the back of my free hand. "Sara told you?" I said, my voice thick with tears.

"She did. She said you saw Juno and ran away."

I shook my head. "I couldn't face her," I admitted. "I couldn't..."

"I understand," Sybil said. Her tone was soothing yet firm. "You can't run away forever, though."

Sure, I felt upset after seeing Juno in person. It was a shock and reminded me of everything I'd given up. I might have wished things could have been different, but I didn't regret my choices, and I wasn't going to let Sybil pressure me into some kind of happy family reunion. It wasn't going to turn out the way she expected, I thought. Not everyone got a happily-ever-after.

I straightened up, sniffing back the last of my tears. "I made a choice," I said. "I'm still convinced I made the right one. I don't want to have to justify it to her. I will only disappoint her." I took a deep breath, feeling steadier.

Sybil looked at me, assessing my words and attitude. "You think that's why she's here? To make you justify yourself?"

I felt some of the steel return to my spine. "It doesn't matter why she's here," I said. "I don't plan on seeing her. She can go back to New Orleans, where she belongs. It's for her own good."

"Is that really what you want? You don't want to talk to her, listen to what she has to say, or get to know your daughter a little bit?"

I stood up, put the photos back in my dresser, and closed the drawer. I turned to my sister. "I don't think it's a good idea. Aren't things complicated enough right now without starting some sort of family feud? No. It's better if she goes home. The sooner the better. I would appreciate it if you talked to Sara and passed on the message."

"No. I won't do that. Juno is an adult now. She's not a child to be sent home, and you gave up your say on what she could or couldn't do long ago." She pressed her lips together and stood up. "I think you're more worried about yourself than Juno. I think you're still clinging to some idea of who you have to be for this town, for our family. Well, you're wrong. Your family is over at that house, wanting to see you. Wanting to get to know you. You might not regret giving her up to be raised by a loving family, but you will regret it if you turn down this chance to talk to her. She's reaching out a hand. I'm not sure she'll hold it out forever."

With that, Sybil turned and left the room, leaving me alone with her words hanging in the air like a thick cloud. She didn't understand. She didn't know how hard it had been to leave that child behind and return to our valley with empty arms and an aching heart.

I'd done what I had for both of us. I'd done what I had to, and I wasn't going to spend any time second-guessing my choices. Getting to know Juno now would only make that harder, I thought.

It was better for everyone if she left.

18

KATE

"She said 'little brother'?" I asked, still confused.

Sara looked at me over the top of her mug of tea before taking a sip. "That's what she said, 'little brother'."

"And did Marcus say anything after that?" I pulled my legs up onto the chair, hugging them to my chest. It was late afternoon, and the sun was still up, but none of our housemates were around. The vampires were all asleep, Juno was taking a nap, Silas was working on the other side of the Pass, and Bruce had gone into town. It was a good time for us to talk if we wanted a bit of privacy. I did feel a bit bad for gossiping, but this was just too good.

"No. He talked to Juno for a few minutes, and that's when you and Bruce came back downstairs," Sara took another sip of tea. "After that, I tried calling my aunt and then spoke to my mother, and you know the rest."

The rest was that we'd all had a late dinner together, thanks to Bruce, and then the non-vampires had gone to bed. I hadn't gotten a chance to talk to Sara privately until now. "Well, now I'm dying of curiosity." I looked at my phone. It would be hours before either of them was awake, and I could ask about this family relationship. I thought back to my first impression of E. She'd been very familiar with Marcus in a way that made me uncomfortable. And when she moved into the house, she went right into his room, his very bed, but he'd assured me they weren't a couple. It made more sense now, I thought.

A noise from the road brought my head around. "Someone's here," I said. "You expecting your mom or Lucia today?"

"Mom, maybe. Lucia, definitely not," Sara said. "I talked to my mom again before bed last night. It seems like Lucia is going to try to ignore that she has a daughter and that the daughter is here in our house. You know, the 'If-I-don't-acknowledge-it,-it-will-go-away' tactic. Juno and I spoke this morning, and it seems she's as stubborn as her mother. She's not going anywhere until they've had a chance to talk."

The sound of tires on gravel made me look back toward the front of the house.

Sara set down her tea and pushed to her feet. "I'll get it," she said. "I hope it is my mom. She is supposed to come over later to meet Juno. Maybe she's early."

I waited, curled in my chair, as the car parked outside, but I was somewhat puzzled as I heard *two* car doors open and close, and the sounds of two people slowly coming up the steps.

"Holy shit," Sara said as she peeked out the window.

I zipped to her side at the speed only a vampire could, startling Sara. I grabbed her elbow to steady her, so she wouldn't topple to the floor, and felt her surprise and alarm. I was afraid I'd caused it with my entrance, but she still stared toward the door, eyes wide.

I looked out the window and saw two figures on the porch. One was an older man with darker skin, grey curly hair, and a serious expression. The other was a tiny, stooped, old woman with ghostly white hair and matching white clothes. "Who are they?" I asked as they stepped closer and rang the bell.

"Two of the Elders, including Elder Coburn, their elected leader," Sara whispered back at me in a hiss. She stood up straight and tugged her blouse down, smoothing the fabric before she opened the door. I positioned myself just over her shoulder to get a clear view of the pair.

Sara pulled the door wide and stepped to the edge of the ward. "Elder Coburn, Elder Paulson, would you care to come in?" Sara said, her voice smooth, but I could smell the subtle scent of fear coming off her.

"Sara Heartwood," the man said, flicking his gaze briefly to me before continuing. "No, thank you. I wish I were here under better circumstances. This is not a social call."

"Then what is it?" I said, not patient enough—or polite enough—to wait for the man to get to the point. Sara sucked in a breath, but didn't say anything.

Both the Elders looked over Sara's shoulder at me. "And who is this?" the older woman said. Her voice cracked with age, but there was power behind her words, and her cloudy eyes were shrewd.

Sara stepped back to look at me, and I took the opportunity to move up beside her. Before Sara could introduce me, I thrust my hand out to the woman, meeting her gaze. "Hi, we haven't been introduced," I said. She eyed me and then extended her hand. As our palms met, the temperature difference registered on her face, and I felt her smug attitude dip toward shock. "My name is Kate," I said. "And I am the leader of the House of Ward." I grinned at her, flashing my fangs, and her eyes widened.

I felt a jolt of electricity from her grip, but I didn't let go. I blinked, maintaining eye contact as I slowly released her hand. My gaze flicked up to the man. The baffled look on his face was comical. I would have laughed if I weren't so angry with the pair. I knew why they were there. Before Lucia ran the night before, she mentioned that the Elders had made a decision, and Sara's conversation with Sybil confirmed our suspicions.

They wanted us gone.

The man, Elder Coburn, looked up at the sun-tinged sky and blinked back at me. "How is this possible?" he said, his voice somewhat strangled.

I clearly hear the woman mumble, "Blood magic," under her breath.

I sighed, as if his question was boring me. "I'm not built like other vampires," I said. "You should remember that if you think you can push us around." Sara cleared her throat behind me, and I wondered if I was laying it on too thick. I glanced back at her over my shoulder, out of view of the witches, and mouthed, "*Sorry.*"

She stepped up beside me. "Yes, Elder Coburn, Elder Paulson, this is Katherine Ward, the leader of our House," she said.

That got their attention. "*Our* House?" Coburn spat. "Do you mean to tell me that not only has a vampire established a House in our valley, but a witch from our own community has joined that House? As a member?"

"Yes," Sara stated.

Coburn drew himself up, regaining some of his lost composure. "It will probably come as no surprise that we have come on behalf of the witches of this valley and the surrounding area to inform you all that the House of Ward is not welcome here in our territory. You will remove yourselves within the month." He glanced at his accomplice, as if for reassurance. Her mouth was set in a hard line as she stared daggers at me from behind her grandmotherly disguise.

"Or what?" I said, crossing my arms. "I don't see how you can make us go if we aren't willing. You have no legal right to force us off the property. We aren't even within your town's limits."

"We provided a demonstration of our abilities," Paulson said, cocking her head and narrowing creased eyes. "It was just a taste, mind you; we could have caused real damage if we wanted to." Electricity crackled around the tiny woman, lifting her wispy hair and sending blue sparks dancing along her exposed skin.

I'm not going to lie, it was impressive. It was what Sara could do with her hands, but all over her body. I could feel a buzzing in my bones, starting at my feet and working its way up to my hairline. Sara shifted uncomfortably beside me, and I wondered if she was about to summon her power as well.

I would not let this woman threaten my House, and I would not tolerate her or anyone else hurting a member of my family. I lifted my lip and growled deep in my throat as my fangs slid from my gums. I wanted this woman to see what I was capable of too.

"Diane, please," said Coburn, and turned back to Sara and me. "We are not here to start a fight. We are here to deliver the message. What you decide to do with it is up to you."

The energy coming from the witch winked out, but the fire in her eyes remained. *We would have to watch that one*, I thought. Coburn might act as though he were the one in charge of this mission, but she was the one who made the hair on the back of my neck stand up.

"You've said what you came to say," I said. "We will not be moving."

Diane looked from me to Sara. "This is how you both feel?" she asked.

Sara took a breath and stood a bit taller. "Kate is my House leader, and I agree with her decision. Now it's time for you both to go."

"I never thought I would live to see the day that a witch would side with a vampire," the old woman said. "Come on, Theo. There is no arguing with these creatures." She turned her back on us and shuffled toward the steps.

Theo blinked, and then the Elder followed the small witch back to the car. Sara and I stood on the porch, waiting in silence until the car disappeared from view, before we went back inside.

Sara shut the door and stood in the foyer, hands on her hips, breathing deeply. "I can't believe I just kicked two Elders off the property," she said. I couldn't tell if she was about to laugh or cry.

"That was just rude," Felix's voice sounded from the darkened hall to the kitchen, and I nearly jumped out of my skin.

"Felix!" I exclaimed. "You nearly gave me a heart attack."

"Vampires don't have heart attacks," he said. "Would you two care to join me in the kitchen, so that I don't have to suffer the sun, please?"

"You would just instantly heal," I said, as Sara and I headed toward the kitchen, one of the only rooms on the main floor without windows.

"I know," he said. "But it makes me so hungry, and I loath the idea of having to drink what you've got in the fridge."

He might not like it, but the bagged blood was my main source of nutrition, and I wasn't as picky, so I went to the fridge on my way to the dining table. "I presume you heard all that?" I asked, plucking a wine glass from the dishwasher as my blood heated in the microwave.

"I did," he said. "I thought Sara was particularly brave."

"I was the one who growled and showed my teeth," I protested.

"Yes, and a wonderful growl it was too, but Sara was the one standing up to tradition, to her Elders."

I smiled at my best friend, who was looking a bit washed out. "Would you like anything?" I asked her before sitting down. "Do we have any whisky?" she asked with a lopsided smile.

"I'm not sure," I said, glancing around the expansive kitchen and its many cabinets.

"We do have a lovely Macallan single-malt," Felix said, rising and going to the dining room. He was back seconds later with the bottle in one hand and a tumbler in the other. "It's a scotch. I hope that's okay." He poured a healthy amount into the crystal tumbler before setting it in front of Sara.

"Why do we have scotch, and why do you know where it is?" I asked. "You don't drink it."

He smiled a wide, toothy grin at me and held the bottle up, inhaling from the neck before resealing it. "No, but Bruce drinks it for me from time to time," he said, setting the bottle down and returning to the table.

I held up a hand. "Okay, that's enough. I get it," I said, taking a seat beside Sara, who was smelling her own drink and pretending she hadn't just heard what Felix said.

"Sara, I'm interested to hear your take on what just happened with your Elders," Felix said in all seriousness.

She took a small sip of the scotch; the look on her face said she was preparing for it to be painful, but then her features relaxed, and she raised her eyebrows in surprise. "This is really nice stuff," she said, saluting Felix with her glass. He dipped his head in thanks and waited. "I think I'm very glad Kate was there. I don't think they are going to know what to make of a vampire who walks around in the daylight, like it was nothing. It's going to make them rethink whatever they have planned. It might not stop them, but they will have to regroup and tell the others what they've learned."

Felix nodded. "That's good for us," he said. "Maybe it will intimidate them enough to back off altogether." He turned to me. "Did you push on them with your abilities? If so, do you think they noticed?"

I blinked at him. "To tell you the truth, I didn't even think of it. I was so pissed off, the only thing I could think of was taking a bite out of them," I admitted.

"It's understandable," Felix said. "They were on your territory, and they were making a direct threat. You have more than physical strength on your side, though, Kate."

"I know," I said with a wince. "It was hard to keep a clear head while that little witch lit up like a Christmas light."

"I'm sorry I missed that," Felix said.

"Is that what you'll be able to do someday?" I asked Sara, and took a drink of my own beverage.

She was swirling her glass now, a much more relaxed expression on her face. "I hope so," she said. "That was really cool. I would bet she was the one who brought down the lightning the other day."

"It's crazy to think a witch that tiny could control lightning," I said.

"A witch's power has nothing to do with their size," Sara said. "It's about experience, practice, and it strengthens with age. Elder Diane Paulson is one of the oldest witches in the entire country, let alone this valley."

"That's good to remember," Felix said. "Let's just hope she isn't feeling homicidal. What about the other one? The male. Do you know what his gift is?"

"Air," Sara said. "He's a powerful Air or Wind Witch. He's been at the helm of the valley's weather for decades."

"He's the one we have to thank for all the rain?" I asked.

"Him, and his team of Air and Water Witches. Yes." She drained the last of her scotch. “I think we should ccall my mom and get her overrr here,” Sara said, her speech slightly slurred.

“I think you should have something to eat unless you want your mom to see you wasted,” I said. “Remember when she caught us drinking beer in tenth grade? I do not want to hear that woman’s lecture on alcohol again.” Felix chuckled. “Don’t laugh,” I chided him. “Or I’ll make you sit through it too. It’s your whisky after all.”

“You could try,” he said, giving me a wink as he got up from the table. “Just call me when she’s here.”

“I’m your House leader,” I teased. “It would be a command performance. She had a PowerPoint presentation, Felix. There were slides,” I called after him as he left the kitchen.

19

SARA

Kate was right; I needed food. Bruce got home just in time and made me an omelet that helped soak up the alcohol. By the time my mom arrived, I had sobered up enough to be horrified again by what I'd done.

"Don't worry, dear," my mother said. "I'm not sure what they expected, but they got what they deserved. I'm surprised that Theo brought Diane at all."

"She's older than Theo, right?" Kate asked. "That would make her more powerful."

My mom nodded. "She is, but she's always been a hot-head and has never been elected to lead the Elders. She resents it too."

Kate narrowed her eyes. "She's going to be trouble, I can tell."

Felix let out a laugh. He was relaxing on the sofa in the spot where he and Bruce often sat, wearing jeans and a faded T-shirt. "I'm sure she's somewhere saying the same thing about you, Kate." He crossed one leg over the other. "Marcus and E just woke up," he said. "And the shower in Juno's room shut off about ten minutes ago. In case anyone was wondering."

My mother sat up at the news. She'd been waiting for Juno to come down and meet her for the first time. I could tell she was nervous by the way she kept fidgeting with the pockets of her linen dress. She'd left her apron at home and was dressed a bit neater than I'd seen her in ages.

"Stop eavesdropping, it's creepy," I said, trying to distract my mother, but I winked at Felix so he knew I was joking. "Where did Bruce run off to? I went back into the kitchen after finishing my omelet to thank him, but he had vanished."

"He's gone to call Chelsea, the new hire, to let her know she got the job. She works nights, and he didn't want to disturb her earlier, in case she was asleep," he said.

"I'm sure Bruce will be relieved once she starts work," Kate said. "I'm afraid we've become a lot to handle since he signed on for the job of running this place."

"Don't worry," Felix said. "He's more than capable. But, yes, it will be nice for him to have an extra set of hands around here, especially with the wedding coming up."

The mention of the wedding made my stomach drop. I still wasn't sure there would be enough attendees to justify the celebration we had planned. It's possible that Bruce—and the rest of us—were putting in a lot of work for nothing.

Just then, we heard footsteps on the stairs, and my mom jumped to her feet. She ran her hands up the sides of her hair, smoothing the few strands that had come loose from her neat bun. I got up and took her arm, leading her toward the foyer. "Don't worry, Mom. You look great," I said. I patted her hand and offered her a smile as we rounded the corner and saw Juno. She was dressed all in black again, wearing a fitted tank that showed off her toned arms, slim black jeans, and black leather boots. She'd layered on multiple long silver necklaces, with chunky silver rings on most of her slender fingers, and large hoops in each ear.

My mother gasped. "You're so beautiful," she said, and her voice cracked. I released her arm and stepped back, giving them their moment.

Juno broke into a warm smile as she reached the bottom step. "You must be Sara's mom," she said in a voice that echoed my aunt's.

My mom let out a sob and opened her arms. Juno's smile grew wider, and she stepped into the embrace. The two women held each other for a full minute before pulling apart. "I can't tell you how wonderful it is to see you," my mother breathed as she reached up and stroked the side of Juno's face. "I've thought of you often."

Juno wasn't as emotional as my mother during the greeting, but what could you expect from Lucia's daughter? She was much more relaxed than my aunt, and her curiosity showed on her friendly face. "You knew of me?" Juno asked. "Before yesterday, I mean."

My mother stepped back and smiled. "Yes, sweet girl. I've known about you from the start." She shook her head as she looked at Juno. "You look just like my sister did when she was your age. Except for the eyes. I guess you have your father's eyes."

"You didn't know him? He's not a member of your community?" Juno asked, and I admit I wondered the same thing.

"That's Lucia's story to tell you, not mine," my mother said.

Juno sighed. "If she ever gets up the nerve to talk to me," she said, lowering her brow in a way that made her look just like my aunt.

"Give her time," came E's voice from behind us. I glanced over Juno's shoulder to see Marcus and E at the top of the stairs leading down to the lower level. E, it seemed, had dressed up a bit more too. She was wearing a wrap dress in soft green, the same shade as her eyes. Marcus, on the other hand, was in his usual jeans and black t-shirt. Juno turned as they approached, nodded to Marcus, and flashed a small smile at E.

"Will you be staying for a while?" my mother asked Juno, pulling her focus away from E, who was smiling back at my cousin.

"As long as it takes," Juno said. "I came here to meet my mother. I'm not going to leave with my tail between my legs just because she didn't jump at the chance for a reunion. I've got time, and I'm patient."

"Good," E said. "Your mother is tough to get to know, but I like her a lot. It'd be a shame if you didn't get to know her too."

I was just about to suggest we all go to the living room when Bruce appeared. "I'm about to get dinner started, but if anyone is hungry, there are snacks in the kitchen," he said before turning and heading back into the kitchen.

Juno watched him go, blinking. "Is he magic or something?" she asked. "I was just thinking about food."

I chuckled. "It seems that way, but no. He's human, just very good at his job."

"But he's also a member of your House, right?" Juno asked.

"Yeah. He is. But he keeps things around here running as well. And he's a great cook. Oh, and he's with Felix."

"That's the vampire I met last night? The flirt with the long hair?" she asked with a smirk.

"Yes," E said, leaning in conspiratorially and lowering her voice to a whisper. "He might look like a college kid, but he's over two thousand years old."

"And he has very sharp hearing," came Felix's voice from the living room.

We all glanced his way, and E giggled. "And he has very sharp hearing," she echoed in a teasing tone.

Marcus, my mom, and I went to the living room to join Kate and Felix, while E led Juno to the kitchen for a snack, claiming she could smell Juno's low blood sugar. I don't know if that was true or not, but Juno seemed happy to go with her and wasn't at all creeped out by E's assertion. I wondered, not for the first time, what life in New Orleans was like for a witch and if she spent much time around vampires or shifters.

I sat on the smaller sofa with my mom, and Marcus sat in one of the chairs beside the one where Kate was sitting. He glanced her way and reached over, offering her his hand, and she took it. Seeing it made me smile. Not long after, E and Juno joined us. Juno carried a small plate piled with sliced fruit and sat herself between E and Felix on the long sofa. Felix tilted his head to look at her as she set her plate on her knee and began munching on an apple slice.

"You seem quite comfortable with our kind," he said thoughtfully.

"I take it we're not the first vampires you've encountered?" His question neatly mirrored my own thoughts.

Juno shook her head, swallowing. "Nope. I've seen them around from time to time," she said. "We don't really interact, though, as a general rule. The vampires mostly live in the Garden District in their big, fancy houses. The witches stick to the French Quarter, and the Shifters live on the outskirts. I've certainly never heard of a mixed vampire House before. Things must be more progressive here than I was led to believe. My other witch friends always said the witches up here were a bit more traditional."

"Oh, they are," I said. "You should have been down here an hour ago."

I told her about the visit from our local Elders and how they were trying to force us out of the valley.

"That's terrible, but not surprising. I believe my Elders would react the same way—if not worse," she said. "Will you go?"

"Absolutely not," Kate said. "We won't be chased from our home by small-minded witches, no matter what their titles."

"Good," Juno said. "I can respect that. I've always thought there's no reason why we shouldn't all get along. But my Elders are just as uptight as yours. I got into a fight once with a vampire at a bar in the Quarter. We worked it out—no bloodshed on either side—but I was called in before the Elders and read the riot act for 'socializing' in the same place and for disturbing the peace. I see that guy around occasionally; there are no hard feelings between us. We're not friends, but we don't run from each other either." She shrugged.

She was right. There was no reason why we shouldn't all get along. It's what Kate and I were demonstrating in our House every day. Here we were, humans, witches, vampires, and a shifter, all living together. If only the proof of what we were doing was enough for our Elders.

We had traditionally kept apart as well. The witches lived in the valley, the shifters on the other side of the Pass, and the vampires stuck to the city. It's true that some witches lived in Seattle, but most preferred staying in the valley, where they could be among other witches and use their gifts without fearing detection by humans. It seems that the communities of Others were living similarly in other parts of the country as well. I'd never really thought about it, but New Orleans did sound like a fascinating place, even if it wasn't as progressive as I'd hoped.

I was pulled out of my daydreaming by Marcus, who was asking Juno about what she did for work. I imagined she did something wonderfully magical, or maybe related to music or the historic downtown of New Orleans. Her answer was much more practical and dimmed more of the sparkle from my fantasies. "I'm kind of between jobs right now," she said. "I used to work at a grocery store and before that at a bookstore, but when I decided to come out here, I had to quit my job. I couldn't get the time off." She winced at the thought.

"What about your parents, dear?" my mom asked. "Are they supportive of you coming to look for your birthmother?"

Juno hunched slightly and tilted her head from side to side. "I may not have told them where I was going," she admitted. "They think I'm visiting friends in Chicago."

"So you flew out here without telling them?" my mother asked.

"Oh, no," Juno replied. "I drove."

"You drove? All by yourself?" my mother said. "That's an awful long way."

"I love to travel," Juno said. "And going by car, I get to see all the sights along the way."

"Do you know any shifters?" I asked, curious for personal reasons, just to see if there was any overlap.

"No," she said. "There aren't as many of them in the city. They like having room to run. There are some in the area, but they mostly live in groups in the Bayou."

"Hmm," I said, hesitantly wondering what Juno's Elders would think about my 'socializing' with Silas.

"Your fiancé is a shifter, right?" Juno asked. "Silas, isn't it?"

"He is," I said. "He's from the other side of this mountain range, about an hour away."

"And is he a member of Kate's House too?" she asked.

But before I could answer, a flash of light streaked through the large living room windows, quickly followed by the thunderclap. The vampires in the room all covered their ears, except for Felix, who merely winced as the windows shook. The steady rain hadn't stopped for days, but we had been blessedly lightning-free since the demonstration a few days earlier. Until that moment.

"That will be Diane," my mother said, a look of disdain on her face. "What a shameful way to use one's gift."

It might have been shameful, but it was no less impressive. I was about to say so when lightning struck again, just as close. Bruce walked in from the kitchen, wearing his striped apron, his eyebrows raised. "Should we be worried?" he asked, as a third strike shook the house.

I shrugged. I wasn't sure what to tell him. I had no idea how far this would go or how long Diane could keep up the assault.

Kate got her feet, the anger on her face illuminated by yet another flash. "I'm going out there," she said, dropping her hands from her ears. "She can't be that far away. I'm going to make her sorry she messed with us." The steel in Kate's voice was a bit alarming, and I wasn't sure going up against the Elder was a wise choice. I'd seen what electricity could do to a vampire. And if my gift was enough to knock one unconscious, I shuddered to think what Elder Paulson could do.

Marcus jumped up to intercept her. "Kate, this is not the way," he said. "If we want to stay here, we can't go ripping off heads. We need to consider a more nuanced approach."

"He's right," Felix said as the group was rocked by yet another flash and rumble from outside. "You want to be able to live here after this spat is over. So far, all she's done is put on a light show. A very loud light show, but still. We should wait it out. I'm sure she can't keep this up forever."

As it turned out, thirty minutes was the length of time the small Elder brought the electrical storm down on us. And it felt like an interminably long half hour. No one was permanently harmed, and although close, the lightning never struck the house or any of the cars. It was painful for the vampires, however, and we had to talk Kate out of going out to find the witch two more times. She took the assault as a direct attack on our House and the vampires in particular. But in the end, she saw the wisdom of waiting. I just wondered how much more it would take to push my best friend over the edge.

20

KATE

My fangs had elongated, and I could feel my heart pounding in my chest. I was pissed. The electrical storm had finally stopped, but my anger remained. I hated staying still. Every muscle screamed to move, to run out into the night and confront the threat. I reached up and grabbed the locket around my neck. It rested against my sweater, but as soon as my fingers closed over the cool metal, a wave of love and gratitude swept over me. I could do this. I could hold myself back. For them.

I slowly breathed in and out, focusing on the feelings flooding in to replace my anger and annoyance. Marcus must have noticed I was struggling, because he leaned over and pulled on my sweater to get my attention. "Kate, would you sit with me on the hearth?" he asked.

I blinked at him, confused at first, but then I realized that our chairs were spaced a ways apart, and he wanted to be closer. Given that the sofa was packed full, that left only the hearth. "Sure," I said, and we both moved over to the stone platform, facing our housemates.

As soon as I was seated, he scooted up close and offered me his hand again. I glanced at him. "Are you sure?" I asked. "I feel like a leech."

He quirked a smile. "Vampire," he smirked, still holding out his hand.

I dropped my hand from my locket and placed my palm in his, and his warmth and steadiness filled me. I relaxed and gazed around the room. I was glad that the lightning had stopped, but it didn't feel over. Bruce and Felix were in the kitchen, but most of us were still huddled together, waiting. "Now what?" I asked no one in particular.

"I would bet she's done for tonight," Sara said. "I can't imagine how much effort that must have taken. I know I'd be wiped out."

Sybil nodded. "I think we're safe for now," she said. "If anyone needs to go out."

"We can't live like this," I said. "I don't care how long it is before the next assault. It has to stop."

"Could we enlarge the perimeter of the wards?" Marcus asked, rubbing his thumb over the back of my hand in soothing motions.

"It wouldn't do any good," Sybil said. "She doesn't need to be close to do what she's doing. She could be half a mile from here. It's the same with the Air and Water Witches. They can affect the weather in the entire valley from any one spot."

"I still want to do something to head them off if we can," Marcus replied. "I don't like that we are sitting ducks either."

"Is there a diplomatic way out of this?" E asked. "I mean, if we can't protect ourselves and we don't want to antagonize the witches, is there someone we could talk to? Someone besides this Diane person?"

"It's a thought," Sybil said. "I'll make some phone calls in the morning and see what we can do." She cleared her throat. "I know Lucia has some connections to several of the Elders, but I'm not sure she's going to be much help."

"She still thinks we should leave?" Sara asked, her voice tinged with hurt.

Sybil sighed. "She's not sure it's a good idea to go against the Elders. But she doesn't want any of you to have to leave."

Sara shook her head and pulled her cellphone out of her pocket.

"Who are you texting?" I asked.

"I'm letting Silas know it's safe to come home," Sara said. "He's been waiting on a side road for the storm to pass." She glanced at Juno, who was sitting wide-eyed on the sofa next to E. "I promise, it's not usually like this around here."

Juno nodded. "It is pretty exciting, but that's good to know."

"Well, there was that one time Bruce ended up with a knife in his chest," I objected, drawing sharp looks from around the room. I raised my free hand up, warding off any comments. "I'm just saying, don't give the girl the impression it's always smooth sailing here. We've had our issues, but we've always handled them."

E leaned closer to Juno. "Don't worry. Those were humans who attacked Bruce, not witches. And they're dead, so there's no reason to worry," she said brightly.

"Okay," Juno said, not sounding convinced by E's reassurance.

I felt it was time for a change of subject, before E offered to show Juno where the bodies were buried and we scared her off forever. I cleared my throat. "So, E, Sara tells me you introduced Marcus as your brother last night," I said. I felt a flutter of nervousness through the connection to Marcus. I could have asked him directly, but I didn't want to sound accusatory; what I really wanted to say was, '*What the hell? Why didn't the two of you tell me?*' Asking E in front of the others seemed like the best choice. She had already told everyone in the room besides Sybil and me, anyhow.

She beamed at me, and my annoyance disappeared. It was truly impossible to stay mad at E. "Yes," she said. "We have the same sire. It was Marcus who brought him back to our House after his capture." She said all this cheerfully, as if I knew exactly what she was talking about.

I looked at Marcus and raised my eyebrows. "Why didn't you tell me you and E were turned by the same vampire?"

He shrugged, and I thought I felt a hint of regret. "When we decided to move out here to Seattle, we chose to keep the connection a secret. It's been a long time since we last discussed it." He smiled fondly at E then, and I saw and felt the adoration in his eyes for what it was—brotherly love.

"I imagine there are plenty of vampires turned by the same sire, but they don't hide it," Sybil said. "Why would you keep it a secret?"

"Well, you have to understand what it was like for us at the time," Marcus said. "Not only were we related through our sire, but we also loved each other and felt protective of one another. Seattle in the 70s was a different place for vampires. We were outsiders. It was dangerous for us to give the local vampires anything they could use against us. We both knew we wanted to stay independent, work for the Council, and not belong to a House. It would have given vampires a way to manipulate us because of our relationship, but also because of our proximity to the Council. Once we decided to keep it a secret, we never revisited the decision, until now."

"And you rescued your sire?" Juno asked. "Who kidnaps vampires?"

"The US government," Marcus said, shifting uncomfortably.

I was glad when Felix appeared to let us know that dinner was ready for us at the table. I didn't know how much of Marcus's story he wanted to share with the entire group. Everyone rose to go to the dining room, but I held Marcus back with a tug on his hand.

E stopped to wait for us, but Marcus told her to go ahead. "Okay, little brother," she said with a twinkle in her eye as she turned and followed Juno into the dining room.

When Marcus looked at me, he was grinning and shaking his head. "What is it?" I asked, unable to interpret what he was feeling.

"It's just nice to hear after a half-century without it," he replied. "When I first met her, I was in a very difficult situation. It was a hard time. I'd lost my wife, my family, my livelihood, and my humanity. After finding my sire, releasing him, and bringing him home, I was pretty messed up. I don't know if I would have made it a year, let alone eighty years, if not for E. She's tiny, but she's a wonderful big sister."

I returned his smile. I felt a bit foolish for my initial jealousy. I was glad he had E and that she had him. I missed my own brother terribly and wished every day that I could still be a big sister to him. "I feel like there is so much about you I don't know," I said.

He shook his head. "You know everything that matters," he replied.

I tilted my head, looking at him. There was more I wanted to say, a lot more, but there were too many ears nearby. "Would you come with me for a minute?" I asked. I hope we wouldn't be missed if we didn't go far.

Marcus nodded, and I turned, leading him through the foyer, through the hall that connected to the kitchen, and into the small powder room located there. Marcus pulled the door shut behind him, and I flipped on the overhead fan, dampening our conversation even further.

I held up a hand, listening and waiting until the conversation in the next room picked up, so we would have a bit more privacy. Then I leaned close. "I want to spend some more time together. Alone. Things have been a little crazy lately with everything going on," I said. "But... I want to try again. I... I want us to be together, Marcus."

I felt his reaction through our clasped hands before he answered. He cleared his throat. "Yes. That would be nice," he said, and I could tell he was holding himself still, trying not to overwhelm me in the small space.

Urged on by his feeling, I stepped even closer, until our bodies met, and tilted my face up to him. He leaned in and brushed my lips with his, inhaling and closing his eyes. His kiss was feather-light and tender, almost teasing. I wrapped my arms around him and pulled him to me, wanting more, but aware that there was a room full of people close by, and that we would be missed soon.

After a moment, he stepped back, breaking the kiss, and smiled down at me. "Later, after dinner?" I nodded, licking my lips, loving the taste of him. He growled low, so that I could barely hear. "You go on in, I need a minute," he said.

It was several minutes before he joined the rest of us at the table, where Felix was doing a good job of keeping us all distracted with tales of life during the Italian Renaissance. "I'm not saying the likeness is perfect," he said. "But..." He stood, balanced on his back leg, with his head tilted to one side, and raised his left hand to his shoulder. "My hair isn't curly, that was Michael's addition," he added.

I burst out laughing. "You're not saying *you* were the model for The David?" I snorted.

He flashed me a fangy smile and took his seat. "I'm not saying I wasn't," he replied. "There were several of us, and I was only available at night, but I'm pretty sure I was the only one he was sleeping with at the time."

Now it was Bruce's turn to snort. Unfortunately, he was drinking wine at the time, and I'm pretty sure some of it went up his nose. After the coughing fit ended, his cheeks stayed red for quite a while. I suspected it was the first time he'd heard that story.

"I can't believe you're actually that old," Juno said, scooping herself another helping of a dish Bruce called 'Plov'. It was fragrant yellow rice with savory chunks of lamb, sprinkled with dried fruit. It smelled intriguing, and the witches all seemed to love it.

"It has been something special to see ages come and go," Felix said, growing serious. "I've spent most of that time focused on the world of vampires, trying to improve how we live our very long lives. However, I have been fortunate enough to witness both human achievements and mistakes. There is much to be learned from both." He gazed at Marcus, then his smile returned, and he continued with another unbelievable story about his time with Queen Elizabeth I.

Silas showed up just in time for dessert and a tale about the French Revolution, and then Sybil excused herself to return home. She embraced Juno again and told her she would talk to Lucia, but couldn't promise anything. My heart went out to Juno. I longed for my mother as well, but I couldn't imagine what it would feel like to be rejected by her—twice.

I felt a twinge of sadness until Marcus stepped up beside me, and I was distracted by the closeness of his body and the reminder of my request for more time together later.

After Sybil was gone, Sara and Silas lingered in the foyer. Sara glanced at Juno, then back at her mate. I was about to step in and suggest that Juno and I watch a movie or something, despite my desire to be alone with Marcus, when E took Juno by the arm. "Would you like to go for a walk?" the tiny vampire suggested.

"E, it's pouring rain outside," I pointed out.

"It's fine," Juno said, glancing between me and E. "I don't mind the rain."

Bruce jumped in and offered Juno an umbrella and a warm coat, and it was decided. Sara winked at E and gave me a smile before disappearing upstairs with Silas. The rest of us headed to the living room. I was still a bit shaken by the events of the evening. I figured some time decompressing with our housemates was probably a good idea.

Marcus sat on the end of the sofa, and I sat beside him, leaning back against his chest. He draped one arm around my shoulder, holding me close. It felt good.

Bruce poured drinks as we settled in, blood for Marcus and me, and a scotch for himself. Felix didn't drink anything, but I noticed how he eyed Bruce's glass and smiled to himself. I just shook my head, feeling happy for the two of them. And a little jealous. As much as I would love to sink my teeth into Marcus, we weren't anywhere near there yet. Plus, I would feel like a hypocrite, wanting to bite him but asking him to keep his teeth to himself. I shook off the thought.

We talked about nothing in particular, each of us seeming to need the company more than anything else. When Bruce's glass was empty, Felix made an excuse about needing a break from all the excitement. He excused himself, but not before offering his hand to Bruce, who shot us a half-smile and a shrug before being led upstairs.

And then we were alone.

21

LUCIA

The sound of a car door closing signaled my sister's return. I was busy wiping down the counters—for the third time—when she entered the kitchen. My stomach was in knots. She told me where she was headed when she left. I knew she had spent the evening with Juno, and while I was dying to ask all about her, I couldn't. I told my sister it was better if I kept my distance from the girl, and I still believed that was true. But knowing Sybil had seen her and talked with her made it very tempting to grill her for details.

"Wow, this place looks great," Sybil said, taking off her coat. "Thanks for cleaning up."

"It's no problem. The kitchen needed it. I plan to brew again tomorrow and wanted it clean."

"What are you making this time?" she asked as she pulled out a chair to sit at the table.

Great, she was sticking around. That was just what I needed.

"I thought I would try something with all that extra lavender from last harvest," I said.

"It's a good idea. It's just going to get older the longer we wait to use it," Sybil said cheerfully.

I sighed. "I heard the thunder earlier," I said. "It sounded like it was coming from the direction of Sara's."

Sybil's face fell a bit. "Yes, it was." Her lips pressed into a thin line. "I'm sure it was Diane," she said.

"It's dangerous to accuse a fellow witch of something like that," I said, feeling annoyed. "Especially an Elder, especially without proof."

My sister huffed out a laugh. "Who else could it be? And Diane stopped by and threatened Sara and Kate. I would say that's proof enough."

I snapped my gaze to hers. "She did what?" I asked, and Sybil filled me in on the Elders' visit to Sara's and the "discussion" they'd had with Kate.

"Was anyone injured?" I asked.

"Well, it seemed painful for the vampires, but no. Everyone was okay."

I sniffed. "It's just going to get worse. Have they changed their minds about moving?"

My sister's brows furrowed, and she fixed her gaze on me. "No. And what's happening is wrong. Had one of those strikes hit the house... it could have been very bad. I can't believe that the Elders as a whole would approve of using a gift so recklessly."

She was probably right. I'd known Diane my whole life. She rarely checked with anyone before acting. I wouldn't be surprised if she received a visit of her own from Theo, telling her to chill out. I didn't condone what's happening, but I could see it from the Elder's perspective. The valley had always been just for us. And no one could deny that the vampires had brought trouble with them. I was just glad that the Elders didn't know the full extent of it.

"Well," Sybil said, getting my attention. "Are you going to ask me about her?"

I bit the insides of my cheeks again and kept my eyes on the table. I should have stood and left the room. I should have realized that not answering wouldn't prevent my sister from talking, from telling me. Even if I had wanted to, I couldn't have left.

"She's wonderful, you know," Sybil said. "Whatever you're imagining, however funny, kind, and smart, she's all that and more. She's tall, like you. Her movements and mannerisms remind me of you, especially when you were young." Sybil smiled. "She's brave and likes adventure. She drove all the way here from New Orleans by herself." Sybil sighed. "I think you would like her very much."

I swallowed and brushed away the single tear that had managed to escape. "When does she go back?" I asked.

Sybil cocked a half-smile. "Did I mention she's stubborn? She's determined to stay until she's had a chance to talk to you."

"Well, that's just ridiculous."

"She said she's giving you two days, and then she's coming here," Sybil replied.

"She can camp out in the driveway, I suppose, but it's fairly wet out there," I said.

My sister scoffed. "I'll pull her across the wards myself," she said.

"You wouldn't."

"I would. I'll even make up Sara's old room for her."

I crossed my arms and stared at my sister. Part of me hoped she would. But a larger part of me was terrified to come face to face with the child I'd given up. "What will she think of me?" I whispered.

My sister's face softened. "You won't know until you meet her. But if it helps, the person she seems closest to in the House is E, and I know E has a soft spot in her heart for you."

"E? Really?" I asked.

"Yes. You should see the way those two are with each other," Sybil said.

"But E's a vampire," I protested.

Sybil laughed. "Yes. I'm aware, and so is Juno. She doesn't seem to mind."

"Well, everyone likes E," I said dismissively. I sighed. It would be easier to meet Juno there, at The House, than to have her come to us. If Sybil did what she threatened and invited her to stay, things could indeed become awkward, I thought. "Fine. I'll go over there tomorrow. I'm going during the day, though. I don't need an audience of vampires eavesdropping."

Sybil just smiled.

"And you're staying here," I said. "I want to do this by myself."

"Very well," she said. "I'm just glad you're going."

I shook my head and stood up. "I'm going to lie down," I said, leaving my sister alone at the kitchen table.

I knew my sister meant well, but her attitude about the whole thing set my teeth on edge. It wasn't that her life had been without challenges, but she had a different outlook than I did. I was more practical than my little sister. She liked to believe the best of everyone, that everything worked out as it was supposed to, that there was a silver lining to every bad thing that happened. I knew better. That's not how the world worked.

Life was what it was. You handled what you were given, and often it sucked, was boring, or felt pointless. But you did what you had to, what was expected of you, and moved on. The only satisfaction in life was doing a job well. This mess with Juno was completely different. I had made a choice I believed was right, and I was sticking with it. I didn't see why everyone couldn't respect that. It wasn't the easy choice, or the sentimental one, but it was the best option at the time. Now, the women in my life were determined to make things difficult.

I almost turned back to tell Sybil I'd changed my mind, but I didn't. I went up to my room to be alone. I retrieved my earbuds from my nightstand and lay on the bed. I found my music app, turned on a three-hour loop of ocean sounds, and closed my eyes.

I breathed in and out, listening to the sounds of water hitting the beach. The gentle crashing of the waves calmed my mind. Ocean sounds weren't my usual listening choice, but I wasn't in the mood for one of the small-town romances I preferred. I needed to relax and not think about romance, or family, or the scandals that often were a part of my favorite stories. I needed an escape.

I placed my hands on my stomach and felt it rise and fall with every breath. I tried to drown out my thoughts, but no matter how hard I tried, my mind kept coming back to my daughter. I flexed my fingertips, realizing they rested over my lower stomach. It felt like yesterday that I reached down and felt the hard swell of my rounded belly. Another unwelcome tear rolled down the side of my face.

I would go the next day to see Juno. I would answer her questions the best I could. I was prepared for her to be angry or resent me, but I would do it if it made things simpler. Then it would be over, and Juno and I could move on with our lives. I hoped it would give her some closure, if that was what she needed. For me, it would simply reopen a wound I had healed decades ago.

22

KATE

We listened to Bruce and Felix climb the stairs to their room. I exhaled and looked at Marcus. As he shifted, I took the opportunity to push myself off the sofa. I stood facing him, with my hand extended.

"What are you doing?" he asked, momentarily confused.

"I thought you said you wouldn't mind some time alone this evening," I replied, a slow smile spreading across my face.

He lifted his gaze to my eyes, and his breath caught. The intensity of his stare made heat course through my body, and my fangs punched into my mouth.

"I, I… did," he managed to say. "But I thought you might want to stay here, on the sofa."

I tilted my head but kept my eyes fixed on him. "We could," I said. "But E and Juno are on the porch. It's pretty cold out, and I doubt they'll stay out there much longer. If you want privacy, maybe we should go down to your room?"

I'd given this some thought. The fear of having him at my throat lingered, but Sara was right. I needed to go after what I wanted, and what I wanted was Marcus.

"Yeah," he said, slowly. "That makes sense."

He seemed to hesitate, and my mind considered an alternative to going to his private space, but there really wasn't a better option. My studio was being used as a staging area for upcoming construction, and the guest room I was in was squeezed between Sara and Bruce's rooms. I grimaced at the thought of so many beings with supernatural hearing just a wall or two away.

"Or we could stay here?" I said, studying his reaction.

He shook his head and rose quickly to his feet. "No," he said, stepping closer. I placed my hands on his chest. He was calm, but I could sense the anticipation too. I inhaled his scent; it was a blend of pine forest and cloves, and it felt as if the aroma was pulling me in. Before I realized it, I was on tiptoe, chest to chest with him, my lips grazing his jaw, intoxicated by his scent.

There was a rumble in his chest that made me press myself closer, but then his hands came up to grip my shoulders. "Kate, you do want to go downstairs? Because I really want to," his voice was rough. He swallowed. "If you do, I would just as soon we go now."

I nodded with my mouth still on his skin, feeling the roughness of the slight stubble on his chin. "Yes," I breathed. "Now."

Marcus reached down and lifted me up like I weighed nothing. I wrapped my arms around his shoulders, pressing my face into his neck as he carried me out of the living room, across the foyer, and down the stairs to the lower level. Our emotions intertwined. Knowing that he felt the same way I did brought me comfort. I nuzzled my face closer to his skin. While I was nervous about having him at my throat, I had no hesitation about being at his, and he seemed to enjoy the nipping and kissing.

I hardly noticed my surroundings as he carried me. I was so absorbed in the feel of him, the scent of him, and his ragged breathing in my ear. The urge to bite was intense. My fangs throbbed as I shivered, and I tightened my grip, unable to ease the growing need inside me.

Finally, we were in his room. He closed and locked the door, pressing my back against it as he tilted his head back to reach my mouth. His building desire fueled mine, and it was difficult to tear myself away from his neck, but his kiss was even better. He thrust his tongue into my mouth. It was nothing like the kiss he'd given me earlier. There was no lightness or hesitation; it was raw desire and need, and I responded to him with my own.

I reached around his back and started to pull at his shirt, wanting more of him, wanting my hands on his skin, when he pulled back. He lifted me higher and then set me on my feet, stepping away from me. I paused, breathing hard, watching him as he reached for the hem of his shirt. "You want this off?" he asked.

I nodded.

The room was illuminated by a single lamp on his bedside table. Even if I weren't a vampire, I could have seen perfectly as he undressed for me. And oh, the body he revealed with each piece of clothing he removed. He was built like a god. His chest was a landscape of curved muscle flowing into a deeply grooved V at his hips. I reached out to touch him, but he shook his head. "Wait," he said. He grabbed the waistband of his pants. "And these?" he asked, his voice velvet. I nodded again, and he let them fall to the floor.

"All of it," I whispered.

I watched as the last of his clothes hit the ground. I realized I wasn't breathing. I was just waiting for him to release me so that I could devour him.

When he stood completely naked in front of me, he spoke. "I want you to be comfortable with everything we do," he said, his voice low and smooth. "I'm going to lie on the bed and let you come to me. Feel free to leave your clothes on, or not—it's up to you. I don't want to crowd you or make you feel trapped. I want you to be able to pull back whenever you need to, to stop the moment you feel threatened. And I promise to stay away from your throat. I will not bite you."

I swallowed and let my eyes travel over his body. There was no doubt about his desire for me. This wasn't just for my benefit. "And what about you?" I asked. "What are your boundaries? What would make you uncomfortable?"

He chuckled. "I have trouble imagining anything you might do to me that would make me uncomfortable, but I'll let you know."

I smiled. "That sounds like a challenge," I teased. But instead of laughing, his eyes darkened, his gaze deepened, and a prominent part of his anatomy twitched as if it enjoyed the idea. I moved forward again, but he raised a hand.

He walked backward toward the bed, holding me with his gaze. When he reached the mattress, he lay down on the green duvet, propped up by the pillows, and rested his head against the tufted leather headboard. Smiling, he crooked a finger at me, and I staggered forward, pulled by my need to touch him, to feel his skin against mine.

I paused at the foot of the bed. "Do you have the coin I made you?" I asked.

He pointed to the bedside table where the coin rested against the polished wood. "It's within reach," he said.

I nodded, feeling more relaxed, then glanced down. I was still fully dressed, and that wouldn't do. Grasping the hem of my sweater, I pulled it over my head and tossed it aside. Marcus's eyebrows lifted with interest as I revealed the sheer bralette I was wearing. Pushing down my jeans, I stepped out of them and stood before him. My matching underwear was just as revealing, leaving nothing to the imagination. I decided I wanted to keep them on for now.

"Gods, you're beautiful," he said as I crawled onto the foot of the mattress.

Once again, as I touched him, I realized our emotions were the same: excitement, anticipation, desire, and affection. I gradually worked my way up his body, pausing to run my hands over the hard muscles of his calves and thighs. When I reached the tops of his thighs, his entire body twitched, and he sucked in a breath as I reached up and grasped him in my hand. He arched his back, and I smiled, never taking my eyes off his gorgeous face. I loved the way he reacted to my touch.

Feeling bold, I leaned forward and took him in my mouth, and heard another gasp. "Your fangs," he panted. "Watch the fangs."

Horrified, I pulled back and looked down. Sure enough, there was a thin red welt on his most sensitive skin. "I'm so sorry. I didn't think,"

I said. "I've never done this before with these teeth." I glanced up to see his reaction.

He shook his head and smiled. "Don't worry," he said gruffly. "I'm okay. I just don't necessarily want to be bitten there."

I quirked a smile. "I guess it didn't take long at all to find a boundary," I said. He let out a low chuckle, and I switched to using my tongue, keeping my fangs safely behind my lips. He stopped talking then, and I spent a few more minutes making him gasp before I wanted more.

I worked my way higher, exploring with my hands and mouth, learning how all those muscles felt under my touch. My fangs ached as I brushed my lips over the firm muscle of his chest, and I had to fight the urge to strike at him. When my knees straddled his hips, I pressed my weight down onto him, trapping him beneath me in a way that applied pressure to all the right places. Pausing, I allowed myself to enjoy the rising pleasure inside me before lowering my face to his and capturing his mouth with mine.

He'd been holding back earlier. His kiss was urgent and rough, but he kept his hands lightly on my hips, not demanding more than I was willing to give. I pulled back just long enough to slip my bralette over my head, then I took his hands and placed them on my breasts. He needed no instruction after that, and I moaned as I kissed him, savoring his decades of experience. My whole body shivered, and no matter how hard I pressed my mouth to his or how deep his kiss was, I couldn't get enough.

"Marcus," I gasped. "Wait."

He immediately stilled, his hands returning to my hips, his touch gentle and comforting. "Of course," he said, and I could feel how he tried to suppress his urgency, to hold back his desire. "I'm sorry if I got too carried away."

I shook my head. "No. It's not that. I... I want more. I want you inside of me," I admitted, feeling embarrassed for some reason. His fingers tightened on my skin, and his anticipation surged. "Is that okay with you?" I asked.

"Yes," he ground out. "It's more than okay."

I tilted to one side, and then the other, as I worked off the scrap of lace and elastic that was holding us apart. He stood himself up, and I eased down over him. Inch by inch, he slid inside as I slowly adjusted to the fullness of him. And God, he felt good. When I finally took all of him within me, I sat for a moment, my body trembling. Then I began to move.

His eyes never left mine as I started a slow rhythm, gently rocking back and forth. I pressed my fingers into his chest as I picked up my pace, and he tilted his head back, breathing heavily. Rocking forward onto my knees, I brought my face down to his, kissing along his strained jaw and nipping at his skin. He groaned, gripping me even tighter as I moved on top of him.

The faster the intensity, the more the pleasure built within me, urging me onward and pushing me closer to his exposed neck. I couldn't keep my mouth off the skin of his throat. I needed him. I needed all of him. I pushed back harder, and he lifted his hips to meet me. He tilted his head back farther, angling it to the side, giving me full access to his neck. His teeth ground together, and I worried I was about to go too far.

I clenched my own jaw, but my body was screaming at me to strike him. I shook my head, but at the same moment, he rolled his hips underneath me, pushing me over the edge. As a powerful orgasm washed over me, I cried out, my scream raw and filled with frustration. "Bite," he demanded in a growl. "Do it, Kate, bite."

In a blink, I struck at his throat, burying my fangs deep. He cried out, his arm coming around my waist, pulling me hard against him as his own orgasm spilled inside of me. The waves of pleasure crashed over me again and again as my mouth filled with his blood. It was nothing like drinking from a human; I could sense it wasn't food, and yet it was better than anything I'd ever tasted. It was his scent, his touch, his roaring desire—it was Marcus on my tongue and sliding down my throat.

I panted through my nose, my fangs still in his skin. I realized I should probably stop. I withdrew my teeth and watched as the trickle of blood stopped and the holes began to close on their own. I bent back down and licked the remaining blood from his throat, and then I sat up to look at him.

He turned his head and looked at me, a lazy smile on his face, his grey eyes soft and full of affection. "Are you okay?" I asked.

His smile widened, and blood stained his bottom lip. I froze, my eyes fixed on the red smear. He blinked and licked the spot. Noticing my expression, he raised his arm in front of me. I looked down and saw blood smeared on his wrist; two pink marks where he'd bitten himself remained. "I didn't bite you," he said. "But I couldn't help—"

"No. I get it," I said, shaking my head. "But did I hurt you?" I asked.

He briefly closed his eyes and took a deep breath. "Gods, no, Kate. You didn't hurt me. It felt amazing."

"Oh, good," I said. Watching his face, watching him recall his own pleasure, made desire well up again, and I realized he was still inside of me, and still hard.

I rocked experimentally, and he grinned. "Do you want more?" he asked. I bit my bottom lip and nodded. "Good," he said, and gripped my hips once more as he pushed deeper inside.

23

SARA

My phone buzzed in my pocket as I sat in the kitchen eating brunch with Silas and Juno. I ignored it and took another sip of excellent coffee. Rarely was anyone awake early enough for a real breakfast, so Bruce always prepared a nice selection of grab-and-go options for when we did wake up. I was enjoying yogurt and fresh fruit, Silas was on his second breakfast burrito, and Juno was finishing a plate of pastry. The phone buzzed again.

Sighing, I pulled it out and flipped it over to have a look. They were text messages from my mom. I scrolled through—they were long. I looked up. "We are going to get a visitor today," I announced.

Both sets of eyes turned my way, but it was Silas who spoke up. "Who?" he asked, leaning back and clutching his own steaming mug of black coffee.

Although Silas was the one who asked, I looked at Juno. "Your mother," I replied. "It seems she has changed her mind and will meet with you here. My mom said she'll text when Lucia is on her way over."

Juno nodded, looking a bit excited, and maybe just a little smug. "It was the ultimatum, I bet," she said. "I thought that might work." She smiled.

"You aren't pissed?" I asked. "Having to threaten the woman to get her to see you? I think I'd have strong feelings about that."

Juno considered. "I have feelings, for sure. But, I'll lay them out for her when she decides to show up." She took another bite of pastry and closed her eyes as she chewed. "This is heaven, by the way. I could get used to living like this."

I chuckled. "It really is nice. I didn't grow up like this, with someone hired to do the housework. I sometimes felt like my mom's housekeeper when I was young. It's been great to get to enjoy it."

"Speaking of housekeepers," Silas said. "When does Chelsea start?"

"Today, I think. She's supposed to show up sometime before lunch. It's going to be busy around here," I said. "I'm tempted to go upstairs to wake Kate so she can help Bruce with the new hire, while I juggle my aunt. The shop's closed today, so at least I won't have that to deal with." Thunder echoed nearby. "But there's always that." I was growing increasingly tired of the constant rain and booming electrical storms. I'd had enough. I realized my face was set in a scowl and tried to smooth out my features.

Juno got up from the table and set her dish in the sink. "I'm going to hop in the shower before my mother gets here," she said and left Silas and me alone.

Silas cleared his throat. "If you're looking for Kate, you might have trouble finding her upstairs," he said in a hushed voice.

"What are you talking about?" I asked. "Where else would she be? I'm sure she's not awake yet." I looked at my watch. It was only 10 a.m.

He took another swallow of coffee and raised his eyebrows.

"No. You don't mean..." I shot a look toward the foyer as if she would magically appear to answer my question. "She and..." I shook my head. "Wait, how do you know where she's sleeping?"

He looked slightly embarrassed. "Well, I could smell that she hadn't been upstairs since yesterday, and... I heard them last night. All night." He buried his face back in his coffee cup as his cheeks turned pink.

I leaned back in my chair as thunder rumbled around us again.

"Well, good for them," I said. "And eww. Usually, I'm jealous of your hearing, but maybe I've changed my mind." I thought it over. "I'm not going down there. Maybe I'll call her or send her a text. I should probably leave them alone. She's got a lot of catching up to do." Silas choked on his coffee and nearly spat it across the table. "What?" I asked as he coughed and wheezed. "She's liked him for as long as she's known the guy. I'm just glad she's getting over her fear of fangs and getting back on the horse, so to speak."

I reopened my messaging app and sent a quick text so she'd see it when she woke up, without disturbing her rest after a much-needed return to romance. I was about to ask Silas what he had planned for the day when the doorbell rang. It was just the doorbell, a sound I'd heard several times since moving in, but adrenaline dumped into my bloodstream at the chime, recalling the last time it sounded, announcing the arrival of the two Elders. I tried to shake off the jittery effects, but my large mug of coffee wasn't helping.

"You okay?" Silas asked, placing his large, warm hand over mine. "You seem alarmed. Are you anticipating your aunt? It's not her, if that's what you're worried about. I can hear Bruce talking to whoever it is. I'm pretty sure it's the new housekeeper."

His touch instantly calmed me, grounding me in the present. "No, I was just startled," I said. "There's been a lot going on lately."

He chuckled. "That's just a normal day around here," he said. "But I understand."

I smiled at my mate. "I'm going to go meet Chelsea. I didn't get a chance to introduce myself last time because Juno had just shown up and I was still in shock," I said. "You want to come meet her?"

"Sure," he replied as we both got to our feet. He offered me his hand and we made our way down the short hall to the foyer, where Bruce stood talking to a woman shaking rain out of her curly auburn hair. She was of average height, but taller than me, with a curvy figure. She had pale, creamy skin, with a scattering of freckles and wide green eyes. She was dressed simply in black slacks and a black button-down shirt, which reminded me of a waitress's uniform.

I raised my hand in greeting. "Hi," I said as we entered, getting their attention. "I'm Sara. Sorry, we didn't get a chance to meet properly last time you were here. And this is my mate, Silas." I gestured to my shifter-shadow, who stood silently by my side, still holding my hand.

"It's nice to meet you both," Chelsea said, smiling and dimpling her kind face. Bruce was nice enough to give me a rundown on everyone who is currently living here, but if there is anything you think I should know, please don't hesitate."

"A rundown. Did you spill *all* the beans, Bruce, or should we get specific so there are no surprises?" I asked.

"Well, I thought it best to leave some things for you all to reveal on your own. To be polite," Bruce said.

"Ah, I see," I replied. I could tell from the look on her face that Chelsea didn't see at all and had no clue what we were talking about. "And she's signed all of Felix's paperwork?"

"Of course," Bruce said. "Before the interview."

"Cool. In that case," I said, turning to Chelsea. "Let's do this again. Hi. I'm Sara, and I'm a witch. And this is my mate Silas." I peered up at him, and he nodded. I glanced back at Chelsea. "He's a wolf shifter. And my Aunt Lucia will be by later, she's also a witch."

Chelsea stared at me, her smile frozen on her face. She glanced at Bruce, who nodded in confirmation. "Oh," she said, looking back at Silas and me. "That's... great. I'll be sure to check with Bruce to ensure that any special needs are met." She blinked rapidly as if she were still processing the new information.

"We're pretty low maintenance, much more so than vampires," I said. "No human sacrifices or howling at the moon."

"Speak for yourself," Silas said in a tone so earnest, I burst out laughing.

"Don't scare the poor woman," I said. "She just got here."

No sooner had the words left my mouth than the table in the center of the foyer slid sideways as if by itself, knocking the orchid in the middle to the floor. The table skidded ten feet and slammed into the wall, nearly hitting Bruce, who dove to the side just in time. I screamed and shot a jolt of electricity into Silas, who still held my hand. Chelsea jumped backward, flattening herself against the front door.

"Gods damn it," I huffed. "Silas, are you alright?" He nodded, shaking out his hand, and then examined his fingers for burns. "Bruce, you okay?"

"Yeah. I'll do. Is that what I think it is?" he asked.

"Yes," I said and turned to look at Chelsea. By the look on her face, she was seconds from bolting.

"Ghosts?" she whispered, her complexion was as white as paper, and her lips looked a bit purple.

"No," I grumbled. "Cranky witches." Chelsea visibly relaxed, but still looked as if she might topple over. "Bruce, would you explain?" He nodded just as one of my precious bookshelves started to shake. "They better fucking not," I spat. But they did. Seconds later, the entire shelf and all the shelf-trophies inside it came crashing to the floor. I sighed, suddenly feeling tired, overwhelmed. "I think I'm going to have to go wake up Kate."

"Do you want me to come with you?" Silas asked.

I knew he was trying to be supportive, but it wouldn't make it any easier. "No, but thanks," I said and excused myself before heading downstairs.

I paused outside Marcus's door, fist raised to knock, when it cracked open. Kate looked out, her brown eyes wide, and her hair messy. "Is everything okay up there?" she asked. "I heard a loud noise."

I filled her in on the situation. As I kept talking, her expression grew colder, and by the time I reached the part about the books, her lip curled up, exposing her fangs. "I'm coming," she growled, and then she slammed the door in my face.

I didn't take it personally. She really loved those books. And the witches were irritating her just as much as they were irritating me, if not more. I knew it would be bad if she lost her temper and did something impulsive, but part of me wanted to see my best friend unleashed on those who were out to get us. It wasn't until I was walking back upstairs that it dawned on me that we hadn't even addressed the fact that I'd found her in Marcus's room, wearing nothing but one of his shirts. I smiled to myself. She was going to have to fill me in later. I wanted details.

I paused at the top of the stairs and texted my mom. She needed to know that things were escalating. Silas was the only one left in the foyer, waiting for me. We went back to the kitchen, where Chelsea was having a cup of what smelled like chamomile and lavender tea, and Bruce was at the sink, holding a dish, with the water running. He scowled at the sink as if it were some kind of logic puzzle.

"I think we have a clog," he said, shutting off the tap.

Just then, Juno came into the kitchen, wrapped in a bathrobe. "I think there's a problem with the shower," she said. "It's not draining."

My stomach dropped. "There's nothing wrong with the shower," I said. "Or the kitchen sink." The whole room turned to look at me with varying expressions of confusion. "It's not a coincidence that these things are happening all at once. It's the Elders. I'm not sure how they've done it, but it's them."

"Are there witch plumbers?" Bruce asked.

"Um, no. But I could call Beth," I got my phone back out and started to dial.

"The human who works next door? With the dog?" Chelsea asked.

"Yup. Her stepdad's a Water Witch, and he likes us," I said, listening to the phone ring. "Even though we splattered his wife in human blood—Oh, yeah. Hi Beth," I said, turning away to talk to Beth, but not before I saw the look of surprise on Chelsea's face and the scowl Bruce gave me. I pulled the phone away from my ear and winked at Bruce. "Sorry," I said. "Baptism by fire?"

"I sincerely hope not," Bruce replied as I walked out of the kitchen.

24

LUCIA

I'd pulled over three times on my way to Sara's. There were many reasons why meeting Juno face-to-face was a mistake, but I didn't want her just showing up at my house either. It was that thought, combined with my desire to get the meeting over with, that motivated me to get back on the road each time. With the delays, however, I was running later than I'd intended. There were only thirty minutes left before dark.

When I pulled up outside the house, I didn't hesitate. They would know I was there, and I didn't want to be seen hiding in my car like a coward. I also wanted to get it over with before all the vampires were awake. I grabbed my umbrella and went to face the drubbing I knew I deserved.

Leaving my wet umbrella on the porch, I took a deep breath and went in. Bruce was there to take my coat, and he was followed by someone I'd never met. “This is Chelsea,” Bruce said. “She's joining us to give me a hand around here.”

“About time,” I said, and nodded to Chelsea. She seemed nice enough, but even her smile couldn't untie the knot in my stomach. “I assume she's waiting for me somewhere,” I said. There was no reason to specify who I meant. Bruce wasn't stupid.

"Yes," Bruce replied. "Ms. Juno is in the living room. I suggest you avoid the reading area. We had an incident earlier."

"Hmm. Yes. Sara called Sybil and told us all about it. Has anything else happened since then?"

"No. But Louis Carter is back to look at the clogged pipes. He's out back with Sara and Kate. He thinks he can pinpoint the trouble, but Sara's still convinced it's magical in nature."

"I see," I said and swallowed, looking toward the living area. I knew I was stalling.

Bruce followed my gaze. "I'll leave you to it then. Please let us know if you or Juno need anything."

I looked back at the man. I was glad that Sara and the others had him with them. And not because he cared for them better than a mother might. No. He was a steady presence here, calm and reliable. He brought order to the chaos that swirled around the place. "Thank you, Bruce," I said, feeling strangely sentimental.

He raised an eyebrow and then offered me a smile. "My pleasure," he said, before he and Chelsea left me standing alone in the foyer.

Taking another deep breath, I moved forward toward the living room. Putting it off any longer wasn't going to make it easier, I thought. She probably already knew I was there. With each step, my body felt farther and farther away, and by the time I saw her, I wasn't sure if my feet were still on the ground at all. My breath caught, and I stopped, held by her gaze.

She got up from the loveseat where she had been sitting and stepped toward me. "Hello," she said, tilting her head. "Please join me?"

I nodded numbly and made my way to where she stood, keeping my eyes on the floor until we were no more than five feet apart. I glanced up to find her watching me, her face blank. She was as tall as me and dressed in a sleeveless blouse, a pair of dark jeans, and black boots. She looked strong and beautiful. "I'm sure—" I started, but she cut me off.

"No. Please. I have a few things I want to say before we begin.

There are a couple of things I need you to know," my daughter said, and I nodded my head.

I was ready for whatever she had to say. I knew that she had things she probably needed to get off her chest, and if this was something I could do for her, I was willing. I loved her, no matter how she felt about me, the woman who'd given her up, the person who'd abandoned her.

"Good," she continued. "I've thought of you often over the years. I've wondered about you—about who you are and what must have prompted you to give me up. Coming to find you has always been something I wanted very badly. Something I needed to do." She shifted her weight and took a breath. "Thank you for being willing to come and see me. It took courage to agree to this. I know I didn't really give you a choice, and I'm sorry, but the fact that you were so close made me determined to have this moment with you. But still..."

She twisted her hands together in front of her, and I could tell she was working herself up to whatever she'd actually come here to say. "So," she went on. "I wanted to say I'm so glad you made the choice you did. I don't know the situation you were in, but I trust you made the best choice for yourself, and probably for me as well. In doing so, you gave me a great gift. I've had the most supportive, loving, and caring parents anyone could ask for."

I replayed the words in my mind, trying to make sense of them. When they finally registered, I felt the breath leave my lungs, and my knees felt like they were about to give out. She wasn't angry with me. She hadn't come there to berate me for what I'd done. She was grateful...

"The last twenty years haven't always been easy, but I've never wanted for anything. I've never felt anything but loved by both my adoptive parents and you," she said. "I do have a lot of questions for you, but just because I'm curious. I don't want anything from you. I don't expect a relationship, but that's up to you. I only wanted to come meet you face to face to tell you, thank you."

I felt the room tilting sideways, and then Juno's arm was around me, easing me onto the nearest sofa. "Sorry," I said, a bit breathless. "I just wasn't expecting that."

She sat beside me and chuckled. "What? Did you expect me to scream at you?" she asked.

I blinked and looked up into her beautiful, golden brown eyes. "Well, yes, actually," I said.

She reached forward and brushed a tear off my cheek, startling me. I hadn't realized I was crying until then. "I didn't mean to scare you," she said softly. "I just needed to see you, to talk to you, if only once." She smiled, and I let out a choked sob.

Before I knew what was happening, her arms were around me. I wrapped mine around her and pulled her close, breathing in her warm scent of citrus and woodsmoke. She smelled like a Fire Witch, I realized. She smelled like a Heartwood.

I pulled back and looked at my daughter, really taking in her features. She did look a lot like the woman I saw in the mirror every day, but she bore a resemblance to my mother and a hint of her father. I brushed away my tears and swallowed the last of my shock. "Ok," I said. "What would you like to know?"

We spent the next hour talking about me, about her, and about how she came to be. I told her about my love of travel and how I had met a beautiful man during one of those trips. He worked at a restaurant I visited, and we started a conversation that turned into a date, and then three. We only spent a few days together, but they were wonderful. It wasn't until I was back home for several weeks that I realized I was pregnant. Her father and I hadn't stayed in contact. We hadn't exchanged numbers and hadn't made any promises, so the decisions were up to me. And she knew what I'd chosen.

I told her how hard it was to leave her behind when I'd left Louisiana, and that I thought about her every day. She shed a few tears, and I did the same. She asked if I had ever married or had children, and I explained that no, I hadn't wanted more kids. I felt like I had already had my child, and that was enough for me. I didn't think it was fair somehow to have another baby since I had given her up. I couldn't quite explain how that made sense; it was just how I felt. She nodded, but I could tell she didn't understand.

She told me about her life with the Everhearts, cousins of the New Orleans Heartwoods. She had a good childhood. She played sports and was still an avid runner. She liked movies and video games —something I knew nothing about. The hot weather didn't bother her, and she enjoyed the muggy Louisiana nights. She loved cooking and enjoyed eating even more.

She'd been delighted when she'd found out she was a witch like her cousins. She'd always hoped, being adopted, that she would have magic, unlike her adoptive parents, who were both human. She loved being a Fire Witch, although she wasn't very strong in her gift. She often wondered which of her birth parents passed the gift along. I proudly showed her my ability to summon a large ball of fire in my palm, and as I watched the flames dance in her eyes, I thought it might be the happiest moment of my life.

"Can you teach me?" she asked, and I thought I would burst with joy.

"Of course," I said, extinguishing the flame.

"My gift is like a Bic lighter, compared to that," she said, laughing. "I hope I have that much firepower someday."

"You might," I replied. "It takes a lot of practice. And just because one of your parents was human doesn't mean you couldn't train up to it."

She beamed at me. "I'm so glad I came here. This has been wonderful," she said.

I felt some of my happiness drain out. "How much longer will you be here?" I asked.

She tilted her head from side to side, considering. "I don't know. I don't have a job to go back to, so there's no rush, but I'll need to let my parents know where I've gone." She smiled again and twisted her lips to the side, as if she were deciding what to say. "I might stick around for a little while, though. E's convinced me to stay a week, no matter how things turned out between you and me."

"Has she?" I said, and smiled. "Well, I hope you do stay. I would like to get a chance to know you better. If that's okay with you?"

"For sure," she said. "I would love that."

It was then that we heard a loud crash from the reading area. Juno gasped, and we both stood up to see what had happened. Peering over the furniture, we saw that another bookshelf was on its face, with books scattered across the room.

Then all hell broke loose.

The rest of the furniture in the reading area, closest to the front of the house, began to jump from side to side. The anchors on the other bookshelves began to pull away from the wall, and the light fixture overhead swung back and forth.

The noise was enough to bring every witch, vampire, and human running. The vampires were the first to get there, and Kate rushed forward to try to prevent more of the shelves from going over. Marcus ran over to help her, although it looked like it was an impossible task. E sped directly to Juno, not sparing a glance for anyone or anything along the way. She immediately asked if Juno was okay and put an arm around her. The others stood back out of the way of the wreckage, watching and waiting for the attack to end. I spotted Louis standing with the rest of the House and wondered what he thought about this whole thing.

"Is this the worst it's been?" I asked E, whose slender arms were wrapped around Juno's middle. I'm sure she meant to protect her, but it looked like Juno was comforting E, the way they stood together.

"As far as I know," E replied. "This seems a lot more violent than even the lightning." She shuddered, and Juno rubbed her back.

I watched as Kate and Marcus held two of the largest bookshelves in place while they shook along with the rest of the furniture in that part of the large room. It wasn't exactly violent, but it was unsettling. Abstractly, scaring people off by flexing your gift seemed fairly reasonable. But seeing it close up made my skin prickle. I wondered how much longer the House would hold out. The Elders appeared committed to their course. If this continued much longer, I would have to go out and try to talk to whoever was out there, I thought.

Finally, the shaking stopped, and we all breathed a sigh of relief.

Kate let out a viscous growl. "What. The. Hell. I'm getting really sick of this shit," she said.

"That's what they're counting on," Felix said calmly from where he leaned against the living room wall. We all turned as the ancient vampire spoke. "What they're doing isn't enough to kill or even harm any of you. They're trying to piss you off enough to provoke a reaction."

"Why?" Kate demanded. "They know how strong vampires are. Do they want to get hurt? Because right about now, I'd be willing to give them what they're asking for."

Felix shook his head. "The moment you harm one of them, they will have grounds to unleash themselves upon you. You will be the aggressor, and they can bring all their gifts to bear."

"According to who?" Kate spat.

"Well, me, I guess," Felix answered. "The Three have made pacts with various Elders over the years to keep the peace. It's preferable to all-out fighting between the species. One may not act violently against the other without provocation. Serious provocation. The injury of a witch or the death of a vampire."

"That's, that's..." Kate fumed.

"It makes a lot of sense," Sara said, from where she stood with Silas. "Think about it, Kate. It might not help us keep them off our backs, but at least we know they're not trying to kill us."

Kate stood with her arms crossed. She didn't seem to like the rule, but she also didn't look like she was about to race out of the house.

"Have all the attacks focused on the front of the house?" I asked.

"Yes," Sara answered.

I nodded. "I would bet whoever it is can't reach farther into the building than the first set of rooms. Why don't we all move toward the back of the house and keep clear of the front for now?" I suggested.

The others appeared to agree, and we left the reading room and foyer, going farther into the house, and gathered in the living and dining rooms.

"You've got goosebumps," E said to Juno as they sat on the sofa together. "Are you scared?"

"No," she replied. "Just a little cold."

"It's chilly in here," Sara said. "I'll light a fire. It'll help improve the mood as well."

Kate huffed but helped Sara lay the logs and arrange the kindling. When Kate grabbed the long matches, I'd finally had enough.

"Stand back," I said, going over to light the fire.

"I'm going to go grab my sweater," Juno said, standing up.

"Want me to get it?" E offered.

"No. I'll be right back," she said cheerfully as she hurried toward the stairs.

I had my back to the foyer, so I didn't notice when E began to move. I only heard her scream.

I turned as a deafening crash echoed from the front of the house. I ran as fast as I could, but still had to push past the bodies of the vampires blocking my way. When I saw what was in the foyer, my blood ran cold.

The massive wrought iron chandelier that hung in the entryway had crashed to the floor. The table seemed to have absorbed most of the fall, but it wasn't enough. Lying on her side, partially under the large iron hoop, was the mangled body of E. I looked up at Juno, who lay unharmed on the far side of the foyer just as she started to scream.

25

MARCUS

I'd heard the distant creaking when E bolted to her feet and rushed after Juno. Understanding came later, when I heard E scream, followed by the loud crash.

My only thought was reaching E. Felix and Kate were close behind me. I smelled E's blood before I rounded the corner into the foyer. I knew it was serious, but my imagination hadn't prepared me for the reality of E's injuries. The heavy iron light fixture, about the size of a small car, had come crashing down on the table and E. She lay to one side, the lower half of her body pinned underneath, her left arm broken in at least two places and sticking out at a gruesome angle. She was bleeding from several locations, and her head was bent back in a way that could only be achieved if her neck was broken.

I took all this in as I entered the room at full speed. It took me longer to figure out the safest way to lift the weight off her, and I paused for a moment. By the time I had my hands under the wrought iron circle, Juno was screaming, and the witches and humans had reached the foyer. I tuned them all out as I decided how best to help E. Felix quickly understood what needed to be done and joined me in gently moving the chandelier aside so as not to cause her further injury.

E's eyes blinked rapidly, and her lips moved, but little sound came out due to the angle of her head. I glanced up to see Felix scanning her other injuries. "Broken leg, and a broken pelvis, I'm thinking," he said, not taking his eyes off E as his hands moved lightly over her small broken body.

"Her neck is broken," I said.

I looked up at a streak of movement, too quick to be a witch or human. I suspected Kate was on her way to enact revenge. "Felix," I barked. "Kate." I didn't need to say more. He was already on it. I refocused on E.

"Is she dead?" Lucia asked firmly, her voice cutting through the crying and murmurs.

"No," I said. "But she's badly hurt."

"What do we do?" Lucia asked.

"We stand back and let the vampires work," Bruce said gently from somewhere in Lucia's general direction.

"Hey sis," I crooned as I leaned closer to her so I would be within her line of sight. My entire world narrowed to those soft green eyes. "I know it hurts. We're going to fix it soon." Blood-red tears slipped from the corners of her eyes, clinging to her blond lashes and streaming down the side of her nose. I stroked her hair and waited for Felix to return. Luckily, it didn't take long.

"Okay," Felix said. "Kate's good for now. Let's get the worst of this over with, shall we?" His voice was calm, but there was a crease between his brows, and all his usual humor was gone, replaced with what I thought of as his 'ancient demeanor.' I was glad he was there for what we had to do.

"We're starting," I told E, as I carefully cradled her head in my hands.

"Onto her back, on three," Felix said. "One, two, three."

We moved quickly but carefully, turning E onto her back. As I positioned her head back at the proper angle, she sucked in a breath and let out a long, loud scream.

"That's right," I said. "Let it out. Just a bit more to go." I tried to be reassuring, but I knew she must be in agony. Being crushed wouldn't kill a vampire, but we felt all the pain from our injuries. No matter how many times you were injured, it still hurt like hell. We needed to get all her limbs in the right positions so her body could take over and heal her properly.

"Someone get me a long towel or sheet," Felix called out, as I gingerly rotated E's broken arm and straightened it out. She ground her teeth together, and her breathing was ragged, but she didn't scream. She was a strong little thing, my big sister.

Bruce came running and handed Felix a white sheet folded into a long rectangle. I saw what he meant to do and scooted over to where I could lift E's hips while he slid the cloth underneath her. It was soaked in blood by the time we got in position, but it would still work. Felix stood and held both ends of the cloth like a sling, with E's hips in the center. He crossed the ends almost like he was going to tie the cloth around her hips, and then lifted and pulled with just the right amount of force so that her broken pelvis would be in a more natural position. She winced and cried out, a thin, reedy sound, but didn't move.

"Silas, could you give us a hand?" I asked. In seconds, he was at my elbow. "Would you take over for Felix? I think we're going to need him for blood." I lifted my head and met Felix's hazel gaze. "If that's okay with you."

He nodded. "Of course," he said. He flicked his eyes to Bruce, who nodded in return, giving his consent. The exchange made me realize that things were more serious between the two than I thought.

When Silas was in position, Felix joined me at E's head. The laceration on her temple was mostly closed, and I didn't see any obvious bleeding. She had some movement in her fingers, indicating her spine was healing, but it was taking a long time. There were just too many injuries for her to handle all at once. She was going to need help if she didn't want to lie in traction for weeks.

"E, darling," Felix said, bending down by her face. "I'm going to give you some of my blood to help things along. If that's okay with you, blink twice for me." E's eyes blinked hard twice in succession. "Good, that's really good." Felix scored his own wrist with his teeth, and with his other hand, gently parted E's lips. He held the wound to her mouth, letting his ancient blood flow into the tiny vampire. "Now, don't go blaming me if you wake up early for a week or so. I warned you," Felix said as he fed her. It was good to hear him joking. It meant he was no longer worried for her.

I took a deep breath, sitting back on my heels, and looked around for the first time since hearing the crash. Silas still held the ends of the sheet, keeping E's pelvis in place. Next, my eyes found Kate. She had her arms crossed and stood between Sara and Bruce, who, I presume, were assigned guard duty. Kate looked ready to rip off heads. I was glad Felix had caught her in time, before she did something rash. Chelsea, our newest addition, stood next to Bruce, and I sincerely hoped this wouldn't be her last day as well as her first.

I pivoted and saw that the witches were all huddled together. Louis stood next to Lucia, who sat on the floor with her arms around Juno. Juno stared straight ahead at E, her look of shock unmistakable. "She saved me," Juno mumbled.

"What's that?" Lucia asked.

"E saved me," she repeated. "I was standing there." She pointed to where E was lying. "And she knocked me out of the way just as that thing came down." Juno's body began to shake all over, and Lucia pulled her tighter.

I turned to Chelsea. "Would you get Juno something warm to drink and maybe a blanket off one of the sofas?" I asked. She nodded, her expression grateful, and headed for the kitchen.

I glanced back down at E. She had her right hand up and was able to grip Felix's arm as she fed. Just then, Kate stepped up beside me. "Is she going to be okay?" she asked.

"Yeah, I think so. She'll need a few days to recover and some blood. They are both going to need blood," I said.

"Why did you have Felix stop me?" she asked quietly.

I swallowed. "Because she's going to survive, and I didn't want you to do something you couldn't take back."

"I still might," she said, her voice icy. "What if E hadn't gotten there in time? What if it were Juno that was crushed?"

Lucia lifted her head at the mention of Juno, and her eyes blazed with the fire within her. "If it had been Juno, I would have helped you kill them," she said, and I didn't doubt that she meant it. "This has gone too far."

Louis nodded in agreement. "I'd heard what was happening from Beth, but I had no idea it was this bad," he said. "This is wrong on so many levels."

Kate stared at the witches and gave one firm nod. "This ends. I'm done. I'm done with the harassment, the noise, and the threats," she said. "Let the witches know, one more lightning strike, one more clogged pipe, one more piece of furniture moves, and I'm coming after the one who did it."

"Kate," Felix said, his arm still in E's mouth. I suspected she wasn't drinking very fast because of her injuries. "You can not injure one of them."

"Like hell I can't," she seethed. "They injured one of us. Hell, they would have killed one of their own if E hadn't gotten there in time." She fell silent, looking down at the floor. She was going to need some time to process what had happened, I thought.

Felix carefully drew his arm away from E, who licked her lips. Her broken arm and leg began to twitch as the mending sped up. As Felix edged away, Juno crawled to E's side. "Hey," she said, kneeling beside her. "Can you hear me?"

"Of course I can hear you," E said, her voice soft and a bit rough. "Nothing's wrong with my ears."

Juno let out a sob, her hand hovering near E's shoulder. "You can touch her," I said. "It won't hurt her. In a few minutes, when her pelvis has had a chance to reknit, I'll carry her downstairs."

Juno nodded and rested her hand on E's shoulder.

"How are you doing, Silas?" I asked the shifter, who still stood over E, holding the sheet. "You need someone to take over?"

"Nope. I'm good," he replied.

I leaned over E so she could see me without turning her head. "How about you, sis? How's the pain?"

She smiled at me. "It's mostly faded. I just feel really sleepy now," she said.

"Good. You're healing faster than I thought," I said.

"Thank Felix," she said. "I've never tasted anything like him." She closed her eyes, a small smile still on her lips.

Felix still sat on the floor, looking exhausted. Bruce had moved beside him. Kate noticed where I was looking.

"Are you going to be able to handle his blood needs, Bruce?" she asked.

"I think so," he said. "If not, I know who to call."

Kate nodded just as Chelsea returned with a steaming mug and a blanket draped over her arm. "Chelsea," Kate said, gaining the woman's attention. "I know you just started, but would you mind organizing the cleanup? I'm sure Bruce will want to care for Felix."

"Of course," she said. "I'll take care of it. Let me know if you need anything else."

"When I'm done here, I can make something for everyone else to eat," Silas offered.

"That would be great, Silas," Kate said. "I'll get blood warmed and in a thermos for E."

I told Silas he could let go of E's sheet and then bent down, as carefully as I could, and scooped her up into my arms. "Where are we going, Little Brother?" she asked, her eyes still closed.

"I'm tucking you into bed, where you can rest."

"Is Juno coming?" she asked.

I looked behind me and met Juno's stare. She nodded and handed her mug to Lucia. "Yup. She'll be right there with you. I'm sure she'll take good care of you, but let her know if you want me. Okay?"

"Okay," she said, nuzzling into my chest. I carried her down the stairs to the room that was usually Kate's. It still smelled strongly of Kate, and I inhaled, letting the scent curl up my nose. Memories of the night before flooded back, but I pushed them aside for later, reminding myself of why I was there. Juno moved the blankets aside and gently laid E onto the soft mattress. She was still streaked with blood and bits of wreckage from the table.

Juno noticed my concern. "I'll wash her," she said. "And make her as comfortable as I can."

"Thank you," I said and touched her on the shoulder. "She means a lot to me."

Juno smiled. "She's pretty special," she said, her eyes on E.

I gave her a soft squeeze and then left, shutting the door so they could have some privacy. Back upstairs, everyone had cleared out of the foyer except for Chelsea, who held a broom, and Louis, who was manning the dustpan.

"I can do that, Louis," I said, holding out my hand for the pan.

"No," he replied. "Thank you, but witches did this. I'm going to help clean it up. And then I'm going back into town, and you'd better believe I'm going to share what I saw here tonight. Most people in town have no idea this is going on. They need to be told."

"Well, thank you," I said. "On both accounts."

I walked back to the living room to find that Kate was the only one remaining. "Where is everyone else?" I asked as I sat beside her on the sofa in front of the fire.

She tilted her head, staring into the flames. "Sara, Silas, and Lucia are in the kitchen. Lucia said she would heat the blood for E. And Bruce took Felix up to bed."

"And what about you?" I asked. "Where are you right now?"

She turned her head, her expression completely blank in a way that frightened me. "I'm deciding," she said. She was feeling her role as a leader, and E was apparently one of hers. Part of me delighted in Kate's protectiveness of E, but part of me feared there could be greater consequences if Kate acted on that instinct.

"Just promise me, Kate, that you will tell me before you act," I said and offered her my hand. If I couldn't get through to her with words, maybe the touch of my emotions would help.

She glanced down at my hand and shook her head. She heaved a sigh and turned back to the fire. "I'm still deciding."

26

KATE

Flames crackled and flickered in the fireplace. Consuming. Destroying. Doing what came naturally. I longed to join them. I longed to do what came naturally to me, a vampire. Inside, I was screaming, growling, gnashing my teeth, but my body sat still, staring straight ahead, watching.

"Kate," Marcus said for the second time. "Kate, look at me, please." He was scared. It wasn't his voice that told me this. My walls were down, and the emotions of everyone in the house hit me sharply. I'd dropped my defenses the moment E let out that blood-curdling scream as she ran from the room. And I felt it all: her terror, her anguish. I felt the horror that filled Juno when she saw E, shattered on the floor. I felt Juno's grief and helplessness. I experienced every minute of worry, fear, and anger in that room. And now it was mine, and there was nowhere to put it.

I turned my head and looked at Marcus. His features were familiar, his expression was concerned, and his grey eyes stared into mine. Even though I could sense everything he felt at that moment, I couldn't quite connect with him. This beautiful man I'd spent hours touching, kissing, biting—yet the rage and frustration were too strong. I wanted to reach for what he was offering, I wanted to latch onto the calm and determination he was trying to push at me, but I couldn't.

He held his hand out again. "Take my hand," he said softly. "Let me help you."

"I don't want help," I said, in a voice that sounded numb and distant. "I don't want to feel better. I want to hurt something, someone."

"You could hurt me," he replied in his maddeningly steady tone.

That caught my attention. I blinked and frowned at him. "Why would I do that? Why would you want me to do that?"

"It could make you feel better, and I'm pretty much indestructible," he said with a smile.

I shook my head. "You're being ridiculous. I couldn't hurt you," I said. "I want to know who did this. I want to hurt them."

"That's a relief," he said. "I don't really enjoy pain."

I snorted. "You seemed to like being bitten just fine," I said.

"Well, that was the opposite of pain. I assure you." His voice was smooth, and his eyes darkened.

I felt my body respond to him. My fangs throbbed, and not from anger. I heaved a sigh. "Ok, your distraction is working," I said. "But I'm still going to make them pay."

"Understandable," he said. "Might I suggest starting with a good old-fashioned chewing out before you start in on chewing necks?"

"I was thinking more along the lines of ripping out throats, not neck chewing," I scoffed. "Chewing sounds too soft for my taste."

"Ah, yes. I can see where ripping would pack a bigger punch," he said. Humor twinkled in his eyes now, and I knew he had me.

I took a few deep breaths and finally put my shields back in place. As I did, the thrum of everyone's emotions softened and then grew silent. Marcus held his hand out to me for a third time, and I took it. "How are you so patient with me?" I asked. "I'm hardly your typical vampire, or typical anything, actually. I have no idea why someone would want to sign up for my particular... mess."

"Are you kidding me?" he asked. I could feel that he was actually curious.

"No," I said. "I mean, I'm a lot."

"Well, I'm not someone who's looking for 'less'. I want you just the way you are. I feel lucky to be near you, let alone with you, as your lover," he said, and I felt a bit of hesitation. An uncertainty.

"I have to be honest," I said. "I can feel that part of that statement made you feel unsure." I sighed. "This is exactly what I'm talking about. I'm not easy to be with. I can't be fooled or lied to; I can sense a person pulling back and losing interest before they even realize it. It makes me a problematic date."

"Because you catch people in their lies?" he asked. "I would think that would just make for very straightforward communication."

"You would think so, but you're the first person I've been with who knew about my little talent."

"Ah," he said, understanding. "Well, I'm not worried. And I don't plan on lying to you. If you felt that I was unsure, it's only because I felt a bit presumptuous claiming to be your lover after one night together."

"Oh," I said, feeling uncertain myself. Not uncertain about being called his lover, but uncertain how much to share with him about how I felt. The truth was, I was falling for him, had been falling for him for some time. "Lover, is good," I finally said. "Um, I know we didn't talk about an actual relationship beforehand, but I don't like the idea of sharing."

His confusion shifted to amusement. "Nor do I," he said. "Maybe I'm being presumptuous again, but exclusivity was what I was offering and hoping for. You don't have a string of lovers, I don't know about, do you?"

I snorted out another laugh. "Yeah, right. You've seen firsthand how hard this is for me. I wouldn't put myself through this for just anyone. Let alone a stable of lovers or casual hookups."

"Good," he said. "Because I don't want this to be casual. I care about you deeply, Kate." With his words, a flood of warmth, affection, and longing washed through our connection. It was deep. It was complicated. And it was honest. It was what I'd felt each time we'd touched the night before. I realized I already knew how he felt about me. I just needed to trust it.

"I care about you too," I said softly. I steeled myself for what I was going to do next. It only seemed fair, at this point, to let him see how I felt about him. I wanted the relationship to be even on both sides. It was unreasonable for me to know everything he felt but then keep my feelings closely guarded. "I've got you at a disadvantage here, and I don't like it," I admitted. "I… want to show you how I feel. Is that okay?"

I could tell he wasn't expecting that, but was open to it. I wasn't surprised when he nodded his assent. I steadied myself, pushing away the nervousness to make room for what I wanted to show him. I drew up the emotions I felt when he was near, when I thought of him, when he touched me, and when I touched him back. I concentrated on those emotions and gently let them flow from me to him through our clasped hands.

His eyes widened, and with the flow of emotion, I had a hard time telling what it was that he felt. "I know," I began to say. "It's a lot—"

"Kate," he said, interrupting me. "I told you. I'm not looking for less." His grip on my hand tightened, and he pulled me toward him until I was in his lap and his arms were around me, his mouth on mine.

As we kissed and held each other, our feelings surged back and forth, intensifying our emotions until we were breathless and craving more. I pushed us apart, intending to stop, but I noticed that my fangs had nicked his bottom lip. I leaned back in and licked the drops of blood from his lip, tasting him, his scent filling me up. I put my hands up. "If we don't stop, I'm going to rip your clothes off here, and we'll end up traumatizing the witches and Silas when they come in for dinner. Not to mention Chelsea," I said, laughing. "It's her first day, for God's sake. If she's not ready to quit already…"

"I see your point," Marcus said, still breathing hard, and clearly ready to go. "Feel like going downstairs for a few minutes?"

"Only a few minutes?" I teased. "Well, yes, but no. I need to stay up here. The House has just been through something major. I… I'm not sure I handled it very well. But I want to be here for them now. If I can."

He nodded. "Good." He smiled at me, tilting his head as he studied my features. "I'm glad you're back."

I heaved out a breath. "Thank you," I said. "I was in a dark place for a moment there. I can't say I'm over it, but I don't think I'll go running out of the house any time soon." I pushed myself off his lap and sat beside him, threading our fingers together, so as not to lose contact just yet. I gazed back at the flames dancing in the fireplace. They seemed cheerier now. "I scare myself sometimes, Marcus."

He squeezed my hand tightly, and I felt what he wanted me to: calm control. "I'm not scared," he said. "You've always done the right thing. You will always do the right thing, Kate. You need to believe in yourself as much as I do."

"If only it were that easy," I teased, but didn't take my eyes off the flames.

Just then, Sara appeared in the dining area, setting a plate of sandwiches on the table. "You guys want to join us?" she asked.

"Sure," I called out. "Be right there." I turned to Marcus. "Hungry?"

"Yeah. I could feed," he said. "I'm feeling a bit low." He smiled at me in a way that reminded me of why that was.

"Hmm," I replied, rising from the sofa and pulling him along with me. I leaned in close as we headed to the dining table. "Drink a little extra. Just to be safe," I whispered.

Marcus growled low in his throat, and I was seriously tempted to take him up on his offer to go downstairs and skip dinner altogether. "How much do we have in the fridge?" he whispered back as he leaned in and breathed in my ear.

"That's enough of that," Lucia said. She placed a large tureen of fragrant soup on the table. "I don't want to lose my appetite." She turned and went back into the kitchen.

I giggled at Marcus. "I'll go see how the cleanup is going." I patted his arm and headed for the foyer.

The debris and blood were gone. Chelsea and Louis managed to carry off the table pieces, but the wrought-iron chandelier still lay off to one side, partially blocking the front door. I examined the structure of the thing. While I was fairly certain I could move it, it looked awkward to handle.

"You want help with that?" Louis said from the hall. He had his shirtsleeves rolled up and was drying his hands on a towel.

"I could use someone to help me balance one side," I said. "Let me test the weight." I bent down, grasped the large hoop, and lifted. Had you told me a year before that something of this size and weight would be easy for me to lift, I wouldn't have believed it. But it was easy. "Maybe help me guide it to the side? Steer me so I don't bump it into anything?" I walked backward with the massive weight held out in front of me.

Louis nodded and jogged over. He placed one hand on the hoop and guided me to a clear spot. I waited until he had backed out of the way to put the thing back on the floor as carefully as I could, so as not to mar the wood. Louis tossed me the towel when I stood up. I wiped the dust and oil smears off my hands. "Will you join us for dinner?" I asked. "There's more than enough. I have a feeling it will turn into a planning meeting—these things often do—, and I'd like to have your input on where we go from here."

Louis nodded. "In that case, I would love to stay for dinner. Thank you," he replied.

We went through the kitchen to see if anyone needed anything and to snag some warm blood for Marcus and me on my way to the table. Chelsea and Lucia were the only ones there. Chelsea was pulling rolls from the oven, and Lucia was pouring blood into a metal carafe. "Is that for me?" I asked.

Lucia raised her head and a neat black eyebrow. "Well, it's not for me," she said. She pointed to another carafe by her elbow. "That one's yours, this one's for Marcus."

"Here, I'll take them in," I offered, smiling fondly at her. It was a gesture, and I was happy to accept it. Lucia nodded and pushed them in my direction. On my way over, I noticed a place setting at the small kitchen table. "Who's this one for?" I asked.

Chelsea glanced over. "Oh, that's for me," she said.

"We eat together here. Join us at the table," I said, trying to sound more encouraging than authoritarian.

"No. That's okay. It doesn't seem right. I mean, you are all family, I just work here," she replied.

"You made it through a day from Hell without bolting. I'd say you more than earned your place at the table," I said. She smiled and nodded. "Lucia, will Juno be joining us?" I asked.

"I took her a tray," Lucia said. "She's keeping a close eye on our E. She'll let us know if anything changes."

"I'm glad to hear it," I said, smiling to myself. I went into the dining room with the pitchers. I was happy to see that Bruce was there, already seated in his usual spot. He looked pale, and I noted happily that he was letting the others do the work of getting the food on the table. "How's Felix?" I asked.

"He's good," Bruce replied. "He's resting, but I needed some food, something warm."

We all took our seats and started passing food around. Chelsea took the seat Felix usually sat in, and I was pleased to see her finally relaxing with the rest of us. Before long, Bruce had a steaming bowl of soup and several breadrolls in front of him. Food would help but the young man looked like he could use some real sleep.

I was looking forward to getting some sleep myself. I wondered which bed I would end up in, however. The thought of the guestroom I was staying in made me realize something. "Bruce, where is Chelsea sleeping?" I asked. There were only four rooms upstairs, and two downstairs, and they were all full.

Bruce set his spoon down and wiped his mouth. "I've set up a temporary space for her at the far end of your studio," he said. "I would have asked but—"

"No. That won't do," I interrupted. "I can't let her sleep down there."

"I really don't mind," Chelsea interjected.

Marcus put his hand on my arm, getting my attention. I looked at him, and he gave me a pointed look and half a smile. "I'll sleep downstairs in Marcus's room," I said, glancing at him. He nodded and took a healthy swallow of blood. I pinched my lips together so that I didn't burst out laughing.

"Well, in that case, we can get that guest room ready for Chelsea this evening," Bruce said. "If different arrangements need to be made..."

"I'll let you know," I said.

Lucia cleared her throat. "Well, if we're done talking about whose bed everyone is sleeping in, can we get down to the business of what we're going to do to keep this House safe?"

27

LUCIA

Finally, the conversation shifted to the matter at hand. I was less worried about who was sleeping where and more focused on moving things forward. We needed to act. My skin prickled all over as I thought about how close we had come to losing one or both of the girls. I couldn't breathe when I considered what might have happened if E hadn't gotten there in time. I don't know if I could have survived losing Juno on the day I got her back.

"So," I said. "What's the next move?" Mostly blank faces stared back at me. Kate, though, had a fire burning in her, and I was going to capitalize on it. "Kate?"

She blew out a breath and stared at the table in front of her. She shook her head, not yet ready to answer.

"Can we assume you no longer expect us to move? To bow down to the wishes of the Elders?" Sara said. She was sitting back from the table, her arms crossed over her chest.

"They've crossed a line. It might not be the line Felix was talking about, but they've gone too far. It's become clear that the House is in the right here." I breathed in, trying not to let my temper get the best of me. I knew I'd been inclined to side with the Elders at first, but no more. "I have to believe whoever brought the chandelier down did so on purpose, just as they saw someone walking underneath it. It was no accident. They had to have been close enough to pull on such a heavy object; they would have seen Juno through the windows. If the Elders condone what's happened here, I can no longer side with them." I shrugged and turned to look at Kate.

Kate reached her hand across the table toward Marcus, who slid his palm in hers. She kept her eyes on me and waited a beat before speaking. "I'm glad you feel that way," she said. "It's best if we are all on the same page. Speaking of which, we should call Sybil. She should be part of this."

"I've already texted," Sara put in. "She's already on her way. I've told her what happened."

Kate nodded. "And, Bruce, someone should probably get Felix. We can let E rest, but I want his input, if he's not too worn out."

"I'm already here," his voice came from around the corner, shortly before he appeared. "I could hardly rest with all the chatter down here." He smiled, and I was glad to see that he looked better. Healing E seemed to take a lot out of him.

I noticed that his chair was taken just as his eyes flicked to Chelsea. "Felix," I said, getting his attention. "Would you sit with me?" I pulled out the empty chair next to me.

"I would love to," he replied smoothly. "It would be a pleasure to sit next to you, my dear. And I promise to keep my fangs to myself."

I sniffed and ignored his comment. He really was too cheeky for his own good. "We were just discussing my changing feelings on the behavior of the Elders," I said.

"Yes, I heard," he replied. "I'm happy to have you on Team Vampire."

I scoffed and shook my head. "I'm not on any team, but I won't let the people here get hurt." I took a steadying breath, my thoughts with Juno and E below. My nervous system still hadn't recovered.

Felix placed a gentle hand on my arm. Despite being ice-cold, it was reassuring. "They're both okay," he said softly, as if he could read my mind.

My body involuntarily shuddered, but I nodded. "Of course. But we need to make sure nothing like that happens again," I said.

"And we will," Kate replied. "I want a meeting with the Elders. Tomorrow afternoon, evening at the latest."

"No one summons the Elders," I objected. "They set the schedules for gatherings."

"I don't care how it's been done in the past," she said. "They will hold a meeting tomorrow, or I will visit everyone's house personally."

The vampires all turned their heads together, and I was not surprised when my sister entered a moment later. "I see you've all started without me," she said. "What have I missed?"

Sara caught her up on everything, including my change of heart about the Elders. Hearing it from Sara's mouth was a bit of a blow. She explained things clearly, but as she spoke, I felt the future I'd always wanted for myself slip away. The Elders and the witches of the valley were on one side of this thing, and I was on the other. There would be no going back for me, but that was how it had to be.

"So," Kate went on. "Do you know who to call to arrange this, Lucia?"

I blinked. It made sense that she would ask me. I knew the witches involved better than anyone present. "Yes. I know who to reach out to."

"Good," Kate said. "Do it tonight. Please," she added.

"I'll take care of it," I said. "But what are you going to say?"

"What does she have to say to get this thing resolved to our satisfaction?" Felix asked.

I was about to answer when Louis spoke up. "She needs to make sure that there's more than just the Elders present, and then she just needs to tell everyone what's been going on," he said. "I can assure you that very few are in on this. The majority of the valley wouldn't go along with what's been happening."

I considered what Louis said and nodded in agreement. "He's right," I said. "I think we need to reach out further than the Elders."

"All three of us should make some calls," Sybil suggested. "Let's get as many community members as we can to show up. That way, even if the Elder's responsible don't show, it won't matter. Word will get around, and the pressure will be on them."

"Good," Kate said. "How many of you here would like to go?" Hands shot up all around the table, including Felix and Marcus. Kate glanced around. "In that case, let's set it up for after dark. Is there somewhere in town that could accommodate those who might want to attend?"

"I would suggest the meeting house," Sara said. "But it would be too charged to bring vampires and a shifter in there. Let's meet at the park. It's public; they can't force us to leave. There's a gazebo there, and seating for those who need it."

"Let's make it happen," Kate said. "Thirty minutes after sunset. I want this over with. Please make those calls right away. I'm afraid I can't handle any more harassment tonight."

Sybil, Louis, and I excused ourselves from the table. I walked out to the foyer—the scene of the crime. I hadn't planned on coming to this spot for the privacy to make the call I knew would be my first, but it seemed like the perfect place to get into the correct frame of mind. I pulled out my cell phone and dialed. It rang once.

"Hello?" came the clipped voice on the other end.

I saw no reason for a civil greeting. "This is Lucia," I said.

"I've been expecting your call," Ruth replied. "I thought you might call after the Elders gathering you attended."

"After your comments about my niece and her House, I didn't see how that would be productive," I replied.

"Are you calling to tell me that the Vampires are moving, or have you called to try to get us to stop?" she asked.

"*Us*?" I said, feeling fire ignite in my veins. "And just who exactly is *us*?"

"Diane and I, along with a few others. That vampire really pissed Diane off when they met. It was a bad move. And there was no way I could stand idly back while vampires moved into our valley to enslave the witches here with their blood magic," she said, her voice growing dark. "I'll continue to do all I can to drive them out. Both the vampires and any witch they control."

"Are you telling me you had something to do with what happened tonight at Sara's house?" I asked. Ruth, in addition to being an Elder, was also an Earth Witch.

"And what if I did?" she said. "They brought this on themselves. They shouldn't have disrespected an Elder. They should be gone by now."

My molars ground together, pain shooting through my jaw as my body began to shake. "You almost killed my daughter," I ground out. "She's no vampire. She came here looking for me. And she almost died."

"Your daughter?" Ruth said, and the line then went quiet.

"Yes," I spat. "I have a daughter, and you almost took her from me this evening."

"You said she came to find you," Ruth said calmly. "And she knew to go to a house full of bloodsuckers. I'd say you and your daughter are part of the problem."

Strangely, her assertion calmed me. She was drawing the line for me, and I felt very comfortable on the side she'd placed me on. "I called with a purpose," I said. "Tomorrow evening, thirty minutes after sunset, at the Gazebo in the park, Katherine Ward, leader of the House of Ward, would like to meet and discuss terms. Seeing that it was you all who injured one of hers, she would like to establish a truce until then." I omitted the fact that the injured person was a vampire. I thought it best to let her assume whatever she liked if it brought some safety to the House.

The line went quiet again, then Ruth spoke. "Fine. I can't promise that any of the Elders will show up, but I'll spread the word."

"So will we," I said, making it a threat. "It will be known that the members of this House asked for peace after you physically assaulted someone on their property."

"Fine," Ruth said.

And then I hung up.

I'd said all I needed to, and I had heard quite a bit more. I now knew who was responsible for trying to kill Juno.

Oh Juno, I thought. I couldn't put into words how grateful I was for what she had offered me. I knew I didn't deserve it, her kindness, her openness, her curiosity, and her respect. What a joyful surprise she was. I never imagined our meeting could have gone so well. I swallowed the lump in my throat. I might not deserve what she offered me, but I was going to take it, nonetheless. I was going to protect it.

I pulled myself together, tucking away my phone and getting my emotions under control before I went back to the dining room, where I reported all that had been said, for those without super-hearing. Louis had called a couple of friends—witches he knew might be sympathetic or at least open-minded—and asked them to spread the word. Sybil had placed her call directly to Theo Coburn, the head of the Elders. He'd been surprised to learn of how violent the "Pressure Campaign" had become. He promised to meet the next evening to see what Kate had to say and to extend the invitation to the rest of the community's Elders. It was the best we could do for the moment.

"Theo agreed to pause the campaign for now," Sybil said. "*If* he has the power to do so. I don't think anyone tells Diane what she can and can't do."

Kate snorted. "Let her try. I'm not playing around anymore, and she's been told to stand down." Despite her words, Kate seemed much calmer. She still gripped Marcus's hand, and I had to think that had something to do with it. Maybe it was for the best that she'd be sleeping in his bed. If his emotions didn't keep her calm, perhaps their activities would wear her out.

"At least we'll get a night and day without the constant rain," Silas said. "We could all use a break, and it's not great for the land we hope to break ground on in the coming weeks. Everything is too soft."

"It will be nice to not have to worry about lightning or crashing furniture, too," Bruce put in. "But what are we going to do about the pipes? We can't go very long with clogged pipes."

We updated Sybil on the plumbing issue. Louis checked the pipes and found they were clogged around the property line. That was where he sensed the water was trapped.

"I think I may have an idea about what's causing it," Sybil said. "Louis, would you show me?" she asked.

In the end, Bruce, Louis, and Sybil all went, with Felix for backup. No one wanted to take a chance that someone else might get hurt.

I helped Sara and Chelsea clear the table. We asked Chelsea if she wanted to join us in the living room, but she begged off. She was tired and needed to get the guestroom changed over before she could rest.

"Thank you," Sara said, before Chelsea left the kitchen. "For taking a chance on us. It will get better, but if at any time you feel like you can't handle it, we would understand. I'm sure you're aware that Felix included in your contract the right to quit at any time and still be covered. You wouldn't be left in limbo."

She smiled at Sara, dimpling her cheeks. "I know. But I'm not ready to quit," she said. "Sure, this place has been a surprise. But the biggest surprise so far has been how lovely you all are. I can see why Bruce likes it here so much. You all really are a family."

Sara gave Chelsea a quick hug, and then she and I went to the living room. Kate and Marcus were side-by-side on the sofa. Sara took her usual spot, cuddled against Silas. I took a look around the room, trying to decide what to do with myself. "I'm going to go check on E and Juno," I said. "See if they need anything."

"Thanks," Marcus said, and I slipped out of the room and down the stairs to the lowest level.

I went past the gorgeous carved door of Kate's studio to the bedroom down the hall. I tapped softly but didn't hear a reply. I didn't want to go back until I made sure that they were okay. I cracked the door open and peered inside. The lamp in the corner was on. E was resting on her back, clean and dressed in fresh clothes. Juno was curled up in the chair beside the bed, fast asleep, her hand extended holding E's.

I stared at both the girls. They looked so peaceful, so comfortable with each other. I smiled, realizing that I loved that for both of them. E was special to me, and I loved Juno more than I could explain. The friendship between the two filled my heart to bursting. I eased the door back shut and tiptoed back down the hall to the stairs. I would die before I let anything happen to those two.

28

SARA

My best friend leaned back against Marcus as if the two had been a couple for years rather than just days. It made me so happy to see her comfortable with that kind of intimacy. I was even happier to see the effect he had on her mood. She was facing a major test of her leadership skills, yet she was relaxed and seemed completely in control. It was encouraging, especially since it was my community she would be going up against.

"What will you say?" I asked Kate, curious to see if she had a plan or was just going to wing it.

She shrugged, and Marcus stroked the back of her arm, where her sweater was pushed up to her elbow. I watched his fingers move up and down her arm as she considered it. "I guess I'll just tell the truth," she said. "From what Louis says, it might be enough."

Silas cleared his throat next to me. "It might be a bit more complicated if what Lucia said is true, and some of the witches think you all are practicing some kind of Blood Magic."

Kate's brows furrowed. "What does that mean anyway?" she asked. "I didn't even know that was a thing."

"Oh, it's a 'thing' all right," Lucia said as she reentered the room. "It's not something usually talked about in polite company." She looked around the room and sniffed as she sat in one of the chairs. "But this is not exactly polite company," she muttered under her breath. "It's exactly what it sounds like," she finally said once she had arranged her linen blouse to her satisfaction. "The witches in this valley practice Nature Magic. We are each born with a gift that corresponds to a particular force of nature: Water, Earth, Air, Fire, Electricity. You get the idea," she explained. "But some witches are not satisfied with the gifts the Gods have given them. They want more. They try to boost their natural gifts with Dark or Blood Magic, both of which are strictly forbidden here in our valley." She sighed and recrossed her long legs. "Some witches have found that by using blood, either their own or the blood of others, they can do more with what they have and sometimes achieve results beyond what any Natural Witch can."

"Then why is it so taboo?" Kate asked. "I don't see much of a problem with using one's own blood to boost your magic. Someone else's might cause issues, but who am I to judge?"

"Hmm," Lucia stared at Kate, her expression unreadable.

It was strange to hear my aunt explain all of this to Kate. I had grown up in the witch's community. All of it was deeply rooted in what I knew and what I'd been taught since I was a child.

"I suppose you wouldn't see a problem," Lucia said. "But we are not vampires. To use blood in that way, to mix it with our natural gifts..." She shook her head. "It's addictive. The more you use it, the more it takes to achieve the same results, and the more you need. Eventually, the lust for it is insatiable, and that way leads to murder, madness, and the possibility of summoning more than a witch can handle."

Kate looked at Lucia, confusion clear on her face. "She's talking about things from beyond our current plane of existence," I said.

"Demons," Lucia said, her voice sharp as a knife.

I sighed. "That bit is debatable. Most people believe the story about demons is more of a fairy tale, a story to scare young witches," I said.

"You're talking to an actual fae, who drinks blood," Lucia pointed out. "What's not to believe?"

I had to give her that one. "Anyway," I continued. "There is a deeply ingrained bias against Blood Magic in our community, and some of the witches here believe that vampires themselves are a manifestation of Blood Magic."

"Who's to say they aren't?" Lucia said.

I ignored her and kept going. "So, you might find that some witches, especially the older ones, won't be very welcoming. They believe that vampires are a perversion of what they can do. They might even assign special powers or Dark Magical abilities to vampires."

"Abilities?" Kate asked.

"It's thought that vampires have magic," Marcus said. "It's nonsense, of course. But some people believe we can fly, turn into bats, or dematerialize. Some believe that vampires can control people's minds, enslave them, or make them act against their nature. Some even believe we can erase memories."

Kate snorted. "It sounds like you're talking about fae, not vampires."

"I suppose the legends get mixed and muddled over time," he said. "Especially if what Felix thinks is true and the fae left, wiping most of what they are from the memories of vampires, witches, shifters, and humans."

"Okay," Kate said. "So many of the witches in the valley are going to hate me for reasons completely out of my control. Not a new situation for me. I've just got to convince them somehow that we mean them no harm. We are just here to live our lives, like anyone else."

"But you're not like anyone else," Lucia said. "You're a vampire. Don't forget it. They won't."

"Thanks. That's a great help," Kate smirked.

Just then, we were rejoined by the plumbing committee, who came in through the front door. They were all muddy and soaked with rain, but there were satisfied smiles on more than one face. Louis wasn't present, but Bruce explained that he had to get home.

"I think we've solved your problem," my mom announced, once she, Bruce, and Felix were all within earshot. "I was right, it was roots."

"Roots?" Kate asked.

"Yes. Some Green Witch sent a massive clog of roots through the pipe that carries wastewater from the house," Mom said cheerily. "I was able to drive the growth back and even use some of the roots to plug the cracks in the pipe caused by the infiltration. It will hold for a while, but you all will need a real plumber out here within a few days."

"I've already put in an emergency call," Bruce said, collecting jackets. "If you all will just give me a minute, I'll get towels both to dry off and sit on."

I smiled to myself. It was great to have him helping and thinking of the details, such as protecting the furniture or calling the plumber. It was technically my house, but I was more than grateful to give up the operations to Bruce and Chelsea, especially with everything going on.

I thought about the meeting the following day. I didn't know how it would turn out. Louis seemed sure that the majority of the witches would be upset by what had been happening, but that didn't mean that they would be on our side. I wish I could say that I had as much confidence as he did. I knew all too well how closed-minded our community could be.

A wave of sorrow washed over me when I considered all my plans that would probably never come to fruition. The Bride's Gathering was canceled, and I was having serious doubts about our wedding plans, but it was more than that. It was the loss of my community, my neighbors, my friends. It was the denial of my heritage. It was being excluded from the rituals and milestones that were my birthright. I wanted those things. I wanted to be a witch, and still marry a shifter, and still be best friends with a vampire. It didn't feel like too much to ask.

"What are you thinking about?" Silas asked, leaning down close and brushing my ear with his lips.

I felt goosebumps rise on my skin. "Nothing," I said. "And everything." I looked up at him and smiled. His golden eyes glowed in the firelight. Looking at him, I was reminded of what truly mattered. I might be on the outside of the community I'd been part of my whole life, but I was making this choice for a reason, and that reason was love. I loved this man, I loved the House I belonged to, and I loved all the people in it. They were what mattered. This strange family of ours was worth missing out on everything else.

I reached up with one hand and gripped the back of his neck, bringing his mouth to mine. The kiss was light, brief, but it was enough. "I love you, you know?" I said.

His gaze warmed. "I know," he said. "And I still can't believe I'm that lucky."

"Okay, you two," Felix said as he grabbed a towel from Bruce. "Any more of that and I'll have to throw Bruce over my shoulder and carry him upstairs."

"Try it," Bruce said. "You'll be sleeping in the hall, and there are no blackout curtains out there."

I chuckled, and Silas kissed the top of my head as I leaned back onto his shoulder.

"Not the way I would have handled it, but thank you for getting their attention, Felix," Aunt Lucia said. "Now, it would be nice if we went over exactly what the plan is for tomorrow."

"Plan?" I asked. "We have a plan, the meeting, Kate talking to the Elders and community members who show up."

"Yes, but I think it's important that we discuss who should stay here. I don't believe we should leave this place empty," she said. "And I think it would be a good idea if E and Juno at least stay back."

Ah, Juno. It was obvious their reunion went well. I was a bit surprised to see Lucia comforting Juno when E was injured, but I was also very pleased. I understood why E should stay behind; she was still recovering. It was telling that she didn't want Juno to go to the meeting, though. Not that I doubted my aunt's love for her daughter.

"That's a good idea," Kate said. "I expect Chelsea to stay behind as well. Who else? Bruce? Felix?"

Felix looked at Bruce, who shrugged. "Sure, we'll stay here and babysit," Felix said. "I trust that you all can handle whatever the witches might be tempted to throw at you. And if you need me, just scream really loud." He gave Kate a fangy smile. "I can be there quickly if you need backup."

"Thanks," she said. "We shouldn't be home too late, and don't let them watch scary movies while we're gone." She smirked at Felix, who just winked back.

"Okay, everyone," my mom said, rising. "If that's about it, I'm going home to get out of these muddy clothes and take a hot shower."

"I'll go with you," my aunt said, getting to her feet. She turned to me. "Juno's asleep, but if you would let her know that I'll be back tomorrow after breakfast. Please pass my number along to her, in case she wants to call me," she added softly.

I smiled. "Of course, Auntie. I think she would like that," I said.

Lucia just nodded and followed my mom out.

When they shut the front door behind them, Felix spoke up. "I take it the mother-daughter reunion went well? At least until Juno was almost crushed by a thousand pounds of iron?"

"Yeah, I think it did," I said. "We'll have to get Juno's take on it tomorrow." I glanced over at Marcus. "It seems like your sister and Juno have become close... friends."

Marcus smiled. "Yeah, it does seem that way," he said. "She's partial to pretty girls, but she's a bit different around Juno. More serious than her usual bubbly self." He shrugged.

"It would be fun if they both stayed with us," Kate said. "I like them both very much." Marcus nodded and pulled her closer.

The rest of us agreed. We would have to see how things turned out, but it would be nice to have more family and found-family around, especially if the community here refused to accept us. The more, the merrier.

It was hardly bedtime, but Silas and I excused ourselves next and went up to our room. I turned on the lights next to our bed and slipped into the dressing room. When I returned in a comfy pair of sweats and an old t-shirt, Silas was already waiting in bed. He'd opted for no clothing, and I was questioning my sartorial choices. I grinned at him.

"Sorry if I'm being too presumptuous," he said, the covers pulled up to his waist, exposing his bare, muscled chest. I drank in the sight of him. His body was something I never grew tired of.

"No," I said. "Not at all." I shed my cozy clothing as I came to bed, trading terrycloth and worn cotton for the smooth warmth of my mate's skin.

It was a blessing to lose myself in his touch. The evening had been a trial, but in his arms I could shut the world out. I could pretend that nothing and no one could upset our happiness, could disrupt the peace we found when we came together.

We made love slowly, deliberately, savoring each kiss and touch. It was exactly what I wanted, and somehow he knew. Or maybe it was what he wanted too.

When we were both sated, I lay in the crook of his arm, his shoulder my pillow. I traced my fingers over the plains of his chest as our breathing slowed, and our bodies cooled. "Do you want me there tomorrow?" Silas said softly.

"What?" I asked. "Of course, I want you there."

"Good," he said. "That's good. I want to be there. To stand with you, but I don't want to make things harder for you or for Kate. I know our engagement isn't approved of by some in your community. Sometimes I feel like an added complication."

I pushed myself up onto my elbow so that I could look at his face, but more importantly, so that he could see mine. "You are far from a complication, and I don't care what the community thinks about our engagement," I said. "I'm proud to be your mate, and nothing—and no one's opinion—will ever change that. I will always want you by my side. I will always *need* you by my side."

He smiled and pulled me down for a lingering kiss. "Good," he growled into my mouth. "Because that's the only place I want to be."

"The only place?" I asked, nipping at his bottom lip.

He growled again. "The only other place," he breathed before he flipped us both over so that I was on my back. This time, he wasn't slow or careful, and it was exactly what we both needed.

29

KATE

Putting my book down on the bedside table, I rolled over toward Marcus. I wasn't afraid I'd wake him, either with my movement or the light from the lamp beside me. He had told me that in an emergency, I could probably rouse him before sunset, but it would take some effort.

He was as still as a corpse. I could easily see where stories about the undead originated. As I watched him for several minutes, he neither breathed nor moved at all. I placed my hand on his bare chest. His skin was the same temperature as mine, as was the rest of the room. To a human, he would have felt cold. Despite the strangeness of his sleep, he was still beautiful.

There was a quiet thrill in being able to look at him so openly without anyone watching me. I could stare as long as I wanted without feeling self-conscious or awkward. I'd memorized the contours of his face that first night, the shape of his shoulders and arms, and how his short hair rested against the pillow. Even though he wouldn't have noticed, I held back from pulling back the covers and exploring more without his permission. That would have been just creepy. Still, I couldn't help but think about it. Every inch of the man was perfection.

Even after spending hours the night before, indulging in each other's bodies, just looking at him, asleep next to me, I wanted him. I still craved his touch, longed to sink my teeth into him, and feel how much he wanted me back.

While I was blissfully happy, there was a part of me that felt unfulfilled and cheated at the same time. I knew that the very thing that made me crave more of him was what made me feel safe enough to let him touch me. He was always in complete control of himself. That was the only reason I could let him come to me, but I desperately wanted to see him unleashed. Deep down, I longed for the raw energy I knew he kept inside. *Why couldn't I just be content with what I had?* I was being ridiculous.

Sighing, I withdrew my hand and rolled onto my back, grabbing my phone from where it was plugged in. It was 5 p.m. It would still be an hour before he woke up and an hour and a half before I was supposed to meet with the Elders and the community members who dared to show up. Staying in bed was making me restless. I needed to get up, get dressed, and find something to distract myself.

Less than fifteen minutes later, I was upstairs heating myself some breakfast in the kitchen when Bruce walked in. "How did you sleep?" he asked.

"Fine, thanks," I said. "How about you? You and Felix both recovered after yesterday?"

"We're both doing well, and I've had a chance to talk to Juno, who reports that E is healed and feeling better than ever. She's also awake and cranky about being trapped in the room downstairs. Felix went down a few minutes before you came up to keep her company. He feels responsible," Bruce said.

"I completely understand. That used to be the worst part of my day until I realized I could withstand the sun. I assume she's up early because of Felix's blood?" I asked. Bruce nodded, but I noticed a hint of a cloud cross his face. "Does it bother you that she fed from him?" I wasn't sure how a human would feel about it, but I could imagine how I would feel if Marcus fed someone else. Just the thought made my skin prickle and my fangs tingle.

Bruce narrowed his eyes as he considered it. "I know it shouldn't," he said. "But I will admit to certain feelings of possessiveness. They aren't attractive, I realize, but they are there nonetheless. However, I wouldn't have had it any other way. We would both do whatever it took to help E, or any other member of this House."

Reflecting on Bruce, his past abuse by Margaux, and his ongoing relationship with a vampire sparked a thought. "Bruce, can I ask you something very personal?"

"Of course," he said, but I could see him stiffen slightly, waiting to see what I would ask.

"You had a terrible experience at the hands of a vampire," I said, pausing. I licked my lips, hoping I wasn't going too far. "I know Felix... bites you. How were you able to let him? After what happened with Margaux?"

Bruce nodded slowly. "Our situations are different, of course, but it came down to trust," he said. "I trust Felix with my life. I have to, given our relationship. He's significantly stronger than me. He could easily take too much, and I'd be helpless to do anything about it. But I trust him. I trust in his love for me. I trust that he doesn't want to harm me."

I thought about his words. Our situations weren't that different. I was scared for myself, too. Was it because I didn't trust Marcus? I wasn't sure that was the reason. I remembered the time he'd kissed my neck, and the flood of memories and fear that had washed over me. "Do you ever get scared? Even though you know he's not her? Do you ever think about what happened?" I asked.

Bruce smiled with understanding and sympathy. "Yes. Sometimes it's too much. In those moments, I'm very clear with him about what I'm feeling, and he's there to reassure me and make me feel safe and in control again. I never feel pressured to let him feed. He's always made sure I can pull back or push for more. On my terms."

That sounded familiar, and I wondered if Felix and Marcus had had a similar conversation. I smiled at the thought. "Thank you, Bruce. I know you hate talking about this stuff, but it's been really helpful," I said.

"I'm happy to help," he replied, and then paused, studying me before going on. "I know it's not easy, but I also know Marcus doesn't want to hurt you. If you can let yourself trust him, it's possible you could eventually overcome the trauma of what Alexander did. You won't forget his attack, but you may not think of it every time Marcus bites you."

Trauma. Yes, that's what it was, I thought. Just the idea of Marcus biting me sent shivers down my spine. But I wasn't sure anymore if it was from fear or desire. "I know you're right," I said. "I'll think about it." Despite all evidence suggesting it would probably be okay, I still felt uncertain. I know Alexander had taken a significant amount of my blood and didn't seem obsessed with getting more. And E had tasted my blood and wasn't lurking outside my door every night, but I was still anxious. I had seen how James acted, how Marcus had struggled with the scent of my blood in the car on the way back from Alexander's manor. I didn't know what to do.

The good news was that all my worries about my relationship were distracting me from the meeting later that night, at least until Sara and Sybil walked into the kitchen. "Hey, Kate," Sara said. "You ready for tonight?" Her tone was pleasant enough, but her face looked grim. I didn't need my gift to tell that she was worried.

"Yeah, I guess so," I said, glancing down at the cold mug I held.

"Here, let me reheat that for you," Bruce said as he reached for the mug. I gratefully handed it to him. "What did you want to wear tonight?" he asked while he put the mug back in the microwave.

"Wear?" I asked. I looked down at myself. I was back in my "uniform" of jeans and an oversized sweater. "I assume this meeting won't require a team of stylists and a rack of designer clothing," I said, addressing the witches in the room.

"Nope," Sara said. "In fact, it might be better to dress casually. You want the witches to feel sympathy for you. You want them to see you as a member of the community. Gucci and Prada won't accomplish that."

"Good Point," Bruce said. "What would you ladies suggest?"

Sybil examined me from head to toe, noting the old knitwear and canvas slip-on shoes. "I'd say she looks perfect," she said. "Maybe just run a brush through your hair and brighten up those cheeks. You look rather pale, dear."

"Yes, a side effect of being a vampire, I'm afraid," I teased. "But, yeah, I'll try to look a little less un-dead."

"That would be lovely," Sybil replied sincerely. "I'm going to go sit down in the library and rest before I go back out."

"Can I bring you something?" Bruce asked. "Tea? A glass of wine?"

"Oh, tea would be wonderful," Sybil replied. "Whatever you have on hand that isn't caffeinated."

"I'll bring it right out," Bruce said, filling the kettle at the sink.

"Where is Lucia?" I asked.

"She's on the porch with Juno," Sara said. "The two of them have been out there a while." She smiled. It clearly pleased her that the two women were getting comfortable with each other.

"What about Silas?" I asked. "Is he planning on going with us tonight?"

"He wouldn't miss it," Sara said. "He's out working on the pipe issue with his brother, Beau. Mom is about to go out and see if they're ready for her to move back the root ball she put in place to hold things together." Sara grinned. "Don't tell Beth Beau was here when you see her. She'd kill me if she knew he'd been here and I didn't call her."

"Beth has a crush on Beau?" I asked. This was news to me. I'd met Silas's brothers and father, but I wasn't aware that there was any connection between Beth and the second-oldest Hemming brother.

"Oh, she's never even met him," Sara said. "She's just determined to find herself a shifter boyfriend. I tried to tell her that's not how it works, but she's convinced she could pull it off."

I chuckled. "Well, she won't hear it from me," I said. "How about we watch something until the others wake up? Unless you all have plans." I was starting to feel the nerves I had been running from.

"Nope, we went out to eat earlier. I have no plans until the meeting," Sara said, following me into the living room. We called up an episode of an early 2000s medical drama we'd both seen a dozen times. It was perfect. Just enough intrigue to draw my attention, but familiar enough that I didn't have to work too hard to follow along.

Before I knew it, the episode was over, and the room had filled with the other members of the House, including E, Felix, and finally Marcus. He sat down beside me and offered me his hand. "You ready?" he asked.

I nodded. "I think so. I just hope we are doing the right thing. I don't want anyone else to get hurt."

"I knew the guy didn't have Lupus," Felix said, engrossed in the final scene of the show.

"It's never Lupus," E said seriously.

"Okay," Sara said, standing and turning off the TV. "We should get going unless we want to show up fashionably late."

Marcus and I got up to follow Sara into the foyer, where I could hear Lucia, Juno, and Silas talking. "Felix, E, we'll be back soon," I said.

"Don't worry, we'll behave," Felix said.

"Speak for yourself," E chided, but gave me a wink.

On our way to the front of the house, we ran into Bruce. "I wish I were going with you, for support," he said.

I placed a hand on his arm. He was genuine and a bit concerned. "Thank you for staying behind. We'll be okay," I reassured him.

"Just yell if you need us," Felix said from the living room. His voice was at a normal pitch, but I could still hear him clearly thanks to my vampire hearing.

"Will do," I replied, catching a quirked smile from Bruce. He'd heard Felix, too. "You're practically already a vampire, aren't you?" I teased.

"Hmm, not quite, but soon enough," he said.

He walked us to the door, where the others waited. Lucia, Sybil, Sara, and Silas would ride over together, while Marcus and I would take my car. Juno was staying behind with E, and Silas's brother, Beau, had already headed back across the Pass.

Butterflies the size of eagles fluttered in my stomach as we made the short drive up the highway, across the river, and into town. It was after sunset, but a full moon had already risen, and the sky was clear for the first time in weeks. I was sure even the witches could see well despite the hour.

We drove through the small settlement, turning onto the main street. There were hardly any other cars on the road, but the businesses were all lit up, and there were people on the sidewalks. I'd only gone through the town a few times since I was turned, mainly to get to the Heartwood house, and this was the most people I'd ever seen out and about.

I followed behind Lucia's car and parked beside her when she pulled over into a lot behind one of the shops. Getting out and locking up, Marcus and I joined the witches and Silas. "We're not far," Sara said. "Just on the other side of this building."

I looked up at Marcus, who smiled down at me and offered his arm. I accepted it gladly. We fell behind the Heartwoods and Silas a little, letting them lead the way. As we rounded the building, the park came into view, and I gasped. "I didn't know there were this many people in the whole town," I said to no one in particular.

Sybil glanced back over her shoulder. "There aren't," she said. "These are witches from up and down the entire valley."

"Oh, great," I said. "What could go wrong?"

30

LUCIA

There was no going back now, I thought. Several witches had already spotted us. Some I knew and many I didn't. I scanned the park as we crossed the small street. There must have been over three hundred witches gathered there, milling about. Considering our small town had only about one hundred residents, it was impressive. Word had spread farther than I'd expected about our little meeting. I didn't know if that was a good thing or not. I guessed we'd find out.

The sea of bodies parted as we made our way toward the gazebo in the middle of the small park. I was unsurprised to see several Elders already clustered inside the open-air structure. As we got closer, I realized there were actually two groups of witches on the covered platform. I recognized Theo standing with four Elders, one from our town and three from the surrounding area. Off to the side, Diane, Ruth, and two other local witches stood. One I knew was a Green Witch, and I was reasonably sure the other was an Air Witch. *Interesting,* I thought.

We paused at the steps of the gazebo, all looking at Kate. This was her moment; it was important for her to lead. She stepped forward, releasing Marcus and locking eyes with Theo as she moved up the steps. "Thank you for coming," she said, addressing Theo and his group. "I see there are a few others interested in hearing what we have to say."

Diane's group fell silent as Kate stepped onto the raised platform. The hostility on their faces said they weren't just there to listen; they were there to challenge Kate and the rest of us. Their separation from Theo made it clear that they were their own faction, and I thought that might bode well for us.

Theo nodded at Kate. "It would seem they are. I hope you've come to say something worth listening to," he said, his voice tight. I suspected he was used to being in control of a situation, and given the sizable crowd and the way every eye tracked Kate, he was not the one everyone had come to hear.

Then Theo turned his gaze and looked down at me, where I stood with the rest of our group. "Lucia," he said, his tone one of disapproval and judgment. "I'm sad to see you here with these... Others. I'd thought you had aspirations for leadership."

I was momentarily stunned. I hadn't expected to be singled out. Even though I'd made my choice and was firmly on the side of the House, I still trembled inside at his words. I'd wanted the Elder's approval my whole life. My new position would take some getting used to, but I wasn't about to back down now.

"My only aspirations are to uphold fairness and order, both of which have been in short supply with some who hold the title of Elder," I said, raising my chin to show I wasn't cowed.

He dismissed me silently by raising his gaze back to Kate. "You asked us to meet you here. Well, we're here." He crossed his arms, his face set in a scowl, waiting for her to reply.

I looked around as the crowd pushed in closer. Among the shifting bodies, I saw Louis standing beside Maureen and Beth. Like everyone else, they waited expectantly, all watching the gazebo, eager to hear what Kate would say.

I wasn't sure if the crowd's curiosity stemmed from Kate being a vampire or from her standing up to the community's Elders—something no one had ever done before. Eventually, the movement stopped as everyone gathered closer. The murmurs faded, leaving only the sound of rustling leaves.

Kate turned toward the crowd, with her back to Diane and her group. I saw Marcus step to the side, keeping his eyes on the old witch. Though he was there to support Kate, as a trained security professional, he also had good instincts about where potential danger might be. I nodded in approval and refocused on Kate.

The leader of The House of Ward was nervous. She shifted her weight from one foot to the other and swallowed as her eyes darted over the gathered witches. I was glad that Bruce hadn't dressed her in anything fancy. It would have made her look even more uncomfortable, and that wasn't what she needed in that moment.

Kate cleared her throat. "Thank you all for coming," she said in a voice that carried throughout the small park. "My name is Katherine Ward. I'm sorry I haven't had the chance to meet more of you in person before tonight. That's my fault. As some of you may know, I've established a House here in the valley, not far from here. My intention was to escape the city and live with friends. I've known the Heartwoods since I was a girl, and when given the opportunity to live with my best friend Sara, I jumped at the chance. I didn't come here to cause trouble or to make anyone uncomfortable.

"Recently, I was told by Elder Coburn and Elder Paulson that we are no longer welcome in the valley. My House and I will not be leaving." Kate paused, took a breath, and gave everyone a moment to process her words. The rumble of low voices rippled through the crowd of witches. I couldn't tell if the mob was supportive or not. I wondered if Kate was aware of the overall mood, or if the presence of so many people would overwhelm her if she lowered her defenses.

Kate continued, and the voices quieted again. "When Elder Paulson became aware of our position, she started a systematic attack on our House, or a 'Pressure Campaign' as she called it. This campaign has not only brought weeks of rain to the valley, which you have noticed, but has also involved lightning strikes on and near our property, damage to our infrastructure, and now the near-fatal injury of one of our House members.

"Our home is located outside the town limits, and we have done nothing to harm any witch or human in the surrounding area. We are peaceful, and our main goal was to be left alone. We made a mistake," she said, and I was curious to see where this was going.

"We should have been better neighbors. We should have, at the very least, introduced ourselves and let you all get to know us," Kate said.

"We don't need to get to know you," Diane said, gaining everyone's attention. Her voice was like a whip of stinging power compared to Theo's. Kate turned to face Diane, and the rest of the crowd followed suit. "You're a vampire, and vampires are not welcome in our valley. They never have been. They never will be. Just because the Heartwoods don't mind mixing with Others," Diane continued, making the word 'Others' sound like a slur. "Doesn't mean that the other witches in this valley feel the same." She might be tiny, but there was strength behind her words, and many of the heads in the crowd nodded in agreement.

"Why?" Kate said. "Why aren't Others welcome here? Why can't we live with one another, work together, and be good friends and neighbors?"

"Because you and your kind are a perversion of life," Ruth spat from beside Diane. "You're blood drinkers. Blood Magic is what keeps you alive. By rights, you should all be dead."

There were gasps from throughout the crowd, but there were also nods and shouts of agreement. Kate reached up and clasped her hand around her locket. Her expression was strained, and I could tell this was not going as she hoped.

A shout from the crowd drew everyone's attention. "They haven't hurt anyone," the voice called. "Give them a chance."

But then another person yelled out, "They're murderers, all of them." This prompted shouts both in support of the vampires and against. The crowd began to erupt in loud voices and rough tones until Kate shouted above the noise.

"We have done nothing wrong," Kate said, raising her voice over the noise. Everyone grew quiet again, wanting to hear what the vampire had to say in her own defense. “Our home has been attacked, and a witch, one of your own, was nearly killed by their actions.” She pointed her free hand at Ruth and Diane.

“Says you,” Diane replied. “There is no proof that anyone was attacked, let alone injured. It’s the word of a leech against the word of an Elder witch.”

“No,” Louis shouted from the crowd. The witches around him parted, either to give him room to speak or to avoid being associated with a dissenter. “It’s not just her word. It’s mine too. I was there. I saw what happened, and it’s true. A witch was nearly killed, and a vampire saved her, getting seriously hurt in the process. If it weren’t for the vampire, the witch would be dead because Ruth used her gift to do harm.”

Conversation bubbled up all around me. Using one’s gift to purposely harm another, especially another witch, was strictly forbidden. It was a powerful accusation, and one leveled against an Elder nonetheless.

Theo held up his hand, trying to get everyone’s attention, but the crowd continued to talk, ignoring the lead Elder. He clapped his hands, trying to calm the increasingly agitated group. A stiff gust of wind blew over the crowd as Theo attempted to use his gift to focus the mob. Things were getting out of hand, however.

I flicked my gaze to Kate. She stood beside Theo, clearly unsure of how to proceed. I moved forward, touching Marcus as I passed. “Keep an eye on Ruth and Diane,” I said as I made my way up the stairs to stand beside Kate. “Hey,” I said to her. “You okay?” She nodded, but there was worry and frustration in her eyes. “Can you do anything to calm this down?” I asked.

She shook her head. “There are too many people and the emotions are too strong,” she said. “I’m having enough trouble controlling my own.” The muscles in her jaw flexed, illustrating her point.

Theo was now attempting to shout above the rumble of the crowd. Scattered blue sparks of electricity and bursts of red flame lit up among the agitated witches, only fanned by Theo’s blasts of air.

This was quickly becoming dangerous. I didn't really want to hear what Theo had to say, but it was important to keep everyone safe, and if getting everyone's attention back on him was what it took, I was willing to help.

"Theo," I shouted. His gaze flicked to me, and I could see the fear in his eyes. "Still the air and I'll calm the crowd," I said. He nodded, and I stepped to the edge of the gazebo. I raised my palm, making sure my arm was outside the covered area. Pulling on my gift, I summoned the largest ball of fire I could manage, and as a seasoned witch in her fifties, it was a sizable flame. Heat rolled over me and those nearby, and I welcomed it. This was what it felt like to be a Fire Witch. It was hot, noisy, and wonderful. I spun the orb of fire, lifting it higher off my palm until most of the clearing was lit up and all eyes were fixed on me. "That's enough," I shouted, over the crackle of the fire. "Elder Coburn would like your attention."

Slowly, I drew the flame back to my palm, dampening it as it touched back down until there was only a flicker left in the center of my hand. Then I closed my fist, and the flame winked out.

I looked at Theo. Despite the cool night, he was sweating, his hair plastered to his forehead. I wondered if it was from the stress or the heat of my flame. Either way, it gave me some satisfaction to see him unsettled.

He nodded at me. "Thank you," he said, then turned back to the crowd, who were now watching quietly with wide eyes. "This is a serious charge against one of your Elders. It will be investigated. And if there is wrongdoing, there will be consequences," he said, mollifying the witches somewhat. "As for the vampires, it is still the decision of the Elders that they should leave our valley. The actions of any given witch don't change our decision. A vampire House has no place in a community of witches."

There were some more grumbles and muttering from the crowd, but Theo held up his hand, stilling them once more. "The campaign —" he began.

"Harassment," Kate said, interrupting Theo.

He shot Kate a stern look. "Will cease for now," he said. "We will not have anyone hurt, whether on purpose or by accident." This time, he turned and glared at Diane and Ruth, who were still huddled together with their entourage.

I didn't bother to turn around to see their reactions. I didn't really care. They would do what they would, and suffer the consequences. It was good to let the community know what they were up to, however. Diane and Ruth might not care about what Kate or even Theo thought, but I suspected they wouldn't want to lose the support of the people.

"We will not leave," Kate said again, this time directly to Theo.

Theo sighed. "We will go directly to your Council and appeal if we have to."

She grinned, showing her fangs. Theo paled. "Go right ahead," Kate said. "They like me about as much as you do, but I doubt they'll do much about it." She sobered then, growing more serious. "Please know, we really do just want peace. The Heartwoods are like my family. I would never do anything to harm them or anyone in this community. Whether we leave or not, I would hope you would not hold our friendship against the Heartwoods. They're good people."

Theo nodded and glanced at me before looking back at Kate. "Thank you. We will take it under advisement," he said, and then he turned away.

"Come on, Kate," I said, taking her arm and steering her down the steps. "Let's get ahead of this."

"Agreed," Marcus said as we joined the others on the grass. "I'd feel better if we were all back behind the wards before all these people get on the road."

Silas took the lead, and we pushed our way back through the crowd as it was breaking up. We hurried to our cars, both Silas and Marcus scanning every shadow for potential threats. I doubted there was any real danger, but it seemed like the right move to get back to Sara's as quickly as possible. Everyone had heard Kate's refusal to leave the valley, and there might be one or two witches willing to test themselves against the young vampire if they thought it could boost their standing in the community.

Sybil offered to drive, but I refused. I was fine, and the drive was short. It was just over five minutes before we pulled into the gravel parking area. Bruce and Felix were on the front porch, sitting in the rocking chairs like an old married couple, waiting for us.

"No one yelled for me, and you are all back in one piece, so things must not have gone too badly," Felix said as we all made our way up the steps.

"No one got killed," I said.

"Well, that's a start," he replied cheerily.

Kate paused halfway up. "I don't know that we really accomplished anything, though," she said. "I wished I could tell how many people were sympathetic to our cause."

"It doesn't really matter," Sara said. "The important thing is people were there to listen, and for now, the harassment has stopped."

"I suppose you're right," Kate said, and she kept going up the steps just as the sky opened up and rain started to pour.

31

MARCUS

We made it undercover just as the heavy rain started. I stood on the porch with everyone else as the rain fell so hard we could barely see the cars in the driveway.

"I thought you said the harassment was over," Felix said, staring out through the downpour into the darkness.

"Maybe we should all move inside," Kate suggested. "Just in case."

I felt much better once everyone was safely indoors. We gathered for a House meeting to update the rest of the group on what happened in the park. Chelsea met us in the living room with drinks and food for the witches. Kate invited her to stay, but she excused herself to finish up in the kitchen. She was warming up to us, but it would take some time before she saw herself as one of the group, I thought.

Once we were settled, Kate and Lucia took turns recounting the meeting with the Elders, starting with the overwhelming number of witches who turned out to witness it. E was especially interested in how the crowd reacted when they found out that a witch had nearly been killed because of the harassment. She sat on the sofa, curled up beside Juno. Even though it was E who had been badly hurt, she was clearly worried for the young Fire Witch.

I was satisfied with how things had gone in the park. Lucia stepped in at just the right moment and regained control of the crowd. I'd had my eye on Diane and her cronies the whole time, trusting that Silas and the others would handle the rest. I had to agree with Sara; the most important thing was that the valley's residents knew what had been happening. I also agreed with Kate; the vampire Council wouldn't lift a finger to make the witches more comfortable. And, since Felix, one of The Three, was a member of the House the witches were trying to displace, the Council would expect him to handle any legal or diplomatic issues. Where that left us, I wasn't sure.

"I think Kate was correct," Felix said, lounging with Bruce at the other end of the long sofa from E and Juno. "This calls for some diplomacy. As vampires in a valley of witches, we've done very little to reach out and get to know the community at large. It might be beneficial for us to make an appearance in town and get to know some of the locals better."

Sara winced. "I understand where you're coming from, and I'm not saying you're wrong, but these witches can be very... old-fashioned about the different creatures mixing. I've gotten more than a few looks and whispers since announcing my engagement to Silas, and he's a shifter." At the mention of the town's reaction, Silas pulled Sara closer on the loveseat as she went on. "Witches deal with shifters on a regular basis. Besides the people in this room, there is basically zero contact between witches and vampires that doesn't happen on an official level."

I looked at Sara, then at Sybil and Lucia, who sat side by side in the two living room chairs. "You know these people. You understand them in a way we don't, but I agree with Felix. If we expect to live here, we will have to do better. We need to understand them too, and they need to be able to get to know us so they can judge us for themselves," I said.

Lucia nodded. "I agree. It might be a good idea to get Kate into town during the day. It will make her seem more like a regular person, more approachable."

"I could do that," Kate said. "What do you think, Sara? Would you take me out and introduce me around?"

"Yeah," she said. "If you're going into town, I'll go with you."

"*We* will go with you," Silas said.

After it was decided that Kate, Sara, and Silas would go into town the next day, weather permitting, conversations shifted to neutral topics. The witches were interested in when the next family dinner would be. E wanted to learn more about the possibility of fresher blood for the vampires in the House, and Felix was asking Sara about the new release coming out in the Demon Hunter series he and Kate were both reading.

Kate and I sat on the hearth, and she reached over and took my hand. She seemed fairly relaxed after the events in the park, but it was hard to tell. "How are you feeling?" I asked quietly.

She smiled at me, rubbing her thumb across the back of my hand. "I'm good. I just wanted to touch you," she said. "I didn't mean to..."

I raised our hands and kissed hers. "You can have whatever you need," I said. "My touch, my steadiness, anything I've got to give."

"I think the rain is letting up," Sybil said. "It might be a good time for Lucia and me to head home."

Lucia shot her sister a look, then glanced around the room at the three couples and Juno and E, and nodded.

"I'll walk you out," Juno said, standing up. Lucia smiled shyly at her daughter and nodded again.

We all said goodnight, and Juno walked the two women to the door.

Kate leaned closer, resting her head on my shoulder, and pulled my hand to her. She returned my kiss on the back of my knuckles, but didn't let go of my hand. I felt her breath against my fingers and then the sharp sting of her fangs. I glanced down, but her hair had fallen in front of her face, hiding her from view, as she sucked gently at the blood welling from my hand, just below my thumb.

I fought to keep my breathing steady as my body responded to her bite. I shifted my position on the stone hearth and looked away, trying not to make it obvious what Kate was doing. I focused on what

Bruce was saying to the group. He and Silas were talking about some of the upcoming renovations. I swallowed hard, trying not to think about Kate's tongue on my skin or the gentle pressure of her sucking.

The rest of the housemates were absorbed in the conversation, but Felix's nostrils flared, and he flicked his gaze to mine, raising an eyebrow. A slow smile spread across his face. Somehow, his knowing look pushed me over the edge. I clenched my jaw, trying not to growl and launch myself at Kate. I'd had enough. "Excuse us, please," I said to everyone and no one in particular as I got to my feet and swept Kate into my arms. She let out a surprised yelp and laughed as I carried her out of the room, passing Juno on her way back from the foyer.

"What are you doing?" Kate breathed into my neck.

"What did you expect would happen when you bit me in front of everyone?" I asked, my voice coming out rough with need.

She laughed again and nipped at my neck. My fangs lowered, and I tilted my head, inviting her teeth on my throat. I increased my pace and didn't stop until we reached my room, where Sara's light laughter and the surprised murmur of the others faded into the distance.

Once the door was shut, I threw her on the bed, eliciting another shriek of delight. I pulled my t-shirt off over my head and then stepped back and undid my jeans with one hand, pausing to see her reaction. She smiled up at me, nodding, and I shed the rest of my clothes.

She watched me with hooded eyes as I moved toward her. She removed her clothes and tossed them aside. Then she crawled backward on her hands and knees to give me space to join her on the bed, never taking her eyes off me. The sight of her, naked, bent forward, her perfect breasts on display, as she looked up at me from under her dark lashes, had me forgetting my own name. All I knew was I wanted her, needed her.

Her eyes heated, and as soon as I was within reach, she lunged for my mouth, kissing me roughly, showing me the force of her need and her frustration. I met her stroke for stroke with my own desperation, flipping her onto her back and pressing myself down on top of her. I pulled my head back as I pinned her body under mine. "Is this okay?" I asked.

"Yes," she moaned, wrapping her legs around my waist, pulling me closer, and catching my mouth again with hers. I pressed deeper, filling her, and she gasped, digging her fingers into my shoulders where she held on to me.

It felt wonderful to be the one in control this time. I was happy to let her take the lead as long as she needed reassurance, but there was something so sweet about her surrendering to me—trusting me. I found myself wanting more, wanting to lose myself in her. It would be so easy, and yet the thought was terrifying too. She was different, unique, possibly addictive, and I knew I needed to keep my head clear. But it was easier said than done.

As I moved inside her, I wanted nothing more than to press my face to her neck and act like the vampire I was. In the times we'd been together, I'd been able to keep from biting her, but it hadn't been easy. The more I was near her, the more I touched her, tasted her skin, smelled the blood just underneath, the more I wanted her. If I took a taste, I wasn't sure I would be able to go back. I concentrated on my breath, the steady rhythm of my hips, and on the feel of her soft skin against mine.

It wasn't long before her breathing grew ragged as she thrust her hips up to meet mine, and she opened her mouth, fangs fully extended. I could feel the moment she was ready, and I bent my neck toward her, hoping to share in her release. She struck hard, and her neck in turn was bared before me. I barely got my arm up in time, sinking my fangs deep into my own flesh, tasting my blood as it filled my mouth, wishing desperately that it was hers.

When we'd had our fill, I rolled onto my back, and she curled herself beside me with her head on my chest, as we both caught our breath. Kate tilted her head and brought her hand up to my neck, touching the spot she'd bitten as she'd come. Her fingertips on the sensitive healing skin sent a ripple of pleasure through my body, and I inhaled sharply.

"Does it feel as good to be bitten as it does to bite?" she asked, still fingering the closed punctures.

It was so distracting that it took me a minute to understand what she'd asked.

"Yes," I groaned. "It does."

She licked her lips. "I think I want to try that sometime," she said breathlessly.

I looked down at her. There was a hunger in her eyes, an excitement. She was serious, but at the same time, she was caught up in the moment, in what we'd just done. "I don't think that's a good idea, Kate," I said, wishing that it weren't true, wanting to call back the words.

The light in her eyes dimmed. "If we were careful, maybe..."

My mind cleared, and my body tensed. "What changed your mind about this? I thought that it scared you," I said, swallowing hard at the thought of what she was offering me.

She put her head back on my chest, hiding her face from me. "It does, a little—okay, more than a little," she admitted. "But I also feel like you're holding back. I want to understand what it's like to be taken that way, when I want it, not when someone's trying to hurt me intentionally."

I shook my head and sighed. "Not with the way I feel right now. Not with how much I want to bite you, want to taste you."

"But that's what I'm talking about," she said, placing her hand flat on my stomach. "I want that. I want you to indulge in those desires the way I do."

My fangs pulsed, and my mouth watered. I swallowed again, trying to clear my mouth as well as my mind. Just thinking of sinking my fangs into Kate nearly brought me to orgasm.

"Kate, I don't know how I'm going to react. You don't know how I'll react. Yes, we've talked about why it might be okay, but this is still new. I don't think rushing this is a good idea," I said, having to force each word out. What I really wanted to do was open my mouth and drink her in.

She went quiet, and her breathing became shaky. I didn't need her abilities to know she was hurting, and it sobered me, reminding me what was important. It was her, who she was, this woman I was growing to love. I would not hurt her.

"Kate," I said. I breathed out heavily, touching her shoulder and urging her up closer to my face. I wanted to kiss her, hold her closer. "Come up here."

She crawled up my body until her head rested just below my chin. I kissed her dark, silky hair, breathing her in. She smelled so good. "But you do still want me? Right?" she asked softly.

I gripped her tighter. "I'm not rejecting you," I said, my lips brushing the top of her head. "I'm trying to keep you safe."

She pulled back and looked up at me. Tears glittered in her eyes, on her lashes, and spilled down her cheeks. Before I could doubt myself, I leaned forward and licked a bright red drop from her skin, holding it on my tongue. She watched with wide eyes as I closed my lips and swallowed. My body shivered as her taste penetrated my senses. It was everything she was—warm rain, the sweet scent of spring flowers, the comfort of old books, and something unnameable, so intoxicating it wiped out all thought.

I opened my eyes, only just realizing they'd been closed. Kate still stared back at me, and I smiled. "You're amazing," I said. "You taste amazing."

"Do you want more?" she asked shyly.

I shook my head. "Still not a good idea," I replied. "But I haven't had my fill of you yet, if you still want me, that is."She nodded, and I kissed the remaining tears from her cheeks as she straddled my hips, savoring every sensation.

When I bit myself the second time, my blood was flavorless and hollow after the taste of hers. I wondered briefly if my blood was as disappointing to Kate as it was to me. Would anything ever taste as good, feel as good as she did to me, I wondered.

It was then that I realized I was already ruined. She was it for me; there really was no going back.

32

KATE

I gripped the seat as Sara and I drove into town. It had been less than a day since I was here in the park, trying to make myself understood and win the local witches to our cause. Going back so soon made me uneasy. Leaving the night before, the way we did, felt like fleeing. And now here I was, voluntarily going back. Luckily, this time there wouldn't be a crowd. It would be easier to use my gift one-on-one or in smaller groups. I was fairly certain I could handle it, but I was also glad I had Sara and Silas with me.

"Where do we start?" I asked as we crossed the river and the first buildings came into view. It looked different during the day, less intimidating.

"Silas and I are meeting with the photographers for the wedding over at the cafe. The same couple that did the pictures for the shop. They are nice, but emblematic of the general attitudes around here. I thought it might be good to see how you do with them, and the other people at the store."

"Store? I thought you said cafe?" I asked, somewhat confused.

"Well, the cafe is inside the General Store, which also functions as a small diner, and where we pick up our mail. It's a one-stop shop for most people in this area. The selection isn't great, but it's convenient if you don't have time to drive into one of the bigger towns. Oh, and it's the only place to get gas," she said.

"Got it," I replied. "I really have done a crappy job of getting to know this place."

"Don't give yourself such a hard time," Silas said from the backseat. "You've only been going out in the daylight for a little while now. You've been adjusting to a lot."

"Thank you, Silas," I said, acknowledging the comment from the usually quiet shifter.

"And you have Bruce, and now Chelsea to run errands," Sara put in.

"That doesn't make me feel better. That just makes me sound spoiled," I said, in a light tone.

"Eh, be spoiled," Sara said. "You've earned it."

"Either way, I'm glad they're both around to help out," I said more seriously. "I like having the house full. Is it wrong that I hope Juno stays too?"

"No," Sara said and smiled at me. "I love her. And I know my aunt, and one blonde vampire, would be happy if she stuck around."

"And if you give us a few months, we might just have room for everyone," Silas said. "By the way, will you and Marcus be sharing a room permanently?" Silas asked. "For planning purposes," he added.

"Ummm, I'm not sure we've given it much thought. It's still a fairly new situation," I said, feeling strange talking about it when Marcus and I had yet to define our relationship or talk about sharing a space together. It was true that I'd spent the last couple of days sleeping in his bed, and I felt welcome there, but it was still his space. I didn't think of it as my own.

My mind drifted to the night before, to the look on Marcus's face when he tasted my tears. Watching him was almost as satisfying as touching him. And, despite my initial fears and his hesitation, I was eager to push further, to have his fangs in me. The thought of it sent a thrill of fear and anticipation down my spine.

"Kate," Sara said, staring at me from the driver's side. "We're here.

You planning on getting out, or you just going to sit there and fantasize about your boyfriend?" She grinned at me, knowingly.

I blinked and looked around. Not only were we parked in front of the café, but Silas was already waiting for us on the sidewalk. "Oh, yeah," I said, hurriedly unbuckling my seatbelt and opening the door.

I had to remind myself to slow down. We had discussed how I should behave in town before the meeting, and I knew the same rules still applied. We all agreed that moving at human speed, or witch speed, was best. No feats of strength. And no hissing, growling, or threatening behavior. Basically, I wasn't supposed to act like a vampire. The goal was to seem normal, friendly, and non-dangerous.

The rain was still falling, but not as hard as the night before. We stepped onto the front porch of the cafe/store/post office/gas station. It was a large, wood-sided building with two big front windows and a bigger front porch crammed with items for sale and signs advertising everything from fishing bait to ice cream. It had a cozy, inviting feel. I hoped that was a good sign.

Silas stepped forward and held the door open for Sara and me, and we went inside. The interior of the building was similar to the outside, but warmer and more cluttered. There was little clear separation between the different areas. On one side, a tall wooden counter lined with stools offered diners a place to sit and enjoy coffee or a soda. A sign on the wall behind the counter designated it as the post office, with about 30 P.O. Boxes. On the other side, there was a checkout counter for shoppers, just behind which were half a dozen round wooden tables and chairs. The back of the shop was filled with shelves stocked with items for sale. All the areas blended together, yet it somehow worked.

There were four people in the shop, not counting the two behind the counters. All of them smelled like witches, but I didn't recognize any of them. Sara went directly to a table where a man and a woman were sitting, drinking coffee. The couple looked up as we approached. They both appeared to be middle-aged, with graying hair and lightly lined faces. They smiled at Sara but then thier smiles froze when they saw me.

Sara turned to me. "This is Kate," she said. "And you already know Silas. Kate, this is Gina and Dale. They are the local photographers I told you about."

The three of us pulled out chairs and sat while the witches just stared back with blank expressions. Gina looked at Dale, blinking, then back at us. "Yes, well. Thank you for meeting us," she began. "We didn't expect… you would bring guests." She tried to smile, but it came out as a pained grimace instead. She clasped her hands in front of her, squeezing them until her knuckles turned white. I didn't need to drop my walls to realize this wasn't going well. "We actually wanted to let you know that we won't be able to shoot your wedding this summer," she finally managed to say. "It's not that we don't want to," she rushed to add. "We do, it's just that things have become a bit political lately." She swallowed and glanced at me. It wasn't necessary. We all understood what she meant.

"I see," Sara said, her tone even but sharp. "And, because of these *politics,* you can't provide your services to a member of the community? Do you have a problem with my housemates or my choice of groom?"

Dale shot a look at Gina, who avoided eye contact with any of us and shook her head. "It's just better if we stay out of it," she said.

"If this is because of me—" I started to say, but Sara cut me off.

"No. It's fine. We will take our business elsewhere," she said.

Sara pushed back from the table and stood. Silas and I took her cue and got to our feet as well.

"If things change…" Gina said, trailing off.

Sara gave the older witch a hard stare. "Things will only change if people like you change them," she said. And with that, we turned to leave.

Before we'd made it to the front of the store, however, the door opened and Elder Theo Coburn entered. He looked flustered, his hair damp and plastered to his head. His eyes found us immediately, and he headed straight for us. "Good afternoon," he said cordially.

I don't know what prompted me to do so, but I pushed my way past Silas and Sara to stand in front of them. The meeting with the photographers was Sara's to handle, but the Elders had made themselves my problem.

"Good afternoon," I replied.

The older man blinked rapidly and tilted his head to look at Sara. He was obviously hoping to deal with her, but I wasn't going to make this easy for him, whatever *this* was. He licked his lips and refocused on me when it became clear he was going to have to talk to the vampire in charge. "Yes," he said. "I was told you were here and I wanted to have a word." He shifted his weight from foot to foot. "I just wanted to let you know that the rain... It's not my doing," he blurted out.

I just stared back at him. "The rain?" I asked.

"Yes, we had an agreement that the pressure campaign would stop. I just wanted you to know that it's not me messing with the weather this time," he said, drawing himself up and regaining a bit of his composure. "I've talked to Diane, and she's promised to stop the lightning strikes and the other... measures. But I am aware that she has allies in the community who are continuing to bring the heavy rain and wind. I've warned them. We're starting to see some minor flooding and pooling water, but she pleads ignorance." He breathed a sigh. "Anyway. I didn't want you to think it was me."

I scowled at him. "You are supposed to be in charge, right?" I said.

He bristled at my question. "I am the elected leader of the Elders gathering, but I don't control them. We make decisions together. We are not a dictatorship."

"Uh-huh," I replied. "Okay, well. It seems like your problem, not mine."

He huffed out a breath. "This is difficult for all of us," he said. "It would be a lot easier if you would accept the inevitable and leave."

"Easier for you, yes. I can see that," I said. "But I'm not here to make things easier for you. I'm just here to live my life."

"Hey," a voice called from behind us. It was one of the other two patrons in the store, a tall woman in her thirties with long red hair and a fierce scowl. "What's your problem?" she said. "They aren't doing anything to you or anyone else. Why are you giving them a hard time?"

At first, I thought she was talking to me, or to our group in general, but as she stepped up beside us, glaring at Elder Coburn, her position became clear.

"Candace. This isn't your business," Coburn said.

"Not my business? You're a community leader, representing me, and I don't agree with what you're saying. I was in the park last night. I heard what the vampire said, and it's clear that Elder Paulson and several others here are misusing their positions of authority. The authority granted to you all by us," she said, her blue eyes flashing in anger. "Many of us have no problem with the vampires in the valley. Considering all this damn rain, they've been better neighbors than you all have recently. Now stop pretending you speak for the rest of us on this matter. This is all of our business. You all made it our business."

Elder Cobun looked like he'd just swallowed a very large toad, and I wondered if anyone had ever spoken to him that way. He opened his mouth to say something, then closed it again. His eyes scanned the four of us standing there, and then he turned and walked out of the shop without saying another word.

I reached out my hand to Candace. "Hi, I'm Kate," I said as she took my hand and shook it. "Thank you for that." I liked the way her emotions felt. She was calm and confident, radiating welcome.

She waved off my comment. "It's my pleasure," she said with a smile. "I've been wanting to give him a piece of my mind for years."

"But still, thank you for saying something. It's nice to know that some people here don't hate us."

She shook her head, causing her long red hair to wave around her shoulders. "There are plenty of us," she said. "Most are just too afraid to stand up to the Elders. The Elders themselves are more of an outdated tradition than anything else. What I said was true; the only reason they have power is because we all buy into it. He claims to be the 'elected leader,' but the only ones voting are other Elders, and they pick themselves. This might not be a dictatorship, but it's definitely not a democracy, that's for sure."

I nodded and smiled at her, inadvertently flashing her my fangs.

Her eyebrows lifted, but her smile remained. "Nice hardware," she said. "Now, if you'll excuse me, my dinner is getting cold, and I'm sure you all have places to be." She surprised me by reaching out and squeezing my arm before turning and going back to her table.

We went back out into the rain and got into Sara's car. "Well, that went both better and worse than I expected," Sara said.

"I'm sorry you have to find another photographer," I said.

"Eh, we'll give them some time," Sara said. "Running into Candace gave me hope for this town. I'd like to think what she said is true and that more people feel the way she does. Gina and Dale aren't bad people, but they need to grow a spine, and it might take seeing others stand up for them to do that."

Silas reached forward from the back seat and put his hand on Sara's shoulder. "Say the word and we'll fly to Vegas for the weekend."

"Ha. My mom would kill us," Sara said, starting the car and backing out onto the road.

The drive home felt more uplifting than the drive there. Despite the encounter with Gina and Dale and the confrontation with Elder Coburn, I still felt hopeful. We needed to reach out to more people like Candace. She seemed really cool, and I thought it would be nice to make friends like her in the valley.

We got back home before dusk. The sun was just starting to slip below the cloud cover, and the sky was lighter than it had been for most of the day. We had a moment of illuminated clouds and an orange sky before the rain started falling harder, and everything was washed in a gloomy late-afternoon haze. I wondered if word of our adventure into town had just reached Diane and her cronies.

I was shaking the rain out of my hair when a low rumble rose up in the distance. It was deep and sounded unlike anything I'd ever heard. I could feel vibrations through the floor, and the rumble turned into a roaring that I was certain even a human could hear.

And then the screaming started.

33

LUCIA

The pot on the stove was simmering nicely, and the warm fragrance of ginger, spearmint, honey, and lemon wafted through the kitchen. The latest batch was for an antiseptic skin tonic. Not only was it popular online, but I'd noticed that Chelsea had red patches on her neck and chest. I also decided to bring her my chamomile-infused witch hazel, in case the recent stress was causing it.

It felt good to do something useful, something proactive. There was nothing I could do about the rain or the stubbornness of the community's Elders, but this I could do. Thinking about the Elders reminded me of the attack on the House, and I felt the familiar fire licking through my veins. I wasn't sure I could ever forgive Ruth and the others for nearly killing my child. And seeing E crushed beneath the heavy chandelier was an image I would never forget. The way her body was bent, and her mouth gaped as she tried to talk. I shivered at the thought.

I stirred the large pot on the stove, trying to clear the picture from my mind. If that didn't work, listening to an audiobook always helped. The rhythmic motion of moving the wooden spoon through the liquid in the pot was soothing. The movement, along with the scent of the tonic, helped to calm my nerves and put me in a better frame of mind. When my sister came in through the kitchen door, shaking out her poncho, I was as close to relaxed as I'd been in days.

"It's no use," Sybil said. "The whole garden is flooded. We're going to lose more than half of what's out there." She hung the bright blue poncho on a peg near the door so the water would drip onto the linoleum entryway instead of the wooden kitchen floor. She smoothed her green apron and its empty front pocket. On a normal day, it would be full of things she'd harvested in her late afternoon garden check. "I'm tempted to march over to Diane's and give her a piece of my mind," she continued. "This is getting ridiculous."

"Come sit. I'll put the kettle on," I said, heading to the sink and filling the battered silver water kettle. After placing it on the stove, I went to the tins on the counter, selected the one with my sister's favorite calming blend, and added two hefty scoops into a teapot. Her teacup was clean and in the drying rack. In just a few minutes, I had everything arranged and steeping before her.

Sybil sighed heavily. "Thank you, sister," she said, pulling the pot toward her and warming her fingers along its sides.

"Cold out?" I asked as I turned off the fire and took a seat across from her at the table.

"Gods yes. Cold and wet and infuriatingly bigoted out there," she huffed.

"Hmm."

"What, you don't agree?" she asked.

"No. I agree with you. I'm just not used to it."

"The rain, or siding against the Elders?"

"Agreeing with you," I said, giving her my best smirk. "But, yes, being on the opposite side from the Elders is a new experience. It feels... I don't know. It feels somehow wrong, and yet I can't go along with what was happening."

Sybil nodded and poured herself a cup of tea. "You've given up then, on your dream?"

Now it was my turn to sigh heavily. "I've thought a lot about it.

And I think I've come to the conclusion that it's not so much that I've given up on it as outgrown the idea."

"Good," Sybil said. "You're too good for them anyway."

"It's not that I'm too good for them," I chided. "It's just what I believe in no longer aligns with the values they uphold. I don't know if my beliefs ever did, actually. I liked the idea of myself as an Elder, a community leader, but it was never right for me. It was a mold I was trying to push myself into."

My sister smiled at me, as if I were telling her a story she'd already read. "I've always known you were too good for them. They aren't what they were when our mother was an Elder. Or maybe, they haven't changed since then. But either way, you're right, you don't belong with them. You belong with us."

"Us," I said. "You and Sara, and the House, I suppose."

"And Juno, and most of the witches who live in this valley," she replied.

"Yeah, that sounds about right," I said. "You hungry? I could cook up something besides product."

"Nah. I'm good for now. Maybe later," she said, and then lifted her head like she was listening for something.

A moment later, I heard it too, or rather, I felt it. It was a rumbling, like a large truck going by on the highway, or a train passing just beside us, vibrating the entire house, coming closer.

And then all hell broke loose.

The rumbling turned into a roar, and the vibrations shifted into the shaking of an earthquake. But it was no earthquake. Sybil and I jumped to our feet as the sounds of cracking trees sounded all around us. "Go for the stairs!" I yelled as the house began to move under our feet. Cabinets flew open and dishes crashed to the floor. We hurried toward the stairs as the windows shattered in their frames and cracks opened up along the kitchen wall.

I tripped several times, not able to keep my feet under me as the floor pitched from side to side. Grabbing the railing of the stairs, I looked ahead to see my sister pulling herself up to the second floor. I crawled after her on my hands and feet, knocking my shoulder painfully against the wall.

I hurried the last bit of the way but stopped on the landing. I looked toward Sara's old room, where my sister had gone, but hesitated. I lunged for my own door across the way.

"Lucia!" my sister shouted.

"I'm coming!" I yelled back as I wrenched open my door and fell to my knees in front of my dresser. As quickly as I could, I pulled out the bottom drawer, grabbed the packet of photos, and stuffed them down the front of my blouse. As the house groaned and rocked, I scrabbled back into the hall and across to the bedroom where my sister waited.

This room was a smart choice. There was only one small window, and although we huddled on the far side of the bed, we could see the world pass by in the late afternoon gloom. It was a surreal sight. Not that I'd ever been in one, but even with adrenaline rushing through my body and fear muddying every thought, I understood what this was. We were caught in a landslide. The sounds we were hearing were a flood of mud, sticks, and dirt plowing into the side of the house.

The shaking and trembling of the house got worse. "Sybbie, stay down," I said as the window shattered, sending shards of glass shooting across the room. I pulled her to the floor behind the mattress and held onto her as we crouched there.

There was a powerful crash that shook the house, and then it wasn't just the world around us that was moving—it was us moving, too. Sybil screamed, and I held her tighter as the house tilted sideways and we toppled onto our sides, still clutching each other. The crashing, creaking, and shaking grew worse until I thought the house would be ripped apart—and us along with it.

A river of mud, rocks, and trees was carrying us away. How long it would last, how far it would carry us, I didn't know. All the while, we held on tight, and I prayed to all the Gods that we would survive. That we would be okay, and I would see my daughter and my niece again. And E, Felix, Kate, and everyone else. It was then that I realized how deeply I loved them all. How much I would miss them.

Then we stopped.

It was abrupt, and it was violent. Sybil and I were tossed back against the bed. There was a moment of hope. Perhaps it was over, and we had come to rest, but I was wrong. We *had* come to rest on something, but the force of the slide continued to batter our poor home. I could hear the water, or mud, rushing beneath us, on the first floor of the house. The home that my parents had built with their own hands shook and creaked around us. I looked up at the ceiling as a giant crack opened up, and as the house crumbled around us and the floor under us dropped, I prayed it would be fast. That death would smile on us and make it quick.

And then everything went black.

34

KATE

I glanced at Silas, who was taking off his coat next to Sara. The two of them were frozen. Silas was looking toward the front door, eyes wide and mouth slightly open. Sara was staring at him, waiting for some sort of explanation as to what he was listening to. He just shook his head and held up a hand as he strained to hear what I did. The roaring had stopped, but the cries of pain were just picking up.

Felix appeared beside me so suddenly, I let out a small yelp. He was wearing a t-shirt and jeans, his hair was wild, he had a thick beard, and he was barefoot. The fact that he hadn't yet shaved spoke of how early it was for the vampires in the house. "Do you hear it?" he asked in a hurried tone.

"Yes. What's happening?" I asked, my panic starting to build as the screams intensified and the shouts of many could be heard from off in the distance. Whatever was happening out there was a massive event.

Felix shook his head. "I'll go see," he said, and then he was gone, the door left hanging open.

"I heard the rumbling," Sara said. "What do you hear now?" Silas lowered his head and whispered to her the sounds the wind carried.

All color drained from her face as she hurriedly started putting her jacket back on. "We have to go now."

"No, wait for Felix," Silas said, still looking toward the open front door. We were joined by Bruce, Chelsea, Juno, and Beth, who'd come in from the shop. "Please, everyone, quiet," he said.

We all stilled, listening. Faintly, but clearly, I heard Felix's voice, calling out to us. "A landslide," he said, his voice strained, and he was panting as if he were lifting or moving heavy objects. "It's bad. We need all the help we can get. Tell the humans and witches to go carefully."

I ran to the doorway and yelled into the gloom, "We're coming." I turned back to the assembled group as Silas was relaying what Felix had said. Everyone looked at me, and I suddenly realized I was in charge. They were waiting for direction, all but Sara. Silas had a hand on her arm, holding her back, but he, too, was waiting to see what I wanted everyone to do.

"Silas, you and Sara go right away," I said, as Sara pulled out of his grip and headed for the door. He nodded and followed after. "Bruce, would you stay here for now? Call emergency services. You and Chelsea can coordinate our movements, as long as the cell phones are working."

"Will do," Bruce said.

I glanced over at Beth, and tears were streaming down her face. "I can't get through to my mom," she said, holding up her cellphone.

"You and Juno head toward the town. Stop as soon as it gets bad, though. We don't want to have to rescue you guys, too, but we'll want you close by. Arrow could be useful," I said, feeling dread at what the statement implied.

"E is downstairs, going crazy," Juno said. "Should I go get her?"

I looked back out the doorway. The sun was still technically up, and the rain had stopped, the sky clearing. There was very little light, however, given the time of day and our position in the valley. "I'll go get her," I said. "If she can withstand the light, I'll send her your way."

Juno and Beth grabbed coats from the closet and headed out to

Beth's car, Arrow following along behind. Chelsea was on the phone with 911, and Bruce had his phone up to his ear. "There's no answer from Lucia's phone. I'm trying Sybil's now," he said, then shook his head. "It's not going through."

"Okay," I said, heading toward the stairs. "I'll be right back."

I hurried down the stairs to my old room. The door was already open, and E had her head poking out. "I heard," she said. Her fine features looked fierce, and instead of worry, her eyes were full of anger. "They did this. Those witches," she said.

"Let's fix it first, then we can lay blame," I said. The muscles of her jaw clenched, but she nodded. "With Felix's blood in you, you might be able to go out. The sun won't set for another thirty minutes or more, but it's not bright out. Do you want to try it?" I asked.

She nodded again and went to the hall door that led to the staircase. She took a deep breath and flung it open, letting the faintest light filter through. "It's not bad," she said. "Let me go check." She zipped upstairs and was back a moment later. "I can stand it," she said. "Are you coming?"

I glanced at Marcus's door. "No. I'm going to try to wake your brother," I said.

E cocked her head at me. "Even if you could wake him up, he wouldn't be able to stand the light. He's not full of Felix's blood like I am."

"No. But we don't have time to wait for the sun to go down. We need all the help we can get," I said, looking at E's confused stare. "We might not need Felix."

She nodded slowly, understanding what I intended. "I'm staying," she said. "Just for a few minutes to make sure you're safe. If he hurt you, he'd never forgive himself."

"Thank you," I said as I opened the door to his room. I glanced back.

"I'll wait here in the hall," E said.

I bit my lip, thinking about how he'd reacted when he'd licked away my tears. "That's probably a good idea," I said.

"And, Kate. Hurry," E added.

I gave a sharp nod and went inside, closing the door behind me. Wasting no time, I headed to the bed where Marcus lay on his back, sleeping like the dead. I shrugged out of my long-sleeve sweater and leaned over him, gripping his shoulders. I shook him gently. "Marcus, wake up," I said. Then more loudly, "Marcus, wake up now." He did not stir. I shook him more firmly, and his eyes twitched.

"You're going to need to slap him," E said from the hall.

"Are you serious?" I asked.

"Just do it," she said. "You're not going to hurt him."

I took a deep breath and then, wincing, I slapped him across the face. The crack made me close my eyes. When I opened them, Marcus was staring back at me, blinking, not quite awake. "Marcus," I said again. "Wake up. You have to wake up. We need you."

The confusion cleared from his eyes, and he pushed himself up as I stepped back. He cocked his head, listening to the crying and shouting I could still hear in the distance, then whipped the covers back. "I hear them," he said, standing up.

I put my hand on his chest to stop him. "You can't go rushing out there," I said. "The sun is still up."

"But we can't wait," he said, his expression growing frantic. "People need our help now. What's happened?"

I quickly explained what we knew and where everyone was at that moment. He grabbed my shoulders and seemed to notice for the first time that I wasn't wearing anything on top except a lace bra. He frowned down at me.

I took his face in my hands, lifting his gaze to meet mine. "If you take my blood, you might be able to go now," I said. "It's your choice, but we don't have time to argue about it. I need to go help."

He looked at me and licked his lips, swallowing, then nodded. Despite the surging desire I felt coming from him, I tilted my head, exposing my throat, but he stepped back, throwing his hands up in front of his face, keeping me out of reach. "No." He shook his head. "Not from your neck. Give me your wrist, if you don't mind," he said.

"Of course," I said, rushing forward, my arm outstretched.

He backed away until he was sitting on the edge of the bed. He took my arm in both hands and then looked up into my eyes. "You sure about this?" he asked. I nodded and pushed my arm closer. "And you said my sister is out in the hall?"

"She is," I assured him. "Now, please. We need to hurry."

35

MARCUS

Kate's bare arm rested in my hands. I looked down at the soft skin, tracing my thumb over the vein in her wrist, and my mouth started to water. Like all vampires, she didn't smell like food; Kate smelled a hundred times better. Since the car ride back from Alexander's months before, I'd fantasized about sinking my teeth into her, tasting her blood, letting it fill my senses with the essence of her. And now I knew what she would taste like. How wonderful it would be. But I'd never imagined my first real taste of her would be like this.

We didn't have much time, and I knew I was stalling. I had to get on with it and see if this would work, but I hesitated. Hesitated because of how badly I wanted it, how much I craved it. I licked my lips, my fangs fully elongated. My body had no reservations about what I intended to do.

"Marcus," Kate said. I looked up, wondering if she'd changed her mind. "You need to hurry." She blinked down at me, her face was serious but not unkind. "I trust you," she said.

Thinking wasn't getting me where I needed to go. I nodded, took a deep breath, and then bit her.

The sound of her gasp made me groan. And, oh Gods, I wished we had the time. I wished we had hours to do it right. I wanted her beneath me. I longed to be inside of her, holding her close, hearing her quick breaths and gentle moans as I tasted her. But she was right, we needed to hurry.

I could still hear the cries in the distance, the churning of rock and earth, and the cracking of trees and buildings. All of it helped keep me focused on the task and the importance of what I was doing. But it was a struggle. Her teardrops were nothing compared to what pumped into my mouth. The velvety taste of her on my tongue was overwhelming, and I growled, my lips pressed against her skin, my fingers digging into her flesh as I tried to pull her closer.

She stroked my hair as I fed. And it was feeding more than it was biting. I nursed at her wrist as if my life depended on it, and it probably did. There was no way I could withstand the rays of the setting sun on my own. Or maybe that was the excuse I told myself as my mouth filled again and again and I swallowed her down, never wanting it to stop.

As I took more and more, a new awareness spread through me. I wasn't sure what it was at first. It felt like an echo inside my head, a thrumming. Then my heart rate increased, and I sensed a thread of fear mixed with satisfaction and a desire I knew all too well. I flicked my gaze up to Kate's and saw those same emotions etched on her face. With a slight shock, I realized it was her I was feeling. Not only was I tasting the very essence of who she was, I was experiencing exactly what she felt.

"You guys doing okay in there?" E's voice sounded from the hall.

"We're just fine," Kate said. "Right?" she said more softly, looking down into my eyes, my mouth still sealed to her skin.

Instead of nodding, I pursed my lips and reluctantly removed my fangs, holding my tongue over the punctures until I could feel the trickle of blood slow and then stop. I pulled back, running my tongue around in my mouth, savoring the last of her before I called out to E. "Kate's going to need some blood," I said. "Please tell Bruce or Chelsea on your way out."

"Got it," E said, sounding more relaxed as she sped off.

"Are you okay?" I asked. She was staring down at me with a

bemused expression on her face, and I could sense how she felt. I could tell she was pleased and feeling a bit smug that it had gone so well. "I can feel you," I said, somewhat shocked.

"I know," she said. "I'm good. And we need to get going, but we are definitely going to be doing this again." She stepped back, giving me a fangy smile, and I could feel her desire. She shook her head and snagged her sweater off the end of the bed. "I wish..."

I nodded mutely—she knew how I felt—and reached for clothing of my own. I covered as much skin as I could, as quickly as I was able, and we were heading out of the room less than a minute later, going for the stairs.

I paused just before reaching the door that led to the illuminated world above. My instincts told me to turn away, warning me of danger, making me recoil, ready to run back to the safety of my room. I shook the feeling away just as Kate took my hand.

"Give it a try. If you can't stand it, if you're burned, I'll heal you," she said.

I swallowed and stepped into the open doorway. There were faint traces of light coming down from above. It looked so foreign. Not at all like electric light or moonlight. The view above was one I'd seen thousands of times, and yet it was nothing I'd seen before.

I walked slowly up the steps, letting the fading sun's rays bathe me in their golden hues. I held my breath, waiting for the searing pain, for the fire to rip across my face and hands. But it didn't come, and I marveled at the fact that I was standing in the sun's light for the first time in almost a hundred years.

"You can breathe," Kate said. "I think if you were going to burn, it would have already happened."

I nodded again, unable to speak, and continued up the last few steps to the foyer. By the time we reached the top, Bruce was waiting for us. He held out a large thermal mug to Kate and handed us both backpacks.

I took mine and looked at the man. "What's this?" I asked. I could feel his anxiety, but he remained calm and steady on the outside.

"Blood," he said. "Enough to get you through whatever you might encounter out there. I figure there will be many wounds to treat. You're going to need a top off eventually. E has one of her own."

I hadn't even thought of it. "Thank you," I said as Kate handed her empty mug back.

"And tell Felix, when you see him, to come home if he needs to. I'll be here," Bruce said. "Remind him, if necessary, that he needs to take care of himself too." He radiated both concern and resolve. I found it interesting that his feelings matched exactly what I saw in the man.

I glanced at Chelsea, who stood just beyond Bruce. Her face was lined with worry, but she seemed calm on the outside. Inside, however, she was a jumble of fear and overwhelm. She wasn't quite losing it—not yet—but she was close.

"Marcus," Kate said sharply as she touched my shoulder. Her impatience drummed through me. "I understand what you're experiencing is new, but you have to focus. We have to go."

"Right, sorry," I said. Before I turned to follow her, I leaned closer to Bruce. "Keep an eye on Chelsea. She's not doing as well as she appears." Bruce's eyebrow rose, but he nodded.

"Marcus," Kate said, standing at the open front door.

"Right," I said, and followed her out into the fading light.

We decided not to take a car. It would just be one more obstacle on the road that could hinder emergency vehicles. We would go faster on foot anyway. In seconds, we'd caught up with E, Juno, Beth, and Arrow. They stood on the roadway next to the bridge that crossed the river and led to the town. Or, more accurately, used to cross the river.

The river was swollen and overflowing, clogged with full-sized trees, mud, and rocks. The force of the debris had taken out one of the bridge's supports, leaving a sizable gap in the center of the bridge. There were no emergency vehicles on the road, and the devastation on the opposite bank was shocking.

Kate stopped just short of the others, and I came up beside her. "Marcus, before we do this, I need to warn you. You are about to come into close contact with people who are hurting and scared. People whose emotions will easily overwhelm you if you let them. You won't be able to shut them out. You'll have to try to ignore what you're feeling. It won't be easy."

"Got it. I'll do my best," I assured her as we joined the others.

"What's the situation?" Kate asked as we came upon the group.

"I was waiting for you guys to help get us across. No sign of Silas and Sara. I imagine they made it over," E said, and I noticed she was wearing a black backpack of her own. Bruce was a Godsend.

"Let me check it out," I said, racing to the bridge and assessing the situation. I went back to the group. "I think we can do it one at a time. The structure on either side of the gap looks okay. Kate, E, why don't you two jump across, and I'll take the others over one at a time?"

They both agreed and headed over together. I watched as E made the leap across the ten-foot gap with ease. Kate hesitated. She was some distance away from me, but I could still feel her fear as she launched herself over to the other side. She landed perfectly, and E pulled her farther from the edge. Both women turned to face the rest of us waiting to help the others.

"Beth, why don't you come with me first. Then I can take Arrow," I said.

Beth stared back at me with wide, fearful eyes but nodded. We walked as far as I dared with her, then I stepped close and lifted her into my arms. As soon as I wrapped an arm around her back, I felt her terror and grief. It hit me like a punch in the gut, and I gasped. It took a moment to get the emotion under control, to not be drowned in it. I adjusted my grip on Beth, then took two large steps and jumped. I landed on bent knees, with Kate and E there to steady me and pull Beth from my arms.

I let go of Beth gratefully and returned to the other side for Arrow. Arrow was crying and whining, clearly upset at being separated from Beth. As I scooped the large German Shepherd into my arms, I was shocked to realize I could sense her emotions, too. She was worried, anxious, but also excited. I whispered calming words to the animal and jumped the distance. As soon as we landed, Arrow's emotions turned to joy and expectation. I released her back to her human and went over again for Juno.

Juno stood there in her black clothes and combat boots, full of grim determination. She looked and felt like a warrior. She was afraid, like everyone was, but she was ready to dig in and get to work. I was glad she was the last to go, and I found that I carried her resolve with me as we jogged off the bridge toward a town that was unrecognizable to me, despite the fact that I'd been there a day before. The closest thing I'd ever seen was Europe at the end of the war. The overwhelming impression was grey-brown rubble.

We heard a muffled human voice and a groan of pain, and Kate and I both rushed over to where a man and woman sat leaning against the side of the closest building. Kate checked in with them, and while they were filthy and bruised, they seemed okay. Felix had apparently pulled them from their car and then sped off to help others. We left them where they were and ventured farther down the road.

We came out to where the main street should have been, but in its place was a river of mud, tree limbs, and pieces of buildings. The tops of cars stuck up from piles near the sides of the road. The "ground" we were looking at was feet above where it should have been, and everything was still shifting and moving around us.

"Everyone, be careful," Kate shouted over the noise of the river behind us and the sound of the landslide in front of us.

"I thought it was over," Juno breathed. "But it's still going on."

"It might keep shifting," Beth said. "A landslide can last for quite a while." It was then that I remembered that she'd trained for search and rescue. She probably knew better than any of us how to handle the situation.

"What is the best way to approach this?" I asked her.

She shook her head. "We are supposed to get away from a landslide, not run toward it. It's not what Arrow and I typically do, but I know that searches don't usually happen until it's deemed safe." She swallowed. "My mom and stepdad live down the river on this side. About a half-mile."

We all looked at the rubble in front of us. At the shifting tree trunks and downed telephone poles. "Okay, E, will you go with Beth toward her parents' place?" Kate said. "Stay on the edge of the slide if you can. Do not put yourselves at risk."

E nodded, but I stopped her before she turned away. "Hey, Sis," I said. "Be careful, please?"

"I will," E said, giving me a wink. The two women and the dog headed off, slowly picking their way through the mess downstream.

"Juno, we're going to want to push through toward the Heartwood home, helping those we can along the way," Kate said, pausing.

Juno looked out over the treacherous landscape. She let out a sigh. "I want to go with you, but I don't want to be a liability. There's nothing I could do that you couldn't do better," she said. Her body trembled as if fighting what she knew was the right choice. "I'll stay here and help whoever I can. Please send people my way as you get them clear, and I'll try to find some water and warm blankets. Maybe the couple over there can help me. At least I know I can manage a fire."

"Thank you, Juno. One of us will come back and let you know when we find your mother safe," Kate promised.

"Thank you," she said, taking another deep breath. I could feel her worry and grief threatening to overwhelm her resolve. Kate stepped forward and placed a hand on her shoulder, and I felt the transformation. Juno's sorrow eased, and her anxiety calmed a bit, replaced with purpose. I'd never witnessed Kate's gift quite like this. It was beautiful, and I was more in awe of her than I'd ever been.

Then Kate turned to me and nodded, and we left Juno there to handle what she could on her own.

36

SARA

The journey was slower than I anticipated. Crossing the bridge was scary and tough, but it was nothing compared to slogging through the muddy, shifting mess that was the town. It seemed like it took Silas and me forever to get from the bridge to where the park should have been. The park was about halfway between the bridge and my family's house. At our current pace, we'd barely make it before dark.

Silas had to help me every step of the way. I knew he could have moved faster if he had shifted and gone alone, but he patiently helped me over every obstacle and through the thick, deep mud. We stopped a few times to help others, but there weren't many people around, and that frightened me more than anything.

Everywhere we looked, nothing was untouched by the disaster. I barely recognized the town I had been visiting and living in my whole life. Trees had been uprooted, cars were buried or on their sides, buildings had been knocked from their foundations, windows were shattered, and water and mud filled every crack and crevice.

I'd tried calling my mom's and my aunt's cellphones on our way to the bridge, but couldn't get through. I told myself it was probably because the lines and cell towers were down, but the deeper we pushed into town, the harder it became to convince myself that the house had escaped the slide.

Looking east, we could see the scar on the mountainside up ahead—the place where the land had given way. There was just too much devastation between us and where the slide had started. My family's home lay somewhere ahead, among all that debris. We'd both seen the bare spot on the mountainside, but said nothing. There was nothing to say. Either my mom and aunt were okay or they weren't; it didn't change our purpose or our drive to get to them.

We continued past the park. The gazebo Kate stood on the night before was crushed by fallen trees and had been pushed out of the park onto what should have been the road. We skirted a tangle of wood and plastic siding to find a group of three people huddled against the side of a brick building. They were so covered in mud that I didn't recognize them at first. I scanned their faces hopefully, but none of them was my mom or my aunt. One person I did know, however.

We increased our pace to reach the group. "Candace," I said. "Are you all okay? Have you seen my family?" I knew these people had other concerns right now, but all I could think about was finding my mom and aunt.

Candace stood up, her long red hair caked with mud. "Sara?" she said, sounding dazed.

"Yes. It's Sara," I replied. I could hear the hope in my voice as I waited for her to answer.

"Sara. I tried. I tried to hold the water back, but there was too much, and it was mixed with heavy earth and stone. I couldn't..." Candace trailed off, staring into the distance. She looked weak and tired. I couldn't imagine the strain of trying to use her gift against a force of nature of this magnitude.

I looked down at the other two witches. One was a woman I recognized as Faith, a Light Witch, and the other was a man named Trevor. He was a Green Witch, like my mom, and a friend of hers.

"Trevor," I said, bending down. "Are you okay? Have you seen my mother?"

He looked up at me, blinking. "Your mother?" he said with the same faraway tone as Candace.

"Yes, Sybil Heartwood. Have you seen her? Or my aunt Lucia?"

He shook his head. "No. I haven't seen them. It's just us," he said ominously. "Only us." He sighed and leaned back against the building, closing his eyes. I noticed one foot was twisted at an unnatural angle. It looked painful. I was wondering what kind of assistance I could offer when Silas touched my arm.

"Sara," Silas said. "It's getting late. We need to keep going."

I nodded. He was right. We needed to get moving. "Candace," I said, getting her attention. "We're going to try to find my family. Stay here, together, and we'll try to send someone to you."

"Okay," Candace replied, seeming more like herself. "Yes, we'll stay here. I don't think Trevor can walk. He's hurt his leg." She rubbed her hands along her arms. "Please hurry. It's getting cold," she added.

We promised we would, and set off toward the Heartwood family home. We hadn't gone far before we encountered more people. Several were badly injured, but there were others there to help. I told the people we passed about Candace and her group, hoping that if they headed in that direction, they would all meet up and be able to help each other. We kept going, determined to reach our destination.

Seeing others lifted my spirits. If those close to the disaster survived, then my mom and aunt could, too. I kept a hold of that thought like a light in the dark. *They would be there,* I told myself. I was convinced that when the house came into view, they would be there on the porch, waiting for help, waiting for us.

We approached my family's property from an angle to avoid the worst of the rushing water and mud, which still made travel impossible in some areas. The light was fading, and I wasn't sure we were in the right place at first. The forest that encircled the house was flattened or just gone altogether. I glanced around, looking for familiar landmarks. There was nothing. No familiar trees. No roadway with marked signs.

No house.

"Silas," I said, my throat tight. "I'm lost, I think. Everything looks wrong." I felt panic rising as I scanned the landscape.

He stepped close and put an arm around me. "No, love. This is the spot," he said, and it was his tone more than his words that chilled me to the bone.

"It can't be," I said. "There's nothing here. It's all just mud and rock. Where is the house?" I kept walking in the direction of where the house should have been, but Silas reached out and caught hold of my arm.

"It's not there, Sara. It's been washed away. If it's still intact, it will be farther down the valley," he said, turning to look west, toward the other end of the valley, downriver.

All I could see was more destruction. More rubble. More mud. And more giant snags of trees. *How could anyone survive being swept away amongst all that?* I shook my head. It all felt so impossible. I was tired, and sore, and sinking in the thick muck underneath me. I sank down onto my knees and began to cry.

Silas touched the top of my head. His fingers stroked my hair briefly, and then he stepped back. I wasn't aware of what he was doing until he touched my shoulder and held out his clothing and boots. "I'm going to go scout it out and find out what's happened. I'll only be a few minutes, but I think it's best if I run ahead. You stay here?"

I nodded and wiped at my face. "Okay," I said, sniffling. "But come back and get me. I don't want to have to try to find you or walk out of here alone."

He squeezed my shoulder harder, then brought his face close to mine. "I will always come back for you," he said. "Never doubt it." He turned and crouched down, placing his hand on the muddy ground; his muscles flexed in his back and shoulders. Then, his whole form seemed to ripple, and he shifted into his wolf. The giant wolf shook his coat and cast his yellow eyes on me. He huffed as if saying goodbye before taking off toward the biggest of the tree snags, due west.

I watched the wolf run across the rocky, tree-filled landscape and marveled at how swiftly he moved over the rough terrain. I hoped he found them, and I prayed to all the Gods I knew that they would be okay. But as I waited there, kneeling in the wet mud, the warmth and hope drained from me.

The sun was setting, and the hazy glow of the afternoon gave way to a deep twilight. I stared at the spot where Silas had disappeared, every little movement catching my eye in the fading light. I waited for what felt like hours, but could only have been minutes. As the sunlight dimmed, I saw small fires flickering in the distance, and it rekindled my hope. Maybe one of those flames was my aunt.

As I started to shiver and wish I'd brought a warmer coat, I caught a glimpse of reflected light. I squinted into the darkness and saw it again. Soon, I could make out a dark form moving fast in my direction. I exhaled in relief. Silas was back. I forced myself to stand, clutching his clothing to my chest to keep it out of the mud. My knees were stiff, and my legs began to shake with the effort of standing after so long in the cold.

Silas shifted back and was talking before he'd even stood up straight. "I found the house," he said, his voice firm and his tone level. "It's in bad shape." My legs trembled harder at his words. He shook as much of the filth from himself as he could before reaching for his clothing. "My wolf is certain they are inside. I shifted some of the wreckage, but didn't spot anyone. I came right back to get you so you could help me. I hope I did right," he said, pulling on his boots and quickly lacing them up.

I nodded, feeling numb in both body and mind. "Yeah, okay," I said, my lips stiff from cold. "Take me to them."

The movement helped warm me, but the darkness slowed me even more than the mud. After stopping for the third time so that Silas could help me get unstuck, he'd finally had enough. "Here," he said. "Climb on my back. I'll carry you."

"Are you sure? It's hard enough to walk without having to carry someone."

"At least I can see where I'm going. It'll be faster. I promise." He bent down, and I put my arms around his neck. I wish I'd had the energy to boost myself up, but I didn't. He hooked his arms around the backs of my thighs and lifted me into place. I clung to him, resting my cheek against his warm back. The closeness was a comfort and overwhelming at the same time. Tears began to flow down my cheeks again, and I buried my face into his jacket and wept.

He turned his face to look over his shoulder. "We're going to do everything we can to get to them. I swear it," he said.

His vow comforted me. I wasn't alone. His strength carried me in more ways than one. No matter what we found when we got to the house, he was with me. I would be okay. Maybe not whole, but okay.

Silas was right. We made better time with him carrying me on his back than if I'd had to walk it by myself. He set me down against a fallen tree, and I got my first look at the house.

It was the Heartwood family home, but not as I'd ever seen it. I recognized it only by the gingerbread trim that jutted up at an angle from the ground. Instead of the tall three-story building I was used to, it had been reduced to a pile of wood and broken glass no more than ten feet high, sticking out of the mud and rocks.

"Silas," I gasped, my voice cracking. I clutched his arm to steady myself as I took it all in. As my eyes swept over the remnants of our family home, I felt an energy build within me. It crackled and sparked, racing up my legs, through my middle, and down each arm. My hair stood on end, and I felt my fatigue fade.

"Ah, Sara," Silas said, getting my attention.

I looked at him, confused at first, and then I saw the blue light arcing from my hand where I touched him. I quickly pulled back. "Sorry," I said, staring down at myself. Blue light raced over my skin and snapped around me. I understood the significance of what was happening, but we didn't have time to stop and marvel over it. "I… Let's get to work," I said.

Silas nodded, looking at me with wide eyes. "Let's start over here," he said, pointing to a spot where the house opened up in a large gash.

We went to the spot and peered in. There was dim light from my gift, but not enough to penetrate into the rubble. I took a deep breath and shouted into the darkness. I called my mother several times, pausing to listen, to give Silas a chance to listen. And then, on the third try, we heard it. A faint cry rose up from somewhere inside, and my gift flared bright with my hope.

37

KATE

Getting to the Heartwood home proved easier said than done. It wasn't the broken landscape slowing us down; instead, it was the dozen or so people we encountered along the way, all of whom needed help. We had the advantage of strength, speed, and our ability to heal their wounds. We couldn't deny them our aid while we had the chance.

The slide was over, and the cries that urged us into action had mostly died out. I hoped it was because of rescue, and not the alternative. As soon as we set off from Juno, however, we heard someone calling for help. We came to a building, the first floor of which was flooded with muck. The person was on the second floor, calling from an upstairs window. The woman's voice carried down to us below. "Hey, you there. We need help," she said, sounding scared.

"Are you alright?" I called up to her. "Is anyone injured?" She leaned out the window, straining to hear us. She appeared unharmed.

"We're okay, but we can't get out. We're trapped up here. The door downstairs is blocked."

I turned to Marcus, and he shrugged. We both went inside and managed to shift the furniture that was shoved against the door. I pushed the mud out of the way and finally got the door open. The woman waited on the other side, standing on the steps with a young girl in her arms. I glanced back at the wreck of a building and the twelve inches of mud.

"Um, I think we are going to have to carry you guys out of here," I said. The woman looked at me skeptically. "We're capable, I assure you." I smiled in a way that was meant to be friendly, and she blanched. *Oh yeah.*

"It's you," she said, and I could feel her fear and repulsion like an oily thing slithering down my center. I tightened my defenses and shut her out.

"Yes," I said, trying to maintain my friendly tone. "We're here to help. We won't hurt you or your little girl. There's a friend of ours, a witch, waiting near the bridge. We can take you to her."

She looked nervously from me to Marcus, but then nodded. "Okay," she said, her voice shaking. "Just so you know, I'm a Storm Witch. I'll fight back if you try anything."

"A Storm Witch?" I asked.

She sighed and held up a hand, balancing her child with the other. Blue electricity sprang up in her hand, dancing around her fingertips.

"Oh, right," I said. "Electricity, my best friend Sara has the same gift." I nodded encouragingly at the young witch and held out my hands. She frowned and clutched her child. "I promise, we're just here to help. Let us help you both."

She leveled a fierce stare at me but handed the child over. The child's fear was like a shuddering wail echoing through me, and I rubbed her back as I settled her in my arms, to comfort us both. Marcus stepped forward and picked the woman up, holding her with one arm around her back and the other under her knees. She reluctantly put her arms around his neck, and we set off for the spot where we'd left Juno.

It took less than a minute for us to find her. She'd moved back toward the bridge and was with the couple we'd encountered first. We dropped the woman and her child off with the three of them and went back to search for more people. It didn't take long.

We made several trips back and forth, dropping off more injured people or those stranded by the slide. The number of people with Juno grew beyond those we assisted, and she informed us that Felix had caught on and was bringing people to her as well. By our third trip, there were nearly twenty witches all huddled together, waiting for rescue from across the river.

We could see emergency lights on the opposite bank, but help still hadn't reached the town. It was just us for now, and even though we could have used more help, the lack of humans let us move quickly and use our abilities to assist those we could without being discovered. So we pushed on, going back for another try to reach Sara and her family.

I'd already had to dip into my backpack for a blood infusion. I hadn't needed to heal anyone myself, but the energy expenditure, along with feeding Marcus, was wearing on me. Marcus, too, had finished about half of what was in his bag, and I suspected that the fading sunlight had something to do with his need to eat.

On this trip, we moved farther into town, heading roughly toward the Heartwoods. We didn't see or hear anyone along the way until we reached a pile of cars that had come to rest against the side of a large rock formation. We peeked inside, checking for anyone who needed help. We didn't see anyone and were about to turn around when I smelled it. Blood. A lot of it. Witch's blood.

"Marcus," I called and ran toward the source of the scent, carried by the gentle breeze. He followed me to a small red car crushed against others. "Hello," I called out. We paused and listened. There was no reply, but I knew someone was inside. I listened more intently, searching for softer sounds. I tuned out the distant river and the creaks and cracks of the surrounding trees. And then I heard it—the soft, rhythmic thumping of a heart.

We carefully pried the door off the crumpled vehicle. There was a man inside. We could only see part of his body, but it was clear that he was gravely injured. Once we'd located exactly where he was, we were able to be more forceful with the surrounding cars, pushing and pulling them out of the way to reach the man beneath it all.

Once the mess was cleared away, we lifted the top of the red car to reveal his injuries. And they were indeed severe. Several of his limbs were at odd angles, which was disturbing, but it was the branch sticking out of his shoulder that was the source of all the blood. As carefully as I could, I scooted into the car beside him, trying to decide how best to help. As I did, his eyes flicked open.

"Hey," I said softly. "We're here to help."

"Help," he repeated, taking a shuddering, painful breath.

"That's right," I said, examining his wound. He'd been impaled by a branch about the size of a broom handle, and from the looks of it, it went clear through, pinning him to his seat. We were going to have to break it off or pull it out in order to get him to safety. I'd heard you were always supposed to leave an impaled object in place, so that was going to be my objective. "Okay, this is going to hurt," I warned him.

He blinked at me and gave a slight nod. *Here goes nothing*, I thought, and grabbed the branch about ten inches from his shoulder with both hands. When I touched it, he winced and started to pant. As quickly and steadily as I could, I snapped the branch in two. The man screamed loudly, which I took as a good sign.

I looked around and saw the other end of the branch sticking out of the back of his seat. I repeated the grabbing and breaking, and the man screamed again, nearly passing out this time. But he was still pinned to the seat.

"Let's try pulling him and the branch off the seat," Marcus suggested. It seemed like our best bet.

I went back around to face the man. "We are going to try to get you free of the car," I said. "But to do that, we have to separate you from the seat."

The man clenched his jaw but nodded again. I smiled back, encouragingly. He wasn't shocked by the teeth, like the woman had been. He'd seen us moving about, seen the way I'd easily broken the thick branch with my bare hands. I gripped his shoulders this time, and Marcus took hold of the branch sticking out of the man's shoulder. "Slow this time," I said to Marcus. "Let's keep an eye on his bleeding."

"Got it," Marcus replied. I counted to three, and we started to pull.

The man let out an earsplitting shriek of pain, and blood began to flow freely from the wound. "Stop," I said to Marcus. "It's not working."

We eased the man back onto the seat. He was still breathing heavily, his eyes closed. "Sir," I said, and his eyes opened again, his stare unfocused from the pain. Blood was still flowing from his shoulder. I looked at his pale face and rolling eyes. I didn't think he had much more blood left. "You're bleeding too much. There isn't time to get a paramedic here. I could heal you, though. If you'll let me. But I can't do that with the branch still in place. We're going to have to pull it out." It wasn't ideal, but I was convinced it was his best chance.

"Heal me," the man said, sounding dazed.

"Yes, I could heal you," I repeated. "Will you consent?" I felt, given the witch's feelings about "Blood Magic," it was best to get his okay first, if he could give it.

"Yes," the man wheezed. "Heal me."

"You got it," I said, glancing up at Marcus. "You take the branch. As soon as it's free of his shoulder, I'll get to work on the healing."

"One more time, on three," Marcus said. On three, he quickly pulled the branch free and tossed it aside.

This time, the man did pass out, and it was probably for the best. I pulled his body to the side, laying him flat across the passenger's seat, and bit my wrist, allowing the blood to flow directly into his shoulder. Just as it had for Bruce months earlier, the wound filled and overflowed. My wrist healed on its own, and when the man's bleeding stopped, I wiped at the shoulder to find only smooth skin.

Satisfied, I examined the rest of him. He had two broken legs and an arm that didn't look right, but no other punctures or lacerations. Marcus picked him up, and we took him back to Juno and the others. He woke up as we arrived, and Marcus set him gently on the ground, mindful of his broken bones. The man breathed easier, but was obviously still in pain. "Thank you," he said, sounding much better than he had before.

"You're very welcome," I said. And then Marcus and I left him there and headed back out.

This time, we were moving in the dark. The sun had set, making it a bit harder to see, but Marcus seemed to regain some energy now that the sun was completely behind the horizon.

We picked up the pace, leaping over downed trees and sliding across the tops of buried cars. We made it most of the way to the Heartwood's property when we caught the sound of a voice calling out. Not cries for help. Not cries of the injured. But the cry of a child for her mother. It was Sara's voice. And it was close.

Both of us turned our heads toward the source of her voice and changed our direction. We rounded a building and were about to move on when a large figure rose in front of us. It was covered from head to toe in mud, hiding all clothing and most features, except for two hazel eyes staring out from a bearded face, reflecting the moonlight above.

"Felix?" I said, hoping it was the vampire.

"Yes," he said. "I assume you're heading for Sara. I'll go with you. I looked for the Heartwoods earlier, but the house was gone, and then I found more witches in need of help."

"The house was gone?" Marcus said.

"Yes. Gone," Felix said, all his usual humor missing from his tone. "Shall we?" He nodded toward the direction of Sara's voice.

We found the Heartwood home far from where it should have been, and in terrible shape. It looked as if someone had held it hundreds of feet in the air and then dropped it. The roof was practically on the ground, the walls were buckled outward, all the windows were broken, and there were gaping holes where pieces were missing entirely.

Off to one side was a faint blue light, and we followed it around to where Sara and Silas stood, looking into one of the large openings in the ruined structure. The destruction was enough to take my breath away, and I was beyond worried for Sybil and Lucia, but as my best friend came into view, I was distracted from all that.

Sara was glowing.

38

LUCIA

My head was pounding, and there was something wrong with my leg. It hurt to breathe, and my hands and feet were cold. So cold. It was dark, and I was lying on my side. It took a moment for me to realize that the upper half of my body was pointed downward, resting below my lower half; my shoulder pressed painfully against something hard, supporting most of my weight. *What the hell had happened? The landslide.* It was slowly coming back to me.

I blinked my eyes open, but the darkness persisted. When I lifted my head, sharp pain shot down my spine and into my legs, making me feel nauseated. I rested my head back down and reached out with one arm, trying to feel what was around me, but nothing made sense, and the motion made my ribs cry out in pain. There was wet fabric, the hard, smooth surface of what was probably furniture, and something soft that felt like... Sybil.

Struggling, I managed to get my other arm out from under my body and reach for my sister. "Sybil," I called out—or tried to. My voice was raspy and too quiet in the close confines. "Sybbie," I said again, but there was no answer. She lay just feet away, turned with her back to me. Fumbling with numb fingers, I located her shoulders and moved up to her head, searching for a pulse in her neck. I struggled to feel anything because of my shaky hands, but she was warm. *Thank the Gods.*

There was a little space around me, but I still couldn't see. I decided to take the risk and summon my gift to get a better idea of our situation. I held my hand out away from myself, careful not to let it get too close to Sybil, and lit a small fire in my palm.

We were wedged into a tight space. The ceiling was no more than a foot above our heads, and we lay on boards that used to be the bedroom floor but seemed to have fallen, because the furniture pressing against my shoulder was a hutch from the dining room below. There didn't seem to be a way out of the small shelter. We were in trouble.

I extinguished the flame and slowly turned, pressing my back against the hutch. I managed to scoot closer to Sybil and wrap an arm around her. She didn't move at my touch, but I could feel her steady breathing. It was the best I could do for now. We were together, and as warm as I could make us without setting the house on fire. Now it was time to get someone's attention.

Turning my head away from Sybil's ear, I yelled as loudly as I could. Sybil didn't even flinch, and for a moment, it stole my breath. I needed to get her help, and I needed it soon. I called out six or seven times, then fell silent, listening. There was nothing but the sounds of the house around us—the creaking of shifting wood and metal, the groan of rock against rock.

I kept calling and listening repeatedly until my voice was gone, along with my hope of rescue. Sybil lay still but breathing in my arms, and I pressed a kiss to the top of her head. My little sister. Ever since I could remember, it was her and me. We'd been through a lot together—losing our parents, the death of Sybil's husband, and my giving up Juno. We'd been there for each other through it all. I was glad we were together in this too. If she was going to die, I wanted to be with her.

Then I heard it.

"Mommmm!" came a voice in the dark. Sara's voice. She had found us. "Mommmm!" she called again, and again, and then silence.

I swallowed, my throat dry, and the air around me stale and thin. "Help," I called back, but my voice sounded so weak, so small. Breathing in deeply, I cried out again. "Sara!" I managed in a wobbly, but loud voice.

"Hold on," I heard in reply.

My body sagged in relief, and I began to shake. Not from the cold, or any injury, but because my body knew I didn't have to hold it all together on my own anymore. Someone was here. Someone would save us. "Sybbie. Sara's here," I breathed into my sister's hair. "You're going to be okay," I murmured to her, and pulled her closer, as if the force of my grip could keep her with me until help arrived.

Luckily, we didn't have to wait long. I knew when I heard the sound of wood being torn apart that Sara had brought help. I felt the boards we lay on shift, and a surge of fear went through me. I sincerely hoped they wouldn't kill us in the process of rescuing us. The next thing I knew, a cool, fresh breeze hit the side of my face, and the feeling of claustrophobia vanished. We were exposed to the night air, and I greedily gulped it in, sucking oxygen into my lungs.

After lying in the dark for who knows how long, the moonlight was bright, a soft blue glow surrounded us, and I could see figures moving toward Sybil and me. I recognized Kate, with Marcus by her side, but it took me longer to figure out who the third figure was. He looked like he had crawled out of a swamp, his long hair and beard matted, and his face smeared with mud. "Hello, dear," Felix said, bending over me to take Sybil from my arms. "I've got her. You're okay."

I'd never been happier to see the cheeky young man. I let out a sob, unable to hold back as relief flooded over me. Then I was in Marcus's arms, and he carried me away from the wreckage of my home. I rested my head against his shoulder until he set me down beside my sister. Felix was bent over her, carefully checking for injury.

I caught sight of Sara.

She stood nearby, Silas at her side, and her gift rippling across every inch of her exposed skin. She was the source of the blue light. It was her amplified gift that I had seen. It wasn't often that our gifts grew in leaps, but it did happen, often under great stress. Looking around, I couldn't imagine a greater stress than this.

Felix sighed, catching my attention, and leaned back on his heels. "It's her head. I'm pretty sure she's got some sort of head injury," he said, and the seriousness of his tone frightened me.

I pushed myself up to sit and nearly fainted from the pain in my ribs. "What do we do?" I asked. I looked around, hoping to see an ambulance nearby or any way to get Sybil to a hospital. But of course, there was nothing. Just the ruin of the town I'd grown up in. I didn't even know where we were. There were no landmarks besides a few dark buildings nearby.

"I could race her out to the waiting humans across the river and hope that they can help," Felix said. "Or..."

"Or?" I asked, not ashamed of the bite in my voice.

"I could feed her," he said. "If I could get some of my blood into her, it would help. It could save her."

"Will she turn?" I asked.

"No," Felix said. "No, I wouldn't give her that much; besides, she would need to be drained first. And, frankly, I'm not even sure it would work on a witch."

"Fine," I said. "Do whatever you need to. Just don't let her die."

Felix looked up at Sara, who was standing over us. The blue crackle of electricity was dying down around her. She nodded sharply. "Do it," she said.

Felix sat down beside my sister and placed her head on his lap, tilting her chin down. Then, parting her lips gently, he brought his wrist first to his own mouth, and then to hers. It was hard to see. I couldn't tell if it was working. I couldn't even tell if any was getting down her throat. "How will we know if it's helping?" I asked.

Felix shook his head. "We should see some change in her soon," he said, withdrawing his wrist.

"You fed E for much longer," I pointed out. "Do you think you should give her more?"

"No. E was already a vampire. It didn't matter how much of my blood she took. Sybil, on the other hand, is mortal and can only have a bit before there would be real… changes."

"What kind of changes?" I asked.

"The kind we couldn't undo," he said, flatly. "If a mouthful doesn't heal her, we can discuss giving her more."

I wondered if his knowledge came from whatever he and Bruce had been doing lately. I'd noticed the man's improved hearing, his increased strength, and how quickly he could move when needed. I was fairly sure Bruce had crossed that line somewhere along the way.

Just as I was about to ask how long we had to wait, Sybil's eyelids fluttered open and she began to cough. Sara crouched down at her mother's other side, grasping her hand. "Mom," she said, and Sybil focused on her daughter. "Mom, hey. How are you feeling?"

Sybil blinked up at Sara and gave her a slow smile. "I'm okay," she rasped. "Where's Lucia?"

"I'm right here," I said.

"Are you okay?" Sybil asked, her voice sounding somewhat normal.

"I'm fine—" I began to reply when Felix interrupted.

"She's got a broken leg, and probably some fractured ribs, given the way she's holding herself," he said.

I scowled at the vampire. "I'm fine," I sniffed. "There's no reason to fuss over me." I looked back at my sister. "How about you? What hurts?"

She took a deep breath and frowned. "Nothing," she said. "I'm tired, really tired, and my throat is dry, but no pain."

Her eyes were clear, and she seemed to be doing better. "Good, but you're going right to Sara's and resting," I said as her eyes began to close. "Felix," I snapped. "What's the matter with her now?"

"Nothing," he said. "She's going to need to sleep. My blood helped her, but it was her body that did the healing. She'll be just fine."

"Would you take her to Sara's place?" I asked the vampire.

"Of course," he replied. "I could use a bit of a pick-me-up myself, and maybe some shoes."

"Shoes?" I looked at his crossed legs, still supporting my sister's head, and realized for the first time that he was barefoot, his long toes just as muddy as the rest of him. "You ran out of the house without shoes on, young man?"

"Yes, I did. It usually wouldn't be a problem, but with all the sharp rocks and debris, I've cut them about a thousand times, and the repeated healing is taking a toll."

I sighed. "Fool," I mumbled. "Take care of her. We'll meet you back at the house."

Felix looked up at Kate and Marcus. "Would one of you see to Lucia's injuries?"

"Sure," Kate said. "We'll take care of it."

I bristled at the idea of drinking vampire blood. It didn't seem necessary. I wasn't that badly injured after all. Felix rose to his feet, careful with Sybil's head, and then scooped her up, taking off into the dark with the speed only a vampire could manage. I turned to Sara. "Are the humans here yet to help? Is Felix likely to run into any of them?"

Sara shook her head. "I don't know. We didn't see anyone on our way."

Kate spoke up then and filled me in on the condition of the bridge, the rallying point for the survivors, the lights she'd seen across the river, and the possibility that the rescuers had already made it across. I nodded. "I'm sure Felix will handle it."

"Okay," Kate said, stepping near and kneeling beside me. "Let's see what we can do about you."

"I'm fine," I said. "I don't need any..."

"Auntie," Sara snapped. "Don't be stubborn or stupid. You can't walk out of here with a broken leg and cracked ribs. One of them will just have to carry you, which is bound to be painful and slow us down. Now drink what Kate's offering so we can be on our way."

"Fine," I said from between clenched jaws. I let out a breath and looked up at Kate. "It's not you. It's just the idea of the thing."

She held up a hand. "I get it. I really do, but Sara's right—you'll feel a lot better. I promise," she said.

I sighed. "Let's get on with it."

Kate bit into her wrist and then held it out to me. I grimaced as I brought my lips to the wound, but did as I was told. It was cold, but not entirely unpleasant. There was a nice flavor, actually, and something sort of comforting about the taste. Kate withdrew her wrist, and I finished swallowing what she'd given me. The taste lingered in my mouth as warmth spread through my body. The ache in my side subsided, and my leg felt noticeably better. The sharp stabbing pain I experienced with each movement had disappeared, and the pins and needles retreated from my fingers and toes. Even the back injury, which I hadn't admitted to, was improved, and the nausea vanished. But it left me exhausted.

"Hey, there. Do you think you can stay awake long enough to walk out of here? Or I could carry you?" Kate asked.

I stood up, testing my healed leg. It would hold, I thought, and standing helped to wash away some of the fatigue. "I'll do. No one's carrying me," I said. "Where do we go now?"

"Back to the bridge where we left Juno and the others we helped. We can decide what to do from there," Kate said.

I took a step and stumbled into the mud. Silas's arm wrapped around me, and I looked up into his yellow eyes. "I've got you," he said.

"Thank you," I said as Sara moved up to my other side, ready to support me if I needed it. I had to hold back tears that threatened to fall. Sybil was alive and safe. My niece and nephew-in-law were with me, and my daughter was waiting for me up ahead. It was going to be okay, I thought. "Kate," I said, suddenly wondering about a detail she'd left out. "How many people were rescued? How many were at the bridge?"

She didn't answer for a moment, and then she said, "Around twenty."

I gasped. *Twenty.* That was less than a quarter of the town.

39

SARA

Silas had his arm around my aunt. She was mostly okay, but walking was difficult. It would have been easier if she'd stopped being so stubborn and let someone carry her, but she insisted on walking. The darkness made it more difficult. There was no light except the moon's glow, at least since my skin had returned to normal.

The light show I put on at the house was a shock. I had only manifested my gift outside of my hands once before. And then, like during the landslide, it was triggered by fear and stress. But it had subsided, and I felt confident enough to hold my aunt's hand as we walked along. The last thing she needed was to be electrocuted on top of everything else that had happened.

While the walk was tough, at least it helped us warm up. Everything was wet and covered in mud. We needed to get to shelter soon and into dry clothes. I looked at what I could see of the ruined town. There were lights from fires in the distance. It was reassuring to see signs of life, but there was a lot of darkness and empty stretches too. I couldn't see all the way to the bridge or the river, but I thought I saw the red and blue glow of emergency vehicles in the distance. It was then, as I was scanning the dim horizon, that I spotted it.

"Silas," I said. "There." I pointed to a spot off to our left, where a faint blue light glowed, not unlike the one my gift made. We all stopped, Kate and Marcus looking to where I pointed as well.

"I see it," Silas said.

"I'll go check it out," Marcus offered. "Be right back." He trotted off in the direction of the light, maneuvering over and around the obstacles along the way. I envied how easy he made it look.

After only a minute or so, Kate lifted her head. "He needs help," she said. "He's found someone."

She took off after him, and I glanced at Silas. "Should we go?"

He listened for a moment, hearing whatever it was I couldn't, and sighed. "Yeah, we'd better," he said. "All of us."

"Well, who is it they've found?" Lucia asked.

"Diane," Silas said. "And she's giving them a hard time."

The three of us headed over. It took us longer than the vampires, and by the time we reached them, it was hard to tell who needed the most help. Diane was lying on the ground, propped up by a fallen telephone pole. She was in rough shape, covered in muck like the rest of us, and bleeding from her head. She was also lit up like a bug zapper—electricity snaking over her entire body—, and she was spoiling for a fight.

"Don't come any closer," she snarled, her eyes fixed on Kate. "I'm warning you."

"Diane," Lucia called. "Why don't you shut up for once?"

I don't know what surprised me more, that my aunt would tell an Elder to shut up, or that Diane actually did.

"What's going on?" I asked, stepping up beside Kate, who had her arms crossed and was scowling down at Diane.

"She's hurt but won't let us help her, even to carry her back to the others," Kate said, not taking her eyes off the old witch.

I turned to Diane, who still had blue traces of electricity wrapped around her like a protective net. "You know this is your fault, right?" I said, my anger growing. "All of this. If you hadn't tried to drive our House out of the valley with the constant harassment, the pouring rain, none of this would have happened." I stepped closer, not afraid of her, and not able to keep a lid on my temper. "My mother almost died because of you. People *are* dead because of you. You and your prejudice and hatred. All because you couldn't stand to have Others in the valley." I pointed at Kate, who was standing behind me. "And now, when you're injured and in need of rescue, you won't even let them help you?"

Diane set her mouth in a thin line, glancing back and forth between Kate and me. I wasn't sure who she hated more at that moment. She still held onto her power and didn't seem willing to budge. I'd had enough of her shit. I reached forward and roughly grabbed her shoulder, letting her gift lash out at me. But instead of experiencing a sizable shock like others might, I latched onto her power and let it flow through me, across my skin, and into my body. Her eyes widened, and she tried to pull away, but I held on firmly, drawing more until the light around her dimmed, and I felt completely filled with the power I had siphoned off. Only then did I let go.

"I'm sure if your positions were reversed, you wouldn't help," I said coldly. "Lucky for you, they are better people than you are. Instead of walking away and letting you bleed to death, they are offering to help you, the person who caused all this in the first place. I wouldn't put up such a fight if I were you. You're not likely to find many allies out here."

The stolen power thrummed and thrashed inside me. I looked down at my hands, which were surrounded by what appeared to be blue flames. Instinctively, I knew it was time to let it go. I stepped aside and extended my palm to the sky, the way I'd seen other Storm Witches do. I felt the gathering energy, the storm raging inside me, searching for its proper home. I gasped at the surge of power as a lightning bolt shot down from a cluster of clouds above, joined by a stream of electricity arcing from my palm.

In that split-second power, unlike anything I'd ever felt, rushed through me. I fed the strike with the energy within, and I could feel myself controlling it. Time froze as I realized I could tell it where to go, direct it, hurl it toward my enemies, or spare those in its path. It belonged to me in that moment.

I forced myself to focus. I just needed to let it go. I needed to send it away, somewhere safe. I concentrated on a point ahead in the dark. A spot I knew was rock and nothing more. My body shuddered as the strike crashed violently to the ground at a safe distance, and time picked back up. The crash was loud and the ground shook around us, but given the damp conditions, I was hopeful it wouldn't cause any damage.

A Storm Witch. That was what witches with my gift were called, but this was the first time I had claimed my gift in that way. The first time I'd felt the power of the storm. My anger mixed with pride, but I didn't have time to marvel at what I'd done. There was work to do, and a stubborn witch to get to safety.

I glanced back at Diane, who was surrounded by Kate, Marcus, my aunt, and my mate. All of them were staring at me with wide eyes. I shrugged and gave Silas a half smile. Focusing back on Diane, I met her with a hard gaze. "You ready to go?"

She drew herself up and took a breath. "Yes," she said, her voice reedy and thin.

"Would you like the leader of the House of Ward to see to your wound?" I offered on Kate's behalf. I just couldn't help but needle the old witch.

Diane frowned, raising her hand to her bleeding head. There was quite a lot of blood, especially considering how small Diane was. But she shook her head. "No. I'll be fine for now," she said.

"Great," Kate said grimly, stepping closer.

"Kate," Marcus said. "Would you like me to handle it?"

Kate snorted. "Nope. If she wants help, she's getting me," Kate said, with a wry, toothy smile. She bent down and lifted the ancient witch very gently into her arms. Despite her snark, Kate was a kind person who wouldn't cause anyone harm if she didn't have to.

With that settled, we continued our trek out of the remnants of the town. I took my place beside my aunt, and Silas and I silently helped her along. She looked up at me when I took her elbow to help her get out of a deep patch of mud. "That was very impressive, what you did back there," she said.

In the dark, I wasn't sure she could see how happy her praise made me. She rarely gave it out freely, and I suddenly felt overwhelmed. "Thank you, Auntie," I said. "It surprised me. I've never done anything like that, but it felt right. The energy... It's hard to explain."

Lucia spun her head sharply back toward me, her eyebrows knitting together. "I'm not talking about the lightning, child. I was talking about the way you stood up to Diane," she said. "Don't get me wrong, your power was extraordinary, but I'm proud of what you said. I'm proud of how you defended your House, your family." She sniffed and looked back into the dark, squinting to see where she was going, heavily relying on Silas's vision to guide her.

I didn't know how to respond. It was so unlike anything I thought I'd ever hear my aunt say. She had always been the one advocating for greater respect for our Elders and holding them in the highest regard. She used to practically bite my head off when I dared to speak badly of any of them, and here she was, praising me for tearing Diane to shreds. "Um, thank you," I said. "She has to know this is her fault. The others will know it too. I imagine that most people will feel the same way. It won't be the last time she gets that lecture, I think."

"You may be right," my aunt said. "Her standing in the community is gone. Or what's left of the community. I can't see how she, Ruth, or anyone who was involved can escape judgment."

"There will be a reckoning, that's for sure," I said.

We fell silent then, each focused on taking one step at a time. Several times during our journey, Silas paused, lifted his head, and his nostrils flared. The first time I asked him what he was smelling in the air, he simply shook his head, and I stopped asking. I'd seen several bodies since we entered the town. At first, I'd gotten closer to check if it was Mom or Lucia, but after seeing the first body, I just couldn't. Silas had checked the rest for me. I wasn't surprised when we reached the gathering point near the bridge, and only about thirty people were there. Some, like Beth, weren't in town when the landslide occurred, but many were lying still in the wreckage, or buried under the collapsed buildings and the tons of mud now covering the town.

Red and Blue flashing lights strobed across those who were huddled together in groups beside the bridge. A temporary patch had been installed over the gap, and emergency personnel had reached the survivors. People were being treated for their wounds, given blankets, and loaded onto backboards to be carried back across to the other side, where vehicles waited to take them to hospitals.

Kate handed Diane over to an EMT to have her head looked at, but the rest of us waved off help. There were plenty of folks who needed it more than we did. I was sure we would be able to warm up and clean off soon enough.

Marcus scanned those that were gathered. "I don't see E or Beth," he said. "I'm going to go see if there is anything I can do."

Kate nodded. "Do you want me to come with you?" she asked.

He shook his head. "No, stay with the others. I don't think it will take long," he said. "I can meet you back at the house if you want."

She was just about to reply when Lucia grabbed my arm. "I don't see Juno either," she said. "You don't think she went back to the house, do you?"

I pulled out my phone, which was damp but still working. It had two signal bars. I texted Bruce, thinking he likely had signal, and it seemed smart to check in. I told him where we all were, that Marcus was heading west to look for E and Beth, and asked how my mom was doing and if he knew where Juno had gone.

He responded immediately. My mom was doing well, with no further signs of head trauma. Felix was still with him, resting up and waiting to see if anyone needed anything. E and Beth had found Beth's parents safe and were slowly making their way to the bridge, and Juno had texted to say she was going with a few others to help some witches who were trapped in the General Store. That had been over thirty minutes before.

I relayed the news, and Marcus took off to go help E and Beth, and the rest of us agreed to go see if we could help at the store. We assumed Juno was still there, since she hadn't texted Bruce back to tell him otherwise.

"Auntie," I said. "Are you sure you don't want to go to my house and wait with Mom? You've been through a lot, and you must be exhausted by now."

She shook her head, but I could tell how tired she was. She was almost falling asleep on her feet. But no one told Lucia what she couldn't do, so she tagged along with us back out into the cold, wet, dark. It didn't take us long to arrive at the shop's location. There were several witches standing around, but no humans yet. As we got closer, I could tell that none of them was Juno, however.

I saw Candace, who was hurriedly talking with two older men. It was obvious before I even reached them that they were arguing about what to do. "Hey," I said, touching Candace on the arm. "What's going on? Have you seen my cousin Juno?" I asked.

"Tall young black woman, with short hair?" she asked. When I nodded, the remaining color drained from her face. "She went in there," Candace said, pointing to the shop. "Just before the roof collapsed."

40

MARCUS

It felt good to get away from the people near the bridge. It was even a relief to distance myself from Kate and the others, although their emotions seemed a bit easier to handle for some reason. Maybe because I knew them, understood them, and was actively trying to help ease some of their fears and worries. There was very little I could do for those at the bridge, however. Many of them had lost everything, and I suspected more than a few had also lost loved ones. The intensity of their suffering was almost unbearable.

I pushed through thick brush and climbed over large rocks along the banks of the muddy river. It was the easiest and most direct way to reach Beth's parents' house, but the going was rough. I glanced at the dark water rushing past. It looked strange to see it so muddy and filled with debris. Usually, the river that separated the town from the other side of the highway where we lived was icy and clear. It was quick-moving and deeper than it appeared, but it was usually a picture-perfect mountain river. Not that night.

Every so often, I called out for E. I suspected they would take a more inland route, and I didn't want to miss them. I was worried, however, that she wouldn't be able to hear me over the ever-increasing noise of the sirens from the emergency vehicles that kept arriving.

The flashing lights illuminated the landscape with a strange, multicolored, strobe-like effect. It was nearly as bright as day to my vampire eyes. The thought took me back just a few hours, when I'd stood in the sun's rays. It still felt surreal. I never thought I'd experience that again. All thanks to Kate. *Kate.*

I still wasn't sure how I felt about what happened at the house. Looking back, it was the right decision—having me take her blood to jump in quickly and help with the rescue effort. But what did it mean for us, for me? Just the thought of what it had been like to taste her like that, to give in to something I'd been craving, was overwhelming. And I wanted more. True, I hadn't felt obsessed or overly distracted in her presence, but it was still a concern. Would it be something I'd be willing to try again? Could I stop myself... if I wanted to?

My thoughts were interrupted by movement in the brush off to my left. I caught the scent of what was causing the disturbance and was unsurprised to see a very muddy, very happy Arrow appear a moment later. "Hey, girl," I said, holding out my hand for her to sniff. But she didn't come any closer. As soon as she saw me, she turned around and ran back the way she came. I followed, able to keep up until Beth, E, Louis, and Maureen came into view.

"What a good girl you are," Beth said to Arrow as she returned to her handler. "We should try you out as an air scent dog." She scratched the German Shepherd behind the ears and patted her side.

As soon as she saw me, E rushed over and wrapped her arms around my neck. Her emotions hit me harder than her weight. Her relief mixed with my own at seeing my sister safe. She pulled back and looked up at me with her clear green eyes. "Did you all find Sybil and Lucia?"

I told her what happened, describing how we found them at the same time Felix did, how he helped save Sybil, and took her back to our house. I told her about rescuing Diane and how Lucia and Sara handled the older witch. Telling it all to E, and knowing now that she and the others were safe, brought a fresh wave of gratitude and relief. It had been a tough night, but it was nearly over.

"How are you doing?" she asked, and I knew she didn't mean physically.

"Okay," I said. "Kate transferred more than her ability to withstand sunlight," I admitted. "Dealing with all the emotions has been a bit overwhelming."

E quickly pulled her arms back and stepped away, breaking all contact between us. I could still sense her emotions, but they weren't as strong. "Sorry," she said. "I should have thought of that."

"No. It's alright. I'm just not used to it," I said. Glancing up, I saw the tired, strained faces of the others. "We should keep going. We're not that far from the bridge and the rescuers. Is everyone okay?"

E nodded. "Yeah, both Louis and Maureen are mostly okay. They were far enough away from the main slide. Their house is filled with mud, however, and is probably a total loss." Louis cringed at E's words, and I imagined he hadn't thought that far ahead yet.

"Mostly okay?" I asked.

"Well, Maureen has a twisted ankle, but she won't let me carry her," E smirked. "She thinks I'm too small."

I smiled back. "I'll see if she'll let a big, strong man carry her," I said, giving E a wink.

"What do you say, Maureen?" I asked over E's head. "Will you let me carry you out of this mess?"

She was leaning on her husband's shoulder, one foot balanced on the toe of her shoe. Looking now, I could see the pain on her face, and I could feel the tired frustration coming from the injured woman. She heaved a sigh. "Sure," she said. "We'll probably go faster if you do. The ankle isn't getting any better as I walk on it."

"Did you offer her a sip to fix the thing?" I asked E quietly.

She scrunched up her face. "No," she said. "It didn't seem like life or death, and I didn't want to go there."

"I get it," I replied, and pat her shoulder on my way over to Maureen.

I picked her up, one arm under her knees, and the other around her back. It didn't allow me to see what was in front of me, as a piggy-back ride would have, but I figured it would be more comfortable for her. E walked in front of us with Beth by her side, and Arrow ranging ahead. Louis stayed next to his wife and me. Maureen's emotions were ebbing from fear and anxiety and tipping into relief and gratitude. It made it easier to hold her in my arms as her emotions began to mix with mine, lightening my mood.

"You know," I said to Maureen. "E there is older than I am. She's my older sister, actually. And when I was first turned, she was much stronger than I was."

"Your sister?" Maureen asked. "By birth? Or..."

"We had the same sire," I explained. "She was turned years before me and could have beaten me in arm wrestling for the first few years. I'm stronger now, but just because of my size, she still heals quicker than I do."

"What does your ability to heal have to do with strength?" she asked.

"Everything, really," I said. "Yes, larger muscles help, but it's the ability to heal quickly from damage that truly matters. Much of our strength comes from our muscles not giving out, tearing, or rupturing completely. Our bodies repair any damage we sustain, allowing us to push beyond what a human normally could. It's the healing process that tires us out and makes us slow, not the tissue damage, lack of oxygen, or energy for our muscles. We don't even really need to breathe; we just do it out of habit."

Maureen shook her head. "That's incredible. But why does E heal faster than you?"

"It's her age. The older we are, the faster we heal, the more efficient our blood, and the less we need to eat. It's what allows the very old to withstand the sun for short periods. It's not that they aren't affected, it's that they heal so fast that they don't burn up."

"Huh. So what you're saying is, E could have easily carried me this whole time?" she said.

Absolutely," I replied. "She may have struggled a bit to keep your longer legs off the ground—since she's so short—but it wouldn't have strained her in any way."

"Hey," E protested. "I heard that."

"She has better hearing than I do, too," I said to Maureen.

Maureen chuckled. "You two do seem like siblings." She paused, then asked, "So what explains Kate?"

It was my turn to chuckle. "Nothing explains Kate," I said. "Or at least nothing related to vampires. She's one of us, yes, but she's something else, too. She and Felix are still trying to figure that out. She basically seems like a very old vampire, even though she's less than a year old."

"I see," she replied. "Well, I'm glad you all were here to help everyone. E told me a bit about what she saw on her way to find us. This would have been much worse without your aid."

"That's one way to look at it," I said. "Of course, if we hadn't been in the valley in the first place, Diane and her friends wouldn't have done this. They wouldn't have been trying to push us to act out with all the rain, and there never would have been a landslide."

"No," Louis said, trudging along beside us. "This was in no way the vampires' fault. It was the witches who caused the rain. The witches used their gifts to lash out at you, and it came back to bite us all in the ass."

"Thank you for saying so," I replied. "But no matter who is at fault, it's the community at large that was hurt, and it's going to take a long time to rebuild and heal from this. I can only speak for myself, but whoever needs it will have my help. I believe the rest of the House is going to feel the same way. We want to be good neighbors. We want to do what we can."

"That's very generous, considering what the witches have done to you and yours," Maureen said.

"It wasn't all the witches. And even if it were, they never meant for this to happen," I said.

Louis shook his head. "I tried to push the rain back, from the very beginning. It was too much for any one witch. And when the landslide started, you could have had every Earth and Water Witch in town lined up trying to help, and they wouldn't have been able to stop it."

"I believe it," I said. "I've seen where it was the worst. The trees and buildings were flattened or pushed off their foundations completely."

We were all quiet then as we slowly made our way toward the bridge. It was obvious that, no matter how long it took for the town to recover, it would never be the same here in the valley. The community, like the mountainside, would bear scars and would take generations to heal.

When we reached the knot of rescue workers and those being treated, I placed Maureen on the ground, and she was seen to by a paramedic. Louis stayed with her, and E and I looked around for the others. I scanned the faces and listened as best I could, but there was no sign of Kate, Silas, or the witches. I pulled out my cell and texted Bruce. Within seconds, I got my answer. Bruce texted to ask if we needed Felix, who was still resting, and I told him we'd let him know. E and I headed for the General Store, but Beth chose to stay with her parents and make sure they were okay.

E and I moved as quickly as we dared. The humans had gone deeper into the town, searching for those in need of help, and their presence meant we were basically hobbled, forced to move at an unnaturally slow pace. It was frustrating, but I was glad there were more hands available to help those who needed it. There was only so much four vampires could do.

We found what was left of the General Store, surrounded by people trying to help. There was a mix of witches and human rescuers, and E and I approached cautiously. We saw Sara off to one side, her eyes fixed on the destroyed building. She had her hand up to her mouth, and tears welled in her eyes. I didn't need my new sense to tell that something was wrong. It worried me that she was the only one we could see, and the direction of her gaze didn't bode well.

E and I worked our way around the others, who seemed to be forming a plan to try to reach those trapped in the building. I came up beside Sara and touched her on the shoulder to get her attention. Her fear and anguish flared inside me. "Where is everyone?" I asked, afraid of what the answer would be.

She swallowed and turned to face me. "They went in after Juno. Juno was in there trying to help others when the roof came down." She glanced back at the building as a loud creaking sounded, and a portion of the roof dropped another couple of inches. Several people let out cries of alarm, but no noise came from within the structure itself.

"I haven't seen them since they went in," Sara said. "I don't know what's going on in there, but I promised Silas I would stay out here." She squeezed her hands together, and I suspected she was trying hard not to call on her gift. Having seen her earlier reaction to fear and stress, I imagined it was a difficult task.

I closed my eyes and listened, straining my ears. There was so much other noise. It was hard to hear anything. "E," I asked. "Can you hear them?"

My sister's eyes unfocused as she stared off into nothing, listening intently. "I hear them," she whispered to the two of us. "They found Juno." E's nostrils flared, and tears flooded her eyes. She blinked rapidly. "She's hurt." E's head whipped back and forth as she scanned the wreckage. "I have to get in there," she said. "She needs me."

I grabbed hold of E's arm, stopping her. "Look around, E. There are humans everywhere. You can't tear your way in there without causing a scene. Whatever help you could offer, Kate can provide. Give them time."

E shook her head. "No, you don't understand," E choked. "Juno's dying."

41

KATE

Lucia had her cellphone out, with the light pointed toward Juno. There was no light without it, and none of us could have seen the extent of what we were dealing with if she hadn't held it up. And what we could see filled me with despair.

The entire structure had tilted, pushed by the landslide, and the heavy timbers supporting the roof had come crashing down. We managed to squeeze through the partially blocked back door into the building. Just after we entered, the rafters that had given way shifted and completely blocked our retreat. We crawled on our hands and knees, over groceries, broken glass, and mud—always the mud. Silas led the way, followed by Lucia, and I brought up the rear. It was dark, with Lucia's cell phone as our only light as we made our way deeper into the building.

We had tried to keep her out, but Lucia wouldn't hear of it. Nothing was going to stop Lucia from going in after her daughter. She called out for Juno several times when we entered, but there was no answer. When Silas told us to follow him, she asked how he knew the way. He didn't reply, and I didn't tell her he was following the scent of fresh blood.

The first body we found was that of a young man. He was already dead, crushed by the falling timbers. He lay face down in the mud, unmoving and broken.

We kept going. The progress was slow, and the building around us groaned and shook. Silas had to clear away several pieces of debris so we could continue toward the scent. It was witch's blood I was smelling. Unlike human blood, there was a strong astringent scent that I'd come to associate with witches. When we reached the spot where it was strongest, there was enough room to stand and for Lucia to shine her light over the fallen timbers and muck-covered shelving that lay on its side.

That's when we saw Juno.

She was pinned under a large beam, lying on her back with her head and shoulders out of the mud, supported by the table she had fallen on. She looked peaceful, her eyes closed as if sleeping. There were no visible injuries, but her color was wrong, and the scent of her blood hung heavy in the air. Looking closer, it was clear that the lower half of Juno's body was bent at an unnatural angle; her spine had to be broken.

Lucia let out a cry of grief and pushed past Silas to reach her child. "Juno," she sobbed as she got to her daughter's side and collapsed into the mud next to her. Lucia reached out and touched her face, leaving a streak of mud on Juno's brow. Lucia turned to me. "You have to help her," she cried.

I nodded, the lump in my throat too large to speak around. I moved to Juno's other side and leaned in close. "Her heart's still beating," I said. "It's fast, but faint." I'd never heard a heart sound like that before, except maybe when Bruce had been wounded. I shuddered to think of what it had taken to help him. There was no one obvious wound I could treat in Juno's case.

"Heal her," Lucia gasped. "You have to heal her."

Silas examined the beam lying on top of Juno. "I could lift this," he said. "Enough to pull her out."

I crouched down to examine what I could see of Juno's body

beneath it. Her back was bent at nearly a ninety-degree angle, her legs fully under the beam. There was a large amount of blood mixed into the mud that surrounded her. She was bleeding from somewhere. "Don't move it yet," I said. "She'll bleed out before she has a chance to heal." I moved back up to her face. Her skin looked too washed out, too blue. She'd lost a lot of blood. I knew there were lacerations I couldn't see, but even if I could, it wouldn't put the blood back in her body. Feeding her some of my blood seemed like the best option. "First, we have to get her to drink," I said.

"Juno," Lucia said loudly, patting Juno's cheek with one hand and holding her phone's light up with the other. There was still no response from Juno. Lucia laid her cellphone down next to Juno's head, pointing it up to illuminate the area, and then refocused on her child. "You gotta wake up, baby." Lucia gripped Juno's shoulder and patted her again, more firmly. Her eyelids fluttered. Slowly, Juno opened her eyes. As she came to, her breathing shifted from shallow, steady breaths to rapid panting. She gasped like she couldn't get enough air. I knew this wasn't a good sign.

"Juno," I said, moving my face into her line of sight. "You're badly injured. I can help, but you're going to have to take some of my blood. Do you understand? I'm going to need you to drink."

Juno's eyes widened as she gasped, darting her gaze between her mother and me. "Yes," she groaned on an exhale.

Right, I wasn't going to wait for any more confirmation. She needed help right away. I bit my wrist and quickly brought the wound to Juno's lips. She sealed her mouth over my skin and kept taking sharp breaths through her nose. I had my walls in place, but through our contact, I could feel her emotions. She was scared, so very scared, but also resigned. She wasn't convinced I could actually help her. She was struggling to breathe and deal with what was in her mouth, but she managed to swallow. I pulled my wrist back after I judged she'd had about a mouthful.

We all watched, looking for any sign of change. Her body still looked badly hurt, but I hoped the blood would help ease her pain and stabilize her enough so we could remove the beam and get her to safety. She kept gasping, and while the sound of her heartbeat seemed stronger, it was still pounding just as fast as before.

"It's not working," Lucia said, her voice frantic. "Why isn't it working?"

"I don't know," I said. "It's possible she's lost too much blood. I don't know."

"Give her more," Lucia said. "She needs more."

I shook my head. "I don't know if I should. Felix said it was dangerous. There could be changes, or it might not work at all. I don't know what to do," I admitted. I was scared. I didn't want Juno to die, but I had no idea what it would take to save her. "Silas, call Felix," I said. I needed advice.

As Silas pulled out his phone and started to dial, Lucia grabbed my hand, squeezing hard. "Don't let her die. Please, Kate. Don't let my baby die." Her eyes were pleading, cutting through my panic and refocusing me on Juno.

She didn't look any better. She was panting, but her breaths were slowing, and her heart was starting to stutter in its rhythm. As I considered what to do, Silas was briefing Felix on what we were dealing with, and then his voice came over the speaker on Silas's phone. "Kate, you're going to need to give her a lot more," he said. "Like I did with E, when she was injured."

"Can I safely do that?" I asked, my voice shaking as I listened to the erratic heartbeat in Juno's chest.

"You're going to have to," Felix said. "You're not old enough to turn her, but there could be some changes. Let her know if you can. I'm on my way. I should be there in just a few minutes." The phone went dead, and I was on my own again.

"Juno," I said loudly. "Did you hear Felix? Can you drink a bit more for me?"

Her lips moved, but no sound escaped. Lucia's grip on my arm tightened, her nails digging in sharply. I had to act; we were losing her. I bit my wrist again, holding the skin apart with my free hand

and pressing my wrist to Juno's mouth for a second time. She parted her lips, and I took that as consent.

At first, the blood only pooled in her mouth, and I was afraid we were too late. If she couldn't swallow, I didn't know what to do. But then I felt it. Her throat moved, and her lips latched on. And then she wasn't just swallowing, she was sucking, drawing in large mouthfuls.

I sighed with relief. She was getting stronger with each swallow. "Silas, remove the beam," I said. "Lucia, I want to keep feeding her, and I need you to straighten out her spine, like we did with E when she was healing."

Lucia nodded and jumped to her feet, ready to move as soon as the beam was lifted away. I kept my focus on Juno, watching her eyes regain their focus and the color slowly creep back into her cheeks and lips. By the time I looked down toward the rest of her, the beam was gone, and Lucia had positioned Juno's body back into perfect alignment. "Her wounds are closing," Lucia said to me.

I pulled back my wrist, and Juno sighed, her face softening. But then her whole body jerked, and she let out a howl of pain as she started thrashing around, her legs and arms twitching.

"What is it?" Lucia cried, struggling to hold Juno down.

"I don't know," I said, hoping that Felix would hurry up and get there. Just as I was going to suggest we call him back, Juno's thrashing ceased, and she lay still, unmoving.

"She's not breathing," Lucia said, panic clear in her voice. She leapt forward, placing her hands on Juno's chest and starting compressions.

I shook my head. "I don't know what happened. I don't know what I did wrong," I said, my voice cracking. "She was getting better."

Silas put his hand on my shoulder, his steady encouragement flowing from his touch. "You did all you could," he said.

Just then, we heard a noise behind us, and the groaning and creaking of the building grew louder. I braced myself for more of the roof to shift. I was ready to bear as much weight as I could to protect the others. Silas must have been thinking the same, because he moved closer to Lucia, who was still trying to revive Juno, and looked upward at the pieces of roofing still hanging precariously overhead.

Movement caught my eye from the darkness, and then the head and shoulders of a familiar vampire came into view. Felix pushed himself through the same opening we'd come through and stood up, followed closely by E. As soon as she saw what was happening, E rushed over to Juno's side, a soft moan escaping her lips.

I turned to Felix. "I did what you said. I gave her more, but..." I glanced back toward where Juno still lay, E having taken over for Lucia, who sat blank-faced, staring at her daughter.

Felix approached and put his hand on E's shoulder. "Hold a minute," he said. E jerked her head up, her face stained with bloody tears, but she paused long enough for us to confirm what I feared. Juno's heart was not beating. Felix shook his head, and Lucia let out a sob, followed by a cry from E.

"No, no. You have to help her," Lucia said to Felix. "You can do it. You have to try."

Felix crouched down next to Lucia and placed his long-fingered hand on top of hers. "Her heart isn't beating. There is nothing I can do once the heart has stopped."

Lucia shook her head violently. "No. We just have to keep trying. She's not gone. We can't give up," she cried. "We have to... We have to..." She reached out with her free hand and touched Juno's hair. "She's got to be okay," she whispered. Felix put an arm around her and gathered her to him. She turned into his chest and let him hold her as she cried.

E sat motionless, looking down at Juno's face. "She looks peaceful," she said, the tears still running down her face and dripping off her chin.

I stepped up beside her and held out my hand. She took it and stood, gripping tightly, not letting go. She was emotionally wrecked, almost numb. I moved closer until the side of my body pressed against hers, sending warmth and comfort her way as best I could. I too was feeling wrecked. E sighed, looked up at me, and gave a small smile.

The building let out another loud groan, reminding us where we were. "We should get out of here," Silas said, taking a step toward Juno's body.

Lucia looked up, her face a mask of grief. "We can't leave her," she said.

"Of course not," Silas said. "I've got her." He bent down and scooped Juno into his arms as carefully as if she were merely sleeping and he was trying not to wake her.

Felix pulled Lucia to her feet. "I was able to distract the humans outside by telling them I saw movement on the opposite side of the building. They're digging over there for now, but I'm not sure for how long. Marcus is out front with them, and Sara will alert us if any of them wander around back. I can lead us out the way we came in."

I glanced toward the front of the building. We couldn't see it from where we stood, but I did hear the noise of rescuers working in that direction. "Is there anyone left in here?" I asked as I strained to listen.

Felix shook his head. "No, there's no one. But there's no way to explain to the humans how we would know that. They are going to have to discover it for themselves."

I nodded as Felix turned to the hole he and E had climbed out of. It was not going to be an easy trip back out, I thought, especially with Juno's body in tow. And it wasn't. We had to crawl and carefully move her along with us, using as much care as we could. Lucia wanted to be right beside her daughter, but we convinced her to follow directly behind Felix and let Silas, E, and me handle her. She reluctantly agreed.

It took us more than half an hour to clear the building. We stepped back out into the cold night air, feeling relieved despite the heavy atmosphere. It was good to be away from the ruined building and know that no one else would be hurt by it.

Sara waited for us in the cold. By the time I came out of the building, she was holding Lucia and offering comfort. The two women clung to each other and were joined by E as Silas and I eased Juno's body from the collapsed building. Silas picked her back up and stepped closer to the group. Sara lifted her head and locked eyes with her mate, tears streaming down her face. Then she lowered her gaze to Juno, and her brow furrowed.

Sara withdrew from Lucia's embrace and slowly moved toward where Silas was holding Juno. Gently, she rested the back of her hand on Juno's cheek. Her eyes darted back up to Silas, wide with emotion. A shudder escaped her as she exhaled softly.

"She's still here," she breathed.

42

LUCIA

My breath hitched in my throat. Sara's words echoed in my mind, but didn't register. "*She's still here.*" What did that mean? What was she saying? I hurried to Sara's side, my eyes fixed on Juno's body still draped in Silas's arms. Was she moving? Did we miss something?

Kate grabbed Sara's arm. "What do you feel?" she asked, the hope in her voice mirroring my own.

"She's still here. Her energy. It's what I felt when I saw your body in the morgue. You felt like this," Sara said, pointing to Juno.

Felix moved next to Sara to look at Juno, just as Marcus approached from around the corner of the building, heading straight for Kate. "We have to move," Marcus said. "The humans are searching for another way in."

"Let me take her," Felix said. "I pushed a tree across the river and came over that way. I'll take her back to the house with me so we can avoid the humans around the bridge. You all can go to the bridge, and we'll meet back at the house."

"Wait," I cried, moving toward my daughter. "If she's still alive, we need to get her help." I looked back and forth between Felix and Kate, but both of them stayed silent.

Felix reached out and touched my shoulder. "Lucia, her heart hasn't beat in over thirty minutes. Her body is cold. She's no longer alive."

"But Sara said she's still here," I pleaded. "There has to be a way."

"Everything that can be done has," he said. "Now we have to wait and see."

"See what?" I said, not understanding what he was telling me.

"See if she wakes up," he said. "If Kate was able to turn her."

My mouth hung open. Juno was a witch, and Kate was newly turned. How was that even possible?

I shook my head and started to ask, but Felix interrupted me. "We have to move. Give her to me," he said, taking Juno from Silas.

"I'm coming with you," E said to Felix.

"We'll meet you back at home, unless we find more people in need of rescue along the way," Kate said.

Felix shook his head. "There is little else we can do tonight for the community. Everyone that could be saved has, as far as I can tell."

"In that case, we'll check with Beth and her parents and be along as soon as we can," Kate said.

It tore at my heart to watch Felix and E speed off with Juno. I wanted to insist that I go with her, but I knew I'd just slow them down. As they disappeared into the dark night, the human searchers reached the spot where we stood. Kate pointed out the small entrance into the building, and they got to work looking for any more survivors as we slipped away.

We walked back the way we'd come. The exhaustion brought on by all that had happened was finally catching up with me. My legs felt heavy, and my head swam with the need to lie down and rest.

Just when I thought I wasn't going to be able to go much farther, Kate slipped her arm around my waist. "Lean on me a bit," she said. "I'd pick you up, but it would look strange to the humans up ahead."

I lifted my head to see that we were almost at the bridge as I gratefully sagged against her. She practically held me off the ground; she was so strong. *Could she really have done it?* I wondered. *Did she save my girl?* I would have given anything at the moment to have Juno back, anything.

My thoughts were only of Juno as we approached the group of witches being treated for injuries by the human emergency workers. I almost missed it as someone called out my name. If Kate hadn't stopped, I would have gone past the knot of survivors without a second thought.

"Lucia," came a familiar voice.

I turned my head to see Elder Theo Coburn striding toward us. "Theo," I said. "I don't have time. I need to..." I trailed off. I couldn't get the words out. I needed to go wait by the bedside of my dead child, but how did you explain such things?

"I understand," he said, not understanding at all. "I was just wondering when we could get together to discuss what happened, and what we do next."

I scowled at him, not able to process what he was asking. I wasn't in charge. I had no obligations to help this man figure out what we should all do next. Then I lifted my gaze over his shoulder to the rest of the witches gathered together. They were all looking at us. Looking at me. "How many?" I asked. "How many survived?"

"A little more than half," he said, dropping his gaze to the ground. "Those who are here, behind me, don't feel comfortable with the current leadership. They've asked me to come talk to you, invite you to stand for them."

"Have they?" I asked. It was unexpected, but I understood why they wouldn't have much faith in the Elders, since it was a group of Elders who caused this disaster. "Fine," I said. "I'll meet you tomorrow afternoon. Come to our shop. We can talk there."

He nodded and went back to the small group of survivors, his tail between his legs.

A little more than half. The anger that had been building in my veins all night threatened to boil over. How could this have happened? How did we even begin to move on as a community after this? I wondered.

"Are you ready to go?" Kate asked, startling me out of my thoughts.

"Oh, yes," I said, as the others stepped up beside us. Beth was there with her parents, her mother's ankle in a splint.

"We checked in with the emergency responders," Sara said. "To make sure we were accounted for. We're free to go home now."

I looked at her. Going home was going to be harder for some of us than for others, I thought. However, I understood what she meant, and I was eager to visit Juno to see how she was doing and to check if anything had changed. "Let's go," I said, my anger draining out with the last of my strength. Kate caught me, and Silas stepped in and picked me up. We started toward the patched bridge together, and I fell asleep somewhere in the middle of the crossing.

When I opened my eyes again, I was in a car heading down the familiar road to Sara's house. Apparently, the car Beth and Juno arrived in was blocked by emergency vehicles, but the group had found Bruce and Chelsea waiting with cars just past the blockade of trucks and ambulances. Felix had sent them, knowing that the walk home would be difficult for several of us.

I was in the passenger's seat, Bruce was at the wheel, and behind us were Kate and Marcus. I pushed myself up straighter, slightly embarrassed that I was tucked into the car without waking, like an overly sleepy child. "I'm sorry, I just can't seem to stay awake," I said.

"I'm impressed you're as alert as you are," Marcus said. "After a healing like that, a human would typically sleep for an entire day or more."

"I'm not human," I reminded him. "And neither is Juno." I paused and then asked what had been on my mind ever since Sara had declared that Juno wasn't gone. "Will it work? On a witch, I mean?"

Marcus shook his head. "I have no idea. Kate shouldn't be able to turn anyone—witch or human—but then again, she shouldn't be able to walk in daylight either. Just because I've never heard of a witch being turned doesn't mean that Kate can't do it." He was holding Kate's hand, and the way he looked at her made me hopeful. He believed. He had faith in her. I would have to do the same.

As we drew nearer to the house, my exhaustion faded and was replaced with a nervous excitement. I was out of the car before it came to a complete stop, taking the stairs two at a time. The door was unlocked, as usual, and I let myself in, heading directly for the stairs to the lower level, where I figured they would have taken Juno.

I was right. By the time I reached the bottom of the steps, Felix was coming out of E's room. "There's been no change," he said, anticipating my question. "We won't know if she survives the change until tomorrow at sunset. Either she wakes or she doesn't."

I looked up at him without speaking. I wanted more reassurance than that. I needed to see her for myself. I pushed past him and went into the small bedroom. Juno was clean and tucked into E's bed. E was in the bathroom, and the shower was running.

I went over to my daughter. She didn't look dead. Now that I could see her in the light, I could tell her color and muscle tone weren't those of the dead. I touched her hand resting on the covers. She was cold, but not as cold as she'd been outside. I clasped her hand and sank down beside the bed, resting my head against the mattress. My energy had once again left me, and I wasn't sure I wouldn't fall asleep right where I sat.

"Do you regret it?" E's voice came softly from the doorway to the bathroom. I glanced up over the side of the bed. She was wrapped in a robe three sizes too big, with a towel around her hair.

"Regret what?" I asked, wondering if I was just too tired to understand the question.

"That Kate tried to help her and might have turned her?" E said, her tone soft and almost afraid.

I lowered my brow. "Do I regret that my child might become a vampire instead of dying?" I asked.

E nodded, her eyes full of worry.

"No," I said. "Don't be ridiculous. I don't care what she comes back as, as long as she comes back." I sniffed. How could a mother feel any different? I blinked, and E's arms were around me. The movement was so quick I had to stop myself from yelping in surprise. I patted her shoulder. "She's going to be alright," I said with more confidence than I felt. "We Heartwoods are a tough bunch. She'll get through this."

E pulled back and nodded, red tears in her eyes. "I'm glad you're not angry. It's going to be hard enough for her when she wakes up. She'll need our support."

E's words made me pause. Amid all my grief, worry, and even hope, I hadn't stopped to consider what this would mean for Juno. Would she feel the same way I did? Would she think that getting her back was worth any cost? Would she regret it? I wondered. We would cross that bridge when we came to it.

"If you want to get cleaned up, there are fresh towels left in the bathroom," E said.

I looked down at myself. My clothes were unrecognizable. The green of the fabric was now completely brown with dried mud, and ripped in several places. My pant legs were several shades darker than the muddy top, and I suspected it was blood. Juno's blood. "I don't have anything to change into," I said, glancing back up.

"I'm sure Kate wouldn't mind if you borrowed something," E said with a smile. "You two are about the same size, I would bet." She walked over to the closet, pulled out a pair of jeans, a T-shirt, and a grey sweatshirt, and then handed them to me.

She was right. It would be good to wash and get out of the dirty clothes. I shut myself in the bathroom and faced the large pile of Juno and E's soiled clothing that lay in the corner of the room. Staring down at the mess, I was suddenly overwhelmed by what we'd all been through. I hurriedly turned on the shower and got in before it fully warmed up, and let it all go. As I sobbed, I watched the water at my feet turn shades of brown and red, and reflected on how much I'd been crying lately. I'd cried more over the past week or so than I had in all my adult life. It hurt, it was uncomfortable, and it was terribly healing. Juno would be okay. I fully believed it. I had to. I would not lose her again.

When I was clean, dry, and had cried every tear I had, I went back into the bedroom, dressed in borrowed clothes. E was sitting in the chair beside the bed, Juno's hand in hers. It so closely resembled the pair from before, when it had been E recovering from her injuries. The sight of the two of them made me smile.

"You should go get something to eat," E said. "I can smell how hungry you are. Healing takes a lot out of people."

I hadn't even thought of food. But E was right. I was starving. The thought of leaving Juno's side, however, made me more uncomfortable than any hunger. "I'll stay," I said. "I'm sure I'll be okay."

"No. Go ahead. She would want you to take care of yourself," she said. "I'll be right here and I'll let you know if there is any change."

Just then, my stomach growled loudly, as if to mock any attempt to lie about my condition. I heaved a sigh. "Fine," I said. "But come get me right away if—"

"I will," she interrupted. "Now go. And have someone send down some blood for me, please. A-positive if we have any left."

"Sure," I said and reluctantly walked to the door, casting a last look back at my child. I tried to tell myself she was just sleeping. And she had E watching over her. I couldn't imagine anyone I would trust more. Before I could second-guess my choice, I ducked into the hall and headed upstairs.

I wandered through the living room and into the dining room, where food was already laid out on the table, along with pitchers of warm blood for the vampires. Felix was the only one around and nodded to me as I came in. I grabbed a roll and began chewing, not caring that it was probably rude.

"Lucia," Bruce called as he entered from the kitchen. "I was about to come get you to let you know that Sybil has been settled into one of the guestrooms. You two will be sharing, if you don't mind, until we can come up with something better. I'm putting Beth and her parents in the other."

I waved a hand. "Of course I don't mind," I said, and then passed on E's drink order. Bruce headed back into the kitchen, and I moved to take a seat next to Felix. I sank heavily into the upholstered chair and looked at the ancient vampire. "Thank you," I said. "For saving my sister, for everything."

He bowed his freshly washed blond head. “My pleasure,” he said. “Do you need anything? Are you in any pain?”

“Not the kind you can help with,” I said, and looked down at the half-eaten roll in my hand.

“We just have to wait,” he said. “I think it’s going to work out.” I glanced up and he smiled encouragingly. “I have some truly distracting book recommendations if you need them.”

He winked, and I shook my head, holding back a smile. “Thank you, but no,” I said. “I think I’ll go lie down for a bit.”

I rose from the table, trying to decide which bed I wanted to go to, Sybil’s or Juno’s. Considering that E was watching over Juno, I decided to go upstairs to Sybil. Before I left, I had another thought and turned back to Felix. “You were out there for a while, Felix. How many were you able to find? Were there others besides those we saw at the bridge?”

He nodded. “Yes. But not many. I left a few who were safe in their homes and didn’t want to leave. And there were a handful who left by ambulance before you would have arrived at the bridge. I would bet seventy or more people survived,” he said.

Seventy was much better than just over half. “We found Diane on our way back from the house,” I said. “After you’d left with Sybil.” He nodded again. “Did you find any of the others that were with her?” I asked. “Her co-conspirators?”

“Only one,” he said, his hazel eyes going dark. “I found Ruth.”

“What happened to her?” I asked. “Did she make it?”

Felix took a breath and smiled again, showing his long fangs. “No,” he said. “I watched her die.”

43

SARA

After a tiring night, we all slept through most of the next day. Lucia had an appointment, though, and neither Kate nor I wanted to miss it. We had discussed what we wanted out of the meeting, and although we hadn't been officially invited, we were determined to go and be heard. Lucia understood and welcomed our presence and all we could offer.

At four in the afternoon, Lucia, Kate, and I were all waiting behind the counter in the shop when Theo walked in. He came alone, which I was glad about. I didn't know how any of us would have reacted if he'd brought Diane along this time. He looked appropriately humbled as he entered, with his head bowed and a look of regret on his face. It took some of the spark out of my anger, but I wouldn't forget why we were there or what this man had enabled. He might not have been the one controlling the rain and wind over the past few weeks, but he bore responsibility for what had happened.

"Theo," Lucia said in greeting.

He paused when he saw Kate and me. "I had hoped we could speak alone," he said, approaching the counter and the stool we'd placed there for him.

"Oh, I don't think so," Kate replied, as if she were the one he was talking to. "It's in your best interest that we're here." She crossed her arms, and I took it as a sign she was going to keep her hands to herself. She'd been doing better lately, controlling her more volatile vampire impulses, but you never could tell what she would do to those who threatened her House. I was pleased she seemed so in control.

"So," Lucia began. "You wanted to talk about me helping you out of the disaster you all created?"

I had to give her credit; she got right to the point.

Theo took a deep breath, but thankfully didn't use it to argue. "Basically," he said. Not only did he look humbled, but he also appeared tired. "There was an informal gathering of survivors earlier today. It was made clear to me, and the remaining Elders, that change is needed. I've come to tell you that the majority of those assembled... voted to elect you as the leader of the recovery efforts. After which, we will start holding regular elections for our leadership." His face was screwed up as if he'd just eaten something sour, and I suspected it took a lot for him to agree to the new terms. Then again, being responsible for the recovery efforts seemed like a job he might not want.

"I see," Lucia said, leaning forward and cocking her head. "Well, that should make the rest of the discussion easier."

Theo's brows knit together, and he looked back and forth between the three of us.

"I assume this means that you are no longer asking for our removal from the valley?" Kate asked.

Theo sighed, and his weary face softened. "No. And I owe you not only an apology but also thanks. We all know what caused the slide. It wasn't a natural occurrence, and it was entirely preventable." He paused for a beat. "You had no reason to come to our aid, but you did anyway. There are a lot of folks who are alive today because you all came to help."

Kate studied the man, and as she narrowed her eyes at the older witch, I knew she was using her gift to figure him out. Then her face cleared, and she nodded. "You're welcome," she said without bitterness or snark. "We told you we just wanted to live our lives in peace. But now, we want more." Theo stiffened, quietly waiting to see what she would say. He clearly understood who had the upper hand. "We want to be good neighbors. We want to help this community heal and rebuild."

Theo relaxed but shook his head. "Do you have any experience with rebuilding an entire town?" he asked.

Kate flashed her fangs at him. "Nope, but I have experience making money," she said. "And I want to use some of it to help the town. I think you will find that most insurance won't cover a landslide, whether it's natural or not. You all are going to need quite a bit of money."

"Why would you want to do that?" Theo asked, looking at her suspiciously. "You want control of the town?"

"No," Kate said, glancing at me. "We don't want control. We want this community to be a place where everyone is welcome. You are going to need help, resources, and people. The only condition for taking the money is that the valley not be restricted to just witches. Vampires, shifters, and even humans who are part of our world should be allowed to live, work, and belong here."

Theo nodded his head slowly. "It's worth considering," he said.

"But not ultimately up to you," I reminded him. I looked at my aunt. "What do you say?"

Lucia raised her eyebrows. "I say we hold a vote. Of everyone, not just the Elders. We should let the community decide. This will affect all of them."

"And, might I propose that all Elders be elected from now on, by the whole of the community?" I added.

Lucia smiled. "We will put it to a vote," she said.

"Now wait a minute," Theo said. "That would be upending centuries of tradition. The community doesn't have the authority to elect Elders. Only the Elders themselves decide who is to be counted among us."

"And how has that been working out?" Kate snapped.

Lucia raised her hand. "It is how it's been done in the past. But the authority itself has always been granted by the community, by the people who chose to follow your leadership. It stands to reason that they should select who among them they wish to hold those positions in the first place."

Elder Coburn's nostrils flared. "You go entirely too far," he said. "It is not up to you to decide."

"No," Lucia said. "It will be up to everyone. Now, do you want to be included in the discussions about the clean-up and rebuild? Or would you like to just attend my weekly briefs like everyone else?" Lucia asked.

"Just because the community has asked that you lead the recovery, doesn't mean that I'm not still in charge of the town."

"For now," Lucia replied. "So, do you want to know what we have planned?"

Theo blew out a breath, but nodded. "We'll have to call in some big favors from the nearby witch settlements. You'll need my help. Their leadership isn't going to want to work with just anyone."

"Oh, I don't think we are going to need as much help as you think, but we would welcome it if offered," I said.

"It's going to take millions for the cleanup alone," Theo said. "I'm sure you do a good business here, ladies, but not that good."

"You're right," I said. "But our business will not be funding the relief efforts. Our *House* will. The House of Ward."

"We've consulted with our lawyer and can scrape together around thirty million for the cleanup, followed by fifty million for the rebuild, to start," Kate said. "It's a small town, but we anticipate that there will be interest from outsiders to settle here, once it's rebuilt, so we may want to expand it in the early stages to prepare. Maybe as much as another fifty million to lay in the infrastructure. We will know more when the plans and bids come together."

Theo just sat there, his mouth hanging open. I suspected he was unaware of how much money older vampires like Felix could raise quickly. And, I was sure he had no idea how much Kate could earn once we started auctioning her Relics more frequently. She preferred the money to come primarily from her creations, but it was helpful to have Felix's vast wealth available to get things going.

"There is something else we should address," Lucia said, getting Theo's attention. "We want those directly responsible for the disaster to be held accountable. I'm not sure how many of Diane's cronies are left—"

"Not many," Theo interrupted. "Just Diane and two others. They are being watched, and they will be dealt with. As soon as our leadership... issues are straightened out. Diane is the only Elder of the group, and she has been stripped of her title."

Lucia sniffed. "Very well," she said. "It will have to do for now. I'll start the cleanup and begin looking for community planners, engineers, and architects to draw up the plans. Where can I contact you?"

"With everyone else," he said, waving a hand. "I've secured lodging for everyone who needed it at the Cascade Hotel near the fairgrounds. We've got the rooms indefinitely."

"I bet that cost a pretty penny? How did you swing that?" I asked.

"A philanthropist from Seattle aided us. He's paying for the rooms out of charity, so we won't need your money for the time being," he said.

"What's his name?" Kate asked.

"A Mr. Voss. I think. Originally from Norway," he said.

I held my lips tightly together to stop from smiling. Voss was the fake last name Felix used, and I was sure it was his money already flowing to help the survivors.

"Interesting," Kate said with a raised eyebrow.

Lucia merely nodded. "Good work," she said flatly, but there was an uncharacteristic twinkle in her deep brown eyes. Then she sobered and glanced at her watch. "If you will excuse us, Theo, we have some pressing business. You are dismissed."

Theo blinked quickly, as if he wasn't sure what he was hearing. Then he stood, looked at each of us in turn, and walked out of the shop.

"I think that went rather well," Lucia said. Rising from her stool, she touched me on the shoulder. "It's almost time. I'm going to head inside."

I covered her hand with mine and gave it a gentle squeeze. "I'll be right in, Auntie," I said. When Kate and I were alone, I turned to her. "You're sure about all of this?" I asked. "It's a lot of money."

She nodded. "It's just a bigger version of what we talked about for the House," she said. "I feel good about being able to help, and hopefully affect some changes for the better. It would be great if our House weren't such an anomaly here, or in other places. There's no reason we can't all get along."

"And we might soon have a witch-vampire hybrid as a House member," I said. My stomach dropped at the thought that we might not. Not if Juno didn't wake up.

"Do you think she'll want to stay? Become a member of the House?" Kate asked almost shyly.

"I don't know," I admitted. "We'll have to see when she wakes up." I looked down at my phone. We had about forty-five minutes before sunset. "Do you think the others are up yet?" I asked.

"I bet they are," she said. "Marcus and E will probably be rising early for several days, if not weeks. I'm not really sure how it works."

"Speaking of which," I said. "How is it going with Marcus? He obviously bit you. Have there been any... issues?"

She shook her head. "No, none so far. I was quite literally drained when we got back, and after drinking more blood than I have since right after my transition, I fell into a deep sleep. I woke up with him lying in bed beside me." She shrugged. "We will have to see. What about you?" she asked. "Are you okay with all this?"

"Yes," I said. "The changes we're asking for are long overdue. And living here will be a lot easier if the community becomes more integrated. It would be hard to raise a family of half-witch, half-shifter kids in a place as intolerant as this used to be, and I want us to stay here."

"Are you trying to tell me something?" Kate asked, tilting her head.

"No," I said, raising my hands. "Not yet, at least. But I want to spend the rest of my life here, and I want to help shape this community into a place where my entire family will be welcomed." I reached over and squeezed her knee. "My whole family."

She smiled, her fangs on full display. "Good," she said. "I want to stay here for a long time, too." She straightened then and reached for her locket, a sure sign that she was feeling nervous.

"You worried about Juno?" I asked.

"Yeah," she said, biting at her lower lip. "I wasn't able to have any real discussion with her before I offered her the blood." She swallowed hard. "I was turned without my consent. I never wanted to turn anyone, let alone someone who wasn't in a position to say no." She bowed her head, letting her hair fall in front of her face. "I just hope, if she wakes, she doesn't hate me for what I've done," she said. Her voice came out small and full of regret.

"Kate," I said. "Kate, look at me." She raised her gaze to meet my eyes. "We won't know until she wakes. But you didn't know what would happen. You didn't think this would be the outcome. Surely she'll understand that you were just trying to help."

"I hope you're right," she said and blew out a breath, glancing toward the door. "I guess it's time we go find out."

44

KATE

I followed Sara from the shop back into the house. With each step, my anxiety grew. What had I done? How would Juno react? Would she even wake up, I wondered? Instead of heading toward the potential birth of a new vampire, I felt as if I were walking to my own death.

It was no surprise to find most members of the House already gathered and waiting in the kitchen—the only room on the floor without windows. The sun was nearly set, and even the vampires, thanks to my blood and Felix's, were awake and waiting to see what would happen with Juno. I received warm smiles and greetings from Marcus, Silas, Felix, Bruce, and Chelsea. Even Louis and Maureen were there, while Beth and Arrow were out working on recovering those who didn't survive the slide. The only others absent were Lucia, E, and Sybil. And I had a good idea where they were.

Marcus came to me as I entered, concern etched on his face. He couldn't block out others' emotions, and I, for the moment, was glad he knew how I felt without me having to explain it. "Hey," he said, low and quiet, just for me. "I've got you."

He slid his hand into mine, and I smiled up at him gratefully. "E and Lucia downstairs?" I asked.

Marcus nodded. "Yeah. You want to join them?" he asked.

I glanced at my phone. "In a bit," I said. "I'll just end up sitting and staring at her for the next half hour." Looking around, I spotted Felix and tugged on Marcus's hand, drawing him over with me.

"Kate," Felix said. "How are you holding up?"

"I've been better," I said. "I'm not sure what I'm supposed to be feeling right now, but this isn't a typical turning."

He smiled. "Are they ever? Either way, if Juno pulls through this, you'll be an actual sire. I'm sure it's a bit like how a parent must feel when a child is about to be born: nervous, excited, scared, hopeful, and thoroughly out of one's depth. Whatever you're feeling is okay."

"Thanks, Felix," I said, feeling myself get choked up. I needed to change the conversation, to distract myself. "I heard you're paying for hotel rooms for the entire town. Elder Coburn has no idea it's you, by the way."

"Good. He doesn't need to know it's me. I just didn't want to leave so many out in the cold after everything else they've been through."

"Well, it's nice of you," I said, suddenly remembering something else I'd learned that afternoon. "And I also heard that you were there when Ruth died." His smile dropped, and he nodded. "You didn't help her along, did you?" I asked.

His blond eyebrows lifted. "It was tempting, but no. I offered to help. She had internal injuries, and I offered to heal her. She told me to, 'Keep my fucking hands off her,' so I did." He heaved a sigh. "I stood over her, though, and watched her slip away. Part of me didn't want her to be alone, and another part of me wanted to make sure she was really gone." He clenched his jaw briefly. "I pride myself on being a man who upholds the law. It would have been wrong to take her life, and yet, I don't mourn her passing," he said.

"I don't either," I assured him. "But I'm glad you didn't kill her. It would have eroded trust if it had gotten out, and we want to be united with the witches here."

Felix smiled and nodded. "It's about time, you should go down," he said.

My stomach flipped over, and my already cool body felt chilled. I glanced up at Marcus and then back to Felix. "I guess I'd better."

"Do you want me to come with you?" Marcus asked.

I considered. "Maybe you both could wait out in the hall," I suggested. "The room isn't that big, and I don't want to crowd Juno. But it would be nice to have you both near."

They agreed and followed me past the other members of the House, quickly through the foyer, and down the steps. Sybil had fully recovered from her injury and was already standing in the hallway outside Juno's room. She smiled at me as I passed and touched my arm. She was scared but hopeful, filled with nothing but caring kindness. I paused and wrapped my arms around her. "Whatever happens, it will be okay," she whispered into my ear as she stroked my hair. "We love you, and we know you tried your best."

I pulled back, nodding. I found, however, that I couldn't speak. Sybil was like a mother to me, and having her support meant everything. I mouthed, "*Thank you*," and headed through the door to my old room.

Only a small, single lamp was on in the room, providing perfect lighting for newly sensitive eyes. Juno lay on the bed, still, unbreathing, and with a silent heart. I took a deep breath and went over to the foot of the bed.

E sat cross-legged beside Juno, watching closely. She had spent the day there, just in case she woke up early. She hadn't, and I could tell E was almost as nervous as I was. But neither of us was in as bad shape as Lucia. She was back in the only chair in the room, pulled up close to the bedside. She'd spent most of the day in that chair, watching over her child, just as she was now.

I felt like I should be doing something, but there was nothing to be done, so, like the other two women, I focused all my attention on Juno. I ran my eyes over the smooth skin of her high forehead, her cheeks, her lips, and throat. No movement, no twitching, no subtle breaths, or blood pulsing under her skin. Utterly still.

I reached out with my gift. She felt nothing. No emotion registered at all. I told myself not to worry, though. I could sense a human while they were asleep, but Marcus didn't give off any emotion while he slept.

With my defenses down, I was briefly distracted by the other emotions in the room. The growing hope, mixed with pure terror, belonged to Lucia, while E was giving off something different. She was excited, expectant. She was suppressing her fear and making space for her longing and love for Juno.

"You love her," I blurted out, then immediately realized what I'd said. I hastily put my walls back up and covered my mouth with my hand as both women looked at me, then quickly shifted their gaze back to Juno.

"You know I do," Lucia said sharply. "She's my daughter."

E's lips curled into a smile, and she let out a sigh, never taking her eyes off Juno. "She was talking to me," she said softly. "And, yes. I do. I'm in love with her."

"I'm sorry, E. I was trying to sense Juno. I didn't mean to...," I trailed off.

"Don't worry about it," she said. "I'm not embarrassed. And when she wakes up, I'll tell her how I feel."

Lucia briefly glanced at E before turning her attention back to her daughter. Just then, I saw it, and E gasped. "What?" Lucia exclaimed, leaning closer to Juno. "What happened?"

E started to cry and shook her head silently. Tears ran down her delicate face, and her mouth opened, but no words emerged.

I swallowed the lump in my throat. "Her chest moved. She took a shallow breath," I said, my voice cracking.

A fire roared to life in Lucia's eyes, and a genuine smile spread across her face. She clenched the comforter in her hands as she watched Juno's face. I knew that if I could feel her emotions at that moment, I would have sensed her overwhelming relief and joy.

We waited a few more seconds, and as Juno's chest rose again, her eyes opened and she suddenly gasped, pulling in deep breaths of air she no longer needed. It had worked. She had made it through.

Lucia rocked back and forth, tears on her cheeks as she smiled at her child. E leaned forward, Juno's hand clasped to her chest as she continued to cry. I stayed at the foot of the bed, watching Juno blink her eyes and look around the dimly lit room. "You're okay," I said, drawing her focus. "You're going to be okay." I was so happy she'd survived that I forgot, for the moment, to worry about how she'd react.

She squeezed her eyes shut and then blinked them open again, her breathing evening out. She glanced at her mother and E, then back to me. "I feel strange," she croaked.

"Do you remember what happened?" I asked. "The landslide? The store roof coming down?" It would be a lot harder to explain what happened to her if she had no memory of the incident, I thought.

"Of course," she said, lifting her head off the pillow to stare at me. "A giant beam fell on me." She looked down at her body. Her foot moved back and forth under the covers. "Seems like you fixed me up pretty good," she said, sounding like herself again. "Thank you."

E sat up and wiped her face, and Lucia looked at me. I guessed it was up to me to break the news, and that made sense. I was her sire after all.

"About that," I said, as Juno pushed herself up to sit with her back against the headboard. "I did heal you, but you needed more blood than I thought. I'm not sure if you remember, but I had to feed you twice, and you'd lost a lot of blood. I didn't intend to, but—"

"Wait," Juno said, cutting me off. Her eyes widened, and she leveled her stare at me. "Are you telling me you turned me into a... vampire?"

I looked at Lucia, who was biting the insides of her cheeks and studying Juno's expression. E sat on Juno's other side, looking frightened, as if rejecting being a vampire would also mean rejecting E herself. We were all on pins and needles.

I took a deep breath. "Yes," I said. "It was necessary." I winced at the words coming out of my mouth. They sounded a lot like what James had said to me when I woke up in the morgue, demanding answers. I only hoped my explanations would satisfy Juno and that she wouldn't regret what I'd done. Wouldn't hate what she was and what it was going to take to keep her alive.

Juno stared at me, her mouth hanging open. She closed it with a soft snap and then looked back and forth between E and Lucia as if seeking confirmation. Both women nodded encouragingly, and Juno turned back to me.

"Okay," she said, her face breaking into a grin. "Is everyone else alright? Aunt Sybil? Beth's parents?"

I nodded as tears of relief flooded my eyes. "Yup, everyone's good. Well, not everyone," I amended. "Several people were killed in the slide, but the Heartwoods all made it, and Beth's parents are fine."

I wiped at my eyes as Sybil poked her head in the room and then came forward, arms outstretched. I took the opportunity to step back and let her see her niece. Happy conversation bubbled up between the women as I edged out of the room. I was still dabbing at my tears when I walked out into the hallway to find Marcus and Felix waiting for me.

"Congratulations," Felix said, bowing his head. "Your first... progeny, fledgling, child?"

"That sounds too weird," I said.

"How about issue, or offspring?" he suggested.

"Eww. Do we have to call her anything?" I asked.

"She's your first 'natural born' House member, so to speak," Felix said. "It's sort of a big deal."

"You're not jealous, are you?" I said, my tone joking. "Don't worry, Felix. I love you all the same."

He put his hand on his chest. "What a relief," he said, then tilted his head. "Can I call you mom?"

"Absolutely not," I replied. "You don't trade smut books with your mom."

"You didn't know my mom," Felix said. "I bet she would have loved smut books."

"Okay, you two," Bruce said, breaking up the teasing. He came down the hall, an insulated tumbler with a metal straw in hand. "I thought your new House member might be hungry." I stepped back to let him pass, but he stopped and handed me the container and a dark colored handkerchief. "No, it should be you," he said.

I looked up at Felix and Marcus, and both nodded. "You're her sire, no matter what you decided to call her," Marcus said. "It's tradition for you to feed her first and help her complete the transition. It might not seem important now, but you might feel differently someday and wish you'd done it."

I smiled at the three men and looked down at the black thermal mug and fabric in my hands. I suspected it wasn't exactly traditional, but I appreciated the gesture. "Thank you, all of you," I said. "The three of you have had my back from the very beginning, and I just wanted you to know that I'm grateful."

"You're very welcome," Bruce said.

"We'll wait for you upstairs," Felix said. "Now go feed your baby."

I rolled my eyes. "I'll remember that when it's Bruce's turn." I snarked.

"Ugh, gross," Felix said, wrinkling his nose in disgust. "I take it back."

I blew him a kiss and went to help usher Juno into her new life.

45

MARCUS

It had been one exhausting night after another. The night before was both a physical and emotional challenge, as I rescued those in need and navigated the unfamiliar experience of feeling the heightened emotions of those around me. This night was a different sort of challenge.

I still hadn't learned to block out others' feelings like Kate could. Everyone's worries, fears, anger, sorrow, and excitement were mine to feel along with them. And I had no task to focus on except waiting to see what would happen. By the time Juno woke up and relief spread among those gathered, I was worn out. I needed a break. I wanted to crawl away somewhere far from everyone else and just be still. But there was nowhere to go in a house with more than a dozen inhabitants besides me—depending on whether or not you counted Arrow, and I did.

I found Kate in the living room, after she'd spent quite a bit of time with Juno. "How's it all going?" I asked, taking a seat next to her on the sofa. The other pieces of furniture were occupied, with everyone relaxing after the earlier tension.

"It's going better than I expected," Kate said, shaking her head.

"I'd only hoped that Juno wouldn't be angry or disappointed. I never imagined she would be thrilled to be a vampire."

"It's something many people seek out after all," I reminded her. "But, I'm glad it worked out." I took her hand in mine, and her feelings were instantly amplified: relief, amusement, love. I sighed.

"How are you doing?" Kate asked, looking at me critically.

"I've been better," I admitted. "I'm feeling wrung out from all the strong emotions swirling around here. I'm not sure how long this will last, feeling other people's emotions, but I could use some pointers on how not to let it drive me crazy."

"I should have asked earlier," she said, wincing. "I know how hard it can be. I'm not sure I can help, but I can try. What you need to do is separate your emotions from those of others. Isolate them, and then push back on the rest, creating a space within you."

"I don't know how I would even begin to do what you just suggested," I said. "It all mixes together, everyone's feelings. Even those of the dog." I glanced at Arrow lying by the fire, warming herself after returning from a day of hard work and a much-needed bath. I chuckled. "Hers are probably the least complicated."

Kate smiled. "Yeah. Animals are a great reminder to live in the moment, for sure," she said. "Here, let me help you." She squeezed my hand, and I felt overwhelm and frustration surge inside me. "Those are yours," she said. "Now focus on those."

I did what she said, despite the fact that they weren't the most pleasant emotions I had to choose from. They were the easiest to isolate, however, and it wasn't long before I had a hold of them.

"Good," Kate said, dropping my hand. "Now focus on pushing out against the rest. It's going to feel hard at first, but once you've established that space, it should hold itself fairly easily."

I took a deep breath and focused, but it was of no use. It was helpful to know which were mine, but there was no way I could do what she was describing. "I think this might be one of those times that you're just different," I joked. "I don't think I have that ability."

She grabbed my hand again, and warmth and affection bled into me, washing over me, overpowering the negative emotions I was battling. "Thank you," I said, rubbing the back of her hand with my thumb. "That's a lot better. And I used to think I was pretty good at regulating my emotions."

"You are," she assured me. "But it's not as easy when you have everyone else's to contend with. I think until you're used to it, you might need to put actual distance between you and everyone else." She tilted her head, studying me, and then glanced around at the others in the room. Everyone was caught up in their own conversations, paying no attention to the two of us. "How are you feeling about what we did?" she whispered.

"You mean drinking your blood?" I asked.

She nodded, shifting slightly. Her eyes were wide with curiosity and nervousness, and I could feel it through our clasped hands.

"I feel pretty good about it," I said. "The experience itself was... wonderful. And, I feel no ill effects, besides the emotional bombardment, that is."

She smiled. "Would you want to do it again?" she breathed, almost too softly for even my vampire ears.

I swallowed and gave a single nod. "Very much, any time you want," I said, bringing our clasped fingers to my lips.

"Not so fast, you two," Felix said from the other end of the sofa, where he rested with Bruce. "I wanted to discuss something with you, Marcus, before the two of you disappear for the rest of the night." He winked at Kate and me.

I cleared my throat. "Of course," I said, a bit flustered by being overheard.

"Bruce is going to be busy with the new construction on the house soon. E will be handling teaching Juno what she needs to know about being a vampire. Sara, Silas, and Sybil have a wedding to plan. Beth is running the shop, with the help of her mom and Louis, for the time being. Lucia is heading up the town's reconstruction efforts. Chelsea is busy taking care of all of us. And Kate is... well... Kate. What I was wondering was, do *you* have any plans for the near future, or would you be open to assisting me?" Felix asked.

"In what way?" I replied.

"Oh, you know," he said cheekily. "My little project: rewriting all the vampire laws and reshaping the very fabric of our society. That sort of thing. Or we could take up golf?"

I blinked at him, not sure how to respond.

"You can't tell me that in two thousand years you haven't learned to play golf yet," Kate said. "The other sounds interesting, but you might want to start there."

Felix smiled at her. "Actually, I do know how to play golf, I just wasn't sure Marcus does. I wanted to give him options."

"How very nice of you," Kate said. Then she turned to me. "So what do you think?"

"Um, it sounds like a really big job," I said. I looked at Felix, who was patiently waiting for an answer. "Yes, that seems like a very worthwhile way to spend a life."

He nodded. "Golf is pretty great," he said with mock gravity. "But I was really hoping you'd pick the other."

Kate snorted. "When do you plan to start this whole societal transformation thing?" she asked.

"I've already started," Felix said. "But I need help. You're right, Marcus, it is a really big job, and not without risk."

"Risk?" Kate said. "What kind of risk?"

"Sometimes I do forget how young you are, sweet summer child," Felix said, looking at her with adoration. "The risk is other vampires not appreciating our work, and seeking to eliminate us for it."

"Ah, yeah," she said. "That checks."

"But it will be worth it," Felix said. "If we can make real change, help usher in an era where vampires are more just, more kind, and more connected to the wider community of Others, and a deeper respect for humanity wouldn't hurt either."

I nodded. "I think I would like to help with that very much," I said, regarding the ancient vampire. "Thank you for considering me."

He dipped his head and then turned his attention to Bruce, his hazel eyes lighting up as he gazed at his lover. The sight of them reminded me of where Kate and I had left off.

I glanced at her, sitting beside me. "Will you be missed if I take you away from here for a while?" I asked.

She tilted her head from side to side, a smile on her full lips. "I don't think so," she said. "Juno is safely in the hands of E and Lucia for the rest of the evening, and everyone else seems content for the moment. Did you want my full attention?"

In response, I stood up and pulled her along with me, leading her from the living room and directly downstairs to my bedroom. I shut the door behind us, aware that there were now two vampires across the hall with exceptional hearing. I leaned close to her ear, and she slipped her arms around my neck. "I want to try something," I whispered, flicking my tongue out over the soft skin of her neck.

She gasped, and a shiver ran through her body. It was incredible to touch her and feel everything she was feeling. It was a revelation how much she desired, trusted, and loved me. It gave me courage and ignited my own desire in a way I'd never experienced. I was suddenly ravenous for her.

I crushed my mouth to hers, her lips parting for me. But my tongue in her mouth wasn't enough. I wanted more, needed more. As her hands pulled at my clothes, I marveled at how much our feelings were in sync, pushing us both higher and higher.

Fabric ripped as we moved toward the bed, never letting go of each other, fumbling with our last pieces of clothing. I pulled her close, skin to skin, and slowly eased us both onto the mattress. Our bodies settled into perfect positioning. She tilted her hips, and I slid inside her. She was so ready and felt so right.

This time, I didn't pull my face away from her throat. I nipped, licked, and teased her sensitive skin while I drove into her. She came first, wrapping her legs around my hips and pushing up to meet my thrusts. She struck my shoulder with her sharp fangs and moaned. I cried out, the pleasure of her bite tipping me over the edge as my orgasm overtook me.

I groaned and opened my mouth wider, propping myself up on both arms. I struck her neck, sinking my fangs deep. Gods, it was heaven. The taste of her blood flooding into my mouth as waves of pleasure ran down my spine, spilling out inside her, all the while her own fangs were locked into my skin. It was perfect. I wanted to stay in that moment forever. I wanted to lock the whole world out and spend our lives in each other's arms.

Slowly, she stopped sucking and withdrew her fangs, licking the last of the blood on my shoulder. I knew it was time to do the same, but I was loath to leave her. Reluctantly, I pulled away, watching the two punctures close on their own, then cleaned her skin of the last traces of blood.

She lay back against the pillows, panting and satisfied. I stretched out beside her. "Did you like that?" I asked.

She laughed. "You know I did," she said. "You could feel me the way I felt you."

"I know," I said. "But it seemed polite to ask."

She rolled toward me and put a hand on the muscles of my chest. "Yes, I loved it. It felt... I don't know. Right."

"I know what you mean," I said, and then paused, my throat going tight.

She frowned, clearly sensing my nervousness, my hesitation. "What's wrong?"

I turned my head to really look at her. "Kate, I know a lot has happened recently. I understand that emotions are running high and that everything is in flux. But I don't want this to change," I said, resting my hand on top of hers. "I want us to be together as we are now, for... well, for as long as we have, I guess. I love you, Kate."

She smiled, showing her elongated fangs. "I love you too, and I want that too," she said. "At first, I was worried that I was only attracted to you because of how it made me feel when I touched you. I felt calm, steady, in control. But I've come to realize that that's how I feel all the time around you, whether I'm touching you or not. You make me better because I love you, I depend on you in ways that have nothing to do with my emotional vampirism." She grinned at me. "I'm new to all this, both being an immortal and long-term relationships. I'm not perfect. And you know I'm a lot. But if you can handle all that, then I'm yours."

I leaned forward and kissed her, long and deeply. Her kiss felt like home. Pulling back, I stroked her face and pushed her long dark hair behind her ear. "I told you, I'm not looking for less. I just want you."

46

LUCIA

Sitting in the chair next to Juno's bed was exactly where I wanted to be. She didn't really need to be in bed resting, but E and I agreed that it was best for her to take things easy. She'd been gravely injured, healed, and raised as a vampire all within the past twenty-four hours, and she was kind enough to humor us.

I was glad Juno had E. After Juno woke up and... ate, Kate, Sybil, and I gave E and Juno a few minutes alone to talk. I assume it went well. The two of them were now cuddled on the duvet, talking about all the things E wanted to show Juno and teach her about being a vampire. I felt a bit like a third wheel, but I couldn't bring myself to leave her side just yet. I'd only just gotten her back—again. I desperately needed to keep my eyes on her to prove to myself that she was still here. She seemed to understand, and I was grateful.

"We have to go to the city!" E was saying. "I want to show you all the fun places vampires hang out and feed."

Juno nodded and licked her lips. "That sounds good," she said, but her words were slightly slurred. "Eating sounds good."

"Oh," E said. "I can get you more." She hopped up, but I stood and waved her back down.

"You stay," I said. "I'll get it. Do you want anything, dear?" I asked E.

She shook her blonde head, her short bob bouncing. "Nope. I'm good," she said, a big grin on her face as she settled back into the pillows next to Juno.

I slipped out of the room and shut the door behind me. The house was unusually quiet for that time of night. I figured everyone was feeling exhausted after all the excitement of the past couple of days. I passed Chelsea in the foyer, and she asked if I needed anything. I didn't want to be waited on, however, so I politely declined her offer.

I expected to see Bruce in the kitchen; he was usually there around that time of night, but it was Silas at the stove instead. Sara greeted me from the kitchen table, where she was sipping a glass of wine while Silas cooked.

"That smells good," I said to Silas.

"Thank you," he said. "I'm making chili. I'll leave it on the stove for whenever people are hungry. There's cornbread in the oven."

I nodded and turned to Sara. "Is there more wine?"

"Of course, Auntie," Sara said, rising to get another glass.

"I came to get Juno more blood," I told her, going to the massive appliance they called a fridge. I hefted open one of the doors and peered inside. "I assume it's in here somewhere."

Silas stepped up behind me and pulled open the other door. "Bottom drawer, you'll want the O-negative. It will have to do until we find out her blood type."

"It's A-positive," I said.

"In that case, bring her the A-negative," he suggested. "She might like it better. I'll tell Bruce or Chelsea to order her some A-positive."

I nodded and grabbed a bag labeled A-negative. I turned around to see Sara standing nearby. She held out both hands, one with a glass of red wine and the other empty. I exchanged the blood for the wine and took a sip of wine as she heated the bag for me and filled a thermal mug.

"How's it going down there?" Sara asked. "Is she handling this all okay?"

I sighed. "Yes, actually. She seems very pleased with how things turned out. I'm not sure I would handle it with the same grace," I admitted. "I think E is helping. She's overjoyed that Juno is a vampire now. And, that she plans on sticking around, now that she's tied to Kate, that is."

Sara's brow furrowed. "I'm sure Kate would let her do whatever she wants," she said. "If she wanted to go back to Louisiana, I know Kate would be cool with it."

I stiffened. "No. She said she'd like to stay," replied. "At least for now. She's called her parents and told them most of it. I expect she will need to go back to visit at some point, but..."

"It's okay," Sara said, handing me the travel tumbler and smiling. "I'm glad she's staying. For both of you."

I swallowed. "Thank you, Sara," I said. "I'm sorry I didn't tell you about her sooner. I'm sorry for many things. I feel like I've wasted a lot of time."

Sara shook her head. "I don't think so," she said. "I think all of this happened in the time it needed to."

"You may be right," I replied, and left Sara and Silas in the kitchen, heading back to Juno.

I thought about Sara's words. I was so confident I had made all the right choices in my life. It wasn't until recently, when Kate moved to the valley, that I began to question things, consider different perspectives, and entertain the idea that there might be another way to do things.

I'd worked hard all my life to live up to my idea of the perfect Elder. And in the end, it was my rejection of them and their ways that helped me earn the community's trust and the respect of those I wanted to serve. Would I have been able to see that earlier? Would I have been able to let go of my fear and welcome my daughter into my life? Would I have been willing to accept my community's rejection to stand up for what I knew was just? I thought Sara was right; these things all happened at just the right time. I was different now. I had different expectations for myself and my community.

I tapped softly before opening the door. The girls were exactly where I'd left them. Juno took the mug gratefully, and I leaned back into my chair, holding a glass of wine. I looked down at the glass and the red liquid swirling inside. I decided to be brave. I could do the hard thing, the right thing. It was time to live up to those new expectations. I took a deep breath. "You know, Kate wouldn't keep you here if you wanted to return home to New Orleans," I said.

Two pairs of eyes looked back at me, blinking and waiting. "Not that I want you to go," I quickly said. "On the contrary, I want you both to stay." I sniffed. "Not only do I love you both, but I've got a big job ahead. I could use some help."

Juno looked at me and smiled. "I can feel what you're feeling, you know?"

It was my turn to look at her, uncertain of what to say.

"I can feel how much you love me, and how scared you are. You don't have to be afraid. We love you too," Juno said, taking E's hand. "We've talked it over, and we both want to stay. I have a lot to learn about my new life, and we both like the idea of helping the community get back on its feet."

"Do you think this means you could go outside during the day?" E asked Juno excitedly.

"I don't know," Juno replied. "That would be really cool."

"Have you checked to see if you still have your gift?" I asked. It was something I'd wondered about but not asked yet, for fear of how disappointed she might be if it were gone.

Juno shook her head. "But there's no time like the present." She held up her hand and snapped her fingers, just like I'd seen her do before. Instantly, fire sprang to life at her fingertips. But unlike earlier, instead of a small birthday-candle-sized flame, her whole hand was engulfed in flames, shooting up to the ceiling.

E screamed, and Juno tried to shake her hand to stop the flame, but it made it worse by wafting the fire toward the curtains over the window. I instinctively raised my hands, dropping the wine glass and pulling the flames sharply into my outstretched palms. Clenching my fists, I completely extinguished the fire.

Both girls stared at the blackened ceiling, wide-eyed. "That answers that," I said, drawing their attention. "No more using your gift indoors until you have a better handle on it, I would think."

E looked at Juno and burst out laughing. Juno looked at her with a bemused smile, and then she, too, began to laugh. Just then, the smoke alarms in the house went off, and both girls began to laugh harder, gripping onto each other.

"I don't see what's so funny," I said over the ear-splitting beeping of the alarm. This comment just set the two off even more, red tears streaming down their faces.

I blew out a breath and stood up to leave as the door opened and Kate appeared, her hands over her ears, looking around for the source of the disruption. The alarms stopped, and I explained what had happened. By the time I finished, half the House was in the hallway, drawn by the excitement. Everyone eventually drifted away, all except Kate.

She followed me back into Juno and E's room. She was wrapped in a robe, her hair was a mess, and I was pretty sure there was blood smeared on her neck. I could only imagine what she'd been up to. "So, you've got a few new tricks along with those fangs?" Kate said to Juno, cocking her head.

"Yeah, I guess I do," Juno replied, wiping tears from her eyes. "I'm sensing emotions, flinging fireballs, and polishing off most of what's in your fridge."

Kate nodded. "I was really hungry at first, too. No fireballs, though," she said with a smile. "Maybe it's a good thing that Lucia will be with us for a bit. We might need her to keep the house from burning down."

"I've got a lot to learn from her, to be sure," Juno said, making my chest warm.

"But seriously," Kate continued. "Are you okay? Are you doing alright?"

Juno nodded. "Yeah. I'm actually doing great. The changes have my head spinning," she said. "But, I've got you all to help keep me steady, and teach me how to deal with this all." E leaned against Juno's shoulder as she spoke, and Juno pulled her closer.

"Well, good," Kate said. "I'll leave you in good hands for the evening. But come find me as soon as you wake. I'll be across the hall. Depending on what time you wake, we can test your tolerance for sunlight." She waved goodnight and shut the door behind her. Marcus's door opened and closed moments later as she went back to whatever she'd been doing before.

I picked up my dropped wine glass and went to the bathroom to grab a towel. I came back and started dabbing at the carpet when Juno said my name. "Lucia." She smiled at me as I looked up from the floor. "Would it be okay if I called you Ma? I call my adoptive mother Mom, so I don't want to use that, but calling you Lucia feels too strange."

I blinked up at her and then slowly straightened, folding the towel in my hands. I looked at my daughter, truly looked at her. She was strong, loving, and beautiful. Her beauty was more than her smooth, dark skin, her bright, whisky-colored eyes, or her gorgeous smile. She had been through more in the last two days than most people ever face, and here she was handling it with humor and grace. In many ways, she was everything I wanted to be. She claimed she had a lot to learn from me, but I was sure I had even more to learn from her. "I think that would be nice," I said, my voice sounding rough. "I would like that very much."

47

SARA

The woman looking back at me from the mirror was almost unrecognizable, yet she was still me—just a more idealized, romantic version. It wasn't the hair, perfectly braided and coiled on my head, decorated with small white flowers. It wasn't the flawless makeup or the diamonds dangling from my ears. It wasn't even the stunning gown, handcrafted by Beth's mom exactly to my specifications, that fit perfectly and looked like a dream. No, it was my eyes, my expression. I was completely happy, relaxed, and full of love, and all of that stared back at me.

My mom stepped up behind me, where I sat at the makeup table in my room, and placed her hands on my shoulders. She leaned down, her cheek next to mine, and gazed at my reflection. "You look so beautiful," she said, squeezing me in a gentle hug. "I'm so happy for you and Silas both, and I love the life you are carving out for yourself." The skin around her kind brown eyes creased as she smiled widely. "I'm very proud of you, you know?"

I sucked in a breath, making the lace of my dress tighten across my chest. "Thank you, Mom," I said, swallowing the emotion that threatened my eye makeup. "This feels completely right. All of it.

Silas, having you and Aunt Lucia here, Kate and the House, Juno... everything."

"It feels right to me, too," she said and stood up, adjusting one of the flowers in my hair.

It had been months since the landslide, and my mother and aunt were still living with us. Beth's parents managed to find a small house to rent one town over, but Beth was still under our roof as well, and we were glad to have her and Arrow. Juno agreed to stay and become an official member of the House. Kate was her maker, after all. And where Juno went, E was determined to follow. E signed her name, E (Ethel) Louise Thompson, to the charter before the ink on Juno's signature was even dry. The House had grown, and we were all happier for it.

With the expansion of the House, the building grew as well. Once the rain stopped and everything dried out sufficiently, Silas and his family broke ground on our expansion. The new, three-level wing featured an impressive locker room and laundry facility on the ground floor, with guest rooms on the second floor. It was all built over a full suite of rooms sunk into the ground for Kate and Marcus. Bruce lost the battle over the doggy door, but there was now a beautiful fountain out back that looked like a natural spring, built into a rock wall. It provided fresh water for any thirsty shifter and looked much nicer than any dog bowl.

Felix and Bruce moved into Marcus's old room in preparation for Bruce's transformation. Chelsea had her own dedicated room now, and Juno and E were now sharing Kate's old room, which was now just "the girls' room". Kate was able to move back into her art studio, which was now attached to a lovely sitting room facing the garden, and led to the underground bedroom and bathroom she and Marcus shared.

My mom and her sister now had separate bedrooms, but they wouldn't be under our roof much longer. "Mom," I said, drawing her eyes back to mine in the mirror. "Are you okay with the plans for the new guest house? You don't wish we were rebuilding the Heartwood family home first?" I asked. I knew she missed her childhood home. I missed it too. But the land was still being cleared in the area where the house had been, and the plans for the expanded town would take a bit longer than the improvements to our house had.

"I don't mind one bit," she said. "It will give Lucia and me time to really think about what we want to put on the property. I loved our old home, of course, but I think we could tailor it more to our needs this time." She smiled. "I'm happy to be close to you and the rest of the House for now. And who knows, maybe there will be grand-pups to care for someday."

I rolled my eyes but smiled back. "Not for a while," I said. "But it will be nice to keep you close. I've enjoyed having you here these past months." I tilted my head, considering. "I've even enjoyed having Auntie here. She's changed a lot. I'm not sure if it's because of Juno, or the disaster, or her becoming an Elder finally after all these years, but she's different."

My mom nodded. "She has. I think she's become who she was meant to be all those years. She's more like she was in her youth, but better—stronger and more... I don't know, emotional isn't the right word."

"I know what you mean," I said. "Maybe, 'emotionally available'."

My mom nodded again. "Yes. I feel I can connect with her better. It's like I'm talking and hearing directly from her heart for the first time."

I patted my mom's hand, which still rested on my shoulder. "How are we doing on time?" I asked.

She glanced at her watch. "Good," she replied. "We have a few minutes until we have to go down. Have you seen it yet?"

She didn't have to specify what "it" was. The strawberry moon had risen around sunset, low along the southeastern horizon. We'd aligned the ceremony's location so it would be behind us on its path around midnight for the best effect.

"Yes," I said, feeling my breath catch. "I peeked out at it earlier. It's beautiful, all lit in reds and oranges." It was breathtaking. And, looking at it, knowing I would be married under it a few hours later, had been a moving experience.

Just then, there was a knock at the door. "Yes," my mother called.

The door cracked open, and Kate stepped into the doorway. She'd been with me on and off all afternoon and evening, but had slipped away an hour earlier to get ready for the ceremony. And she looked stunning. Her dark, straight hair was loose, except for a single braid wrapped around the crown of her head and decorated with soft red flowers. Her dress, which she had picked out with my help, was also red. It had capped sleeves, a fitted bodice, and then fell to the ground in waves of crimson.

"You look amazing," I said as she shut the door behind her and came closer.

"Oh, please," she replied, her sharp vampire eyes narrowing at me. "No one will be looking at me." She shook her head. "I've never seen a more exquisite bride."

She grinned, showing her pointed fangs, and I laughed. "I never pictured my wedding exactly like this," I said. "But, I couldn't be happier."

"Well, everything is almost ready," she said. "Bruce is waiting downstairs with your bouquet, the guests are seated—besides the shifters—and your groom is in place."

I felt blood rush to my cheeks at the mention of my groom. I don't know why I was feeling nervous. I'd felt married to Silas for quite some time, but there was something about standing up and declaring it in front of my family and community that made butterflies churn in my stomach.

"Why aren't the shifters seated?" my mom asked, looking confused. "Are some of them running late?"

Kate shook her head but didn't answer, so I spoke up. "No, Mom," I said. "They are coming in wolf form, as is their tradition." I chuckled, imagining a pack of wolves trying to position themselves onto white folding chairs.

Mom's face went comically blank. "I would think that would have been something you should have mentioned," she said.

"It's not a problem," I assured her. "They will all be on their best behavior. And, when the ceremony is finished, they will shift back and join us for the reception."

She blinked at Kate and then at me. "Will Silas be in wolf form?" she asked.

I burst out laughing; I couldn't help it. "No. He will be human," I said. "I'm marrying him, not his wolf. Plus, it will make the exchange of vows easier."

"But, his family..." she trailed off.

"They don't have weddings, Mom," I said. "But when they do celebrate important life events, they usually do it in their wolf forms. It's how their wolves honor them, and how they honor their wolves."

"Ah. I see," she said, but still looked confused.

"Are you ready?" Kate asked me with a smile, changing the topic nicely.

I nodded at my best friend and maid of honor. "Mom, why don't you go take your seat, and I'll be right down," I said, my voice only trembling slightly. She took a deep breath but didn't speak, then softly kissed my cheek before waving and walking out the door.

I stood from the padded bench, and Kate rushed behind me to fluff out the train of my dress. She circled back around and looked into my eyes. "You look really happy," she said. "And I know tonight will be perfect."

I shook my head, feeling the weight of my braided crown. "It doesn't have to be perfect," I said. "It just has to end with Silas and me married. Everything else is just cake."

She grinned. "I'm sure we can manage that," she said. "Now, you go ahead, and I'll make sure your gorgeous dress doesn't trip you on the stairs."

She opened the door, then stepped back to let me go first. I took another deep breath, testing the limits of my bodice, and stepped out the door. The house was dimly lit to avoid casting too much light onto the clearing outside, where the ceremony would take place.

The front clearing wasn't the perfect spot for the event, but it provided the best view of the moon, and that's what mattered. The clearing had been raked multiple times and then covered with soft green ground cover. Chairs were arranged in two sections to form an aisle. A white runner led to an arbor built by Silas and Bruce, where a local priestess would marry us.

I stood at the top of the stairs, hearing the low rumble of voices from the front of the house. The sound made my throat tighten, but then movement at the bottom of the stairs caught my eye. Bruce stood in the foyer, dressed in a beautiful black tuxedo and holding my bouquet of white and green hydrangeas. Seeing him relaxed me somewhat, and I continued down the steps, with Kate trailing behind me and occasionally fussing with my lace train.

"Sara," Bruce said, once I'd made it to the bottom of the steps. "You look absolutely beautiful." He handed me my bouquet and gave me an appraising look, taking in my custom lace gown and my crown of flowers. "Stunning. Silas isn't going to be able to speak when he sees you."

"Thank you," I said, gripping the flowers with both hands like they might fly away.

Kate stepped up beside me and placed a hand on my arm. The effect was immediate. The nervous, sweaty energy drained out, leaving me excited, happy, and resolved. I glanced up at my best friend. "Too bad you're not walking me down the aisle," I said.

"I won't be far," she said, winking at me. "But, it's time for me to go. See you at the altar."

She stepped away, removing her hand. The nervous fluttering came back, but it was bearable and expected. Butterflies weren't going to keep me from my fiancé.

A door opened and closed behind me, and I knew it was nearly time. Bruce smiled at me and gave me a slight bow, and then he, too, left through the open front door. Steps sounded over my shoulder, but I didn't turn. I'd just have to straighten my dress back out.

"I suppose you're ready," came the voice to my right. "You certainly look ready."

I turned my head and looked at my Aunt Lucia, who stood beside me in a stately black, floor-length gown. I'd never seen her so dressed up in all my life, and for a moment I was speechless. I managed a nod. "I am, Auntie," I choked out.

Her eyes softened. "I love you, Sara. Like you were my own," she said. "I hope you know that." Her voice was the same one I'd known my whole life, but her words were loving, cutting through to the heart of me. "Oh, no. I didn't mean to make you cry," she said, reaching up to wipe away a tear. "You okay? I could tell them to wait." She flipped a hand in the direction of the door. "You're the bride. They won't start without you."

I sniffed. "No, Auntie. I'm ready," I said.

She nodded, then straightened her spine, her face adopting the mask she wore when taking charge, when acting as our matriarch. I looked down at her outstretched hand. I took it, and she gently folded my hand into the crook of her elbow, guiding me toward the aisle.

48

KATE

The night was perfect, and the clearing looked like something out of a dream. The trees and shrubs were decorated with tiny white lights, and torches flickered around the perimeter of the house, enhancing the ambiance. The arbor behind me was adorned with flowers and green herbs, scenting the air around us. If you'd asked me to describe the setting for a woodland witchy wedding, this would have been it.

My nerves were starting to get to me as I waited with the wedding party for Sara to emerge from the house. I scanned the crowd in front of me. Everything was just as it should be. I spotted the photographers, Gina and Dale, in position to get the perfect shots of Sara as she walked down the aisle. They had been hard at work all evening, snapping what I was sure were gorgeous shots of the event. Sara had been right; they just needed some time and a bit of backbone. But like the rest of the town, they had come around and were happy to be there to help with the big night.

I glanced beside me, where Juno stood, with E on her other side. E had been essential in helping Juno adjust to her new life. I was grateful. As her maker, it was my responsibility to make sure Juno learned everything she needed to know, but I was still figuring things out myself. Juno needed much more than I could give, and I was thankful she had people like E and her mother.

I looked across the aisle to where Silas patiently waited, hands clasped in front of him, with a sweet smile on his face. Beside him stood Bruce and Marcus. Silas had asked both men to stand with him for the ceremony, and I knew the gesture meant a lot to them. Silas's brothers would have stood beside him if they had been human. Instead, they waited with the other members of their community. And as much as my eyes were drawn to Marcus, looking delicious in his black tuxedo, I couldn't help but be curious about the pack of wolves standing and sitting just beyond the wedding party, and my gaze shifted toward them.

The wolves remained inside the circle of guests, but with nothing but the untamed woods at their backs. I'd met many of the shifter guests earlier that day, and while they all seemed fairly comfortable around me, the other vampires, and the many witches bustling about, I knew their wolves might be a bit more cautious. The thought took me back to the first time Silas and I met, and how on edge we both had been. I respected the wolves a lot for coming to support Silas, his wolf, and Sara in a ceremony they were unfamiliar with.

My eyes scanned the gathered canines. I knew the two older wolves at the front were Silas's parents. Silas's father looked just like him in wolf form—a large, classically colored wolf with golden eyes. I guessed the young wolves fidgeting to one side must be Silas's niece and nephew. His older brother and his wife were there, along with the two younger brothers and several cousins. Overall, I counted thirteen wolves of different colors and sizes, but I couldn't tell who was who.

There was a murmur from the crowd, and all eyes turned toward the house as Sara and Lucia stepped over the threshold. Everyone stood, and I looked up at my best friend as she crossed the porch on Lucia's arm. They waited at the top of the steps for the music to start, and it was as if I were seeing Sara in her gown for the first time. Sara, as a bride standing in her bedroom, was nothing compared to the way she appeared in the moonlit clearing in the forest.

She was breathtaking, as if she had stepped out of a fairy tale. Her off-white lace gown reflected the pink and orange moonlight, and the buttery yellows of the torches highlighted her warm brown skin and black-as-night hair. The tiny white flowers looked like stars among her braids, and the diamonds at her ears sparkled with an otherworldly glow. The quartet started playing, and she descended the stairs on steady, bare feet, her eyes fixed on Silas, Lucia ready to catch her if she faltered. She did not.

When Sara's toes touched the soft green groundcover, I looked up at her fiancé. The expression on Silas's face made my heart tighten painfully in my chest. If I had ever questioned whether the shifter truly loved my best friend, that look would have erased all doubt. The rugged planes of his face were carved with such love and tenderness, and his entire being seemed to reach out toward Sara, as if pulling her closer with each heartbeat. I hurriedly reached into the neckline of my gown and pulled out a black handkerchief that Bruce had given me earlier. I'd initially complained that I had nowhere to keep it in my gown, but he insisted, and I'd shoved it down the front of my dress. I was glad I had it now as I dabbed at the red tears blurring my vision.

I pulled my gaze away from Silas, and my eyes found Marcus behind him. While everyone watched the bride walking down the aisle, he was looking at me. He tilted his head to the side, and I understood that he was checking to see if I was okay. The thought warmed me, reminding me of the love all around me that evening. I took a breath of the herb-scented air and nodded, smiling at him.

At that moment, Sara and Lucia reached the end of the aisle and paused by the front row. The priestess spoke, and even though I'd been there for the rehearsal, it managed to startle me. "Who stands for this woman and supports her in her choice to join with another, promising to aid them both in their union, remind them of the vows they are about to make, and uphold her and the power she brings to this marriage?"

"Her mother and I do," Lucia said loudly, not a trace of hesitation.

Then the priestess turned to Silas and those with him, repeating the question, asking who would stand for him, support his choice, aid the union, and uphold his power. They weren't the words I was familiar with, and Sara had explained that the cerimony had been adopted by their community long ago and had evolved over the years to reflect their values and feelings. I thought they were quite beautiful.

This time, the question was answered by the howl of a classically colored wolf with bright yellow eyes.

The priestess nodded, and Sara stepped forward, handing me her bouquet and offering her hands to Silas, who reverently took them in his own. I stood beside my best friend and listened as she and Silas exchanged their vows. My eyes were drawn to the crescent-shaped scar in the crook of Sara's shoulder that showed plainly with her off-the-shoulder gown. I smiled to myself. These two were already one, and anyone who cared to look could see, I thought.

They had written every word of their vows themselves, and they were both personal and heartfelt. I tried to focus on what was being said, but the swell of love and happiness from those gathered in the clearing overwhelmed my senses, even with my defenses in place. I almost missed it when the priestess called for an exchange of tokens, signaling my part in the ceremony.

I turned to Juno, who swapped the bouquet I was holding for a small wooden box. Taking the box, I stepped forward and handed it to the priestess. Witches didn't wear wedding rings, like humans did, and shifters rarely wore jewelry, but Silas and I had worked together to create something special for the occasion. The priestess opened the box to reveal two wooden rings. Silas crafted each one out of hardwood, ensuring the wood was perfectly dried and the sizes were accurate. Afterward, I took each ring and carved a pattern of interlocking scrollwork and small flowers. Then they were buffed, waxed, and polished until the dark wood shone with a glow.

Sara gasped when she saw them, and I felt a surge of pride. Before Silas could reach for the smaller of the rings to present it to Sara, however, the Priestess turned to me, holding out a hand. I stepped up beside her and plucked Sara's ring from the box, turning to look at

Silas. I held out my hand with a smile. He smiled back, and he took my hand. "Now lend me the love you feel for this woman," I said, as my hand closed around the ring. Tears pricked my eyes again, and I swallowed hard as I tried to force a love so big into something so small.

When I was finished, I handed the ring to Silas and repeated the process with Sara, giving her the ring she would give to him. Tears rolled down my best friend's face as she opened herself to me, letting her love, admiration, and devotion pour out. I handed the ring to her and leaned forward, kissing her on the cheek before stepping back with the other bridesmaids. The exchange was brief, and as the rings slid onto their fingers, the couple kissed, and the priestess raised her hands. The witches gathered, cheered, and the ceremony was complete.

The next few minutes were a blur of red tears, well-wishes, and hugs. Sara and Silas walked back down the aisle, married in the eyes of the witch community. They went up the steps to the house and disappeared inside, where they would take a moment for themselves before joining the rest of us at the reception.

As soon as they were out of sight, the wolves vanished behind the house, heading for the "shifter garden," as Bruce called it, and the door to the locker room where they had hung their clothes for the party. I was watching the last of them leave when I felt a hand on my elbow. I turned to find Marcus standing just behind me. "Ready to go?" he asked, holding out his arm. I smiled, took his arm, and we walked slowly behind the others, heading toward the house.

When we reached the front row of chairs, Lucia and Sybil joined us. Both women were glowing with happiness and had slightly puffy eyes. I glanced at the sizable crowd ahead of us. "This must be everyone who made it through the landslide," I said to Lucia beside me.

"Just about," she said and sniffed. "Theo isn't here, along with two other older witches. Not because they didn't want to come," she said quickly. "Diana is on house arrest. Or, hotel arrest, I guess. And they need a few of the more powerful witches to keep an eye on her."

"That doesn't seem very practical," I said. "How long can they keep that up?"

"Until her trial," Lucia said. "Or until we rebuild the jail if she's found guilty and sentenced to serve time."

I shook my head. "I didn't know the Elders did stuff like that," I replied. "It reminds me of the vampire Council." I shivered at the thought.

"It's not as bad as all that," Lucia said defensively. "But there is room for improvement, I'm sure."

"Congratulations on becoming the first widely elected Elder," Marcus said from my other side. "I hadn't gotten a chance to say it before."

"Well, thank you," she said. "But it's not necessary." Lucia waved her hand, dismissing the compliment, but her chin raised slightly, and I could tell she was pleased. "I'm just happy to be able to serve the community as both the leader of the recovery effort and now as an Elder."

"She's a wonderful Elder. Just like our mother was," Sybil said, grasping her sister's arm and smiling. "We're all very proud of her."

Lucia nodded down at her little sister, but said nothing. Even with her lips pressed tightly together, I could see the slight trembling in her lower lip.

Before there was a risk of any real emotion spilling over, Felix appeared, stepping between Lucia and me. He wrapped his arms around both of us as we reached the porch steps and started up, shuffling slowly behind the gathered witches. "Hello, beautiful ladies," he said. "Wasn't that wonderful? Quite a lovely occasion for the House's first-ever event."

I rolled my eyes, but was secretly grateful for the interruption, saving Lucia from losing her composure. "Hi, Felix. Yes, it was wonderful," I said. "If you plan on throwing many more parties, you're going to have a tough time beating this one."

"Indeed. Speaking of which..." he said, drawing out the last word. "There have been several on the Council vying for an invite."

"An invite?" I asked, confused. "To the wedding?"

"No. To the House," Felix said. "Ever since you proved how special you are at Bruce's trial, they would like to come courting you as an ally. I think it helps that I'm now a member of the House as well." He puffed up his chest and bobbed his head with mock importance.

"Yes, we are both very special," I said, as we reached the porch, still following the flood of well-dressed wedding guests. "But I'm not hosting any vampire dinners for a bunch of spoiled immortals."

"Never say never," he crooned, then patted me on the shoulder before making a sharp left, getting out of line, and heading toward Bruce, who was standing to the side, ushering everyone through the house and down the steps to the lower level.

We'd had to pull down the wards for the occasion and re-ward individual spaces within the house. It wasn't easy, but it seemed simpler than guiding the crowd around the house with its varied landscape. It felt strange, however, to see everyone flowing through the building.

We descended the stairs, and I could feel the cool outside air coming through the newly installed French doors below. Now, thanks to the ongoing renovations, the stairs opened onto a larger lower landing. My beautiful studio door was to the left, just as it had been before, and there was another intricately carved door opposite it now, leading to the "vampire wing" of the house, where there were now four light-proof rooms.

Directly in front of us, two large doors were open to the back of the house. As we stepped through, we found ourselves on a slightly raised walkway. My private garden was to the left, while a newer, matching garden was to the right. The walkway led to a wide, grassy area that served as the reception space for the evening. It was also lit with fairy lights and flames, filled with white catering tents, seating areas around small fire pits, and a large dance floor. Music was already playing, and drinks were being served.

After we reached the reception area, Marcus and I excused ourselves from Sybil and Lucia, who had been quickly caught up in conversation with two other witches. We walked over to one of the smaller seating areas and sat on a rattan loveseat with white cushions. Chelsea came over with glasses of warm red liquid that wasn't the pricey wine Silas's uncle sent over, and we gratefully accepted them.

We stayed quiet as we sipped our drinks and watched the witches mingle and chat happily under the pink moonlight. Sara's mother and aunt had reunited with their cousins and were discussing family matters. The shifters were gradually emerging from behind the hedges that separated the lawn from the shifter garden, all in human form and fully dressed. Beth and her parents stood to one side, holding glasses of wine and talking animatedly about some topic. Beth, however, kept sneaking glances toward the hedges and the shifters. Maybe she'd find her shifter boyfriend after all. Meanwhile, Juno and E had just taken the dance floor.

"This is so very beautiful," I said after a while. "I don't think I've ever been happier..." I trailed off.

"I'm holding your hand, Kate," Marcus said. "I know there is more than a bit of sadness in that statement."

I sighed. "I wish my mom and brother were here," I said finally. "I don't know that they would have been invited under normal circumstances, but with me here, it was impossible. Not only do I miss them, but I feel like I took this away from them."

"There aren't any humans here who aren't related to witches. What do you think Sara would have done had this wedding taken place before you were turned, before you knew she was a witch?" he asked.

"That's a good question," I admitted, looking around again. "It doesn't look particularly witchy, but then again, I would have definitely remarked on the wolves at the ceremony."

He nodded. "I don't think you would have been invited either, Kate," he said. "There would have been a story about a Vegas elopement, I bet."

Somehow, his words made me feel a bit better. I wasn't taking this away from my mom and brother. I still missed them like crazy, but I wasn't stopping them from being there. But with that realization came the truth of the situation. Despite our success, both in the

House and in the community, there was still work to be done. I was committed to working toward a way for Others to better coexist and, perhaps, a chance to someday be close to my family. Who knew what the future would bring?

At that moment, Sara and Silas came out of the house, stepping onto the walkway arm in arm. The wedding guests cheered and clapped as the couple walked out onto the lawn. Seeing the bride and groom greeting their guests and accepting congratulations from witches and shifters alike gave me hope. We were on the right track.

"Would you like to dance?" Marcus asked, bringing me out of my thoughts and back to the present.

I set down my empty glass and reached out my hand. As we headed toward the dance floor, where E and Juno were showing off their moves, I looked around again. I saw all the members of our House talking, laughing, and enjoying each other's company, as well as that of the wider community. It had taken a disaster, a tragedy, to bring the valley and the House together, but here we were: a patchwork whole, not unlike the House itself. A House led by a vampire-fae that never should have existed. A House of witches, vampires, shifters, humans, and combinations of the three. A House I was growing more and more proud of every day.

The House of Ward

Don't let the story end here! Preorder Book 4,
Challenged by Tradition and Desire,
now! Available April 2026.

ACKNOWLEDGMENTS

Words fill the pages of a book, but love, patience, and the people who stand beside you are what truly build it.

To my sister—thank you for being the best little sister anyone could ask for. This book bears your fingerprints in ways both seen and unseen.

To my husband—thank you for being my constant, my home base, and my partner. Your love steadies me and gives me the courage to chase these stories.

To my Alpha Reader—you've always believed in me, from the very beginning. Your encouragement lights a spark that keeps me going, and I am endlessly grateful for your confidence in me.

To my Beta Readers—your thoughtful critiques and sharp eyes made this book stronger, sharper, and fuller.

To my children—you are my everyday wonder. Your imagination and humor remind me why I fell in love with stories in the first place.

And to my loyal Border Collie—thank you for the daily reminders to take breaks, and for keeping me on schedule better than any planner ever could.

With deepest love and gratitude,
A.R. Abbott

ABOUT THE AUTHOR

A.R. Abbott is the author of *The House of Ward* series, a sweeping paranormal fantasy saga where vampires, witches, and shifters navigate treachery, passion, and ancient power. Known for her lush, character-driven storytelling, Abbott delves into themes of found family, desire, and the dangerous bargains of magic. A designer and illustrator as well as a writer, she draws on her love of folklore and paranormal romance to craft immersive worlds. She has lived across the globe with her diplomat husband and now calls Northern Virginia home.

Join the House at arabbott.com

instagram.com/a.r.abbott

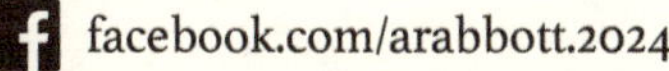

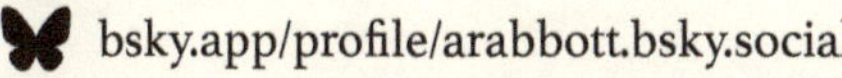

www.ingramcontent.com/pod-product-compliance
Lightning Source LLC
Chambersburg PA
CBHW020247030826
48979CB00030B/2647/J

* 9 7 8 1 9 6 7 5 2 0 1 1 4 *